ICED OUT

USA TODAY BESTSELLING AUTHOR

VERONICA EDEN

ICED OUT SPECIAL EDITION

Cover Illustration: Bitter Sage Designs

HESTON UNIVERSITY KNIGHTS
#24 EASTON BLAKE

HESTON U HOCKEY

TEAM ROSTER

EASTON BLAKE, CAPTAIN, #24, CENTER
CAMERON REEVES, #33, GOALIE
MADDEN GRAVES, #27, LEFT WING
NOAH PORTER, #45, DEFENSEMAN
ELIJAH ADLER, #86, FORWARD
ALEX KELLER, #22, LEFT WING (FORMER, CURRENTLY PLAYS IN NHL)
THEO BOUCHER, #14, RIGHT WING
JAKE BRODY, #47, DEFENSEMAN
DANIEL HUTCHINSON, #16, LEFT WING
MITCHELL MANNING, #66, DEFENSEMAN
ERIC HOLLAND, #38, BACKUP GOALIE
JACK MCKINLEY, #77, FORWARD
NICK BRIGGS, #82, DEFENSEMAN
CALEB ADLER, #68, FORWARD (FORMER, CURRENTLY PLAYS IN NHL)

COACHES

HEAD COACH: DAVID LOMBARD
ASSISTANT COACH: COLE KINCAID
ASSISTANT COACH: STEVEN WAGNER
FORMER HEAD COACH: NEIL CANNON, RETIRED NHL PLAYER

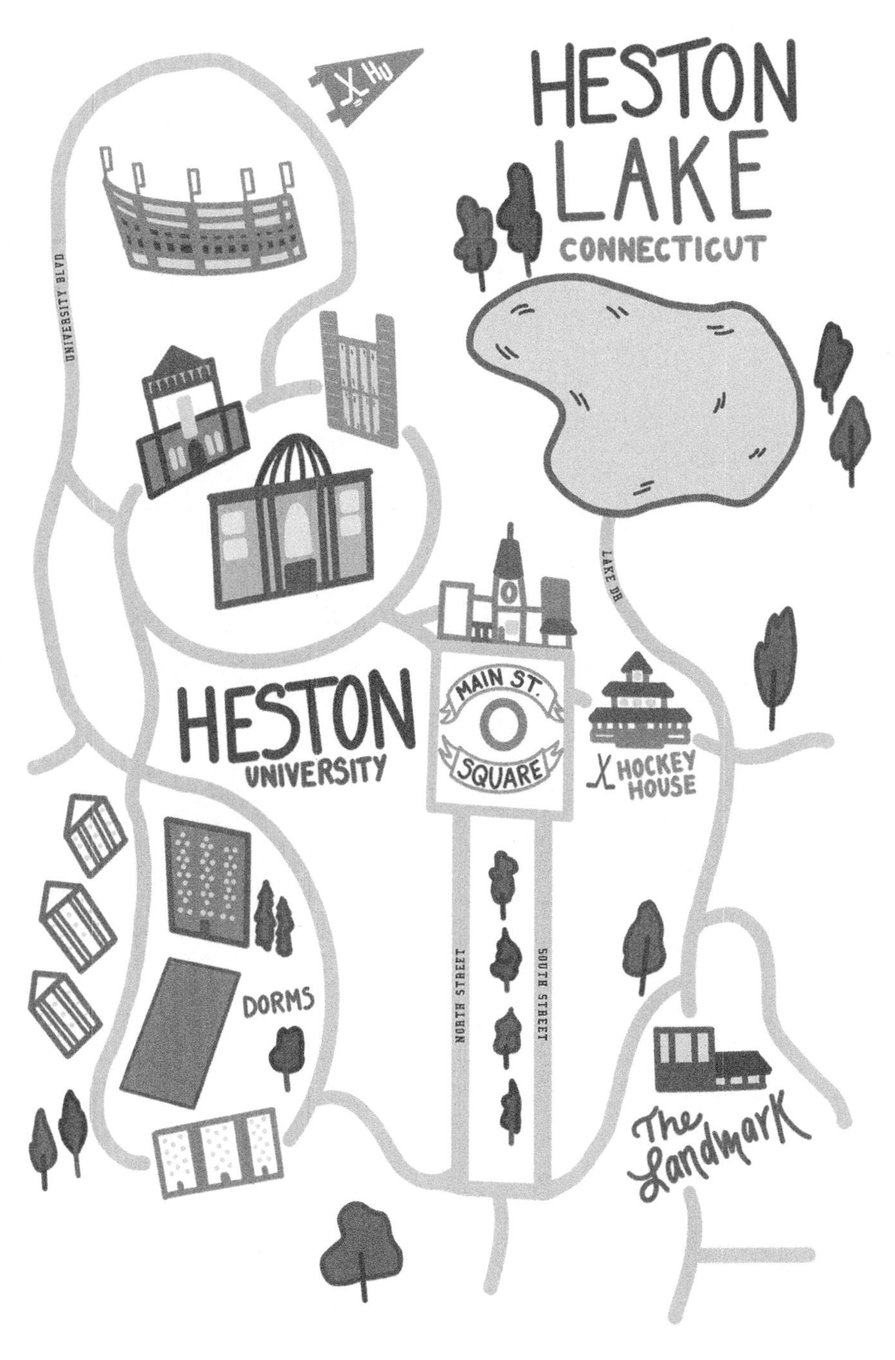

MAP KEY

HESTON CAMPUS	***HESTON LAKE***
HESTON U ARENA	MAIN STREET SQUARE, CLOCKTOWER BREW HOUSE
ACADEMIC LOOP	HESTON LAKE AND ICE SKATING RINK
CAMPUS HOUSING	THE LANDMARK BAR & GRILLE

PLAYLIST

Can We Pretend That We're Good? — Daniel Seavey
DANCING ALL ALONE — Clinton Kane
Tripping Over Air — Aiden Bissett
Got Me Good — DNCE
ROOM FOR 2 — Benson Boone
Coast — Hailee Steinfeld, Anderson .Paak
Lavender Haze — Taylor Swift
Healing — FLETCHER
Until I Found You — Stephen Sanchez
Swoon — Beach Weather
Nonsense — Sabrina Carpenter
uh oh — Tate McRae
Charlie Be Quiet! — Charlie Puth
this is what falling in love feels like — JVKE
Just Friends — Why Don't We
Can I Kiss You? — Dahl
Don't Let The Light Go Out — Panic! At the Disco
NIGHTS LIKE THESE — Benson Boone
i can't help it — JVKE
Cross your mind — ROLE MODEL
Long Story Short — VOILÀ
Call You Mine — The Chainsmokers, Bebe Rexha
YOU AGAINST YOURSELF — Ruel
There's Nothing Holding Me Back — Shawn Mendes
golden hour — JVKE
Figure You Out — VOILÀ
Oh shit...are we in love? — Valley
I.F.L.Y. — Bazzi
i like that — Bazzi
Before You — Benson Boone
Here With Me — Susie Suh, Robot Koch
Stranger — Lauv
Everyone And No One — Ashley Kutcher
It'll Be Okay — Shawn Mendes
Conversations in the Dark — John Legend
Until I Found You — Ayradel

CONTENTS

BONUS DELETED SCENES

ABOUT THE BOOK

Dancing on bartops means the night is going great. Exiting the bar hauled over the shoulder of Heston University's infamous hockey captain? Not my idea of a good time.

But my would-be knight would have to do. I needed an escape route from my brother...his biggest rival.

Easton Blake is the perfect reminder of why I avoid hockey players.

Cocky.
Frustratingly sexy.
Accustomed to every girl in his orbit falling for his charm.

With his sultry smile that tells me he knows all the ways to make girls come undone with his touch, I'm almost the next score on his stats. Except I have no time for distractions when I'm focused on graduating early. Gaining Easton's attention wasn't part of my plans. Of course, from the moment he catches me shaking my assets on the bar, he decides I'm his next goal.

Instead of sticking to my own rules, I do something I shouldn't: *I dare him to try.*

Easton's never met a challenge he wouldn't accept. He makes it clear he won't be iced out without convincing me to give him a chance.

I swore off hockey players for a reason. Can I risk making the same mistake again?

ONE
EASTON

LOSING a game on home ice is one of the worst feelings in the world. It's a kick right to the dick knowing you're down in points as the clock is running out, and no matter how many plays you and your boys try to make happen nothing is connecting. Even more rage inducing is when it all goes down against your goddamn rival.

Ryan Donnelly's punchable smirk makes my blood simmer while the two of us face off for the puck drop.

"Ready to dance again, Blake?" he taunts. "If the NHL doesn't want you, I'd say you have a fair chance twirling around the ice in tights. Magic on Ice is calling your name."

This fucking guy. He's been a thorn in my side since junior league.

My teeth clench hard enough to send an ache throbbing through my jaw. I won't let him get to me. His game is cockier than ever since he was a second round draft pick over the summer during the off season. The only consolation is that the team who picked him has not offered him a contract yet. They must want to keep him in the NCAA for further development.

I'm still fighting for my dream of being drafted by the NHL. It's the goal I've been striving for as hard as I can.

This is my damn year. I'm making sure of it, taking every chance to prove myself. Freshman year I didn't meet the eligible age requirements. I'm still getting over the fact that no teams bit for me as a prospect during this chance, yet they did for Donnelly. Even though Heston U beat Elmwood in the championship to maintain our school's unbroken streak of winning Frozen Four.

Punching this asshole for having a better chance at making it to the pro league than I do won't get me any closer to it, only an ejection from the game I love more than anything for misconduct.

I can't change that he got drafted before me, but I can still beat him here and now.

It's the last period. With minutes left to spare, I don't have time to fuck around anymore. We need to put up points against Elmwood University to take the W.

"It's okay to admit you fantasize about guys in tights, Donnelly." I grin when he jerks his head. "Last I checked, you need to sign a contract. Any official offer from Buffalo yet?" His gloves tighten on his stick and I laugh. "Don't sweat it, man. You can still make it on a team as a free agent after graduation when their hold expires on your signing rights."

Donnelly narrows his eyes, lip curling back with a growl. The ref's whistle blows and we sink into position for the face-off.

The puck drops to the ice and our sticks clash together. I win the battle for possession and dart around him. It's feeling good. My linemates are in strategic positions, evading our opponents' defense.

I'm flying down the ice toward Elmwood's goal when my attention snags on a flash of red in the corner of my eye. It interrupts the sea of dark blue and green in the Heston student section.

What the—?

It's not just someone wearing red in our student section. The brunette in the front row is wearing an Elmwood jersey with Donnelly's number emblazoned across her chest.

What the *fuck*?

Our eyes meet and I barely feel it when Donnelly checks my side hard, the momentum slamming both of us against the boards right in front of her.

Time seems to freeze. My heartbeat drums in my ears, drowning out the sounds in the arena. It's strange. I've played games where I felt like I was at the top of my performance level—skating better, shooting on the net more accurately, and connecting with my teammates.

This isn't like that. The audience's energy is something to feed on, but I've never let them distract me while I'm on the ice. Never picked a girl out of the blur of faces in the stands.

I need to move. Get Donnelly off me and make this play instead of gaping at the girl who sticks out amongst the Heston fans.

Her lips part and form the shape of a name. My attention falls to her mouth.

He manages to swipe the puck from me with the tip of his stick and skates away.

"Fuck!" I shove off the boards and dig hard, willing my legs to move faster to get it back. "We have to stop him! Get in there!"

Two of my teammates converge on him. He avoids them one after the other, making it all the way to our end of the ice.

My chest constricts as Donnelly slaps a shot on our goal. He's good, but our goalie is better, stopping the puck in its tracks with his leg pads. Our defense picks up the rebound and passes it to the left winger for a counterattack.

We have to win this.

* * *

We lost.

"Damn it," I mutter on my way out of the showers.

My jaw locks, then I let out a heavy exhale to release the tension in my sore muscles, making my way to my spot in the locker room after the game. Despite the shower, the imaginary stench of our failure lingers on my damp skin. Coach already gave us a lecture before he sent us off for the night.

We might have gotten our offensive and defensive line chemistry working enough to score a goal in the final period, but all it did was tie us up. Elmwood—*Donnelly*—lit up the lamp in overtime first, clinching the win.

If that girl in the stands hadn't distracted me, the play would've gone differently. The strange moment our eyes met continues repeating in my mind.

I shake her from my thoughts and grab the jeans in my cubby. Coach likes us to arrive to games cleaned up, but we're free to leave in casual clothes.

Some of the guys are talking while they check out their new bruises and wind down. The vibe in the room is somber, but not as heavy as my own disappointed mood. It's not like me to keep my head down after a loss.

Not a great look for the team's new captain. I've only had the title for a few months.

My last play against Donnelly replays over and over as I search for what I should've done differently. My dad always taught me the importance of moving on after a bad game outcome. He's one of the reasons I'm chasing this dream so hard, so for his memory I have to put this behind me.

This is my year. I want that draft pick rather than graduating without any NHL recognition and choosing to go the free agent route to make it to the pros.

These days being drafted doesn't mean you get called up right away without finishing college like it was in my dad's era. Some do—Alex Keller, one of our upperclassmen teammates, signed with the NY Islanders last summer and he killed it during his rookie season. It's becoming more common for drafted players to finish out their development in the NCAA and graduate before they're called up to play professionally. Sports blogs speculate it makes for a more well-rounded player.

Still doesn't make me hunger for that pick any less.

And if I get an offer, I'll leave school early in a heartbeat. I like my classes fine enough, but finishing my degree isn't important to me if I have the opportunity to achieve what I want.

It's got me impatient to get out there on NHL ice where I know I belong. I came to play for Heston University with that in mind when UMass passed me over.

Heston Lake, Connecticut is a small college town not far from Hartford. This close to any of the major teams in the northeastern division, players usually vie for spots on the UMass, Elmwood U, Boston College, and UConn hockey teams. But this is the right team for me, and I show UMass what a mistake they made every time we've wiped the ice with them in the last two years.

I heave another sigh, then rake my fingers through my disheveled hair, sending water droplets at my locker neighbor, Cameron Reeves. He whips me with his towel, clearly in better spirits than me.

"Do I need to tell you to turn that frown upside-down like my mom always does?" he jokes.

My lips twitch, but I can't revive the determined smile I gave him before we hit the ice. "Shut up, man."

"Not doing it for you? Well then, my other sage advice is to hit up The Landmark for a drink and get laid."

Noah Porter and a couple of our other D-men chime in with their agreements. This time my smirk comes a little easier because I'm with them on that cure, too. It'll take nothing to find a girl to help me forget the sting of losing against our rivals tonight.

Once I finish getting dressed, Cameron nudges me with his elbow before tugging on his worn Heston U baseball cap backwards over his mess of thick dark brown hair. Win or loss, it's his ritual after a game to reset himself for his next time defending the crease.

Hockey players are some of the most superstitious people on the planet. We've all got our little quirks to keep our focus dialed in on the W.

"Hey, captain?" Elijah Adler, one of our freshman players, hovers behind us.

"Careful, rookie," Cameron warns. "He's in a mood."

I shoot my best friend a flat look. His gray eyes glint with amusement and his easygoing grin widens as he finishes tossing his goalie gear into his bag.

"Relax." He drops to the bench and slings an arm over my shoulder. "We'll get Elmwood back when we play them again."

My jaw works. "I wish it was tomorrow night instead of us playing another home game."

"Me too," he says. "Damn scheduling. But when we do have our second game, we'll get our revenge."

I give an affirmative grunt in response. He's right. Everything this year feels more intense with my last chance at the draft looming over my head. It's all on the line this season.

"For fucking sure, man."

Cameron clamps a hand on my shoulder and jostles me to get me to loosen up. "There you go, bro. It's early in the season still. It'll be us on the ice at Frozen Four for sure after we kick ass for the next thirty games to make the playoffs."

An enthusiastic cheer of *hell yeah* echoes around the locker room from our teammates. Even though we lost against our rival school's team, their morale isn't as low as mine for costing us the win. They voted unanimously to pick me as team captain during summer training. I'm letting them down if I can't pull myself together.

"What's your go-to postgame pick-me-up?" Noah prompts, phone poised to capture the response.

"Porter," Madden growls from his seat on the bench at the gear cubby next to mine.

He's shirtless, face mottled with red splotches while he hurries to tug a hoodie over his head.

"Chill out, Graves. It's called creative cropping." Noah smirks and shoots me a wink over the top of his phone. "You know what I keep telling you. Any exposure is good exposure."

Noah's the only one of us with sponsorship deals he's secured through flashing his winning California beach boy smile, blond hair, and perpetual golden tan on social media.

Madden ducks his head, thick dark hair hanging in his face as he scowls at his lap. "I'm just here to play hockey."

"And with that winning attitude, who wouldn't want to sponsor you?" Noah quips. "So? Give us your postgame recovery ritual. What about you, captain?"

"Not right now," I say. "Ask us tomorrow."

Ruffling my hair, I cast a glance around the room. The whole team is here. None of them have left yet, though Coach Lombard cut us loose. I clear my throat and step to the center of the room, thinking of the things Dad would say to me after a loss that I need to hear myself right now.

"Don't let tonight weigh on you. A season isn't defined by one game. We've got a long road to go."

The guys thump their feet on the floor and clap. My chest tightens as the lingering tension in the room breaks.

"Let's come back strong tomorrow," I say. "See you all there ready to work."

"Go blue!"

The team shouts our chant as one before they begin to leave the locker room.

"You coming?" Cameron asks.

I pause, weighing my options. "Is everyone going out? I might head back to the house with anyone who's not."

"We need this tonight so we can hit the ice tomorrow with a clean slate," he reasons.

I nod slowly. "Yeah."

He bumps his fist against mine. "Good man. Let's go. Come on, rookie. You too."

Elijah points to himself, green eyes wide. I wave him over so he's not hovering at the edge of the group.

The five of us head out of the arena and start the short trek from the far side of campus to the local sports bar. After a game, The Landmark is where everyone goes. The blast of cool, late October air feels good. It's helping clear my head during the walk through town.

This is a big part of hockey, too. If you don't know your teammates, all the practice in the world can't take you the last extra mile that sparks from the camaraderie built outside the rink. We live together off campus, eat together, and go out together. I see them more than I see my mom and little brother, but it's okay because my teammates are my family at Heston.

When we make it to The Landmark, the place is packed with students and townies that attended the game. They commiserate together with pitchers of beer and the best wings in the state. It smells fucking heavenly. I wish I could cheat on the plans the team nutritionist gave me to enjoy some of that tonight, but the best I can get away with is a couple of beers.

Hambone, the owner's white and tan dog weaves through the room, sniffing around for any scraps of fried chicken that fall. He trots over and I kneel down to greet the pitbull with a scratch behind his ears.

"Hey, Hammy. You making out good tonight?" I chuckle at the

way his whole body wiggles when he wags his tail. "Yeah? Good boy."

"Our usual spot's full," Noah says when I stand up.

"You've gotta be shitting me," Madden growls.

Right as we follow his gaze, the group taking up the end of the bar shouts in celebration. My mood plummets at the sight of red. Some of Elmwood's players are here, in our bar.

"What the hell are they doing here?" I mutter.

"I heard from Coach Kincaid they have another away game on their schedule south of here, so they're staying in town tonight instead of busing back to their campus," Cameron says.

Madden takes a threatening step in their direction, thick brows pulled together. I cut him off and nudge him back with a shake of my head.

"It's fine, Graves. Let's just go over here." I motion to the other end of the bar furthest away from them. "They're not ruining the rest of our night."

"Damn right," Cameron says.

Reagan, one of the student bartenders, makes her way to us once we're situated with a sympathetic smile. "Hey guys. The usual?"

Noah braces his elbows on the bar. "Reagan, I need to drown all my sorrows tonight."

"So a pitcher, four large baskets of grilled chicken strips, and a round of potato wedges?" She laughs when five hungry as fuck hockey players nod in unison.

"Stat, babe." Noah blows her a kiss. "Thank you"

"Just water for me. That's it," Elijah says.

"Not so fast." With the same mischievous smile that steals the hearts of girls all over campus, Noah waves a twenty pinched between two fingers. Reagan accepts the tip he slides her whenever we're here to make sure our song choice plays. "Did you think you'd get out of it because we're so far from the stereo system?"

"Come on," Elijah protests. "Really?"

"Tradition's tradition, man." Cameron rubs his mouth to cover his grin. "You've gotta do it. We've all been through this. Easton. Noah. Your brother did it."

Elijah's older brother was a sophomore on the team during mine and Cameron's first year here. Caleb Adler was drafted after that season and plays for Seattle.

"It's your time." I elbow him when Pony by Ginuwine starts to play.

Whenever he hears it, he's supposed to dance. The rest of the patrons get a kick out of this just as much because it's' a time-honored team tradition.

Cameron chuckles. "You've got this, rookie."

Elijah pulls a face, then his shoulders slump. He keeps his light brown hair trimmed on the sides, but the longer section on top falls in his face. He scrapes it back with a sigh.

Noah hypes him up when he starts to move. He's off beat, but his attempt at a sexy dance has all of us trying to keep it together. Not cracking up is a struggle as he turns around, plants his hands on his thighs, and tries his best impression of twerking.

I lose it first, leaning heavily on Noah. Cameron breaks next, wheezing while he wipes away tears.

Shouts and whistles from the other side of the bar cut through our laughter. My smile fades while I search the crowd to see what the commotion is. The Elmwood guys block the view around the opposite end of the bar where a bunch of people have congregated.

Exchanging a look with Cameron and Noah, I lead them around the corner for a better view. I'll tolerate Elmwood crashing our bar, but if they start any shit, we'll handle them.

The yelling shifts into cheers as a girl emerges in the middle when she stands on a bar stool. She climbs on top of the bar and winks at Reagan as she tugs her ponytail free, sending wavy chestnut brown hair cascading around her shoulders.

Rolling her hips to the sensual beat of the song, she sinks her fingers in her hair and gives the entire bar a show that captures my rapt attention. Mine, and every other guy's in the room.

"Damn, baby," Noah mutters.

I agree.

She drops down low and pops back up with a sexy move that ignites heat low in my gut. My hands ball into fists when she faces our direction.

It's her. The girl from the game.

I'm so awestruck that she's here, I'm not watching where my feet are taking me. I grunt as I walk into a wooden column, clipping my side. Pain flares in the shoulder that Donnelly slammed against the boards earlier while I stumble to regain my balance, nearly knocking over a bar stool.

The guys bust out laughing, but it barely registers. I don't care. How the hell could I care about anything else?

Nothing else matters right now. My eyes remain locked on *her*.

TWO
EASTON

THERE's no mistaking that the beautiful girl swaying her ass to the music on top of the bar is the same one I locked eyes with during the final period.

Her Elmwood jersey is gone—thank fuck.

My gaze drags over her, captivated by every move she makes. She flips her hair to one side, grinning as she lifts her arms into the air and rocks her hips back and forth. The strappy black top beneath her flannel that crisscrosses over her chest rides up to flash the bar a peek of her stomach. Snug jeans hug her soft curves, and—

"Dude." Cameron claps my shoulder, sputtering through his amusement. "You almost ate it."

"Yeah." My answer is distant and I brush him off absently.

"You good?" He waves a hand in front of my face when I don't answer. "Hello? Earth to East."

I'm not listening at all.

The girl dancing owns my focus.

She wore Donnelly's number to the game, but I want her beneath me tonight while I make her scream. Hell yeah, she's exactly the girl I need.

"Guess I'm finding another lucky lady tonight," Noah says.

That gets my attention. I bunch my fists and ride the hot wave of jealousy that slams into me at the thought of her with him. This is a first. I've never been one to clash with my friends over a girl. A moment ago we were both admiring her before I recognized her, but now I'm gripped by an unfamiliar sense of possessiveness.

Noah holds his hands up. "Relax, man. She's all yours. Not really my type, anyway."

"Every girl is your type," Cameron says wryly.

He shakes his head. "Not my friends' girls. I've never slept with someone any of you have been with."

The others follow us over as my feet continue carrying me closer to the crowd watching the girl on the bar. Half of them bob and sway with her, singing the seductive tune as a group.

"You're missing the show," Madden says gruffly.

He grunts behind me as if he's been jabbed in the stomach.

Elijah mutters under his breath, "Don't say anything or they'll make me keep dancing for the whole song."

Noah chuckles. "Our captain's found a much more appealing performance."

Some guy starts to climb up to join her. She shakes her head with a sexy little smirk and nudges him down with the toe of the knee-high boots encasing her long legs. When another guy tries his luck, she says something to Reagan and accepts the drink nozzle attached behind the bar. Sinking to a low pose as the chorus hits, she squirts him with a quick spray of water, earning the cheers of the rest of the Elmwood players.

She's a firecracker. I find myself smiling, my shitty mood over the loss gone.

It falls when someone else moves in on her, planting his hands on the bar at her feet. I recognize Donnelly, even from the back of his head. I can't hear what he's saying but it's clear he's bothering her.

I'm moving again before I'm aware of what I plan to do.

She doesn't listen to him. Rolling her eyes, she moves out of reach.

"Don't just watch, you numbnuts. She's still off-limits." Donnelly searches his nearest teammates' faces. "Help me get her down."

Another Elmwood player edges closer in my periphery.

A muscle jumps in my jaw when I catch the way he looks up at her. Donnelly thinking he can take this girl home is bad enough. Curbing the strong urge to deck this guy for it, I weave through the crowd she drew, intent on making all the Elmwood guys back the fuck off.

I catch sight of his name printed on the back of his red warm up jacket when he pushes past his teammates to get to the bar.

Werner. Sounds like wiener. I smirk, overwriting his name in my head with the fitting replacement. His arm is in a cast from above his elbow all the way down. I vaguely recall playing against him last year. It clicks that this guy is benched this season because of it.

We reach the bar at the same time. I ignore him for the moment, grasping a fistful of Donnelly's pullover to wrench him away.

"She doesn't seem interested. I think that's your cue to go." I leave the unspoken *before you get punched* hanging in the air between us.

He gets in my face. "No one asked you, Blake."

"No one had to. It's obvious to the whole bar she's not into you."

Satisfaction floods my chest when I give Donnelly a warning shove and earn her attention. Her sensual movements slow in the corner of my eye, though she doesn't stop dancing. Tilting my head to meet her curious gaze, I offer her a crooked smile.

"These guys bothering you, sweetheart? I can make them leave if you want."

Wiener fucks up big time by reaching around me and grabbing at her flannel with his good hand. It causes her to wobble when he tugs. I clamp my fingers over his wrist with a forceful squeeze.

"Hey," I grit out. "That's dangerous, idiot. You'll make her fall."

If he doesn't let go, I'll break his other arm to match the one in the cast. He won't ever make it off the injured reserve list after I'm through with him.

He shakes me off with a frown and releases her. "Step off. I can handle her."

Before I get out a response, my mystery girl plants one hand on my head for balance and her boot against Wiener's chest.

"Actually, you can fuck off forever now, Johnny." There's a hard edge to her fierce tone. She pushes off with her foot and he falls back a couple of steps, mouth set in a line. "If I want to dance on the bar, I will. I don't need Ryan's permission to enjoy myself, and I sure as hell don't need *yours*."

She knows them? I guess that explains why she wore Donnelly's jersey. Irritation simmers in my gut. She might know them, but she doesn't want them harassing her.

"Stop making a scene and get down," Donnelly argues.

He reaches for her. I shove him back again, blocking him by standing between him and the bar.

"Try that again, and I'll lay you out flat on your back, asshole. She said no."

He stares at me with his features twisted in a mix of disbelief and anger. I smirk when I catch sight of my teammates squaring up behind him. They've got my back.

"We're not on the ice now, Donnelly." The warning is evident in Cameron's words. "You won't get any more cheap shots in."

"Says the losing team," Wiener replies.

Noah eyes the cast. "Didn't see you out there, pretty boy. Best pipe down."

"*Pretty boy*? You wanna go? I'll still kick your asses."

Wiener—no fucking way am I ever calling him anything else again—takes a threatening step toward my teammates. His buddies hold him back with placating protests.

While my friends distract Elmwood's team, I turn my attention back to my mystery girl.

"Feel like getting out of here?" I ask.

She stares at me for so long, I believe she's going to turn me down. Her gaze bounces between me and the guys arguing behind me.

Finally, she nods. "If it gets me away from them? Yeah."

I offer her my hand. She holds out on me for another beat, scrutinizing me before she slips her hand in mine.

Grinning, I haul her off the bar and catch her over my shoulder. A surprised shriek escapes her, but she clutches my hoodie while my grip settles on the back of her lower thigh to keep her steady.

A laugh leaves me when Donnelly realizes I'm halfway across the room. His shouts follow us as we make our getaway.

I forget the sting of losing the game because this win tastes far sweeter. Having a hot girl over my shoulder puts me in an excellent mood. Even better, she left with me instead of Donnelly. She's not cheering for him now. Satisfaction expands in my chest because soon I'll have her screaming for me instead.

We're approaching the square at the center of town three blocks away from the bar when she taps me on the back.

"So, are you going to let me down soon, or what? I'm just hanging over your shoulder."

Chuckling, I pretend to think about it for a second. "I hadn't thought about it, no. I like you where you're at."

She hums sardonically and pokes me in the side. I grunt when she prods at a tender bruise above my hip.

"Put me down."

Reluctantly, I stop walking. "Alright."

I guide her carefully, hovering my hand over her back ready to catch her as I bend to let her slide off my shoulder. Her feet dangle, wiggling in search of the ground while she keeps an arm hooked around my shoulders to stabilize herself. Her body drags against mine when she drops the last few inches to the pavement.

"There." I clear my throat and ruffle my hair to distract myself from how good she felt pressed against me so I don't pull her back in. "Better?"

"Much."

Oh, damn. It was hard to tell when she was standing on the bar while I was too busy enjoying her dancing, but she's shorter than me. Most people are when I stand at six-foot-five. I've got almost a full foot on her. In her heeled knee-high boots, the top of her head barely reaches my chin.

I study her long legs, guessing she's around five-seven give or take an inch. Her body is banging with flared hips that look perfect for grabbing, and the strappy shirt beneath her flannel provides a tempting peek of her mouthwatering cleavage.

She brushes herself off, shivering against the crisp breeze.

"Are you cold? We got out of there without getting your jacket." I tug at the neck of my hoodie. I don't usually give my clothes away, yet I offer anyway. "Want to wear this?"

She tucks her brown hair behind her ear. "No thanks. I'm fine. I like the cold. It's still bearable for me to go out without a coat. At least for another couple of weeks."

We fall into step together and continue through Main Street square. She's heading for campus, though I'm not sure if it means she has a car parked at the arena or if she goes to school here.

"Do you live on campus?" I ask.

"Is that your way of asking if you can come over?" she counters in a teasing tone. "I do. I'm in the apartment suites in Montgomery."

I breathe easier knowing she isn't about to disappear after tonight. "So you go to Heston. I haven't seen you around before."

She seemed to know Reagan back there. Me and the guys are in The Landmark at least twice a week and I can't say I've seen her. I would've noticed.

"I keep a pretty loaded course schedule. I'm working hard to finish my degree within three years instead of four."

"But you came out tonight." The corner of my mouth lifts in a slow grin. "Looked like you enjoyed yourself."

"Taking breaks is important for your mental health," she says airily.

My heartbeat stumbles at the bright smile she flashes me. I rub at my chest, chuckling.

"I'm sorry your night got cut short since that guy was being an asshole."

"Well, my brother's always been overprotective."

My grin falls. Shock arrows through me and I stop in my tracks. She shrugs, unaware of my brain imploding on the word *brother*.

"Ryan didn't want me to get up there. He thought I wouldn't do it when his buddies dared me, and I love nothing more than proving him wrong. The look on his face was totally worth it."

I open and close my mouth, brows furrowing. "Wait—you're Donnelly's sister?"

All the years I've played against him in junior league and the NCAA I had no idea he had a sister. A seriously *hot* sister, jesus.

She snorts, her hazel eyes crinkling at the corners. "Yup. You know technically that makes me Donnelly, too?"

Her gaze travels over me, sizing me up the same way she did earlier. The radiant smile that's making my heart thump hard fades. I want to bring it back right away, debating which of my best lines to use on her to revive it. Instead, those beautiful full lips purse in a cute little frown.

"Don't tell me you're a fan? No." She cuts off my scoff of disbelief, squinting. "Damn. Tall as hell, muscles on muscles, hanging around The Landmark like you own the place. You're a hockey player."

There's zero recognition.

Is she serious? She doesn't know me?

I scrub a hand over my jaw, hitching a shoulder. It throws me to not be recognized when I'm used to every girl on campus knowing exactly who I am. People rush up to me to take selfies between classes even when I'm not wearing the team's hockey jacket. I haven't had to actually introduce myself in a long ass time.

"I'm Heston's starting center. Team captain," I say proudly.

"Shit." She blows the word out on an unimpressed laugh. "Yeah, that's not gonna work for me."

I step into her, dipping my chin to stare her down. "Is that so?"

"I don't do hockey players."

She says that, but the little hitch in her breath when my chest brushes against her tells a different story.

"Then why hang out at The Landmark? Everyone on campus knows it's where you go to chase jerseys." My head lowers along with my voice, my words coming out on a rasp as I watch her carefully. "Why get rinkside seats to the game? Didn't seem like you were so against hockey players when you were cheering with every other fan in the arena."

Her eyes widen. "How did you—?"

"Hard to miss you, babe. You were the only one wearing an Elmwood jersey in the Heston student section. Ballsy move. Red looks great on you." I swipe my tongue across my lower lip. "Bet you'd look even better in blue and green."

Her eyes glimmer beneath the glow of the lamp lighting the path, and she puts on an innocent expression. "I do happen to look great in those colors. But I don't cheer for the Heston Knights."

The thought of her in my jersey crosses my mind, rewriting what happened at tonight's game to have her in the stands wearing my number instead of her brother's. "You're the reason I got checked before your brother stole possession of the puck from me."

"So you're not as much of a hotshot player as you think. Heston lost to Elmwood tonight."

Another smirk curves her full lips. Instead of pissing me off for ragging on my game, heat pools low in my gut. What the hell?

Usually the girls I talk to go for a flirtatious approach, like getting into my pants is already a done deal when they lean in too close to tell me what a big fan they are. Everyone on campus worships the ground I walk on, but not her. This beautiful girl insults me and it turns me on. I trace my bottom lip with the tip of my tongue, confused by how refreshing I find her. Refreshing and seriously hot as fuck with that exasperated, mildly amused tilt of her tempting lips.

Knowing she's Ryan Donnelly's sister only amplifies how enticing I find her.

"I'm sure you'll have no trouble finding someone to help you cope, captain," she says with mock sympathy in her tone.

Someone else? My usual routine after a game doesn't even register in my mind at the suggestion of finding another girl. It's what I should do. It would be easy—it always is—but it wouldn't be *her*. This intriguing girl who doesn't give a single shit who I am or what my reputation on campus is.

Time to show her why I've got most girls on campus wishing for the chance of one night in my bed.

"Your name is the only one I want on my lips tonight, baby. Tell it to me so I can whisper it against your skin between the hundreds of kisses I'm going to lay on every gorgeous inch of you."

She lets out a breathy laugh and shakes her head slowly as her stunning smile returns. It gets my pulse going into overdrive again.

"Go try that line on one of the girls back in the bar."

She retreats, backing away step by step. I'm struck by an irrational urge to reach out and hold on before she slips through my grasp.

"See you around, hotshot."

"You're really walking away from me, just like that?" I call.

She smirks over her shoulder. "Just like that."

"You have no idea what you're missing out on."

My chest puffs out when she pauses to face me once more. I take my time dragging my eyes over every inch of her, loving that the longer I admire her, the pinker her cheeks turn.

"Let me take you somewhere." My voice lowers to a soft rasp that drives girls crazy, each word deep and rough. "I know how to make you feel real good. So good I'll have you screaming, baby."

She licks her lips, cutting her gaze to the side. "I bet."

A shadow crosses her beautiful features, there and gone in a moment. My fingers curl into my palm to keep myself from striding over to her and cupping her face until I earn her smile again.

Huffing, she props her hands on her hips and squints at me. "You know what? I dare you to try." She lifts her brows. "I'll never say yes to a hockey player."

My head jerks in surprise. First she rejects me, then she throws down the gauntlet? Another slow smile tugs at my lips.

"Challenge accepted."

The corners of her mouth curl. "Bye, captain."

My rival's sister leaves me alone in the lamp-lit square. I watch her until she's out of sight with a strange burn of anticipation tickling the inside of my chest.

THREE
MAYA

My phone lights up with another text, the tenth Ryan's sent since I escaped him at the bar. My brother's been blowing up my phone with countless texts and three ignored calls about the dramatic exit I made thanks to Heston's hockey captain hauling me over his shoulder to carry me out like some dashing knight.

Not exactly my idea of a good time to rely on a hockey player, but it was the fastest way to evade my brother and Johnny.

I finish twisting my freshly showered hair into a towel and grab my phone off the nightstand ready to silence my notifications if he doesn't leave me alone. Reagan won't be home from her shift at the bar for another two hours.

I was planning to enjoy tonight to the fullest, celebrating that I went to my first hockey game in years without wanting to throw up at seeing my ex-boyfriend on the ice with my brother. Johnny wasn't even playing after his accident benched him for the season.

While Johnny's mere presence still causes an uncomfortable knot to tangle in my stomach and my heart to splinter with fractures that throb with the old ache of his betrayal, I made it through the game I used to love without my anxiety winning.

I even let Reagan and my brother talk me into going to the bar afterwards. I tend to avoid it on nights I know the hockey team takes over the place.

Another pushy text from Ryan makes me shake my head.

Ryan
Maya.

Ryan
Maya. Maya Maya Mayaaaa. Answer your phone damn it!

Ryan
Don't think I won't blow you up every five minutes until you answer. We both know I've always been better at getting on your nerves. You'll break first.

Ryan
I finally get you to watch me play again after three years and you ditch me?

Ryan
Why did you let Easton fucking bag of dicks Blake carry you out of the bar?

Ryan
If you're with him right now I'm disowning you as a sister.

I could let him stew for the rest of the night. He deserves it after he tried to go all overprotective on me at the bar for having fun. Sighing, I take a photo of myself in my pajamas giving him the finger.

Maya
I wouldn't have ditched you if you weren't being an ass. You can't tell me what to do. You're only like five minutes older than me.

Ten months older, actually. Irish twins. Our family had a trip raising us, especially our grandfather. Ryan's older, but I've always felt like I'm the more responsible sibling. By high school we were in the same grade because I tested into his year.

We used to be so close growing up. For the last two years I've distanced myself from hockey. After his big NHL draft moment over the summer, I agreed to go to the game tonight so I wouldn't miss my last chance to see him play my college before his professional career.

Ryan doesn't respond for several minutes, then sends a thumbs up emoji as his only apology. Dick.

I scroll back through the messages to the one that gives away my Heston Knight's name.

"Easton," I murmur.

I wasn't sure at the bar if he was a hockey player or not. He's built like one, tall and strong enough to throw me over his shoulder and carry me for three blocks with ease. I might have a soft hourglass figure, but I'm not exactly willowy. Mom used to say the Donnelly women are built solid with curvy hips and generous chests.

My face tingles with warmth remembering the feel of every firm muscle of his body when he set me on my feet. He had the attitude down, too.

I swallow thickly and clamp my thighs together to chase away the unwelcome throb of heat while picturing the sultry look he served up —the one that almost made me the next score on his stats.

Easton Blake is the perfect reminder of why I avoid hockey players.

Cocky. Frustratingly sexy. Accustomed to every girl in his orbit falling for his charm.

Handsome, playful smile. Messy dark brown hair. Warm blue eyes.

"Oh boy."

I rub my forehead, still shocked at myself for winding up with a hockey player tonight. I can't believe I dared him to keep trying to win me over. There's no way I'll ever give in, yet part of me wants to see how hard he'll work for it. My lips twitch.

Nah. He'll move on. A guy like him is bound to forget about me.

Johnny did. Not a second wasted before I caught him with another girl—not like finding an unfamiliar pair of panties in his bed, but interrupting them in the act. I wanted to surprise my boyfriend before I toured his college. Instead, I got my heart broken and learned I should never trust hockey players.

Other than my brother, I want nothing to do with them. I swore them off to shield my heart from ever going through that pain again.

An aggravated sigh escapes me and I flop back on the bed, covering my face with a pillow. I don't need to dwell on him at all. Annoyed with myself, I climb beneath the covers for bed.

This semester I have what most students would consider a normal schedule. It's a blessing and a curse because I'm not keeping myself as busy as I have the last two years. Without the extra classes and assignments to distract myself, all the things I try not to worry about rise to the surface.

At least winter break is soon. That means I get to visit Grandpa in person.

I wait all year for the short amount of time I grant myself to go home. Since I started at Heston University, I've been nose to the grindstone. The intense course load that comes with racking up enough credits to complete my degree a year early is hard work, but worth the summer semesters and crammed schedules from the last two years.

This semester is the first one where I feel like I can breathe. It's weird after piling on credit hours to have such a light class schedule. I'm glad I got as many course requirements as I could out of the way. From here on out, it'll be smooth sailing to finish my studies next semester.

It's all so Grandpa can see me graduate from college.

My throat closes over for a brief moment. In my senior year of high school his health took a really bad turn and he hasn't fully recovered according to Mom and Dad's reports about his physical therapy and doctor visits.

Winter break can't come soon enough.

When my phone vibrates with a notification ten minutes later, I assume it's Ryan texting me again. Time to silence my notifications. It's an unpleasant surprise to find my ex's name on my screen.

Johnny
You shouldn't have left. Come back to the bar so we can catch up.

Johnny
I missed you.

"Ugh. No way." I grimace at the slimy sensation his message causes in my stomach and glare at my phone. "Asshole."

Stabbing the block caller button after so many years feels great. It's something I should've done when we broke up, but I never had to worry. Johnny didn't bother fighting for us or explaining himself. Hard to formulate an excuse for *sorry you caught your boyfriend balls deep in a sorority chick.*

He was my first and *last* hockey player boyfriend. I swore I'd never fall for another self-absorbed jackass like him. He's also the only serious relationship I've had—at least it was for me. Considering he was cheating on me, things were probably never serious for him. The few other guys I've dated either couldn't handle my lack of availability, or fizzled out because I wouldn't let my guard down for any true connection to develop.

What sucks most of all is the wedge the breakup drove between me and my brother. I never told him why I ended things with his friend and teammate because something Johnny said when I told him we were done stuck with me.

You think Ryan doesn't know what's up? Every player messes around.

My heart beats hard and my breathing comes in tight, quick pulls of air just thinking about the ways he would manipulate me. I close my eyes, trying to concentrate on slowing my anxious breathing with meditation exercises, then squeeze my eyelids when I'm unable to focus.

"Screw this." I flip the stuffy covers off.

There's no way I'll be able to sleep. So much for my wins tonight. The pride I felt for being able to go to the game dwindles.

After throwing on a pair of sweats and a plain black hoodie, I pull my hair into a ponytail and grab my grandfather's faded baseball cap. The hat alone brings a small comfort. I always snagged it from him whenever me and Ryan had sleepovers with our grandparents and wore it around their farm. He gifted it to me when I started college. I brush my fingertips over the embroidered Donnelly Dairy logo that's gone soft and frayed with age.

Once it's tugged down low, I pocket my keys, my phone, and keep a sharp cat-shaped safety keychain in my hand just in case. Heston Lake is a safe enough town, but I'm still a girl walking alone after dark. There have also been a few reports of break ins around campus.

When I'm too wound up, I have to move. The jittery sensation that vibrates in my muscles is too impossible to shake without going for a late night walk to clear the racing thoughts from my head. I hate it when my brain won't just shut off.

In the moment I'm fine, then I end up overanalyzing if I said the right thing or acted weird.

This is the only way I've learned to cope so I don't spend a sleepless night of tossing and turning laying in bed alone with my anxiety picking apart every memory on loop.

On my way out, I text Reagan to let her know where I am and turn on location sharing so she'll be able to track me. We've always got each other's back.

Most of campus is quiet after midnight with a few stragglers here and there. One of the fraternity houses is having a party. The thumping music fades behind me as I head off campus toward the square at the center of town.

I love walking this way. The buildings all have a historic charm that feels cozy, plus my favorite coffee shop sits between a local family-owned bookshop and a small art gallery.

Clocktower Brew House got its name for the old tower at the top of the building with a clock face. There are photos inside the coffee shop from the town's records showing the different uses for the building through the years dating back almost to colonial times.

My head feels clearer already. As I reach the end of the block, a cat emerges from the shadows and meows at me. I grin. This is even better than my walk.

"Hi, kitty," I whisper.

Approaching slowly so I don't startle it, I crouch down with my hand outstretched. The cat sniffs me briefly before purring and rubbing against my hand. My mood perks up as I stroke its soft fur.

"No collar. Are you a stray?" I laugh at the sound it makes in response like we're having an actual conversation. "You're definitely well fed. Look at your belly."

The cat flops to the pavement and rolls on its back, wriggling back and forth. I can't resist taking out my phone to snap a few photos.

Animals? One hundred percent better than people in most cases.

"I could pet you all night. Everyone at Merrywood Farms would love you. I'll show them your picture when I go in for work this week."

I've always loved animals, but it was my grandfather who made me understand how therapeutic they can be. It's why I've built my psychology and physical therapy degree around animal-assisted therapies. Part of that is thanks to Merrywood Farms, a wellness and rescue farm that offers a variety of animal activities.

The cat's ears prick, then flick in the direction of the houses on the street connected to the square. I think I hear someone calling for it and shaking a food bowl. The cat twines around my leg before bounding off.

Feeling much better, I cut my walk short and head back towards campus.

FOUR
EASTON

After my Tuesday morning workout, I hustle across campus to make it in time for my post-gym treat. The team's nutritionist stays on us about our intake during the season. I adhere to the recommendations closer than some of the other guys because I'm serious about this. It's all part of playing my best, starting with how I fuel myself.

But sometimes a man just needs a donut.

Coach has been handing our asses to us on the ice to make up for the loss against Elmwood on Friday, despite securing a W for Saturday's home game. Not one guy is slacking. We're shaping up for the next games on the schedule this weekend. Skating with these guys makes me a better player because we all want to earn our next win.

The pastel-colored food truck comes into view. It only parks on campus for a short window on certain days every other month. I rub my stomach in anticipation.

"No line," I mumble cheerfully.

My mind becomes one-track—no thoughts, only donuts. I'm digging for my wallet while scanning the display window before I've reached the truck. Spotting my favorite kind, I grin.

Right as I come to a stop in front of the pink counter and open my mouth, someone cuts me off.

"I'll take the sour cream with cinnamon vanilla glaze, please," she says.

I jolt, snapping my head to the side. It's her. Donnelly's sister. Who is also Donnelly in my head because I never got her name.

Damn, I thought she was gorgeous under the dim bar lights with her soft curves and addictive confident smile, but in the light of day she steals my breath.

She's bundled in an oversized cream sherpa jacket and leggings. It's not in a seductive outfit, yet she has all of my focus. I haven't run into her for four days, and just like Friday night the mere sight of her has my pulse speeding up.

The bright morning sun catches her chestnut hair, highlighting fairer strands. In the heels of those knee-high boots, she came to my chin, but without the couple of extra inches I'm at the perfect height to kiss the top of her head.

She puts her coffee from Clocktower Brew House on the counter —a mocha latte going by the scrawled handwriting on the cup. There's a peppermint stick poking out of the lid that has me picturing her plush lips wrapped around it, sending my mind down a path I need to cut off before I'm standing in the middle of campus with a boner.

Donnelly isn't paying me any attention, more occupied with rummaging in her crossbody saddle bag.

More importantly, she ordered my favorite donut. It's a sign.

"Last one," the perky donut dealer announces.

"Wait," I stammer.

"Great," Donnelly says.

"Hang on." I step in front of her to create a barrier between her and the donut, offering a crooked smile. "We meet again."

Her lips part in surprise now that I've earned her full attention. "Captain."

The lopsided curve of my mouth stretches into a grin. "I like it when you call me that."

Her brows lift and the corner of her mouth twitches with a suppressed smile. "Don't get used to it. From now on, you'll be captain full-of-yourself."

"I can live with that." I swipe a hand over my mouth in an effort to hide the amused noise trying to escape me. "I've gotta say, I much prefer your company to your brother's. You're my favorite Donnelly now."

"An honor." She grants me a sardonic little bow. "Are you going to move so I can pay for my donut? I'll be late for class."

"The thing is, I want that donut. Been craving it all through my morning weight training."

She scoffs in amusement, eyeing me up and down. "Is this you defending the donut from me?"

She's got me there. Basically, yeah, I am defending the donut I've been craving. Plus, the longer I keep her here, the more time I get to spend with her. An unquestionable win-win.

"We both can get what we want. We'll split it. Pick out another kind and we'll share them."

I dip my chin to seal the deal with something that always works: smoldering puppy dog eyes. It makes all the girls I've been with fold like a house of cards. Noah says it's my blue eyes, girls can't resist them.

Usually.

Donnelly is immune to my tactics. Instead of agreeing to what I want, she mocks me with a head tilt and puppy eyes of her own. My pulse skips. She looks cute like that.

"Split it?" She sidesteps me to get to the counter. "A gentleman would let me have the donut. I was here first."

"Actually, we arrived at the same time. So fair is fair."

Before she can pay, I move in beside her and slide a twenty to the girl running the food truck. I give Donnelly a sidelong glance to check if she's still going to fight me. Her stare lingers on my hand resting on the counter, veins prominent from my workout.

"Okay, fine," she agrees begrudgingly a few seconds later. "The maple bacon."

There's no stopping the groan that leaves me at her choice because *fuck yes* that sounds good. "I like the way you think, Donnelly."

She tucks her hair behind her ear. I catch the faint pink tinge in her cheeks while she avoids looking my way and stares at the display case.

"Also a Boston cream, please," she adds hastily, pointing to the custard-stuffed chocolate iced donut in the corner. She peeks at me. "Is that cool with you?"

"Yeah."

I'm not about to say no if it means spending more time splitting donuts with her. She tries to offer me money while our selections are packed up. I shake my head.

"I've got it."

"If we're sharing, then let me pay for half." Her lips slide together and her gaze cuts to the side. "I don't want you to think I owe you something because you paid."

Something cinches tightly in my chest at her hushed yet guarded tone.

"It's just donuts. No strings, I promise." I take the bag and guide her away from the food truck with my hand resting lightly at the small of her back. I keep my tone joking. "I don't need to resort to such underhanded tactics to get you to say yes to me, baby. Unless I can use these donuts to bargain with you to get you to wear a Heston jersey to our next home game this week."

She exhales, seeming more relaxed. "Not a chance. I won't be there or at any other games. Friday was a one time thing."

"Are you doubting my persuasion skills? I got you to give me half of my favorite donut, didn't I? We're just getting started here."

She shoots me a wry glance and points to a round stone table in the shade of some maple trees that still have most of their orange and red leaves. "There's a nice spot over there."

We each take a seat on the stone benches on opposite sides of the table.

I pass her share of our donuts to her once I divide them. "You know, I can't keep calling you Donnelly. We're splitting donuts. That makes us friends in my book. I'm Easton."

"I know." The corners of her mouth lift.

I perk up. She didn't know my name the other night when we left the bar together. "You looked me up?"

She breaks out in a radiant grin and shows me her phone. It's opened to a text conversation with her brother. He rags on her for letting *Easton fucking bag of dicks Blake* carry her out of the bar. My brows shoot up and I laugh.

"That's quite the mouthful of a name. I don't know if it'll fit on my ID. I'll have to go the initials route." I brace my forearms on the table. "So you know my name. If you don't tell me yours, I guess I'll be forced to call you Donnelly forever."

She shakes her head, pretty hazel eyes gleaming. "It's Maya."

"Maya." I like the sound of it. "Maya Donnelly."

"Okay, stop saying my name." She covers my mouth with a hand when I start to murmur it again. "For real."

I give her palm a quick kiss, chuckling when she whips it back to her side of the table. She can't quite stifle a laugh and crams a large bite of maple bacon in her mouth. I mirror her and spend several moments in heaven at the taste. Sweet and savory, what a combo.

"Goddamn, that's good. Bacon makes everything better."

She hums in agreement. I finish off the maple bacon in another bite and go for the Boston cream next, saving my favorite for last. It takes no time at all to demolish my portion of the Boston cream before she's even finished her first donut half. I hold my last one up, anticipation building.

For a minute, I debate sending a photo of my little cheat snack to the guys. It's something we like to do. Another tradition the older players pass down to the incoming rookies that bonds us as a team.

I would send it, but I want this moment with Maya to myself.

"Guess I'll be going for an extra run later for indulging like this." I take a bite and hold a fist to my mouth, fucking blissed out on the best donut in Connecticut. "Worth it."

"So worth it," Maya mumbles, more to herself than me.

She's in her own world, absorbed in enjoying her treat. And I'm wrapped up in watching her.

Does she know she's torturing me with the dollop of custard from the cream-filled one at the corner of her mouth? The way she wipes it with her finger and licks it off has my throat going dry.

The crisp morning breeze catches her wavy brown hair and sends a flutter of orange leaves to the ground around our table. My donut hangs from my fingertips, partially forgotten in favor of studying her while she eats. This is nice. We're not talking, but I don't mind the quiet. I might barely know her yet, but this has the makings of the same type of comfortable silence I have with Cameron and the guys.

It goes hand in hand with an instinctive sense of trust. I don't get to have that with a lot of people. Definitely not with most of the girls I know, except for Reagan at The Landmark. For that reason alone, I know I have to get to know her more.

She pulls me out of my trance when she checks her phone and mutters a reluctant curse. "Thanks for the donuts. I'd better run."

I watch her fold up her napkins into tiny squares and stand, gathering her things. "You're leaving?"

"If I don't go now, I'll be more than ten minutes late for class. Luckily for me, the professor doesn't show up until twenty minutes into the lecture. The TA is more lenient on attendance."

"That is lucky. Can't say the same. All of my professors go hard on us, even the student athletes."

I shove the rest of my donut in my mouth before getting up to take her little origami trash collection. I dump it with mine, then walk with her in the direction she starts off in.

"Were you hoping for an easy ride?" she taunts.

"Nah. I don't mind the hard work. It keeps me focused." I stretch my arms overhead, noticing that the move draws her gaze to my biceps. Her eyes dart away when she realizes I caught her checking me out. "I'm not about slacking or cutting corners."

"Spoken like any good captain," she says.

Pride swells in my chest. I want to be a man Dad would be proud of. Someone capable of taking care of others, and for me that includes leading my team as captain.

"Come to more of the games. You'll see my work ethic in action."

She plays with the strap of her purse. "I don't think so."

"Then let me take you out."

"Not happening." She takes the steps of a building that I think I had a sociology class in last year. A few steps up puts her level with my height when she turns around to face me. "You'll have to try harder. Bye, hotshot."

I grin like an idiot. "I guess I will. Later, Maya."

My phone buzzes in my pocket a couple of times. Probably the guys in our group text wondering where the hell I am since we all left the weight room around the same time. I'm too busy enjoying the view until Maya disappears inside the building.

FIVE
MAYA

It's early on Friday when I poke my head into Reagan's room. She's still passed out in a cocoon of covers. Between the two of us, I'm the early riser.

"It's almost nine."

She groans faintly. "Unfairly early."

"I'm going to Clocktower. Do you want coffee?"

Her sleep-mussed strawberry blonde bun pokes further out of the mound of covers as she wakes up more. "Coffee? Okay, those are the magic words."

"Mhm. That's what I thought. I'm on it."

It's about to get busy in there and I want coffee before my only class today. I push off her door frame and grab my purse from the counter in the kitchenette attached to the living area.

Our apartment is what Reagan likes to call dainty. Off-campus apartments are bigger, but neither of us can afford it. At least the two-bedroom apartment suite is larger than our shoebox dorm from freshman year. We could easily fit that room inside one of our bedrooms and still have some space left over for Reagan's music equipment.

"Have I told you lately I love you?" she calls groggily.

"Back at you." My phone rings right on schedule as I exit the building. "Hey, Mom. How was the appointment today?"

"Good. He's tired, but he got through all of his PT exercises. The trainer was happy with what he got done."

"Don't treat me like I'm an invalid," I hear Grandpa grumble. "Still here, you know."

I look to the sky, mouth curved. "Can I talk to him?"

His scratchy voice comes over the line. "Hi, chicken. How's school?"

Affection blooms in my chest at his nickname for me. "Hey Grandpa. It's good. How are you feeling?"

"Oh, on top of the world. Like I could dance one of my mother's jigs with her, rest her soul."

He never loses his sense of humor, even when he's not feeling his best. I can tell from the tightness in his voice that he's feeling the age of his bones. He's a stubborn man who hates that he has to rely on my parents and the rest of our family to take care of him when he spent a lifetime taking care of all of us.

"I can't wait to see you for Christmas." The words come out slightly strained. "I'm spending the whole break with you. We can do anything you want."

"You don't have to come see me, chicken. Go out with your friends."

"No way. I want to hang out with you."

"Ah, well, in that case turn around, Rosalie. If Maya's coming to see me, I need to be able to walk on my own two feet again instead of hobbling around with the walker."

"Take it easy," I say as I reach the coffee shop. "You know you don't have to show off for me."

It's busy inside with a line all the way to the door.

"Wouldn't that be nice?" He goes quiet for a few seconds.

"We're almost home, Maya. We should go," Mom says.

"Okay. Love you guys. I'll talk to you later."

I keep my voice hushed so I don't disturb the other customers. While I'm distracted with saying goodbye, I accidentally bump into the guy ahead of me in line.

"Excuse me," I offer as I slide my phone into my purse.

There's no response until I look up, coming face to face with Easton Blake in a navy blue Heston U Hockey warm up jacket and gray sweatpants. They highlight his powerful thighs and show off the impressive bulge of his—I snap my eyes up, darting my gaze around the cozy coffee shop.

Fuck me.

"Oh," I choke out. "Sorry about that."

The corner of his mouth kicks up. "It's cool. You can bump into me whenever."

"Yeah, I'm sure you'd like that." I mutter it before thinking, more to myself than him.

"Oh, without a doubt." He winks, shuffling backward when the line moves so he doesn't have to stop talking to me.

"Aren't you late for practice?"

"Away game." He nods to his bulky duffel bag by the door. "I have to head to the rink to catch the bus right after this."

I smirk. "A hockey player-free campus tonight? Score. The Landmark won't run out of wings."

He scoffs. "That only happened like once."

I tick off on my fingers the times since I've been here the hockey team was directly responsible for eating all the wings the few times I've braved the sports bar. "Freshman year, late April. I'll give you that one, since I'm guessing you won Frozen Four."

"Damn right we did."

"Summer semester last year, end of July," I continue. "Then again in March."

He chuckles, allowing me to go to the order counter first when it's his turn. "Okay, so what I'm hearing is I owe you wings. It's a date."

"Don't get ahead of yourself," I toss over my shoulder. "Can I get a mocha latte and a pumpkin spice latte to go? Thanks."

Easton leans around me to hand the cashier his card before I have the chance to pay, rattling off his coffee order. I miss it, stunned by him paying for my drinks.

"What are you doing?"

"Buying your coffee." He holds his hands up at the suspicious look I give him. "Just donuts, just coffee. Still no strings."

"Next time, I'm paying."

He smirks. "You've got it, baby. You're making me wish I didn't have to go get on the team bus. Can I see you next weekend? We're having a party for one of the guys on the team."

I bite my lip to keep from smiling. "Still not saying yes."

Easton shakes his head with a sly expression, lowering his voice to murmur near my ear so the barista giving him mooneyes doesn't hear. "You're going to be kicking yourself for holding out on me, baby. Once I show you what you're missing, you're going to wish you had it sooner. But that's okay, it makes it more fun this way."

I shiver, moving a few steps away. While he waits for his card back, he gives me one of his flirty once-overs I'm becoming familiar with. His eyes flick down my body with confidence, then meet mine again. The heat flaring in his gaze causes my breath to hitch as an excited pulse of warmth spreads through my stomach.

This is dangerous territory because Easton really is my type with his inviting blue eyes and the playfully cocky attitude that used to be my downfall. I was having fun last week with my dare, not expecting him to actually try to get with me. I remind myself of all my excellent reasons to not go for hockey players to keep myself from falling for his moves.

"Why are you so interested in me?" I ask once he gets the receipt for our coffees.

"Easy. I like your smile and I think we'd have fun together. I don't give up easily when I know I like something."

I laugh at the simplistic answer. "I'm not the type to hook up casually, so this is all pointless." I gesture to the coffee counter. "You should really forget me. It's not like hockey players have a lot of free time for girlfriends. Besides, I'm not sure those count as solid reasons to ask someone out. You don't know me."

"Yet," he says pointedly, not put off. "I'm getting to know you."

"Come on. What could you possibly have learned about me?"

"Plenty. You have killer dance moves and a sweet tooth." He pulls a face and shrugs. "Shitty taste in college hockey teams. You're a Bruins fan though, right? Please say yes."

"Duh." I smirk at his dramatic display of wiping his forehead and sighing in relief.

"Crisis averted. It would be so awkward if my girl didn't cheer for me when I get signed to my dream team."

I lift my brows and give an amused scoff. "Keep dreaming, hotshot. I'm not your girl."

"*Yet.*" He winks.

Easton takes my hand to draw me over to the pickup counter. His is huge, engulfing mine with his warm callused fingers. He keeps doing stuff like that, touching me affectionately in small ways. He has conversations with his touch, whispering endearments and seductive promises.

I can't tell if he's just a handsy type of guy who likes a lot of physical contact or if this is another of his charm tactics.

He brushes his thumb across my skin, sending tingles spreading through me. I roll my lips between my teeth, ignoring my skipping heartbeat. I admired his big hands earlier in the week, remembering how it felt when he kept a secure grip on the back of my thigh the night he rescued me from the bar.

"Give me time because I'm still discovering more reasons whenever I see you," he continues while our coffees are prepared, unaware of the effect those tiny caresses have on me.

The barista calls out my order first and sets it on the counter. Easton gets it for me, selecting one of the complimentary peppermint rod stirrers the shop puts out around the end of fall that I'm addicted to.

He pops it in, then offers me the drink. I blink at the cup.

He inclines his head. "What? You like mocha lattes with a real peppermint stick, not that fake crap big chains peddle."

Something tightens in my stomach. It's not anything special. Not even anything major to notice, yet my heart gives an insistent little thud.

"Thanks," I stammer as I accept the cup.

His expression softens, eyes hooding as his stare flits across my face. "See? Damn, girl. Your smile is beautiful."

I'm smiling? I touch my lips. Oh. Yeah, I guess I am.

Easton takes the other drinks, passing the second one to me so he can shoulder his gear bag when we reach the door. He holds it open for me and follows me outside.

"My roommate will be grateful for free coffee," I say.

"No problem." He glances in the direction of campus and sighs. "I need to get going."

"Right. Okay, I'll see you later."

"Yeah? Good." He licks his lower lip. "Wish me luck?"

I tilt my head. "Do you need it?"

"From you, gorgeous? Yes." He steps into me, nearly brushing against me. It traps the warmth of the coffees I'm holding between us. "Say it, baby."

My lashes flutter and my lips part on a shaky exhale. A gust of wind slices through the square and he rubs my arm, blocking me from the brunt of the cold air with his tall frame.

"Good luck," I finally murmur.

The broad grin he gives me forms gradually until the corners of his eyes crinkle with pleasure. He holds a hand over his chest as if he's captured my words and tucked them into his heart. Then he drops it, finding my waist. My gaze locks on his mouth while my pulse thrums.

It's been a while for me, but I can tell—he's a good kisser. One that can take you apart with a single, devastating kiss.

The old bell above the coffee shop breaks the moment. He shifts us so we aren't blocking the sidewalk.

"I should go. Before this one gets cold." I hold up Reagan's drink. "Thank you."

"Anytime." He smirks.

My brow furrows. "What's that look for?"

"I'm getting used to watching you walk away from me. It has its benefits, don't get me wrong." Easton scrapes his teeth over his lip as he checks me out. "But one of these days, you won't walk away."

A laugh catches in my throat. "Bye, Easton."

"Bye, baby. Hate to see you leave—" He gives a low, rumbling hum when I turn around and start walking. "—love to watch you go."

My face is on fire and his enticing tone causes an ache between my thighs that lasts long after I leave Easton behind in the square.

SIX
MAYA

WORKING at Merrywood Farms is a highlight of my week. My advisor is friends with the owner, and recommended me when a position opened up during my summer semester between freshman and sophomore year. I have a few rotating shifts during the week and come in on the weekends for extra help.

The farm is run by a therapist offering a variety of activities and services with their mostly rescued animal residents. Some of it is geared toward mental health well-being, but they also provide animal-assisted therapies that I get to observe for my degree. I do a bit of everything for the farm, often working with the horses.

This afternoon, it's a goat yoga session with my new co-worker that started here last month. Hana Yoo is a freshman performing arts major and way better at leading yoga classes with her lithe dancer build than I am. I love hanging out with the goats, though. Like our guests, I spend sessions cuddling the cute little kids that run around freely during the class rather than bending myself into a pretzel the way Hana excels at.

"And...deep breath out," Hana says serenely from her mat at the front of the pavilion. "Namaste. Great job, everyone. That's it for today's session. We hope you had fun!"

Right on cue, one of the goats yells as it headbutts her, making the group break out in laughter. We wrangle the goats and end the class with some group photos. Once the book club that arranged the session files out, we work together to return the goats to their paddock before finishing our shift for the day.

"Great work, ladies. Thank you," our boss says when we pass her walking through the grounds. "See you tomorrow!"

"Have a good night, Marnie." I wave.

"Want to go for a trail ride?" Hana asks when we reach the stable.

Prince pokes his head out of his stall, ears swiveling to me. He's my favorite horse here for his friendship with the donkeys and his penchant for breaking into the hay shed to help himself. I stop to give him some love.

"I wish I could. I promised Reagan I'd get groceries on my way home."

It's my turn. We've split the groceries between us since we first started rooming together freshman year.

"No worries. Next time?"

"Definitely." I laugh when Prince bumps his soft nose against the top of my head. "I haven't had the chance to ride in forever."

It always reminds me of Grandpa. He taught me to ride on his lazy old mare as soon as he thought I was old enough after I begged him. We used to saddle up and circle the pasture where cows grazed when the dairy farm was operational.

The nostalgic memory makes my eyes sting. Even if he makes a full recovery, Grandpa likely won't be able to ride a horse with me ever again.

Clearing my burning throat, I get my things and go. The drive to the grocery store is short. In the small town of Heston Lake, everything is nearby. Normally I walk to and from work, but on shopping days I borrow Reagan's car.

I wander the store with my thoughts a million miles away, plucking our staples off the shelves without paying much attention. A familiar laugh breaks me out of the trance with a jolt. I hesitate at the end of the aisle.

Easton's here. He's filling a shopping cart with another guy our age with a shadow of dark scruff on his jaw and a backwards cap. The two of them joke around while they grab three large bags of pizza rolls from the freezer.

Tell me why my stomach dips like I'm excited to see him? Because I'm not. I can't be.

Have the athletes at this college always been so hard to escape? How did we go the last two years sharing this campus without meeting, yet now I can't seem to avoid him?

I haven't seen him since he bought my coffee a week ago. It's Friday again, shouldn't he be at the arena playing? I purse my lips side to side, then check the game schedule. They're off tonight after playing Sunday and Tuesday earlier in the week.

I could turn around and sneak away before they notice me. I *should*, but I don't.

"Hockey stars shop for their own groceries? They're just like us," I announce sarcastically to the otherwise empty aisle.

Easton freezes, then whips around so fast he nearly knocks his friend over. I hide a laugh behind a hand, giving them a small wave.

"Maya. Hi." His face splits in a handsome grin that makes my heartbeat falter.

"Hey." The other guy—probably a teammate—nods in greeting, adjusting his backwards cap. "You were at The Landmark the other night. Dancing, right?"

I huff in amusement. "That's me. Is there anyone who didn't see that go down?"

"You were hard to miss." He glances at Easton. "I'm Cameron."

"Go and get the, uh, chips." Easton nudges his friend, shoving him more insistently when the guy snorts. "Yeah. Go, Reeves. I'll catch up with you."

"Uh huh." Cameron smirks, looking between us. "Nice to meet you, Maya. See you around."

"Sure."

"Reeves." Easton frowns, shifting closer to me to block me from his friend's line of sight.

I hate to admit it, but the hint of jealousy is a good look on him. His jawline becomes more defined when he locks it and those thick brows flatten, giving him a sense of ruggedness that stokes an ember of heat within my core.

With our height difference, it's easy for him to become my shield.

"Relax, dude. I'm going," Cameron says through his poorly hidden snickering.

Easton's features clear once he moves down the aisle to leave us alone. He erases the small distance between us. It makes the wide grocery aisle seem more intimate.

"Hi."

The corners of my eyes crinkle. "You said that already."

"Right. Shit." He clears his throat, attention sweeping over me appreciatively. "I'm glad I ran into you. Any day I see you becomes a good one. How was your weekend?"

He's got lines. Better ones than Johnny's. My ex's idea of romance was only talking about himself and trying to hook up at every opportunity.

"It was good. I had work, then kept my roommate company while she worked Saturday night. The Landmark was noticeably more chilled out without the hockey team."

"We got back late on Sunday. That away game was in Vermont, then we had an exhibition game." He pauses, pride gleaming in his eyes. "We won. Crushed both of them, actually. It was a shutout."

"Good job."

I know Heston won, though I don't admit it to him that I looked up the final score on my phone. I checked out the highlights over a basket of fries while Reagan took the small stage to belt out covers for a twenty minute set.

There was a photo of Easton in action with the puck that I stared at for longer than I care to admit. Reagan caught me scrolling through the team's official social media, watching a video of Easton shaking out his damp, messy hair before putting his helmet on. All she had to ask was how many times I let the video loop before I regretted my curiosity.

"You were my good luck charm," he murmurs.

"Shame that wasn't the case against my brother's team," I tease.

"We'll play another game against Elmwood before the end of the season. Things will go differently then." He smirks, unaffected by my heckling. "Will you wish me luck again?"

"Do you need it?" I repeat the same words, though this time they don't sound jokingly skeptical.

He dips his head, bringing his face almost near enough to kiss me. "Maybe not, but I want it. That's what matters."

My breath hitches. He always finds a way to catch me off guard, while also making me relax around him. It's strange.

Typically, guys like Easton set me on edge. I keep waiting to feel that when I'm around him, and yet...

And yet.

"So..." He scans my face and his throat bobs. "That party is tonight."

I know what's coming. I really shouldn't have risked making the same mistake by challenging Easton to try to win me over because part of me wants to say yes to see what happens.

"Is it?" I reply with a neutral tone.

There's something sweet about the way his brows pull together in confusion every time I respond differently to how he expects. Too bad for him—I'm not someone willing to throw myself at hockey players, no matter how hot and tempting he is.

He coughs out a laugh and regroups, rubbing the bridge of his nose as he retreats a step.

"Yeah. You know how to get there? Actually, let me give you a ride. I'll pick you up at, say, seven?"

Smooth. Skipping over inviting me again and acting like I've already said yes. Cuts out the chance of rejection. I didn't miss the offer to pick me up so he knows where I live, either.

"Ohh, close, but no cigar, captain." I pat his arm and pout. "You botched it when you left it open as a question for me to decide. Have fun."

He takes my hand, twining our fingers together. It steals my breath when his blue eyes flare with heat and his voice lowers to be smoky and inviting. "We will, baby."

It takes effort to pull free of his warm grasp. The way his big hand encompasses mine is strangely comforting, making it difficult to remember why I need to say no.

"*Without* me."

Easton heaves a sigh, broad shoulders sagging and the corners of his mouth turning down. Oh god, his sad puppy eyes will be the death of me. It was difficult enough not to cave to them last week at the donut truck.

Be strong, girl.

I know his type. He's into me now because I'm not easy. I present a challenge to conquer. But as soon as I open up to let him in and he gets what he wants? Bam, he's moving on and I'm left with a wounded heart and the unpleasant reminder that I shouldn't fall for guys like him.

Drawing a fortifying breath, I square my shoulders and lift my chin. I'm ready to give him a firmer refusal to end this little game here and now before it goes beyond my control when he nods slowly, ruffling his messy brown hair.

"Okay. Sorry for pushing you. I don't want to do that at all." He offers a rueful tilt of his head, eyes bouncing between mine. "I'm not that guy. You just have me ready to do anything, even if it takes getting on my knees to beg for you to give me a shot."

My shoulders fall. Now he's the one confusing me with unexpected behavior. And distracting ideas of him on his knees for me. That mental image is—

I force out a breath. "I—No. It's fine. If you really overstepped, I'd tell you and shut it down."

The corners of his mouth twitch. "I like that about you. Not afraid to tell it like it is."

There isn't one hint of bullshit in his tone. Only honesty.

My cheeks flush. I swallow thickly, ducking my head.

"If you do change your mind, I can give you my number. I'll come get you. Even if the party is over. I mean, you can have it for whatever you want—to talk, to pretend it doesn't exist in your contacts, to call me in as your cavalry the next time you're dancing on the bar and some guy gives you shit." He chuckles at the last one. "It's up to you."

I stare at him for a beat. Before I decide, Cameron clears his throat as he approaches.

"Sorry to interrupt. E, we've gotta go before the guys get back. Noah keeps texting me SOS. Theo's smart, he's going to figure out this is a surprise for his birthday." He throws an arm around Easton's shoulders to steer him away. "Crashed and burned, man. What happened?"

"I keep asking myself," Easton mutters. "Doesn't make any sense."

They disappear around the corner at the end of the aisle with Easton's teammate laughing.

I'm lucky Cameron interrupted us when he did. If he hadn't, I might've gone against my own rules and accepted Easton's number.

SEVEN
EASTON

IT's after ten by the time we migrate from the bar back to the hockey house.

Laurel hangs off my arm, huddling against me for warmth since she showed up without a jacket. I didn't invite her, but she came with a friend who is dating a senior D-man. She's hovered around me all night, staking her claim to the other girls at the bar I guess. I don't know, I've mostly tried to ignore what was going down.

I should've seen it coming when the guys decided to take the party home that she'd tag along, probably thinking she's ending the night getting dicked down.

"Shut up, shut up." Theo laughs on his way up the steps to the house, tipping sideways when he goes for the phone in his pocket. "Keller and my sister are calling."

Cameron keeps him upright while opening the door. "Night's not over yet. This party's still going strong."

His declaration is met with cheers. Half the people who returned to the house with us head for the living room. I follow Theo into the kitchen along with Cameron, crowding around Theo's side to join in on the video call. Laurel tags along. She hasn't let me out of her sight all night.

"What's up, man?" Cameron asks.

I lean in with an easy grin. "Hey guys. Is the Calder trophy as sweet as it looks in photos?"

"Even better. He let me touch it. NHL rookie of the year, calling me on my birthday? I must be special, or something, huh?" Theo grins at his screen where Alex Keller and his girl, Lainey huddle close for the FaceTime call. "And same goes for you, I guess."

"Happy birthday, dickhead." Lainey sticks her tongue out.

"Back at you," he says to his twin sister.

Keller snorts. "Like I wasn't going to call my best friend. I didn't forget, I just had to make sure my beautiful girl got a special night first."

He turns the phone to show the rooftop view with an intimate table set for two against the New York skyline. The camera pans to Lainey. She looks amazing in a silver slinky dress. Her cheeks turn pink.

"Alex." She hides behind him.

"You look gorgeous, baby," Keller says.

Theo pretends to puke. He pulls a face, snorting at himself. "What's the rule? No details. Ever."

"Did you go out to Dad's?" Lainey peeks around Keller.

"Yeah, we just got back from The Landmark," I say. "We're missing our private kitchen mini-parties without you."

"God, I'd kill for a fun night of pizza rolls and ranch dip right now. Grad school is intense," Lainey says.

"What?" Keller's dopey ass smile falls. "But we do that whenever I have off. I wanted to make tonight special."

She pats his chest, then locks her arms around him for a hug. "No, this is amazing. I'm just reminiscing. Can you believe the nerd is the one missing the hockey house parties?"

He laughs. "I told you a hundred times that divide is only in your head."

"This is really bringing back memories," Theo says. "You know what? I don't miss having both of you here. My eyes and ears aren't assaulted anymore having to watch my best friend mack on my sister."

"Tough shit because we're still getting married," Keller says with a smirk. "I'm spending forever macking on the love of my life."

"Aww," Laurel says. "That's so cute."

"I don't need this. It's my birthday." Theo shakes his head with a smile. He gives them hell, but he's happy for them. He hands us his phone and heads off. "Later!"

"Bye!" Lainey laughs. "We'll let you guys go. It was good to talk to you!"

"You too. Happy birthday," I say.

"Thank you."

Cameron ends the call and tucks Theo's phone in the basket of keys by the door. "Beer?"

"Yes, please," Laurel says.

"I'm good. Practice in the morning."

We follow the victorious shouts coming from the living room. Sounds like Elijah is kicking ass against Madden on the PlayStation. Laurel pulls me away from watching them play the latest NHL game, and we wind up in the back room where we like to chill around an electric heater when it's too cold out to leave the closed in sunroom for the fire pit in the yard.

Seeing how happy Alex and Lainey are has struck a chord with me. I never thought I'd want to be tied down, but now...maybe I wouldn't mind it if I found the right person.

Everyone's having a good time while my mind is back at the grocery store with Maya's hand tucked into mine. I stare at my hand sitting on the armrest, closing it around nothing. I have no idea what it is, but this girl has gotten under my skin.

The same thought keeps popping into my head that hasn't stopped for the last two weeks: I want to see her again.

"Oh my god." Laurel giggles, nudging me. "Everyone in here is making out. I'm actually pretty sure Kelly is getting fingered over there by Jake. Should we show them all how it's done, captain?"

I frown. Her calling me captain sounds way off.

When I don't respond, she exhales through her nose and shifts onto my lap. Her lashes flutter as she slides her arms around my shoulders and brushes my cheek with her lips. I don't make any move to touch her, gaze remaining on my hand.

It occurs to me that this would be a normal night for me not that long ago. Whenever an opportunity to get laid presented itself, I let loose and enjoyed it. I wasn't sleazy about it the way some guys are once they realize how much people want to bag a hockey player for bragging rights. How easy it is to fall into bed with someone—or more than one someone—each night and this isn't even the pro league yet.

Here I am with a smoking hot girl in front of me, flirting with me all night, and I don't care at all.

I'm not interested in anything with her or anyone else when I can't stop picturing captivating hazel eyes with flecks of green like the meadow behind the house I grew at, thick chestnut hair I want to spend hours running my fingers through, and perfect lips that form sarcastic quips and a smile that is quickly becoming my undoing.

"Let's go find somewhere more private," Laurel whispers seductively in my ear. "I've been wet all night thinking about getting you in my mouth. No one's looking. Slide your hand up my dress to find out how much I'm dying to blow you. I want to choke on your cock until your come drips down my chin."

Jesus.

Yeah, no. Not a single twitch of interest in my dick, despite the filthy description of the scenario she offers.

The old me would be all over that, but I need to stop her right there because I don't want any of it. Her hair is the wrong shade of brown and her face shape is different from Maya's. She's hot as fuck. We had fun once upon a time, but she's not the girl for me because she's *not* the person I can't stop thinking about.

I ease her off my lap and get up. She hurries to follow me to the foot of the stairs, smothering an eager giggle. I block the way up, bracing my forearm against the wall.

"You know the rule. No sleepovers."

Laurel's inviting smile falters. "I know." She traces her nails down my chest. "It's not your bedtime yet. We can have fun, superstar."

I gently wrap my fingers around her wrist to stop her from clawing my zipper down in the freaking entryway. "No thanks. I'm not interested. Do you need me to get you an Uber?"

"What?" Laurel blinks at me in disbelief.

Sighing, I nod to the hall leading back to the living room. "Hang out if you want. Hell, find another guy. I'm heading up to bed." I hold up a hand when she makes to join me. "No, Laurel. I'm going alone. I don't think me and you will ever happen again."

"Find someone else? What are you saying, Easton?"

Shit, her eyes begin to shine with tears. "I'm saying I'm not interested in anything with you. Not anymore. I'm sorry."

I watch several emotions play out on her features, evolving from rejection to annoyance, wary of how she'll react. Finally, she huffs and pulls out a lip gloss from her small purse.

"You should've said something sooner. I wouldn't have wasted my time shoving my boobs against you all night if it wasn't leading anywhere, asshole. Fuck this, I'm going to get Theo to rail me after I give him a strip tease for his birthday."

She flips her hair and strides away to find Boucher. I stand on the bottom step, blinking. Shaking my head, I go upstairs to my room and lock the door behind me.

"Good for her," I mutter.

It's been a long ass day, but seeing the black and white cat sitting at my window makes me smile. The stray climbs to the roof of the wraparound porch every night and waits for me.

She paces in front of the window as I open it. With a happy meow in greeting, she enters the room and hops on my bed, curling up like she owns the place. The landlord the college rents the house from for the team would shit a brick if he found out I let her in my room. He's already given me an earful on loop since freshman year when I started feeding her and sitting on the porch to brush her until her coat gleamed.

I probably should think of a name for her other than stray, kit-cat, and my pretty lady. Some of the guys have their own names for her. Keller used to call her Casper for her ability to sneak up on him before he went pro and left Heston early to play for the Islanders.

After closing the window to keep out the chill, I sprawl on the bed. Kit-cat doesn't take long to demand my attention by sniffing my arm and kneading my shoulder. My worries drift away for the time being, eased by the comfort of petting her soft fur.

"We should give you a name. A real one." Her nails prick into me as I rattle off some options. "Luna, because you're always out all night. Or what about Princess Potato? Okay, ow. You don't like that one. No need to attack my hand with your love bites, jesus."

I wriggle my fingers to play with her for a few minutes, dragging my hand in quick movements across the sheets for her to hunt before she calms down again. I skim my knuckles along her back, then massage her ears.

"I think I'm in over my head." All I get in response is a continuous purr while the cat leans into my palm for more petting. "There's this girl. Maya. I think I really like her, which is new for me. It's impossible for me to stop thinking about her."

Kit-cat settles on my chest, curling into a crescent-shaped weight keeping me in place. Within moments, she's dozing. I can't move or I'll wake her up—those are the rules when it comes to pets sleeping on you.

It's not like I'm in the mood to go back downstairs anyway.

Pulling out my phone, I open Instagram and search for Maya. I find her on the third try after skimming through two other Maya Donnelly accounts. The latest photo is one with her brother from the night we met, taken before the game against Elmwood.

Another surprisingly familiar face jumps out—Reagan. I didn't know they were friends since I've never seen Maya around The Landmark on nights I'm there. Has Reagan mentioned her? She must have, right? I'm kicking myself for missing out when I could've known her sooner.

My thumb hovers over the screen. I could ask, but Reagan might be suspicious if I come on too strong with everything I want to know about her friend out of the blue. For now, I hold myself over with glimpses of her life through her social media.

Maya's feisty personality shines in her posts. She makes silly faces. Dances around with Reagan. Hugs an old man with the biggest smile I've seen on her yet. I pause on a shot from the summer where she's on the quad by the dorms giving the viewer a sultry smirk, holding a dandelion over one of her eyes. In every photo, I feel her love of life.

I breathe in sharply when I scroll down. "Yoga pants. Fucking hell."

My dick wakes right up, thickening as I admire the snug fit over her curvy thighs and ass. My fingers twitch with the need to grab her legs and wrap them around my hips to feel them quivering while I fuck her.

Shit, I need to calm down. It feels too weird to jerk off when my cat's cuddling with me. I run through hockey drills in my head until my erection is gone.

Kit-cat cracks her eyes open to peer at me.

I resist the urge to cover my face. "Don't judge me like that."

The yoga pants photo has a geotagged location on it. Merrywood Farms. Curious, I click on it. The map shows a local address for Heston Lake, along with a stream of photos tagged at the same place of people riding horses and stretching on yoga mats in a pavilion surrounded by goats. Maya's photo is there a few more times posted from other accounts than her own.

I Google the farm and find the website offers bookings for a bunch of activities. I save the form for goat yoga to show coach after tomorrow's practice.

If she doesn't want to hang out in my world, I just need to get her to see me in hers so she'll give us a shot.

EIGHT
EASTON

In the morning, most of the guys are moving slowly while we gear up in the locker room for our early rink time before our game later. I grin at Cameron while he gingerly tugs on his leg pads next to me.

"Feeling it?" I pull my practice jersey on before checking the blades on my skates. "That's why I cut myself off at two drinks."

He huffs weakly, whipping me with his jersey. "Shut up. You've been in the same boat."

"I definitely like being the one not hungover." I dodge the glove he chucks at me.

Noah catches it. He's half-dressed, hanging out in the middle of the locker room. He's been selling all of us on surfing after he picked it up over his summer back home in California.

"It's this little beach town my family visited right before I came back for training camp. The dude who runs the surf shop in South Bay is rad." He mimes surfing. "Someone come fan my hair so you can get the full effect of how badass I looked cruising those waves."

Elijah snickers at his antics, stopping when he spots someone in the hall. "What's up, Kincaid?"

"See you out there guys. Let's have a good practice."

Cole Kincaid is one of the assistant coaches. He started about two years ago when our old defensive coach retired. He's seen me, Cameron, Noah, and Madden develop to the players we are now. Having a younger coach much closer to our age has been great.

We go to him whenever we need anything. He's the one we call when we're in the shit. He's like an older brother for all of us.

"Bauer!" Several guys say it in unison at the sight of Coach Kincaid's black lab mix padding after him through the locker room wearing a blue bandana with the Heston U Hockey logo.

The dog eats up the attention, his whole body wriggling in excitement. He's like our mascot after Kincaid got the dog in the middle of the season last year.

"Look how big you're getting," Noah says while the dog weaves through his legs. "Toss me a puck."

Madden pops it in the air with an underhand throw, losing his permanent moodiness for a moment while we all watch Bauer go nuts for his favorite toy whenever Kincaid brings him to the rink. Once he's got the puck to gnaw on, he takes it around to everyone like he's showing it off.

Noah comes over and holds his phone up, rolling right into recording a clip for the team's social media. "Are you a dog or cat person?"

"Get the phone out of my face, Porter," Madden grumbles. "I'm too hungover for this."

Noah chuckles. "That's what you get for not taking my hangover cure last night. I'm telling you, hydration is key. It's how I can still lift in the weight room the morning after to keep these sexy guns pumped up no matter how much I've had."

He flexes and smacks a kiss on his bicep. I snort, giving Coach Kincaid's dog attention when he brings the puck he's chewing to me and drops it once I pet him. The dog's tongue hangs out in a happy pant while he melts down to flop on his back at my feet.

"Better not be too much." All of us straighten at the stern call from Coach Lombard before he enters the locker room. "I see players in my locker room rather than on the ice for practice. Are we going to fix that?"

"Yes, sir." Noah loses his playful nature.

"Let's hit the ice," I announce.

Everyone picks up the pace, putting on the last of their gear. I head for the rink with Noah and Cameron.

Noah pats my shoulder. "That chick was hot last night. Did you hit that?"

We lose our skate guards and step through the gap in the boards. It's always like coming home whenever I feel the crisp chill nipping at my skin and the first glide of ice beneath my blades.

"Nah, I wasn't in the mood." I follow the flow of everyone else with our usual free warm-up of skating a few loops around the rink to get our blood pumping.

"You? Not in the mood?" Noah smirks and bumps his shoulder against mine before he skates around me in a tight circle. He might play defense because of his muscle mass and broad frame, but he's got damn good footwork.

He points his stick at me when he overtakes me, flipping around to skate backwards. "You're still hung up on your mystery girl."

"Maya," Cameron sing-songs beside me. "I'm telling you, man, you should've seen him when we ran into her at the grocery store. E was struggling like I've never seen before."

"Wow, I never pictured our boy with performance issues."

"Keep it up. I'm not going easy on either of you today." I grin, shaking my head. Finishing another lap, I scoop one of the pucks up, popping it onto the edge of my stick. "I'm making defense work. You're both going to feel this one through both games this weekend and every practice until we play UConn."

Noah and Cameron bump fists, then take positions with grins. I flip the puck off my stick and toy with them, zipping back and forth without going in for the attack.

Elijah skates over and links up with me when I evade Noah. I see the drive I had to prove myself in him. I catch his eye and give a small nod to signal it's go time. Madden appears out of nowhere to pick up a three-man attack.

They whip the puck between them with wicked speed to keep Noah on his toes before sending it to me when I'm in the perfect position. My slapshot flies towards the net.

Cameron dives into a slide, arm outstretched for a glove save. The puck misses his glove by a scant inch and glides through the crease.

"Oh!" I hold my arms up. "That's how it's done, boys."

"That was fucking beautiful, East." Noah's glove rubs my helmet.

Coach blows his whistle to signal warm-ups are over. The team circles up near the bench where he leans against the boards. We're ready to work.

Practice goes well. The wingers on the first line with me connect all our passes and our defense tightens up. Coach even smiles, which is a rarity.

As long as we keep this up, we'll make Ryan Donnelly eat Elmwood's lucky win against us.

After we finish, the locker room is almost empty when I'm out of the showers except for Cameron and Elijah.

"Ready to go?" Cameron shoulders his duffel bag.

"I'll meet you outside. I'm going to talk to coach for a minute."

He throws up a peace sign on his way out and the rookie follows him. I get dressed and go to the office.

"Coach?" I hover in his doorway.

He's seated at his desk reviewing game tape with Kincaid.

"Come in, Blake."

"I just wanted to talk to you about this thing I saw. I thought the team could do it." I lay my phone on his desk. "You're always saying we need to train all sorts of ways."

"Right." He holds the phone away, squinting to read. "Yoga, huh?"

Coach Kincaid peers over his shoulder. "It's great for improving stability and range of motion. Especially for goalies."

Surprise hits me. There are plenty of ways to train for hockey outside of practice. Some guys take figure skating and ballet classes. It didn't occur to me that yoga would fall under that, too.

Coach Lombard hums thoughtfully. "Let's do it. I'll sign off on a special class. Keep up this initiative, Blake. Kincaid?"

"I'll take care of it."

* * *

A few days later after our evening workout, I hang back while the guys go inside the house. I take a seat on the porch steps, allowing my bag to slump beside me. I taped my stick before practice this morning, but I redo it anyway to keep my hands busy.

I've let my fixation on Maya take me on a ride. Coach

commended me on my way out of his office when practice ended Saturday morning. He believes I suggested goat yoga for alternative training because of my dedication to the game. I'm always looking for ways to edge out our competition by doing everything to train at peak condition.

The truth is, I really want to see her. There's no doubt how much I like her, which makes me fucking nervous because I've never been in this situation before. This is brand new territory to be more interested every time I see her.

At first she caught my attention because I was curious how she had the guts to sit front and center in the Heston student section, cheering for the opposing team. Then she held my attention with that dance in the bar and her intriguing challenge. After only a handful of encounters, I'm drawn to her, searching campus for her in every brunette I pass, hoping it'll mean I get five minutes with her.

Maybe in the past I'd fuck her a few times and get it out of my system, but this isn't about that. Yes, I want her. Obviously I want her. But it's more than that. I've been thinking about hanging out with her and holding her hand, for fuck's sake.

This is beyond simple attraction to her because she's hot as hell. I've never become so consumed by an unending desire for a girl like this. I want more—way more than I should. If I'm this crazy over her when I hardly know her, I can only imagine what it will be like once I do. The thought is equally exhilarating and nerve-racking.

I haven't even kissed her yet and I can tell once would never be enough. She's not a hit it and quit it girl. Not if the strange sense in my gut like I'm excited and freaked out all at once whenever I'm near her is anything to go by. Not when I want to be around her in any way she'll tolerate my presence.

I just *like* her. End of.

Our upcoming games against UConn and UMass didn't factor in when I talked to coach.

UConn is always a tough team that we fight neck and neck with to win overall in our division on the road to Frozen Four. Playing UMass is personal for me. I fight for every win against them. Their recruiter came to a few of my games in junior league, but ultimately they passed on me.

At eighteen, that shit stung. By now, I know I'm where I should be. Since I started at Heston, I've put the work in to prove to the coaches, to my teammates, and to myself that I've got what it takes to take us all the way every time.

Am I putting all of that at risk if I keep chasing Maya? This isn't the time to split my focus. Being drafted from the NCAA is a slim chance at best, yet it's way better prospects to reach the NHL that way over going the free agent route.

I have been skating my ass off in games, especially against Vermont last weekend. In fact, I played incredibly every time it was my shift on the ice. We won in a shutout, and I'm not going to lie, I wanted to win it for her because she wished me luck. Even if she wasn't there to see it.

If I can win while she's on my mind, it's okay, right?

"Doesn't have to be a bad thing," I reason under my breath.

There are guys on the team who have girlfriends. They find the balance, like Keller used to say to me and Cameron as rookies. He and his girlfriend—now fiancé—made it through okay, so maybe I have nothing to stress out over.

There's never been a deeper connection to worry about before. I've worked so hard at keeping girls as a surface level thing so I'm not distracted from my goals. Screwing that up now when I'm so close to the goals I've been striving for could be the end of everything. It hasn't been an issue until her.

I never expected a girl to catch my eye, least of all Donnelly's sister.

Maya turns me into a man possessed. *Obsessed.*

The only thing I've ever been obsessed with is playing hockey.

When I'm around her, there's nothing I won't do to earn her gorgeous smile. Then when she's not around, I hear her voice, imagine her sarcastic eye rolls that ignite something warm and thrilling within me. She's constantly on my mind.

And half the time, it's like she barely acknowledges that I exist.

A soft laugh leaves me. I set my stick aside and massage my forehead. What the hell am I doing?

The shuffle of feet on pavement draws me out of my thoughts.

Neil Cannon pauses in front of the short pathway leading up to the house, eyeing me. The retired NHL player is a local legend. He comes to all of our home games and usually takes a walk about this time. Some of the guys think he does it to keep an eye on the players coming back from practice. He stops sometimes to offer his advice.

After another moment of scrutiny, he turns down the path and takes a seat beside me on the porch steps with a gruff, crackling hum. Neither of us speak until he sighs.

"I don't have all night."

"Uh." I'm not clear on what he means.

"Talk," he grumbles without making any move to go. "Better be quick, or I'm leaving you to sort out what's on your mind for yourself."

"Oh. Okay, right." I clear my throat, pushing my fingers through my hair as I search for where to start. "I'm just out here thinking about a lot of stuff."

Cannon snorts. "You don't say."

His crabbiness is a staple around town. He's got a hard shell to him, but it doesn't put me off. If anything, it sets me more at ease and gets me to open up.

"Yeah. A lot's changing and the pressure's on. This is my last year to make it in the draft. I'll be above the age requirement before next season."

"You're the team captain this year, I hear. Lombard drinks with me down at the sports bar."

"Yeah. I wasn't expecting it, to be honest. I thought Reeves would've made a better captain." I scrub my face. "And I just need to stay focused. This is when it counts most."

"But you're not focusing," he surmises.

I duck my head when he levels me with an expectant look, lifting his bushy gray eyebrows. Sliding my lips together, I pinch the zipper on my duffel bag to tug it back and forth.

"I am, it's just—there's...a girl."

"Uh huh. Always is."

"Usually it's not a problem, except I can't stop thinking about her." Warmth prickles through my chest. It's strange to unload like this about feelings. Especially to him. "I never expected there to be anything in my life that could possibly rival my concentration on hockey, and I don't know what I'm doing."

Cannon narrows his eyes. "Holding back never did anyone any good."

I blink, nodding at his advice. It gives me a new perspective I hadn't considered. I've always drawn a line in the sand between me and the girls I've been with. No sleepovers. Keep it casual. No repeats if they think what we have is going anywhere, because I don't let it go further.

But none of them have ever made me crazy the way Maya does. It was easy to hold back with them.

With her, I feel like I'm fighting against a whole team to skate towards the goal.

"Like game seven of the Stanley Cup the year before you retired where everything was riding on that win. Down in points until halfway through third period. Your hat trick tied it up and you won in overtime with a wicked assist."

Cannon grunts in acknowledgement. That game solidified him as one of my favorite players. I look up to him. Hell, I picked my number because it was his.

"When it's all on the line, you make it count," he says.

The heaviness sitting on my shoulders lifts, leaving me lighter. "Thanks."

"Sure, kid." He rises to his feet with a restrained groan people his age make whenever they get up, stuffing his hands in the pockets of his jacket. "Buck up. I don't want to see the Knights get your asses handed to you again on the ice."

A laugh huffs out of me and I squeeze the back of my neck. "Yes, sir."

While watching him continue his nightly walk, something Dad used to say to me filters through my thoughts. *The players that seem like they have it all are the ones who put the work in, on the ice and off it to achieve their goals.* At the time, I didn't think much of it beyond remembering when to rest my muscles and when to put my all into practicing, but now it rings a little differently.

Having it all could mean I don't have to draw any lines in the sand when it comes to Maya.

The thought is dangerous, taking root as soon as it slips through my mind. I picture her as something much more than a casual hookup. Coming to my games wearing my number to cheer me on, celebrating my wins with me at The Landmark, eating dinner with me and the guys followed by breakfast the morning after. All things I've never had with any other girl—an actual relationship.

I have Mom to talk to. My little brother, Asher, although he's too young for topics like this. Coach and the assistant coaches. My boys. But it's not the same. Sometimes I get hit square in the gut with how much I wish Dad were still here with me instead of the hole left behind in my heart after we lost him in the accident.

Five years isn't enough to make the grief of losing him go away. It will probably always hurt that I lost my dad too soon. I try to be strong for Mom and Asher. It's my job to take care of them now.

If he were, I think he'd be proud to see how far I've come, how hard I'm working to achieve what we both believed I could. Proud of the man I've grown to be. He'd want me to have it all.

Including the girl.

The corner of my mouth tugs up with a renewed sense of drive. Hell yeah.

NINE
MAYA

"We're going to be late! Let's go. Come on, come on." Reagan appears in the doorway to my room and claps her hands when she finds me sprawled across the bed.

"I can't believe you talked me into going out tonight."

Sitting up, I fight with my favorite knee-high boots to get them on. The battle ends with me out of breath, but successfully ready.

She checks her flawless makeup in my mirror, carefully putting on the final touches by applying deep red lipstick to her plump lips. She has a round face with high cheekbones, and when she smiles at her reflection, it lights up her beautiful green eyes. The ripped black jeans hug her thighs and the wide v-neck sweater falls off her shoulders, accentuating all her generous curves to complement her pear shape. Her gaze flicks to me.

"Girl. Don't you dare back out on me. I rarely get Saturday night off." She offers her lipstick. "Want some?"

"I'm good. You look hot."

She winks and fluffs her strawberry blonde curls. "You know it, bestie. And so do you. What do I always say?"

I love her confidence. She never lets anything stop her from living life and never fails to pull me out of a bad mood. No one is allowed to rain on her parade.

When we became roommates freshman year, she was a vital support system to help me work through Johnny's betrayal. If I didn't have a friend like her to talk to, I might never have put myself back out there.

"We live life with good laughs, good books, and good shoes sharp enough to stomp anyone who tries to diminish our light." I recite the mantra she's been boosting both of us up with since we met.

"That's my girl. Let's go have fun. We deserve it. *You* deserve it after working your ass off to get to this point."

She's right. I front loaded so many of my credit hours so I could have a lighter schedule this year. I don't have to bail out on her to study. It feels like I can actually breathe and let my hair down.

Reagan holds out an arm and I hook mine around it with a smile. "Let's."

A blast of nippy November air hits us as we leave the building. She shudders, but I'm fine. The cold feels refreshing.

"Ugh. Thankfully it's not a long walk," she says.

"Where's the party? You didn't tell me."

I pull her to a stop, really hoping we're not going off campus.

"Pi Kappa Alpha."

I relax. Frat and sorority parties aren't my favorite, but as long as it's not the hockey team's party, I'm fine.

"Really?"

She smirks. "Well, some of my friends from class are going and promised I'd see them there."

"Cool."

"But," she drawls. "There's also this Pike with serious himbo energy that's been coming by the bar whenever I have a set to make moon eyes at me while I sing. There's not much going on behind those pretty brown eyes, but he's fun to flirt with and his dick is huge, look."

"Don't you dare. Reagan!"

I struggle with her as she tries to show me her phone, both of us laughing. She wins, waving a photo in front of my face that has decent lighting as far as dick pics go, but the perspective is questionable.

"Are you sure that's not a trick of the camera angle?"

"Oh, I'm sure. I thought the same thing, so I demanded better proof. Got a nice video."

I huff in amusement. "So we're going to this party and you're going to leave me?"

She gasps, laying a hand across her cleavage. "I'm offended. When have I ever done that?"

"Okay, never. If you want to, though, go for it. I'm not standing in the way of your hookup."

"Thanks. We'll see how the night goes, but we're arriving together and I plan on leaving with my hot best friend."

She waggles her brows and nudges me. Our laughter echoes around us and we draw curious looks from other people walking through campus, but neither of us care.

When we reach Greek Row, people spill out of the frat house onto the lawn. The music is louder when we head inside and she pulls a face.

"Oh no. I'm definitely hijacking their system. This playlist is not it. Can you believe this is what these guys think they need to play to get laid? Honestly."

I can't contain laughter as we navigate the crowded rooms. "You're the music queen, not me."

Once we have drinks, we make our way to the biggest room in the house. A guy hanging out on the couches pops up to greet us. I roll my lips between my teeth because all I can think is that I know what his dick looks like.

"Hey, you came!" He looks Reagan up and down in obvious appreciation, holding out a hand for her. "Come meet my boys."

She gives him a confident, flirtatious smile, then turns to me. "You okay? I'll be back in ten after I say hi."

"Go ahead."

The Pike nods at me with his chin. "Your friend can come, too."

I hold a hand up. "No thanks. I'm fine here for now."

Reagan swats at the guy when he tries to pull her away, leaning in. "You sure? He might have cute friends."

My shoulders shake with amusement. "*Yes*. Standing alone for five minutes at a party doesn't bother me. I might go see who else is here. I saw a guy I partnered with for my bio lab last fall. Go on."

"Okay. I'll come find you in a bit!"

I'm not alone for more than two minutes before someone saunters up next to me. He leans into my personal space, bombarding me with beer breath.

"What's up? I'm Justin."

"Hi," I reply shortly.

When I don't offer any other conversation, he frowns and hits his vape pen.

"What's your name?" he tries.

Scanning the room for anyone else I know to go talk to instead, I freeze. My eyes lock with Easton's as he comes in with a couple of other guys. His attention flicks to Justin and his pleasantly surprised expression shifts into something hard and jealous.

He bumps his fist with one of the guys with him and heads in my direction. My heart skips a beat, but it's not in disappointment.

Justin notices Easton. He stiffens and grumbles something under his breath, moving off before Easton reaches us. "You could've said you had a boyfriend. Later."

Easton doesn't take his eyes off me as he makes his way to me. With each step, his grin grows bigger. A rush of butterflies swoops in my stomach. When he stops in front of me, I tilt my head, propping a hand on my hip.

"I should've known I'd run into you here, captain."

The edges of his mouth curl in a charming smile as his gaze roams over me, lingering on the knee-high boots encasing my legs. "Can't escape me."

"I really can't." Hiding my entertained expression behind my cup, I take a drink. "Who were those guys you came in with?"

"Guys from my mass media class. I wasn't planning to stay long. We played an afternoon game and I've got an assignment to finish for another class on Monday." He cocks his head, teeth dragging across his lip. "That was before I knew you'd be here, though."

A smile breaks free. "Same, but I got talked into coming since mine's not due until Friday."

He smirks. "I see how it is. You'll go to this party, but you won't come to ours?"

I shrug, still smiling. "Maybe I had a better offer for this one."

"Is that so?" Easton steps closer, eyes narrowing. "Which guy was it? Edwards? Nah, never mind. That guy could never score you. You're way too good for him."

I bite my lip, enjoying watching him work through his suspicions. "And you think you could score me?"

He pauses, gaze flickering between my mouth and my eyes. "It's no secret by now I want to, baby."

Tingles spread across my skin in a rush. I gulp my drink to hide my reaction.

"It wasn't a guy. My roommate invited me. There she is." I point Reagan out across the room as she laughs, leaning into the guy sliding an arm around her.

The tense set of Easton's shoulders relaxes. "Oh. Reagan's your roommate?"

"Since freshman year. Sorry. Best friend trumps anything else every time."

"Fair." He chuckles, brushing his arm against mine as he angles his head lower to talk near my ear. "At least I don't have to go fight someone else for trying to get with you."

A shiver flies down my spine. It's followed by a pulse of heat that has me pressing my thighs together at the thought of him in a fight over me.

I take another sip of my drink to give myself a moment to recover.

He leans against the wall, bracing his legs at a wider stance so he's not towering over me as much. Amused, I mirror him, resting my back against the wall beside him, crossing one leg over the other at the ankles. The corner of his mouth lifts.

"So if you know Reagan, how come I haven't seen you around The Landmark before that night we played your brother?"

"I don't know," I reply airily. "I avoid places that involve hockey players unless I know they won't be there. Plus, I've been a little more preoccupied with studying my ass off. How come I haven't seen you around the library?"

He rumbles faintly, playfully narrowing his eyes. "You said going to the game was a one-time thing to see your brother play. So what is it about hockey that you're not a fan of?"

"I actually really like the game. I grew up not far from Boston going to games with my family. I loved how fast and exciting it was." I angle towards him like I'm divulging a secret. "It's the players that ruin it for me."

Struck with an impulsive urge, I ruffle his hair. It's thick and softer than I imagined it would be. He chuckles, letting me get away with it for a moment before catching my wrist. His blue eyes gleam, holding mine.

Then he tickles my sides.

I yelp, darting back. He steadies me with a hand on my arm to keep my drink from sloshing over.

"Careful."

His touch leaves my arm tingling. I suppress the urge to shiver.

"Thanks."

"So the players are the problem, huh?" He braces his shoulder against the wall this time, facing me with interest.

I squint. "What's that smug grin for?"

"Just figuring you out. Now I know more about you, like you're ticklish as fuck, and you don't actually hate hockey. See? We have a lot in common."

I huff, the side of my mouth quirking up. "Good luck with that."

"I told you before, I like hard work. I might be an athlete, but I enjoy studying. Committing something to memory. Learning all about it."

He lets the statement hang between us with the implication that I'm the one he's studying. His fingers brush mine and I don't pull away.

"What are we talking about over here?" Reagan returns from the other side of the room. "Hey Easton."

He pushes off the wall we're leaning on to give her a friendly hug. "Hey."

"Where are the rest of the guys?"

He shrugs. "Noah might be here. He hits the gym with some of the guys from the frat."

She peers between us, catching my eye to give me a *yes girl* smile. I shake my head, laughing her off.

"Squeeze in. Let's take a photo," she says.

"Sure," he says.

Before I have the chance to react, she has her phone up. With a wry exhale, I hug her shoulders from behind since she's shorter than me.

Easton moves in behind me, keeping a small breadth of space between us so I'm hyper aware of everywhere we're not touching. I stare at the small version of us on the screen. His attention is on me rather than posing for the camera.

His masculine scent fills my nose, clean and fresh with a hint of musk. It's heady. Another wave of tingles spreads through me, and I slide my lips together as his chest grazes my back.

Finally, he looks at the camera. Can he see the ways he's affecting me written all over my face? I hope not.

"Ok, ready?" Reagan prompts.

When he steps away, my back goes cold from the loss of his warmth.

"It's cute! I'll text it to you guys," she says.

My phone vibrates in the back pocket of my jeans while I'm trying to recenter myself. She captures my hand, squeezing.

"Hey, are you okay? Your face is all red."

Oh, great.

Easton leans in to check, features morphing with concern. I duck my head.

"I'm okay. Too many people in here, I think. I'm getting overheated."

"Oh yeah, I feel you." She fans herself. "Let's go find some water."

Someone calls Easton's name, stopping him from coming with us. I offer him a small wave, following Reagan.

Once we get two bottles of water, I run into two girls in my animal sciences class. Reagan's frat boy finds us while we're talking to them. When the girls see other people they know, the guy flirts with Reagan, whispering in her ear to get her to smile.

I catch her eye.

We exchange a conversation completely through facial expressions and subtle gestures, understanding each other with ease. She's fine, so I'm going to search through the house for an open bathroom while she's occupied.

I'm directed upstairs by one of the house members, passing a few locked doors where people are definitely having a good time before finding it.

Easton's people watching alone when I come downstairs. Instead of finding Reagan, I wander over to join him.

"I thought you weren't staying long?"

The corners of his blue eyes crinkle in pleasure. "Didn't want to leave without seeing you again."

A flutter tickles my stomach. "I was going to go find Reagan, but I think I'll chill here for a bit."

He angles his body towards mine. "Yeah?"

"As long as you quit trying to get me to another one of your hockey games."

He captures the finger I point at him. I pull, but he holds it, lips twitching.

"How about I ask for your number instead?"

I lift my brows. His easygoing grin stretches.

"Asking as a friend."

"A friend who is forward about wanting to get with me."

"But who also knows damn well you have the final say on that. We can hang out like this otherwise, right? We've shared donuts."

"Oh, so that makes us friends?" I ask slyly.

He's still holding on, playing with my fingers. He uses it as leverage to tug me closer.

"Definitely."

"Okay. Friends."

I'm reluctant to admit it, but he's fun to hang out with. He keeps making me laugh and I like the good natured bickering.

A commotion sounds behind me and Easton reacts in a split second. He takes me by the waist to swing me out of the way of someone spilling their drink. It puts my back against the wall with him shielding me. He leans in, eyes roving over me.

"They almost bumped into you. Did any beer get on you?"

I shake my head, throat dry from his grasp on my waist and the intimate proximity. "Looks like they got your shoulder instead."

He shrugs without checking, not tearing his stare from mine. I wet my lips and his attention falls to them. My heart thuds.

I tilt my head a fraction and he draws in a sharp breath,

massaging my waist with his big hands. My lashes flutter and I feel the warmth of his breath on my mouth as he dips his head lower.

Rowdy shouts from the next room break the moment.

We stare at each other. He goes still, eyes bouncing between mine. His brows pinch together. I swear I hear a frustrated rumble vibrating in his chest.

It hits me that I was about to kiss him, causing my stomach to bottom out.

The shouting turns tense. It sounds like a fight, and it's drawing a crowd.

"Oh, shit." Easton takes a step away, then hesitates. He cups my face with a resigned expression. "I think that's Madden getting into it again. I'll be right back. Wait here for me?"

"Okay."

Relief crosses his face before he pushes through the crowd to find the source of the shouting. Spotting one of his teammates, he motions for the guy to join him. The fight must die off quickly, because once they disappear from my sight, someone turns up the music and the tension leaves the air.

Reagan finds me not long after. "Hey, ready to go?"

Reluctance washes over me. I told Easton I'd wait, but he didn't come back right after breaking up the fight. Chewing on my lip, I nod.

"Um, let me just say goodbye."

"Sure. Let's do a drive by."

We make our way through the frat house. I scan each room for him without any luck.

I give up searching for Easton and trail after Reagan to the door when she finishes her goodbyes. The two guys blocking the door make me pull up short. One of them is Easton, and the other must be his teammate. He's muscle-bound with dark brown hair and a brooding expression.

"Keep that short fuse in check," Easton says. "You good now?"

He drops his gaze. After a moment he gives a jerky nod.

"I'm done for the night," he says flatly.

"Okay, man." Easton squeezes his shoulder.

"Hey," I say.

Easton's attention flies to me. "Hey. I was just coming to find you."

"We're heading out."

"Oh. Already?"

"I'm ready to crash." Reagan leans her head on my shoulder. "Ohh, we should do pancakes tomorrow. Yes? Yes."

"Fine," I say with a laugh.

Easton and his teammate follow us out. He buffs my arms against the cool night air when I linger on the front steps to the frat house. I can't help closing my eyes for a second. He smells nice and his big hands are comforting.

He studies my face. "Want us to walk you back to your place?"

My stomach tightens. If I let him walk back with me, I think I'd invite him inside for the kiss we almost shared. I swallow thickly and shake my head.

"We're okay. Thank you. Stay and have fun."

The corners of his mouth tip up and he releases a soft chuckle. "Nah. No point."

"Why?"

"Because you're not there."

My pulse jumps. I twist the strap of my clutch around my fingers to keep myself from reaching out when he retreats from my space to hold an arm out so I can go down the steps.

Ducking my head in the hope it hides my blush, I hurry to Reagan, hooking my arm with hers.

"See you," he calls.

"Bye, boys. See you at The Landmark." Reagan waves, snickering when I pinch her side.

TEN
MAYA

The moment I almost kissed Easton repeats in my head during the entire walk back to our place. I'm thankful for the cold air because my body is too warm from picturing his grasp on my waist and the desire burning in his blue eyes.

Reagan pauses before opening the door when we reach the apartment. "So," she drawls. "I saw you cozying up to Easton Blake most of the night. He even asked to walk you home, aww."

"Oh, uh." I release a nervous laugh, floundering for a way to explain. "That's not—no. Don't give me that look. We're just, sort of, friends now, I guess. Weirdly."

"Friends who definitely want to fuck each other," she mumbles.

My mouth pops open. "I heard that."

"Heard what?" she says innocently on her way inside.

She makes a beeline for the water jug in the fridge. After filling two glasses, she hands one to me and downs hers.

"Whew, I needed tonight," she says breathlessly.

"I think I did, too." I fold my arms and lean on the small island that separates our kitchenette from the living room. "Tonight was fun. Thanks for making sure I get out of my head for a while."

"You know I've always got your back."

I return her warm smile. "Same. What happened with your frat boy?"

She shrugs. "Turns out he's a terrible kisser. You know how I feel about that. Sex without kissing just feels empty and disconnected."

"That sucks."

She sighs. "Right? He seemed like he could really toss me around easily." She eyes me slyly. "Maybe I need to find myself a hockey player, too."

I laugh at her over the top winking. "Go for it. You can have the whole team."

"Ohh, now we're talking about getting spicy. Night, babe." She puts her empty glass in the sink and heads for her room.

"Night."

Even though I spent most of the night hanging out with Easton, I surprisingly did have a good time. I fight the smile tugging at my lips while I sip my water, failing to smother it.

When I return to my room, my phone screen lights up on the nightstand.

My brows furrow when I check the text from a number I don't recognize. The contact name is *Hat Trick King* with the wet emoji.

Hat Trick King 💦
Wish you were still with me right now.

Worry slices through me for a moment. There's no way Johnny would go through the effort to text me from a different number, let alone somehow have it already saved as a contact. He's not bright enough for such a strategic play.

And to be honest, he's not skilled enough for any hat tricks. On the ice or in bed. I can't recall one good orgasm I had because of him. He's too selfish, only ever focused on his own pleasure. He was the kind of guy who thought his dick was enough magic to get me there without any kind of foreplay, so I'd end up taking care of myself. I'm certain he only plays hockey for the fringe benefits.

Maya
Who is this?

Hat Trick King 💦
The only man for you, baby. I'm ready to prove it as soon as you let me. Did you make it home okay?

Oh. Easton. A wry smile twists my lips and my thumbs hover over the keyboard as I relax.

Maya
I don't remember giving you my number. 😜

Hat Trick King 💦
That's because you didn't. Technically Reagan did.

The photo. She must've sent it as a group text. I didn't check since I was too busy resisting my attraction to him. I shoot a glare with no real heat behind it towards Reagan's side of the apartment.

How the hell did he get his contact saved in my phone as *Hat Trick King*, though? The only time my phone left my hands was when Reagan wanted to change the music and her phone wasn't connecting to the Bluetooth speaker after we left Easton to go to the kitchen.

No, you know what? I don't need to know. It doesn't matter, it's done now.

Maya
So you stole it.

Hat Trick King 💦
You miss every shot you don't take.

Hat Trick King 💦
If you're really not comfortable with me having your number, I'll delete it. Say the word and it's gone from my contacts.

The second message comes through only moments after the first cocky response. I bite my lip. Other guys I've been with were never so considerate of my comfort the way he is.

Johnny never respected me, period. It's easy to see that now in hindsight looking back on our relationship. If I can call it that. Most of the time it was him manipulating me to get what he wanted.

I doubt the time I caught him with someone else was the only time. He probably cheated on me the entire time we dated.

Easton might flirt and joke around, but when it comes to my

boundaries he knows when to stop without making me feel like shit about it.

Maya
No, it's fine. But don't even think about sending me a dick pic or I'll make you regret it.

Hat Trick King 💦
Never. Not unless you begged for it, baby.

Maya
I don't beg, and I'm definitely not begging to see your dick.

Hat Trick King 💦
Yet 😉

Yet. Him and that damn word. He's so sure he's got me, so confident that it's only a matter of time before I realize I want him too.

My stomach dips pleasantly as I recall how it felt to have his breath fanning across my lips just shy of kissing after he swung me away from someone spilling their drink.

Maybe I do.

I suppress another smile, shaking my head. "You're asking for it, hotshot. I'll text you *daddy* and pretend it's the wrong number before I disappear. Let's see how cocky you are then."

The temptation is strong. I bet he'd go feral thinking I meant to send it to some other guy instead of him, but he'd guess it was fake if I do it right now. I'm brainstorming other pranks to pull when he redirects the conversation.

Hat Trick King 💦
I had a great time with you tonight. I wanted to freeze it in time so it wouldn't end.

Maya
Everything ends eventually.

Hat Trick King 💦
So what you're saying is we just need to keep having nights like this. Got it. Have I mentioned how much I like the way you think?

Maya
Hah, nice try. You can't score me that easily.

Hat Trick King 💦
Taking my shots wherever I can. What are you doing?

Maya
I'm getting ready for bed.

Hat Trick King 💦
Sexy.

Maya
If you ask me what I'm wearing right now, I swear to god... 😂

Hat Trick King 💦
It's a classic opener for a reason 😉

Maya
Goodnight, Easton.

Hat Trick King 💦
Sweet dreams, baby.

He sends a photo of himself hanging out by a fire pit with two of his other teammates creeping in at the edges of the frame making goofy faces. His charming lopsided smile is half hidden by the green Heston U Hockey hoodie he's wearing with the neckline tugged up over his chin.

Hat Trick King 💦
I'll be dreaming of you. Tonight and every other night.

"Oh boy," I whisper when my heart flutters. "Don't do that. No swooning for hockey boys. Especially this one."

My heart isn't behaving, thudding rapidly in excitement. I roll my lips between my teeth, gazing at the photo. He really is handsome. When he turns those blue eyes on me, I can't think straight.

With a resigned groan of defeat because I can't control this little crush fighting to take hold, I cover my face with my hands to hide the blush heating my cheeks. I'm crushing on a hockey player.

"This is tomorrow's problem," I mumble before climbing into bed.

For once, I fall asleep easily. Instead of battling anxious racing thoughts, I'm relaxed when I lay my head on the pillow. One of my last thoughts before I drift off is wondering what it would be like to kiss Easton Blake.

* * *

Getting out of bed in the morning is a struggle. Mainly because I woke up in the middle of the night from a dream that left my core tingling and my nipples tight.

I was ready to reach for the box hidden beneath my bed to chase the way the dream left me feeling when I realized it wasn't some random guy spreading me out on the bar after I danced, kissing a path down my body until he slid his big hands up my thighs to lift my dress and cover my pussy with his perfect mouth.

It was Easton.

He was doing all that to me in my subconscious, taking me to the brink and leaving me turned on as fuck when I woke up.

Then I was awake for an hour with my thoughts taking me for a ride to pick it all apart before I finally fell asleep again.

I slide my thighs together and tug the covers over my head. Blowing out a breath, I get up to grab my shower bag. Before I leave the room, I kneel down to drag out the box decorated with cat stickers.

They make me smirk every time I get one of my collection of toys out of it. I grab the little aqua blue one because it's waterproof and add it to my shower bag for a self-care morning.

When I come out forty minutes later, my body is languid from reliving the dream for five orgasms in a row.

Anxiety After Dark Maya can overanalyze all she wants, but in the light of day the dream is just that—a dream. It's not real. He doesn't have to know how many times I came to the thought of his tongue inside me.

Or that I'm crushing on him. As far as he knows, we're still just friends and I'm keeping it that way.

Besides, Easton's hot. If he's starring in my dreams to devour my pussy on top of a bar in my fantasy, I'm not complaining. I can keep this crush under control so that it only has an outlet in my fantasies.

"Don't you look relaxed."

Reagan peers at me over the rim of her steaming mug. The scent of tea with lemon and honey wafts through the kitchenette.

I hum in amusement, flashing her a playful look. "Self-care works wonders."

"Hell yeah it does." She sets her tea down. "Pancakes?"

"Yes. I have work this morning, though."

She pulls down the instant mix from the cabinet while I get a pan out and set it on our small stove.

I duck into my room to get dressed and hang my towel to dry. When I come out, everything is set up for breakfast.

"So last night was fun," she says.

"Yeah, like the part where you helped Easton get my number?" I laugh at the overly innocent expression she puts on. "Your singing might tug at the heart strings of your online following, but you're not fooling anyone with that terrible acting."

She presses her palms together and closes her eyes. "I'm sorry."

"Don't worry about it. He offered to delete it if I didn't want him to have it."

Reagan relaxes, beaming at me. "See? The hockey guys aren't so bad. They tip great at the bar, and if they're there when I close out, one of them always walks me to my car."

"That might be true, but that doesn't mean this is going anywhere between me and him."

She gives me a side hug that's warm and soft. I rest my cheek on her head.

"I'm with you one hundred percent of the way no matter what goes down."

"Thanks."

After we eat, she takes care of the dishes while I go back to my room to dry my hair before work.

I'm sitting on my bed looking for a hair tutorial I wanted to try on my phone when I get a text that makes my stomach fill with tantalizing prickles of heat when I see it's from Easton.

Hat Trick King 💦
Morning beautiful. Did you sleep good?

My mind jumps right back to the dream. Then swerves to remind me of the moment we almost kissed. A flush spreads across my skin. He did wish me sweet dreams.

Maya
Is this going to be a thing now?

Hat Trick King 💦
Yup.

Maya
Fine then. Morning handsome. Did you get a good night's sleep?

Hat Trick King 💦
Aww, see you do love me. And yes, but it could be better. All that's missing is you in my arms all night.

I bite my lip to hold back a smile. Before I respond, Ryan hits me up. Switching to his text, I check what he wants.

Ryan
Did you find a ride home for Thanksgiving break?

Maya
Yeah. My last class is on Monday, and I don't have work. Reagan and I are road tripping down to New Haven early on Tuesday and I'll catch the train there when she drops me off. You can still bring me back on Sunday, right?

Ryan
Your roommate won't be back at the same time? Heston Lake is like an extra two hours out of my way from Elmwood.

I roll my eyes when he follows up with an unimpressed emoji.

Maya
That's what you get for being the one who got to take our car to college. You said you'd do it when Mom asked. Should I tell her you're bailing on me?

Ryan
Fine, I'll do it. Maybe I'll stop by the rink to see if your boyfriend's around.

Maya
What?

Ryan
Bag of dicks.

Maya
Ugh, stop. Maybe if you weren't just as much of a dick, I wouldn't have left with Easton when you were here.

He doesn't answer after I send him a middle finger emoji because he knows I'm right. He's only joking about how I left the bar that night, but him calling Easton my boyfriend sends a mix of jitters and warmth rushing through me.

It gets worse when the latest message from him appears at the top of my screen.

Hat Trick King 💦
What are you doing today? Let me take you out for something to eat.

Maya
I have work. But next time the donut truck is around, you can buy me donuts again.

Hat Trick King 💦
Nice. I'll buy you as many as you want.

He continues talking to me while I get ready for work, and we're still texting back and forth on my way to the farm for my shift.

Maya
I have to go. Just got to work.

My stomach tightens as I impulsively tell him I'll talk to him later. He replies with a winking emoji.

I curse when I realize I'm about to be late. I jog across the farm to reach the pavilion, darting inside to meet this morning's group Marnie scheduled me for.

I freeze inside the door, gaping at the sight before me. What. The. Hell.

Hockey players.

There are hockey players everywhere.

This can't be happening. How is this real?

Easton Blake and the entire team of Heston University Knights are at Merrywood Farms, in the yoga pavilion. Waiting for me.

"Hey," he greets when he spots me hovering in the doorway.

"What are you doing here?" I blurt.

"Goat yoga." He grins, waving an arm at the guys. "I think they're actually looking forward to it."

"Goat yoga," I repeat faintly.

"You should've been there when I suggested it to our coaches. Most of the guys lost it. They thought I was kidding."

"I don't blame them. I can't picture Mr. Macho hockey captain —" I give his arm a friendly push. "—and a bunch of hockey players doing yoga, let alone *goat* yoga."

He lifts a shoulder. "We're here to limber up. Did you know yoga is great training to help improve stability and range of motion?"

My mind goes right to the gutter, picturing Easton's muscles flexing as he moves into different poses. The tips of my ears grow hot.

"And the three other yoga studios in the area were booked? If you want to have a session that's more serious, goat yoga probably isn't it."

He rakes his teeth across his lip. "Yeah, but you don't teach at those. We requested you specifically."

Now my ears are on fire. He calls for the guys to circle up.

"This is Madden—we call him Graves—and our rookie, Elijah." Easton messes up Elijah's light brown hair and dodges when he tries to retaliate with a shove. "Then there's some of our seniors, Jake Brody and Theo Boucher. You met Cam the other day, and—"

"And I'm Noah," says the tall beach blond guy with a gleaming smile. "The hot one."

Easton elbows him in the side, nodding in satisfaction when the other teammates give Noah shit. "Can it, assholes." Once the laughter and smack talk settles down, he gestures to me. "This is Maya. Don't flirt with her."

"Yes, captain," Noah says in a jaunty tone. "We wouldn't dream of making moves on your girl."

"I'm not his girl."

Easton opens his mouth and I silence him with a fierce look, holding up a finger in warning before he can utter his favorite word: *yet*. Smirking, he lifts his hands in surrender.

"Where are these goats?" Noah asks. "I'm ready to cuddle."

"I'll bring them in once Maya goes over some information about the session," Hana says as she arrives. "Sorry I'm late, Marnie needed me."

"Hana?" Elijah sputters.

Her steps falter. "Eli. Hey. I've barely seen you around so far this semester."

"What are you doing here?" Elijah asks.

"I work here."

He rubs at his forehead. "What are you doing in Heston Lake? I thought you were going to go to Stanford."

She gives him a wobbly smile. "I applied here last minute. My grandparents weren't happy with Dad for letting me pass on my acceptance to their science program, but he said I should follow my dreams no matter what they are."

"Wow," he says. "That's awesome. Why didn't you tell me?"

Hana shakes her head, waving him off. Noah looks between them with an intrigued smile. He nudges Elijah.

"Dude. You know a hot yoga instructor? You're holding out on us."

"She's my sister's best friend. We grew up together." Elijah's stare is caught on Hana as she puts her hair up. He gravitates toward her.

"Okay, you can all take a mat. I'll go over everything to expect, and then we'll get started," I say.

Easton picks front and center, sprawling on the mat that faces mine. Once they're all settled, I go over the rules for when the goats are in the room. We get started with some simple breathing techniques to help us dispel the energy we brought into the pavilion.

"Okay, incoming," Hana says. "Let them approach you. Trust me, they're obsessed with attention."

She opens the door to the pen where we keep the goats on standby until yoga sessions begin. They all stream into the room and the guys get a kick out of it.

The smallest kid rubs against Noah's hip and flops down when it loses its balance. He pets it.

"This one's mine," he says.

His teammates laugh, equally enthralled by the baby goats roaming the pavilion.

"Taking a deep breath in, let's bring our hands overhead," I direct. "Then we're going to slowly curve our bodies to the side. It's okay if you can't reach far. Go at your own pace for everything."

I don't know what I expected, but Easton taking this seriously and keeping his teammates in check wasn't how I thought this would go.

The guys are all having the time of their life. They put good effort into the poses, but when the goats interact with them they basically have hearts in their eyes.

Despite my surprise when I found out who was taking today's class, I can't hold back the content feeling I get every time I see animals helping people relax and let go of any worries they're carrying with them.

Easton ends up with a brown and white goat climbing into his lap while we're working on stretching our hips. He smiles down at it, letting it sniff his crooked finger. It settles down for a nap and he winds up spending the next fifteen minutes absorbed in the goat like nothing else in the world exists.

My heart gives a squeeze at the sight. What is it about a guy snuggling animals in his strong arms that is so damn attractive?

Easton catches my eye, stroking his sleeping goat's cheeks. My pulse thunders.

Concentrating through the second half of the session is challenging. I keep getting distracted watching him when I'm supposed to be leading them through the final poses. He can definitely tell because he keeps peeking at me until we finish.

After the photo we take at the end of every session, Easton lingers while his teammates file out. He helps me herd the goats to the paddock behind the pavilion while Hana hangs by the door talking to Elijah.

"You seemed like you enjoyed that," I say.

"Any time I get to spend with you is enjoyable." He winks when I laugh. "Actually, it was pretty cool. Might have to come back again. We bonded."

He points to the brown and white goat playing with another one. It's the one he cradled in his lap when it fell asleep. Once we have them all in the paddock, he rests his forearms on the gate. I do the same beside him.

"So," he starts.

"So."

"There's a party at our place next weekend."

I hum. "Have fun with that."

He angles his head to look at me with a soft smile. "I will if you're there. What do you say?"

"I mean..."

"Say yes."

He hits me with that damn puppy look, smoldering gaze piercing through me. Biting my lip, I mull it over.

"Okay."

His face splits with a heart-stopping smile. "Yeah?"

"I can't believe I'm saying this, but yes."

He whoops, drumming a victory beat on the gate. He wraps his arms around my waist and swings me around. I choke back a scream so I don't startle the goats, laughing at his antics.

"Easton? We're about to leave," Elijah calls from the pavilion.

He puts me down and brushes hair from my face. "See you."

A warm laugh bubbles out of me. "Bye, weirdo."

Hana walks down the small hill sloping off the pavilion and joins me. We lean against the gate, watching the two hockey players walk away.

ELEVEN
EASTON

AFTER POKING the burning logs to stir the fire pit, I sink into a folding lawn chair with a sated groan, patting my full stomach. Nights like these are where it's at. I love being on the ice alongside my boys, but it's just as great to vibe with them around the fire in the yard following a meal.

"I've gotta say, the days you cook are the best, dude." I give him a thumbs up.

Cameron chuckles, running his fingers through his hair to tame the tousled brown locks before fitting his hat on his head.

"You always say that," he points out.

"Truth," Noah chimes in, equally chilled out.

Our resident beach boy is even more laid-back than usual, long, muscled limbs sprawled in his seat.

"If you ever stop playing hockey, you can cook for a living," Madden says.

Cameron jerks his head with a smile that's slightly tense. "Well, we'll see. For now I'm all in on hockey." He kicks out at Madden's folding chair, jostling it. "Maybe you lazy shits could learn how to cook. It's not hard."

Madden shoots out his legs to stabilize himself with a moody frown. "Everything I try to cook burns. It's pointless."

A few of us groan in agreement. He's one of the few team

members we've restricted from our cooking rotation, keeping him on cleaning duty in exchange.

"Wait, is McKinley asleep over there?" Noah gestures with his chin. "Graves, check for signs of life."

Madden grunts, stretching a leg to nudge him with his toe without getting up. McKinley doesn't budge, stretched out on the picnic table with his arms folded as a makeshift pillow. His hoodie is pulled over his head.

"Bro, seriously, how can he sleep like that?" Theo gets up to poke at him.

"Beats me," I say. "I'm jealous he can go out like a light anywhere."

Cameron, Brody, and Noah join him, doing a shit job smothering their snickering while they take photos of him. It doesn't matter. He snores through it all. Even when Brody pulls Jack's hood off to lift his head, throwing up a peace sign while Noah purses his lips to keep it together.

The back door opens and three more of our teammates poke their heads out. Eric Holland, our backup goalie, along with Daniel Hutchinson and Nick Briggs are three of the biggest guys on the team. Hutch is a senior and Briggs is a sophomore that sticks close to him.

"I was wondering where you all wound up," Holland muses. "What's going on?"

I lift a hand in greeting. "We're just chilling."

"Me and Briggs are going to hit the gym," Hutch says.

"Where's Manning?" Theo asks.

Hutch shrugs. "Haven't seen him since we got back from that farm earlier."

"Probably banging that sorority chick he brings around." Brody mimes an O-face, grabbing imaginary hips and thrusting the air suggestively.

Madden rolls his eyes and folds his arms, tucking his chin close to his chest, thick dark brows flattening. He gets extra grumpy whenever the guys flaunt their hookups.

"You joining us?" I ask Holland.

The other two are in sweats, but he's overdressed for a night around the fire pit. He's fresh-shaven, no longer rocking his scruffy dark beard and he's wearing a nice sweater instead of his usual graphic tee. He shakes his head, gesturing to the guys.

"Hutch is giving me a ride. I've got a movie date with my girlfriend."

The guys outside all coo in sync. "Aww."

"Sweet." I smirk. "Is that why you shaved the ecosystem?"

"You look so weird without the beard, bro." Noah squints at him on his way back to his seat. "But in a good way."

Holland rubs his cleaned up jaw. "She likes it when I'm smooth."

"I bet." Noah waggles his brows with a raunchy chuckle. He strokes the light blond stubble he's grown over the last few days. "I've never gotten any complaints for providing a rougher ride."

I hold a fist to my mouth, chuckling. Typically I keep myself trimmed, but curiosity crosses my mind, sending a tug of heat south to my dick. Which would Maya prefer?

Before the intriguing thought consumes my attention, Cameron gives me a friendly tap on the shoulder to get me to move my feet so he can get by. He collapses in the seat next to mine with a content sigh.

"I can't with the upkeep." He scratches the dark shadow of hair covering his face.

"You always look like a baby when you shave." Theo plants a hand on Cameron's hat and gives his head a jostle. "Your rookie year here, I thought some fifteen year old walked out of the bathroom."

"Shut up, man." He swipes at Theo, both of them ending up in a ridiculous wrestling match.

"We're out." Briggs salutes us to follow Holland to the driveway.

"See you guys later," I say.

"Don't forget to take care of the fire when you're done," Hutch says before leaving.

Out of all the seniors, the giant-sized blond is like our house dad after our previous captain graduated.

"We've got it." Madden doesn't lift his thousand-yard stare from the dancing flames.

Cameron and Theo settle, neither of them the clear winner. The crackle and pops of the fire are relaxing, lulling me into a zen state.

"You're awfully focused over there, rookie," Noah taunts a few minutes later. "Looking at some good porn?"

"Oh, for sure. He's gotta be," Cameron says with a sly grin. "That's why he's been quiet for the last twenty minutes. Just don't whip it out while we're present, man. Go jerk off back at your dorm."

"I wasn't!" Elijah bursts out from across the circle.

He nearly topples his chair over when Theo sneaks up behind him to nick his phone.

"Hey—!"

Theo holds him back with one arm, twisting to check his phone. "Relax, rookie. We just want to know if you've found a gem or—oh."

I snort. "What, is it something kinky?"

His chin dips, dark blond hair hanging in his face. He turns the phone to show us. It's not anything naughty. The Merrywood Farms website shows photos of little goats running around the yoga pavilion we were at earlier today.

"Look at this fucking softie."

All of us crack up. Elijah scratches his nose, averting his eyes.

"I was just looking to find out if there was a class schedule to do it again," he mutters.

"Oh yeah?" Cameron pitches forward, fluttering his lashes. "For the goats, or so you can have that cute instructor put her hands all over you?"

"As long as it's not Maya." The warning in my tone is good-natured, but present.

Elijah scrubs his face, head hanging back. "Fuck off. We're just friends."

Another round of mocking laughter goes around the fire pit.

I wouldn't mind visiting the farm again for a repeat at all. Watching Maya in her element was just as awesome as I pictured when I figured out she worked there.

My teeth scrape my lip, reminiscing about her flexibility. Spending an hour with her plump ass and thick thighs right in front of me was an ideal way to spend the morning.

More than how hot she is in yoga pants, it was cool to see her passion for the animals she works with. It's got me eager to find out more about her.

"Oh, hello." Noah pops up with a smug expression.

"What's up?" Cameron asks.

"I've gotta dip." Noah flicks Cameron's hat on his way around our circle. He holds up his phone with a jaunty wave. "I've got the green light from Amanda, half a mile away."

The guys bust out with a drawn out chorus of *ohhhh*, smacking and elbowing him playfully. Madden's the only one that doesn't join in. His jaw works and he keeps his gaze locked on the fire.

"Have fun, man." Grinning, I fold my hands behind my head, propping my feet on the warm stones surrounding the flames.

It's still strange to think I was having the same kind of fun not long ago, yet the idea of going back to random hookups is long gone from my mind. That's just not the guy I want to be anymore. Not now that I'm enjoying getting to know Maya.

Other girls have ceased to exist to me. She's the only one I'm interested in.

We're still taking small steps, but she's not fighting this thing between us as hard as when she first realized I'm a hockey player. I'm holding on to that, willing to take this at her pace while I work for my chance with her.

A startled yell and a thump draws our attention to the picnic table. McKinley swings a bewildered look around from the grass, rubbing his hip after rolling off the table.

"You good, dude?" I check with an amused rumble. "You're in the yard. You fell asleep on the table."

"I dreamed Gritty was chasing me," he mumbles. "I couldn't get away. The ice just kept going and going."

"The Flyers mascot?" Cameron bursts out laughing.

"He's just so—orange." McKinley shudders, scraping a hand through his hair.

The rest of us lose it, our wheezing laughter echoing off the trees with embers from the fire floating into the night sky.

TWELVE
EASTON

WALKING out of my midweek journalism class with an A on my test feels damn good. I've got some time to kill before my next class and head for the coffee cart to see if I can get a snack.

My good mood improves when I spot Maya sitting on a bench with her notebooks. We must have an overlap in our schedules. I never noticed her around campus before, but now she'd be impossible for me to miss.

Her hair is twisted up in a blue flower-shaped clip. I drag my gaze down the uninterrupted view of her neck, fighting back the urge to kiss it.

I smirk. "So you do wear Heston blue."

I'm hoping for a smile, but all it gets me is a tired sigh that makes my chest constrict. I scan her face and my stomach tightens. She's upset.

My bag drops off my shoulder and I kneel in front of her, covering her hand with mine. "Hey. Are you okay?"

She meets my gaze with a guarded look, eyes glistening. They're puffy and bloodshot, like she's been crying for a while. My heart bolts into my throat. I want to make her feel better, willing to do anything to take whatever pain she's carrying away.

"What's wrong, baby?" I rub her skin with my thumb. "Do you have any other classes today?"

Maya shakes her head. "Why?"

The defeated, flat tone of her voice hits me square in the chest.

I take her hand and urge her up. "Come with me. I know what will help."

"Don't you have stuff to do?" She grips my hand like a lifeline.

"It's fine. It's not important right now."

She sniffles, threading her fingers with mine. I brush my thumb over her knuckles to comfort her as I lead her to where I'm parked.

I'll email my professor later to let her know I missed class because I had a personal matter to handle. I haven't missed a class yet, so hopefully she'll be understanding. But if she's not, I don't care.

Maya is all that matters.

She stays quiet once I get her in the car and pull away from campus. I stop at the drive-thru and start an order. She pipes up to ask for a milkshake, digging in her purse. I hold out a hand to stop her. Everything I ordered is for her except for the large ice water I got for myself.

The lake isn't far from the drive-thru. I find a good spot with a view and park. She's halfway through her nuggets already.

"Thanks," she finally mumbles.

"No problem. Better?"

"This is helping." She picks at her fries. "Today sucks. But now it sucks slightly less."

"Want to tell me why today sucks?"

Sighing, she wipes her fingers and bites her lip. "I found out today that one of the last required classes for a typical senior seminar won't be available next semester unless they find a professor that's willing to run it. The one I'd planned on taking it from just took early retirement. I need that class in order to graduate in three years."

"Is it available as a summer class?"

She undoes her hair clip to play with it and thumps her head against the seat. "I think that'll still depend on whether or not they find a replacement."

I frown in sympathy. It's annoying enough to pick my classes so they don't interfere with my athletic schedule.

"Any other classes you can substitute for it?"

"I don't know yet. I have to talk to my advisor to see."

"It'll work out."

"I hope." She sips on her milkshake. "Thank you for getting me food and letting me vent. I'm sorry for dumping on you."

I squeeze her leg. "Please don't apologize. I'm here to listen to anything you want to talk about. Lean on me."

She hesitates, eyes darting away before she continues.

"The thing with the seminar is annoying, but what really upset me today is this." She shows me a text from her brother. "It's my grandfather. He's back in the hospital again after he's been doing so much better lately. And—"

A tear falls and her voice grows tight, cutting off with a strained gasp. I cup her face, swiping at her tears, hushing her.

"It's okay."

Her throat convulses as she swallows. My heart fucking breaks at her quivering lip while she fights back her emotions.

"I've been working so hard to graduate early for him. I want him to see me finish my degree, but his illness is only progressing." She squeezes her eyes shut, more tears leaking out at the corners. "He's such a big part of my life. He's the one I've always gone to with my problems. I'm...I'm so afraid he won't make it. I'm terrified of losing him."

"Shit. I'm sorry, Maya." I unbuckle my belt, then hers, and gather her into a hug.

Instead of pulling away after a moment, she tucks her face against my neck, melting against me. The position is a little awkward, but it doesn't matter if it's helping her feel safe. I'll hold her like this all day if she needs me to. I stroke her hair until she stops shaking.

I wish I could protect her from her grief. When she calms down, but still remains in my arms, I start talking about stuff I've only told Cameron and Noah.

"I know how hard and scary it is. He's gotta be so proud of you, baby. I know it." She releases a shuddering breath, nodding. "I wish I could tell you that it'll hurt less, but I can't promise there won't be days it'll just hit you. It's okay to be sad, though."

"Who'd you lose? One of your grandparents?"

"My dad." She goes still and I skim my lips over her head, speaking against her hair. "It was a car accident five years ago. I was fifteen. It blindsided me. We were really close. Hockey was our thing, so I feel like I have a piece of him with me every time I put on my skates even though it sucks that he's gone."

"That's how I feel when I'm working at the farm," she rasps. "Grandpa taught me how to ride horses. It's how I first fell in love with animals and knew I wanted to have my degree involve them."

I nod in understanding. "Our passion turned into the thing I want to do with my life. I started pursuing my hockey career with him helping me work towards it. If I knew I would lose him, I would've done everything to cherish the moments we had together even more."

She swallows audibly. We go quiet for a short while until she breaks the comforting silence.

"God. I just cried all over you. I'm sorry." She shifts away with a sniffle, flipping down the visor to wipe her puffy eyes. "I'm a mess, huh?"

You're the most beautiful woman I've ever seen, even with snot dripping from your nose.

"Not at all. Here." I give her an ice cube from the water I ordered and wrap it in a napkin for her. "Put this under your eyes. It'll help with the swelling."

"Thanks."

"Hockey players are no strangers to icing our injuries. Here, look at this killer bruise I got at an exhibition game."

I lift the hem of my shirt to show off the mostly healed bruise on my ribs. Her lips twist wryly.

"You should've seen it the other day. Want some water? You should hydrate."

"I'm okay. Just this."

She puts her hair back in the flower clip to get it out of her face, and settles back in her seat with her food.

I watch her crushing her nuggets, wondering how the hell it's possible for me to be even more into this girl. She already has a powerful hold over me.

"Way to be a creep." She sounds more like herself and offers me a nugget. "Eat this instead of watching me."

I chuckle. "I really want some, but I already had my weekly

quota of cheat meals. The nutritionist will have me by the balls if I eat that."

When I give it a longing look, she takes my hand and gives it to me.

"One nugget isn't going to hurt. I thought you wanted to commiserate with me?"

The corner of my mouth tugs up. "Maybe without the skin."

She's flabbergasted as I peel it off the meat. "Dude. You can't eat a naked chicken nugget. That's just sad."

"I know." I laugh at the pitiful meat. "Damn it."

"Here."

Maya takes it away and balls it up in a napkin before shaking her box of delicious smelling nuggets insistently. I rub my fingers together.

"I won't tell if you won't."

Her lips twitch and she leans in. "Your secret's safe with me."

Sharing food with her makes something warm and happy spread through my chest. The feeling grows when I have to fight her for the last nugget.

"This is my sad meal. Get your own." She swats at my hand.

I snort. "I thought you wanted to share with me."

"Yeah, but the last one's mine."

She bites it in half, eyes gleaming with the spark I think I fell for the first night I met her. Catching her wrist, I bring her hand to my mouth and eat the second half.

"Hey." A hoarse laugh escapes her. "That was mine."

I trace a circle on the inside of her wrist. "Mmm. Thanks."

She shivers, watching my tongue swipe across my lips. Pulling free of my grasp, she squirms in her seat to get comfortable, tucking one of her legs beneath her.

Next time I'll definitely make sure to remember I need to order extra food to keep her satisfied.

"Mind if we make a stop on our way back?"

"Sure."

When I pull into the drive-thru for the second time, she gives me a sidelong glance. I put in a new order and follow the line of cars to the pick up window.

"If you wanted some, you should've just ordered when you got mine." She holds up her hands. "For the record, my emotional breakdown is not responsible for your cheat meal."

"It's for the guys," I explain. "Even though we have our nutritional plans, and we can all cook for ourselves. Well, mostly. Some of the guys on the team aren't allowed in the kitchen."

After thanking the girl at the window, I park, then hop out. I'm aware of Maya watching me set the bag in the back seat and clicking the belt around it before I get behind the wheel again.

"You buckled in the nuggets," she points out.

"I know. We do emotional support nugget runs." I hand her my phone. "Here, take a photo and tell the group chat the goods are safely secured."

It gets her to laugh, and that's all I wanted from the minute I saw tears in her eyes.

* * *

It's late by the time I finish the extra practice time I put in at the rink to hone my skills. On my way home I check in on Maya to see if she's okay. Once I get in, feed the cat, refilling the bowl we leave for her on the porch. Then I stop in the kitchen, grabbing milk from the fridge. My attention stays glued to my phone while I chug a few sips from the container before pouring a glass.

"Is this some new hand-eye coordination training? Because you suck." Cameron pops up on the island in the middle of the kitchen. "Try getting it in the glass."

"Shut up."

He steals the jug from me while I'm distracted by three dots appearing in the message thread with Maya.

Easton
How did the rest of your day go? Any updates about your grandfather?

Maya
He's better now. They sent him home.

Easton
That's great 🩶

Maya
I'm so relieved. It stresses me out when he's there.

Easton
Wyd now?

"Earth to East." Cameron nudges me.

"What?"

He smirks. "I asked if you're done with the milk. Twice."

"Yeah." I bump my fist to his.

My phone vibrates on the counter between us. He grins, snatching it up before I read her response.

"Reeves." I stalk him around the island. "Give it back."

"You've been glued to your phone."

Madden comes in with a fork sticking out of an empty container from last night's leftovers. He eyes both of us.

"Help me out, Graves," I say.

He sighs, moving to block Cameron, leveling him with a flat look. "This is stupid."

"Here." Cameron tosses my phone to Noah as he comes in from the entryway.

"What are we playing?" Noah looks at the screen. "Ohh, Maya."

Elijah wanders into the kitchen. "What's going on?"

"Catch." Noah lets my phone fly through the air and Elijah scrambles not to let it fall from his hands.

"Assholes." I narrow my eyes. "If someone doesn't give my phone back, I'll convince coach we need an entire week of suicide drills."

Elijah hands my phone back, clearing his throat. "Sorry."

I wave him off, making sure they didn't accidentally send Maya any weird messages with their game. There isn't, but her answer makes me freeze.

Maya
I'm about to go for a walk. I need it to clear my head.

What? It's almost ten.

Easton
At the gym?

Maya
No, treadmill walking just makes me antsy. I have to walk outside when it's for my anxiety.

Easton
Are you walking alone? In the dark?

Maya
Yeah, I always do. I take protection.

She sends a photo of the metal cat ear-shaped self-defense. I pinch the bridge of my nose for a moment, then scrub at my face.

Yeah, no. I think the fuck not.

Easton
Tell me where you are. I'm coming with you.

It takes her a long moment to respond. I'm about to comb the entire town to find her when she says she'll meet me in front of Clocktower Brew House. I heave a sigh. The protectiveness I feel over her slams into me as hard as a player checking me at full speed.

"I'm going out," I announce.

"Tell Maya we say hi." Noah winks.

Grabbing my keys and wallet, I head back out and jog the short distance to Main Street square. I beat her there, spending a few minutes shifting my weight foot to foot until I finally spot her coming from the direction of the school. She has a worn baseball cap on with her ponytail swinging.

Maya eyes me up and down. "You okay? You're all tense."

"Yeah, because someone told me they like to walk around by themselves at night." I step into her, taking her by the shoulders. "Do me a favor?"

"Sure."

"No matter what time it is, tell me when you feel like going for a walk from now on. I'll go with you so you never have to walk alone."

Her pretty mouth parts in surprise. I want to trace her lower lip with my fingertips and taste it until I have the shape of it committed to memory.

"Nothing's ever happened. Heston Lake is safe." She waves to the owner of the bookshop.

I shake my head. "I don't like the idea of you out late at night by yourself."

"What if I need to go for a walk in the middle of the night?" Her chin lifts.

"I'm there."

She slides her lips together. "The night before a game? You need to be well rested to play."

I squeeze her shoulders. "I'm *there*, Maya. Anytime you need me, I'll be there."

She's stunned into silence for a beat. Something shifts in her eyes, but she nods.

"Good." Tension bleeds from my shoulders. "So, where are we walking tonight?"

"I don't know."

She sets off in a direction and I fall into step beside her. On our way through the square, a guy looks her way. When he spots my glare, he takes his eyes off her so fast his neck almost snaps. I nod slowly in satisfaction.

"What do you mean?" I reach for her hand, twining our fingers together.

She darts a look at me from the corner of her eye. "I don't really walk with a destination in mind. Sometimes it's a short walk. Sometimes I swear I circle town three times over. Whatever it takes."

"To clear your head?"

"Yeah." She peeks at me again, playing with her ponytail. "I'm usually fine in the moment, but at night my anxiety makes it hard to sleep. This is the only way that works to quiet my brain. Thanks for coming with me."

I give her hand a supportive squeeze. "Yeah."

We walk hand in hand without a destination in mind, talking about everything from stories about her work at the farm to me regaling her with stories about the times I've gotten into trouble with the guys to make her laugh. Time slips by without either of us noticing until I check my phone.

"Oh, shit. It's after midnight." I chuckle. "Are you cold?"

She peers up through her lashes. "I'm okay. Do you have to get back?"

"We're not going back until you're ready. I'll walk around with you all night if it's what you need."

She smiles. "I'm okay now. I've been good for a while, actually."

Pride stirs in my chest. I let her steer us back towards the center of town. She tries to part ways in the square, but I insist on walking her all the way back to her apartment.

When she leaves me behind at the entrance to her building, there's a tug in my chest that makes me want to follow her.

THIRTEEN
MAYA

On my way across campus Saturday night, I garner several strange looks. It's worth it. Easton might have me braving a party at the hockey house for him, but just to rile him up, I'm wearing Ryan's jersey as a joke.

I take it from the amount of blue and green hockey fan gear I spot on and off campus, the guys won their home game this afternoon. When I reach the square at the center of town, Reagan sends a text to our group chat saying she's running late, but she'll try to be there later. Hana responds to say she can't make it after all, apologizing for bailing on us to practice choreography for her upcoming solo.

"Shit," I mumble.

That leaves me heading to party with the hockey team and their crowd alone. Wearing an Elmwood jersey.

I hesitate in front of the coffee shop, debating waiting for Reagan in there. Another text pops up on my screen. I roll my lips between my teeth.

Hat Trick King 💦
You're still coming, right?

Maya
Ohhhh, that was tonight?

Hat Trick King 💦
:(:(

Maya
Kidding. Almost there. Picked out my outfit just for you.

He replies with a heart. The rush of delight is ridiculous. I tamp down on it to keep my feelings in check. We're friends. Nothing more.

My pulse skitters again at the thought of him walking with me the other night and because he was the only person to recognize I was upset when he found me on campus. He's the kind of friend who buys me food and lets me cry all over him while he held me.

I close my eyes, murmuring firmly. "Just friends."

The hockey team's house isn't much further. It's just off the square with historic charm and a wraparound porch. I've heard the freshmen have to dorm in the school's housing for athletes on campus, but the rest of them live here like a frat house.

I blend in with the group of people entering ahead of me, planning to slip by Noah as he greets them. An arm stops me in my tracks once I'm through the door. Cameron grins at me, shaking his head.

He whips off his baseball cap and scrubs at his hair before putting it on backwards. "And where do you think you're going?"

I gesture to the sounds of music and chatter down the hall. "The party I was invited to."

"Wearing that? Noah, get a load of this."

His teammate turns around and busts out laughing. When he recovers, he braces a forearm against the wall, subtly blocking me from leaving the entryway with his huge frame.

"What, is there some cover I didn't hear about?" I lift my brows. "I thought girls got into every party here for free."

"Hate to admit it, because fucking *Elmwood,* but you pull off the red," Noah says. "You're asking for trouble wearing that in here."

"So? People have to exist all the time with fans of teams they don't like occupying the same space." I grin. "The Devils and Rangers fans, the Eagles and Cowboys fans—they manage. Mostly. Can't you handle it like big boys?"

Noah opens and closes his mouth. Someone else comes through

the door behind me. The guy takes one look at my Elmwood jersey and boos at me like a shitty ten year old. Or a sports fan.

"There. That." Noah snaps his fingers. "We can't have that. We're celebrating tonight."

"It's for your own good. We'll find you something else to put on if you want to stay." Cameron cups a hand next to his mouth and shouts. "Easton! C'mere."

"I'm good." I flip my hair. "I did my makeup to coordinate with these colors."

Noah snorts into his fist. He claps Easton's shoulder when he rounds the corner from the hallway.

"What's up? Did the beer run fall through? Brody texted to say it's all good—Oh." Easton spots me.

I wiggle my fingers in a little wave. "Hi."

"Hey. You came." His attention lowers and he lets out a rueful laugh. "And you're wearing your brother's jersey to a Knights party."

Biting my lip around a smile, I twirl to show off. "I remembered how much you liked it the night we met. Told you that you'd love the outfit I picked out."

He hums. "I'd like it more if it was on my floor."

My mouth pops open. "Yeah, you wish."

Cameron stands sentry at Easton's side, smirking. "You've got two options if you want to party. Change...or change."

I squint, making a show of tapping my finger against my chin in thought. "I think I'll go with...option three."

Offering an innocent smile, I flip them off. A huff of amusement shakes Easton's shoulders. He prods his cheek with his tongue, eyeing me up and down.

It doesn't bother me that his friends were joking around with me over this, but my stomach tightens. His expression says I'm a five-star feast and he's fucking starving.

"Your call, E." Noah smirks, slinging an arm across Easton's shoulder. "But you'd better stick by her side in case she needs a bodyguard. You'll have to fend off everyone here."

Easton's eyes don't leave mine and a smug grin tugs at the corners of his mouth. "I can't let you in here like that, sweetheart. Not while you're wearing our rival team's jersey."

"And if I don't want to take it off?" I challenge, mirroring his grin with a sassy one.

He gives his friends sidelong glances and comes forward, dipping his chin with a playful smirk. "I can work with that. What's it gonna be? Take it off, or I'm taking it off for you and burning it in the fire pit." He lowers his voice. "One way or another that jersey's coming off, baby."

A shiver works down my spine. I peer up at him through my lashes.

The idea of cocky hockey players pulling something like this on me would normally send me running in the other direction. But that's the version of myself that's been stuck by avoiding guys like Easton, instantly on guard to protect myself from getting hurt again by someone that doesn't care about me.

I've never given anyone else a chance.

But Easton...I think I want to give him a chance.

Rather than uncertainty about his intentions, I'm having fun. This is similar to the camaraderie I had with Ryan and his friends growing up, before I started dating his teammate. Part of me missed this feeling when I closed my heart off from this side of myself.

Easton stares me down, as captivated as he was by me dancing on the bar when he came to my rescue.

It spurs me on with confidence, flooding me with a sense of deviousness. I'm down to play this game, and I'll do it better than them.

"Oh yeah? Sounds serious. So I should take it off?" My lips curve slowly as I lift the hem with each taunting question to reveal bare skin. "Right here? Right now?"

Easton's buddies cheer. His eyes snap up from the expanse of skin I'm showing off.

He shoots an annoyed look at his teammates. "Hang on—"

"I guess unless you want me partying with you in my bra, one of you better go get me something to put on."

Before I lift the jersey to reveal it, Easton moves. Within two strides, he's in front of me, using his body to block me from his teammates' view. I swallow as he pulls me in close, fisting the material at my back. The guys continue to joke about defeating the enemy, but I'm trapped in his intense blue gaze.

He shifts closer, lips brushing my temple. "I don't want to see you wear another guy's stuff, Maya. Not even my teammates' clothes. Come with me."

My stomach dips at his voice in my ear and his scent surrounding me. I bite my lip around a smile.

"Fine, hotshot. You can have it your way. *This* time."

He smirks. "Good girl."

Then he bends to haul me over his shoulder, carrying me up the steps. A laugh escapes me. His boys hype us up and it stirs a comfortable, warm glow in my chest. I cling to him so I don't overbalance us.

"Is this how you get all the girls to your room?"

His big hand squeezes the back of my thigh, holding me steady. "No. Just you."

"So this is our thing?"

Another squeeze of my thigh. "It could be if you were my girl. But you're not mine."

"*Yet*," I tease when we reach the top of the staircase.

"Yet," he echoes, the smile evident in his voice as his thumb rubs absent circles that send tingles up my thigh.

Butterflies fill my stomach when we enter his room. It's surprisingly cozy with a decent sized bed, and it's cleaner than I pictured after growing up with a hockey player for a brother.

When he sets me on my feet with care not to drop me, I'm struck with curiosity because it's hardly the room I'd expect of a notorious playboy that takes a different girl to bed every night.

"No roommate? That's a nice perk."

He chuckles, closing the door. "Team captain gets the big room with my own bathroom. Last year I was rooming with Cameron down the hall."

I peer around at the Bruins posters, hockey gear taking over the corner by the tall windows, and his disorganized desk with half-scribbled scrimmage notes.

Photos of him with his teammates and family dot the walls. The one where he's wearing the same green Heston University t-shirt stretched tight over his broad chest catches my eye. He's holding a boy several years younger than him on his shoulders with a woman that has to be his mom. It makes me smile softly.

I hold my arms out in the middle of the room. "You've finally got me where you've been trying to get me for like half the semester."

"Four weeks, if we want to be exact."

I blink, mentally counting how long it's been since the Heston vs Elmwood game in October. I'm surprised he's kept track.

"Well, you've got me here."

"Just for a shirt."

Without breaking eye contact, he reaches behind his head and tugs, stripping off the shirt he's wearing. My mouth goes dry at the sexy, effortless move. I stare at the hard planes of his bare chest. His muscles flex, abs and biceps contracting.

I swallow.

Then swallow again, because once isn't enough.

Easton hands his shirt to me. The cotton is soft and warm between my fingertips. It's more faded than the photo of him with his family. He offers me privacy to change by turning around.

I wait a minute, studying his shoulders while he tousles his hair. My heart beats hard. Squeezing the shirt, I leap off a cliff I haven't jumped from in years.

"Okay," I say.

He turns around, brows pinching when he sees I haven't changed. I hold eye contact with him while I peel off my brother's jersey, dropping it to the floor.

His lips part. He pushes out an uneven breath, gaze dragging over me while I stand before him in my bra and jeans. The bra isn't anything special, a simple gray racerback that does the job to support my breasts without killing my back.

Still, he can't look away.

His throat bobs. "Damn."

A small puff of laughter falls from my lips at his reaction. This is even better than his face when I showed up in the wrong jersey again.

He watches raptly, eyes burning as I pull on his green Heston University t-shirt. It nearly drowns me, hitting me mid-thigh.

It's like being enveloped by him, wrapping me in his scent as if his strong arms are locked around me.

"Better?" I prompt.

My cheeks flush at my throaty tone. I'm trying—failing—to act cool. It's impossible. Easton's unwavering attention has a stronger effect on me than I anticipated when I invited him to turn around.

"You wearing my shirt? Hell yes, baby," he rasps.

Heat thrums in my core. We stare at each other. Time ceases to exist. There's only the hot ache radiating throughout my body the longer he gazes at me like I'm the only one in the world that he wants.

Everything in me begs for him to—

He takes a step in my direction, then another, moving closer like he's pulled by an invisible tether drawing him in. Each step causes a fresh surge of sparks in my core. His attention drops to my mouth. My heart races and air rushes from my lungs in a dizzying exhale picturing what's coming.

A knock at the door makes both of us jolt.

Noah opens it and pokes his head in. Easton whirls around, partially blocking me from sight.

"Come back to the party. They're here." He makes no apologies for interrupting us. Instead, he smirks at my change of clothes and Easton's lack of a shirt. "You look good like that, Maya."

"I'll be right down." Easton sighs.

He crosses to the door and shoves his snickering friend into the hall. The moment we had is over. We should go join the party.

I twist my fingers together, surprised at the disappointment rising within me.

Easton closes the door once Noah is gone. Then he catches me off guard by striding over, quickly eating up the distance between us. My stomach drops. He almost knocks me over when he reaches me, cradling my face in his hands.

The excitement that subsided races through me once more.

His eyes bounce between mine. I lick my lips. He exhales in relief before his mouth descends on mine, capturing my lips in a kiss.

A tiny cry catches in my throat. He makes a sexy, rough noise in response, sliding one hand to cup my nape.

My hands are trapped between us. I curl my fingers against his chest. The kiss sweeps me away with every slide of his tongue, every ragged sound he utters against my lips.

His grasp on me tightens, as if he still can't get enough of me while he's devouring my mouth. All I can do is hold on and kiss him back.

"If you don't come down, I'm sending in reinforcements!"

Noah's shout from the top of the steps filters through my awareness.

We break apart, both of us short of breath like two teenagers who just learned how to make out. My lips tingle and a soft laugh leaves me when Easton rests his forehead against mine. He brushes hair out of my face with a crooked finger, skimming his knuckles across my cheek.

He kissed me like a man possessed, as if he wanted to erase any man who ever touched my lips before him. Yet now, he's gentle. My drumming heart swells, making my breath hitch.

I swallow. "It's going to be so obvious what we were doing up here."

The corner of his mouth lifts in a crooked grin. He traces my lower lip with his thumb. The touch makes me press my thighs together at the rush of tingles spreading through me.

"I'll distract them. Come down whenever you're ready."

Easton kisses the top of my head, lingering for another moment before he rummages through his drawers for a new shirt. He pulls it on as he heads downstairs first.

Tucking my hair behind my ears, I go into his bathroom to study my reflection. My lips are swollen and tinted a darker pink than the lip balm I put on. A flush fills my cheeks, and my eyes are bright.

Easton's shirt is baggy on me. It makes me look like a girlfriend wearing her boyfriend's shirt.

And I don't hate it.

I slide my lips together. I haven't been someone's girlfriend in a long time. The few other guys I've been with after Johnny were all safe options, but never anything serious enough to progress to a relationship.

The girl in the mirror looks so much more sure of herself compared to the one who got her heart broken by her manipulative cheating ex.

I lift my chin, a smile playing at the corners of my mouth.

Once I fix my hair, roll the sleeves of Easton's shirt, and tuck part of the front hem into the waistband of my jeans so it looks more put together, I join the party.

It's crowded when I make my way through the front hall, passing people in the kitchen circled around the island to get to the living room where most people seem to congregate. Some of the players I recognize from the team's goat yoga session are playing video games while other people watch the beer pong match set up at a table in the corner.

"Oh my god, hi!" Someone rushes me from the side in a blur of dark blonde hair.

"Lainey!" I laugh in delight, giving her a hug. "Hi. I didn't know you'd be here. It's been way too long without you around the psych department. Are you in town visiting your dad? How's grad school?"

"Just for a little. We got lucky there was a break in the schedule for Thanksgiving next week." She leans in to whisper. "Don't tell Alex or my dad, but I'm mostly excited I get to spend some time with Hammy."

Lainey Boucher was one of the first friends I made in Heston Lake after Reagan freshman year. She's a brilliant psychology major and helped me manage my packed course schedules with advice on graduating early.

When we first met, she was shy and practical without many friends, but she fell for her brother Theo's best friend—and teammate. Then she came out of her shell.

He comes up behind her with eyes only for his fiancé.

"Whoa," I tease. "Alex Keller."

"What? You've hung out with me before," he says.

His handsome smile is easygoing as he slides an arm around Lainey to pull her into his side for a kiss on top of the head. It's not hard to see why she fell for him when she gives a happy sigh, resting her hand rocking the stunning engagement ring against his chest.

"Yeah, but that was before. Now I'm hanging out with Alex Keller, the Islander's breakout star and rookie of the year." My eyes go dramatically wide as I put on a fangirl voice. "Like, oh my god, can I get your autograph and a selfie?"

He shrugs with a chuckle. "Wild how things change, right?" He lifts a brow. "Like you at a party here."

I open my mouth, but I'm lost for words.

Lainey tried to get me to come with her and her friends to the countless hockey house parties freshman year, but I was adamant about staying away from hockey players. I only tolerated Alex's presence when we went for coffee or studied at the library because he was chill and in love with Lainey.

A familiar deep laugh tugs at me, drawing my attention like a magnet snapping into place with its mate. I'm smiling before I realize, searching the room.

It freezes when I spot Easton in the corner by the beer pong table. He's talking with Elijah and a few other people. One of them is a girl standing closer than necessary to him.

The rush of jealousy nearly steals my breath, taking me by surprise. He's not doing anything to encourage it from what I can see. In fact, he moves away when he shifts his weight. Is this how he felt seeing other guys talking to me?

Okay, I need to chill out.

We had one kiss. I'm wearing his shirt, but I'm not his girlfriend.

I shouldn't be jealous over anything.

My lips press together when he laughs again, giving a carefree shrug.

"How's Ferguson's class? If I remember, you planned to take that this semester," Lainey says.

"Oh, uh." I run my fingers through my hair, trying to put it from my mind. "Yeah, it's good. She's tough, but you were right. Taking Yang and Nelson's classes in the spring set me up for what Ferguson likes to throw at us."

She beams. "That's great."

Despite my efforts, my gaze finds the corner of the room again. Something pulls taut in my chest.

Easton spots me. I thought he looked happy over there, but once he's staring at me across the room, his smile shifts from cocky to warm and affectionate. He immediately starts towards me, barely sparing the group a goodbye. Relief sweeps over me and there's an answering tug in my chest making me want to go to him.

Elijah moves in closer to the girl, and whatever he whispers in her ear makes her trail a finger over his chest flirtatiously.

When Easton reaches my side, he slips his hand into mine and squeezes.

I blink, willing the unwarranted sting to leave my eyes.

"Sorry I didn't see you come down," he says. "Elijah needed a wingman. Hey, Alex. What's up?"

They slap their hands together. "Enjoying the down time."

Easton's thumb traces random patterns across my knuckles. "It's good to see you guys. Lainey, I've got your favorite in the freezer. And the ranch dip."

She gasps. "You're the best. Alex grumbles whenever I get pizza rolls because the team's nutritionist is even stricter than yours."

Alex pats his stomach with a frown. "Look, those little lava pockets of cheese and sauce and bread are too fucking tempting to resist. If I try to eat one or two, it's like I black out and suddenly I'm twenty pizza rolls deep."

"I feel you, man. We have a house rule now that we only get them for special occasions. Want some?" Easton flashes each of them a secretive smirk, then directs it at me. "We used to have a secret kitchen party when Lainey came around."

"Like VIP? That's cute."

"Exactly."

I fight an amused smile, picturing the big, bulky hockey players on the team bending to make Lainey comfortable back when she was shy. Easton squeezes my hand again, not letting go as he leads us to the kitchen.

"Reeves," he says.

Cameron hops off the counter, understanding what Easton wants with one simple word. He taps Noah on the shoulder. Noah helps him herd the few people nursing beers and chatting through the house to light the fire pit.

Before Noah returns, I hear him call, "Madden! Get out here. Handle the fire."

It's just the six of us in the kitchen.

Cameron puts the frozen pizza rolls in the oven while Lainey mixes the ranch dip. Once the tray is in, he braces his forearms against the island counter, lips twitching.

"Weren't you wearing a different shirt?" His eyes flick to me and he chuckles. "*That* shirt?"

Easton rubs my back sedately before slipping his arm around my waist. He shrugs, an easygoing smirk tugging at his lips.

"Nah. That's all hers now." He leans in, his breath fanning across my neck. "I'm glad you came."

My stomach dips at his proximity, remembering every detail of our kiss.

"Me too," I whisper.

FOURTEEN
EASTON

A few days later, we have our last game before the short break in our schedule for Thanksgiving. I'm amped up for it because this season is shaping up to be our best yet.

We've always been good, but the team is playing better than ever with the chemistry the current roster has built.

Losing to Elmwood is a distant memory now that we're further into the season and crushing our standings on the road to playoffs. We've pushed hard in practice and in games, earning rare words of praise from Coach Lombard.

During warm-ups, I hit every puck Madden sends my way, sinking them into the net before our second match up with Princeton.

It gets the crowd going. People wave felt flags that say *Go Knights* while we run through drills.

A couple of girls call my name when I skate by. It used to be my fuel before a game. The effect it has on me isn't the same.

Not anymore. Not by a longshot.

There's only one girl I want to hear screaming my name right now.

I go through pregame stretches, then pass some loose pucks to Madden and Elijah while I warm up my legs by circling the rink.

On my next lap, I wave to my mom and younger brother on the

other side of the glass. My bag is packed for Thanksgiving weekend. We head out after the game.

"Easton! Do the thing!" Asher shouts, miming a crossover by tapping his foot excitedly.

Grinning, I oblige. Dad showed me this technique when I was around his age. It helped me perfect handling the puck while moving like I'm one with the ice. Asher is obsessed with backwards crossovers and has started asking me to teach him when I bring him to my local rink at home.

"You ready?"

He nods eagerly. I flash him a crooked smile and scoop up a puck, skating in a tight circle before pushing backwards, one leg crossing over the other a few times like I'm running on the ice to pick up speed. Changing directions, I race back to the boards, firing off a pass to one of my teammates zipping around me.

"Woo!" Asher claps and throws his fists above his head while Mom ruffles his hair.

The ref blows his whistle to end warm-ups. I circle up at the bench with my team after the announcer's opening.

"Graves," Coach Lombard barks. "Get out there."

Madden jolts before flinging himself over the boards to join me, Theo, Noah, and Brody on the first line in Hutchinson's place while he recovers from a sprain. We've played this formation in practice, but this is the first chance he's been given to join a game for the first puck drop.

"Like we practiced, boys." Coach hands off the iPad to Kincaid and folds his arms across his chest. "Work up those appetites for tomorrow."

"Yes, sir," I say.

The guys echo me and we skate off ready to take on Princeton.

First period passes without either team putting up points. I'm not worried. In fact, I'm feeling awesome, switching on and off the ice for a few minutes at a time as we work through our lines.

When it's my shift again, I trade off with Elijah. "Good work, rookie."

My skates glide across the ice and my concentration is sharp going into the second period.

Before Princeton's center can react, I win the face-off and avoid their defense by flicking the puck right to Theo.

No lie, I feel so great because I kissed Maya at the house party Saturday night. God, that kiss. It's a miracle I'm able to split my focus from the memory to play the game.

Every other second, I'm reliving the night in my head from the moment I thought she was about to strip in front of the guys to carrying her over my shoulder to my room.

To watching her take off her brother's jersey for me.

To seeing her in *my* shirt.

To the moment I claimed her mouth in that hot as hell kiss.

My grin is unstoppable. I pick up the pass Theo whips my way, closing in on the net. Keller used to be the only player fast enough to match our star right wing, but I've proved since freshman year I'm just as good on the forward line.

The goalie shifts, giving me an opening. He's expecting me to pass to Madden racing in on my other side. We don't call him Mad Man Graves for nothing. He's a skilled winger, yet it's his wild energy that commands the opposing team's attention on the ice.

Seizing the opportunity to use Madden as a decoy, I angle as if I'm preparing to pass to him, then flick the puck off with a wrist shot. It sails across the ice and skips into the air, passing into the net over the goalie's stick to light up the lamp.

Score, baby.

I hope a clip of that makes it to social media so Maya can see it since she's not here. She texted me early this morning when she left for her family's home in New Hampshire.

"Nice play." I high five Madden.

His stare remains trained on the net. A muscle in his jaw jumps. I recognize the hungry expression as the burning desire to be the one on the offensive line scoring the goals.

The beauty of hockey is that it's not like most other team sports. Everyone on the team has a job, but any of us can take over the tasks of all the positions to support each other for every play. Whatever it takes to get the puck to our teammates and into the other team's net. Madden's still learning that.

"Don't worry, man. Coach sees how hard you're working. He'll keep shifting you around the lines to find the sweet spot. This isn't your only shot."

Theo skates up on Madden's other side, clapping him on the back. "Good hustle, Graves." He snorts. "I think you scared the piss out of their goalie."

The comment gets a satisfied smirk from Madden as we return to the red line.

Princeton's forward wins the face-off, shouldering past me hard enough to make me struggle to keep my balance. I take off after the guy while he looks for his teammates. Noah checks one of their wingers against the boards once he has the puck and Brody moves in when the Princeton player tries to throw a punch that Noah dodges.

The refs miss it.

I clench my jaw and come at their center to steal possession back when he reaches the loose puck first. He's just out of my range when he takes a shot on the net, cursing when he misses.

Reeves edges out of the crease to get the puck and two of Princeton's guys go for him while he's not looking. One barrels into him from behind with a sloppy check and trips, taking Cam down to the ice with him.

Oh, fuck no.

There are plenty of unspoken rules in hockey. The most important of all is simple: *never* touch the goalie.

Even with all the padding he wears, the landing is awkward. He doesn't move for a beat, but it's a split second too long in my book.

All of us react in a flash, gloves flying off and fists grabbing jerseys to yank the Princeton player away from Cameron while our teammates yell from the bench. The center slams into my side, struggling with me.

Adrenaline pumps through my veins as we all scuffle, elbows getting in cheap shots on both sides. It takes everything in me not to smash my fist into the forward's face.

The refs blow whistles and work to break it up, one wrestling me away from Princeton's center with the beady eyes.

"It was a clean hit!" Beady Eyes keeps shouting.

"Bullshit," I spit.

"Enough," the ref barks. "Number fifty-two, penalty for charging. Two minutes in the penalty box."

The blare of the whistle directly in my ear is jarring. I grimace, skating off when the ref lets Noah pull me away. Coach's stare bores into the side of my head. I look his way, finding him standing at our bench with his arms crossed and a surly expression. He gives a single jerk of his head in silent approval.

We skate over to Reeves as Theo and Brody help him up.

"You good?" Noah asks.

"Yeah." Cameron gives me a fist bump. "Why the hell do you look like this is a funeral? Jesus, lighten up. I'm fine. Are we playing hockey, or what?"

My shoulders relax. "We've got your back."

"Thanks. Now get out of my zone. I like to chill back here while you do the work over there." He gestures to the opposing end of the rink.

Theo snorts. "Next one's for you."

"Aww, you shouldn't have, big guy." Cameron rests his elbows on the upper bar of the net with a chuckle.

Noah and Brody get back to defensive positions and the rest of us get to where we need to be for another face-off. I exchange glances with Theo and Madden, both of them nodding. We're all on the same page.

The second the puck hits the ice, it's all-out war and we dominate the other team in retaliation for fucking with our goalie.

We press the one-player advantage while fuckface fifty-two waits out the clock in the sin bin, scoring a goal to bring the game to 2-0.

The score remains the same through the third period until it ends. Princeton's players rip off their helmets, skating off our ice with defeat hanging over their heads. Our team follows them to go to our lockers. People lean over the tunnel waving things ready to be autographed.

Noah pauses to sign things and take photos as usual.

Victory is sweet. Even better when we thrashed them the rest of the game, playing with brutal precision to shut down any move they tried to make, out-skating them to keep the puck in our control.

We file into the locker room in high spirits, stripping sweaty pads and jerseys. Someone connects their phone to a bluetooth speaker and plays music while the rest of us grab showers.

"Good game, boys. That was a nice hustle out there," Coach says when he and Kincaid come in. "See you back here on Sunday for practice. If you eat too much pie, you're skating suicides until you can match tonight's speed."

Some of the guys groan. Coach Kincaid takes over the debriefing.

"Anyone not going home, the rink will be open tomorrow during normal hours, closed on Thursday, then Friday afternoon and Saturday it's back to the regular hours. Have a good weekend with your families."

"We know you will," Noah fires off with a smirk. "Man's got it made after he scored the coach's daughter."

"Alright," Kincaid says mildly when the guys whistle. "Get out of my locker room, assholes. Come back ready for the next game on the schedule. We're playing Bexley U."

"Happy Thanksgiving, Coach." I shoulder my gear bag.

"See you, East."

On my way out to meet up with Mom and Asher, Noah falls into step beside me. His younger brother waits for him outside the door to the locker rooms.

"Jonah," Noah says as he catches him around the shoulders before he can dodge him. "What's up, little dude?"

"Hate it when you call me that," Jonah grumbles.

They struggle, Jonah fighting off Noah as he goes to mess with his hair.

"How've you been? We haven't seen you up here for a game yet," I say.

Jonah is four years younger than Noah and attends a boarding school an hour away. Their parents live in California, where both of them spend their summers. The rest of the year, they go to their grandparents' place near Connecticut's coast.

He shrugs. "Not bad."

Noah wins the struggle, ruffling his brother's hair. "He's lying. He's been blowing my phone up every other day about this guy on his team pissing him off."

Jonah pulls a face. "It's whatever. I can't wait to graduate so I can get the hell away from him."

"Oh yeah? You coming to play for Heston?" I ask. "Bet Coach would love that."

"No, this little traitor wants to play for Elmwood." Noah scoffs and pokes Jonah's cheek.

"I like their coaching staff," Jonah mutters stiffly. "It's not personal, just strategy."

I grin, shaking my head. The two Porter brothers couldn't be more opposite in personality.

"I see my mom." I tap Noah's arm with the back of my hand. "See you when I get back."

"Later, dude."

I jog over to meet Mom and Asher waiting near the exit.

"Hey, sweetheart. Great game." I bend so Mom can hug me easier. She gives me a kiss on the cheek. "Ready to go home?"

"Yeah." I squeeze her in another half hug and high five my little brother. "Did you hear it's supposed to snow tomorrow? We can skate on the pond if it's cold enough."

"Or I could kick your ass on Mario Kart," he says.

"Asher," Mom chides with an amused huff. "What did I say about your language?"

He shrugs. "I'm nine."

"Almost nine," she corrects. "Still not allowed to talk like that."

He deflates with a whine.

When we lost Dad, he was just turning four. He's entering middle school next year, and at that point where kids waver between wanting to grow up too fast and remembering they're still just a kid.

I snort. "Dude, don't try her. You won't ever forget the taste of soap if you've got a dirty mouth."

"Your mouth is dirty," Asher mutters. "I've heard you."

I smirk, whispering to him. "The trick is not to get caught."

Mom gives me an exasperated look that melts into a loving smile as we make our way out of the arena.

It feels good to spend time with them. Most of my year is spent training and focusing on the season. If I'm going pro, I have to cherish this time.

FIFTEEN
EASTON

THE HOUSE SMELLS fantastic on Thursday afternoon. Mom loves to start prep early. By lunchtime, she's cooking.

"If you're only going to snack on goat cheese and olives without helping me, get out of my kitchen." She whips my hand with a dish towel to keep me from snagging another stuffed olive. "Go keep Asher occupied."

I grumble in protest, mouth too full of the appetizer cheese-cracker-summer sausage masterpiece sandwich I crammed in a moment ago. Bracing my hands on the island separating us, I chew furiously and gulp it down.

"Do you need help, though? Put me to work."

"I'll call you back in when I'm ready for you to carry all this food to the table."

"Okay."

I circle the island to kiss her head, then head for the living room where Asher's playing video games.

He doesn't take his eyes off the screen, rapidly tapping buttons on the controller. "You were eating all the cheese again, weren't you?"

"Maybe. Open. I snagged you a piece of pepperoni."

He gasps, eyes wide. It's comical to watch him open his mouth while watching what he's doing in the game. I feed it to him and check my phone.

There are a few new messages in the group chat with the guys. A bunch are of the fresh snow that dumped across the northeast and some are photos of the spread on their tables. I press a fist to my mouth at Cameron's and reply.

Easton
Good god, Reeves. That looks good. Is that fried chicken, too? What the hell.

Cameron
Dad's going through another cooking phase and I'm living the life. Bringing the stuffed peppers recipe back with me. You're all about to crown me king of the kitchen.

McKinley
Think I just came looking at that.

Theo
Dude, I'm fucking eating.

I snort. As much as I look forward to my future career, I love this team. These guys are the best brothers in the world.

Another photo comes through not long after, this time from Coach Kincaid. He's got Eve, the head coach's daughter, tucked against his side and they're both grinning while Bauer tries to jump on them to be part of the action.

I sit up once it registers what's going on in the photo. He proposed. They snuck around during my freshman year. I had to keep it quiet that I knew anything about their secret relationship when I accidentally caught them making out at the rink.

Easton
Holy shit, Kincaid. Congrats.

Noah
Yooooo! 🎉

Easton
Locking it down with Coach Lombard's daughter.

Elijah
Nice.

Madden
Congrats.

Cameron
The man, the myth, the legend.

Noah
Did you use my suggestion?

Kincaid
No. Only sent this so you'll stop sending me every viral proposal idea you see.

Easton
Don't lie. You love us.

Kincaid
And I question why often.

Cameron
Fuck off, bro. Go enjoy the good news with your family.

Kincaid
Oh shit.

Easton
What?

Kincaid
I'm marrying Eve. That makes David my father in law.

I hammer the laughing emoji and send a line of them, swiping amused tears from the corner of my eyes.

Asher pauses his game. "Can we play Mario Kart?"

"Yeah."

I stretch out on the couch and he sits on a pillow in front of it on the floor. We play three races and I win all but the last one, allowing him to beat me.

"I want to go back to playing the other one now," Asher says.

"So you can win?" I prod him with my foot until he laughs.

"I like winning."

"Me too, bud. Here."

He takes my controller and switches to the first game he was playing. I end up scrolling social media until I see a random video about a goat that makes me think of Maya. Sitting up, I bring up her last text. She hasn't said anything to me since yesterday when I sent her a photo of me and Asher skating on the frozen pond behind our house.

I don't want a text. I want to hear her voice. No, I want to *see* her.

Hitting the FaceTime button, I wait to see if she'll pick up, rubbing my chin absently.

The call connects and Maya fills my screen. Everything I mean to say flies out of my head at the sight of her. Those gorgeous hazel eyes stare back at me and her lips part. Her hair is twisted half up in a clip that makes me want to run my fingers into the part that's left down. The sleeves of her sherpa jacket are pushed up to her elbows.

And she's wearing my Heston University shirt that I gave her to wear at the party beneath it.

"Hey." She peeks shyly at her parents in the background and leaves the kitchen to talk to me. "Happy Thanksgiving."

"Yeah. You too." I swallow, rubbing at my chest. "Did you eat yet?"

"Not yet. It'll probably be another couple of hours before we sit down for dinner. We always work around my grandfather's medication schedule so he doesn't get thrown off his routine."

"Nice. We haven't either. Mom makes a huge feast, but between Asher starting his human garbage disposal appetite phase and me, we eat the leftovers by Saturday."

"Yeah, they don't last long here with Ryan in the house. And my dad's a midnight snacker."

The edge of my mouth lifts. I'm enjoying getting to see this side of her. It feels like she's letting me in. The fiery girl I split donuts with a month ago never would have told me any of this.

She hasn't stopped moving since she answered the call, strolling from room to room. I catch a big family photo taken at sunset on a farm hung on the wall before she goes into a den to grab a piece of cheese.

The football game is muted on the flatscreen mounted above the mantel and her brother is visible in the background sprawled on the couch.

"Hold on, I have to put you down for a second. I need both hands."

She spends a moment propping me against something so I have a front row seat to her making a cheese and cracker sandwich similar to my own masterpiece earlier. A stupid smile stretches across my face and I do nothing to hold it back.

"Looks tasty."

She smirks. "It's cheese, of course it's delicious."

While she pops it in her mouth, she picks the phone up, humming contentedly as she chews. Her brother appears at the edge of the screen when he stands.

"Is that Blake?" Donnelly leans over her shoulder, squinting at the camera. "What the hell? Why are you calling my sister?"

I blow a kiss. "Just to tell her I miss you."

He grabs at her phone with an annoyed grunt. She laughs, elbowing him to evade him.

"Stop. Go away."

"I'm stealing your phone later to delete his number from your contacts," he says.

"I'd still have her number," I point out cheerfully.

Donnelly's brows flatten. "Blake, if you do anything to fuck with her, I'll—"

Maya scoffs. "Okay, that's enough of that, Ryan."

She moves away to a different room. It feels damn good seeing her wearing my shirt while Donnelly's jersey is still on the floor in my bedroom in Heston Lake, kicked into a corner.

"Nice shirt." I waggle my brows.

Her eyes widen and she pinches the sides of the jacket in an attempt to hide what's underneath. "What—? No, this is—I didn't know this made it into my bag."

"Yeah?"

Her tongue darts out to swipe across her lip. "I'll give it back when I see you around campus."

"Keep it. Looks way better on you."

"I've been helping my parents get everything ready for dinner since I rolled out of bed this morning. I haven't had time to get dressed." Her cheeks turn pink. "I need to go change."

"You slept in my shirt?"

Maya's mouth pops open, the realization of what she implied dawning on her face.

"Yes." She lifts her chin. "I like a big shirt to sleep in."

Immediately, I'm picturing her sleepy and languid in my bed, wearing nothing but that shirt skimming her bare thighs. Fuck, that's a nice thought.

"Mm, don't tell me now, baby. Otherwise, I won't be able to go anywhere."

"Why?"

"I'm about to be stuck on the couch with the nearest pillow or blanket covering my lap because I'm imagining it." My eyes hood at the way she reacts, her lashes fluttering and lips parting. "Now you're definitely keeping it. You've claimed it, so it's all yours."

"Easton," she blurts.

I like it when she gets flustered. It's cute.

We're interrupted by an older man she passes while she paces her house to talk to me. I recognize him from photos on her Instagram. He's in an armchair with a walker next to it.

"There's my chicken. What are you doing?"

There's no question how much she loves him. She lights up at the nickname. He holds out an arm for her, smiling when she perches on the arm to hug him.

A pang echoes in my chest as I recall how she broke down crying in my arms because her grandfather is so important to her. I get it, I honestly do. Loss is a shock to the system and rocks the foundation of your entire world whether you're able to prepare for it or not.

"Talking on FaceTime with a friend from school. This is Easton." She angles the phone so he can see me better. "He plays hockey, too. Like Ryan. Easton, this is my grandpa."

"Hi, sir. Nice to meet you," I say.

He hums, studying me.

"Are you seeing my Maya?"

She jolts. We answer at the same time.

"Yes."

"No, Grandpa." When my answer registers, her eyes widen. "We're friends."

His gaze flicks between us. Although he has liver spots on his wrinkled skin and his eyes are milky with age, he sees right through it.

"You treat my girl right, you hear?"

I sit up straighter, fixing my hair so it lays flatter, but it's hopeless. "Of course, sir."

"Good." He pats her leg. "She deserves the world. Take her horseback riding, she's always liked that. Loves animals. And so good with them, too. You remember when you would get dropped off to visit me, chicken? You'd take my hand and wanted to see all the livestock."

I nod, attention drifting to her bright red face. "She deserves everything. I won't give her anything less."

"You keep her happy." He tips his head down to level me with a serious expression. "Otherwise, I've got a whole collection of hunting rifles on the farm."

A surprised laugh punches out of me.

"Grandpa," Maya protests. "Don't say that."

"Don't worry. I'll always treat her right," I promise.

"Boys," Mom calls from the other room. "Come help me. Dinner's almost ready."

"I've got to go," I tell Maya reluctantly. "Text me?"

"Sure." She gets up and tucks her hair behind her ear. "Bye."

"See you soon," I say.

She flashes a wry smile. "Okay, *bye*."

The call ends. I sigh, running my fingers through my hair until my heart stops beating so hard.

"What's that look on your face?" Asher asks.

"What look?"

He lifts a shoulder. "I dunno. Like happy, but weird."

I swipe a hand over my mouth to hide my stupid smile. "I'm extra happy because we're about to eat. Let's go."

We help Mom bring dishes to the table. She makes up a plate for

Dad. It's a tradition we keep at every holiday. I tense when she sets it next to her instead of where it should go.

She pulls out the seat at the head of the table. "Here, sweetheart."

My chest constricts, making it difficult to breathe for a beat. I shake my head, straining to get the words out.

"No. That's Dad's spot."

This started last year. I refuse to sit there every time she asks. The first time she pulled the chair out for me, a surge of grief welled up out of nowhere because I miss him.

It doesn't feel right to sit where he always did.

She gives me a sad smile. "Okay. Wherever you want to sit is fine."

"Smells so good." Asher's nose is almost in his potatoes. "Happy freaking Thanksgiving."

I tousle his hair and sit down next to him. "You think you're being sly with that."

Mom reaches across the table for both our hands. We each clasp hers. "I love you, boys. I'm so glad we have another beautiful day together."

"Love you too, Mom." I squeeze her hand.

She squeezes mine back. "Let's dig in. And for dessert, we have four kinds of pie."

Asher echoes me, but he doesn't get why we make it a point to say I love you. When Dad went out five years ago to get us ice cream during a snowstorm, he lost his life in a pile up on the highway. Losing him so suddenly, I learned how important it is to say goodbye since I never got the chance to say it to him.

He was gone and I live with that.

Every second counts.

Every moment could be the last.

SIXTEEN
MAYA

It's two hours after dark by the time I make it back to campus on Sunday. Ryan parks in the lot behind the dorms.

"Need me to carry your stuff?"

I can tell he's not that eager to since he still has an hour and forty minute drive between here and Elmwood.

"No, I didn't pack much. It's light." I hop out and grab my bag from the back seat. Before he leaves, I lean in the window he rolled down. "Thanks for the ride. Drive safe."

"Yeah. See you later."

"Text Mom and Dad when you get to school."

He waves in acknowledgement and shifts into gear. I back up, watching him pull out before I head for my apartment. It's just me tonight. Reagan won't be back until tomorrow morning.

Easton texted me during the drive back until he went to practice. I let him know I made it.

Maya
Just got to campus. How'd your practice go?

Hat Trick King 🏒
Hi 🩶

Hat Trick King 🏒
Good, it just ended. Wyd? I need a quick shower but we could hang out if you want to go get coffee.

I grin. Coffee sounds good, but seeing him sounds even better. I let him know I'm almost at my apartment.

Once I'm in the door, I drop my bag and turn on the hall light. Maybe I could see if Easton wants to come over after coffee to watch a movie. My lips twitch because there's almost zero likelihood we'd be able to pay attention to it before our hands would be all over each other.

After that amazing kiss at last weekend's party, he walked me home and gave me another sweet kiss before he left rather than pushing me for more. A bright glow fills my chest at the thought, then turns hotter as heat pools low in my stomach. I wasn't ready for more then, but I missed him while we were gone for break.

I want to see him. I want to kiss him.

Biting my lip around a smile, I start to text him that he should forget coffee and just come over.

I freeze when I swear I hear something in the dark beyond the hall. "Reagan?"

Did she decide to come back early without telling me? I want to believe it's her, but even on my way to her room something feels...off. My stomach clenches and the hair on my arms stands on end as I flick on the light in her room, finding it empty. Heart beating hard, I strain my ears, wondering if I was hearing things.

A muted thump reaches my ears. My heart plummets and ice spreads through me.

I think that came from my room.

The vibration of my phone ringing feels too loud. It slices through the tense silence, startling me.

Shit, shit. I answer it without looking, keeping my voice low. "Hello?"

"You went quiet on me. Where'd you go?" Easton teases.

"Um," I breathe while trying to peer from Reagan's room to mine to see what's going on.

His demeanor shifts immediately, becoming concerned. "What's wrong? Why are you whispering? I'm five minutes away. Are you at your place?"

I close my eyes as his protectiveness washes over me. "Yes."

"I'm coming."

I don't bother telling him I don't need him because I don't want to be stubborn and brave right now. Gulping, I search Reagan's room for some kind of weapon, cursing the fact my metal kitty ears are in my room.

Easton stays on the line with me. I hear his terse breathing as he jogs across campus to reach me.

Reagan has a microphone stand in the corner. I grab it, prepared to defend myself if the intruder comes at me.

The front door slams shut. A freaked out yelp flies from my lips and I whirl around. My heartbeat races faster.

What the fuck?

When I gather the courage to peek out from Reagan's room a few minutes later, Easton yells over the phone. The sound of tires screeching snags my focus.

"Jesus," he snaps.

"What happened?"

"Some asshole in an ugly ass blue Jeep pickup truck with a douchey sticker that says 'ask me how long my other stick is' almost ran me down in the lot by your building."

My chest constricts. I know that truck all too well. I know who was in my apartment.

Johnny.

Some of the trepidation leaves me, replaced by the burn of anger. Sighing, I put down the microphone stand.

I don't think Johnny would hurt me. Not physically, anyway. He likes mental games. Manipulating people's emotions to control them. But he's always loved pranking people in awful ways, and this falls right in line with his brand of fucked up humor.

Stalking to the front door, I check the fake potted plant that hangs from our message board. My spare key is inside. I know it's how he got in. He used to give me shit about forgetting my key in high school and watched me get the spare from its hiding spot countless times.

"Asshole," I growl.

I'm sorely tempted to call Ryan and tell him what his friend is up to. I never should've kept the truth about Johnny cheating on me to myself thanks to him gaslighting me into believing my brother wouldn't care. Except the thought of hashing that out with him right now causes the beginning of a headache to form.

"You're not whispering anymore," Easton says.

I bite my lip, debating if I should tell him. Before I decide what to say, he appears through the door to the stairs at the end of the hall. Even knowing I wasn't truly in danger, intense relief washes over me at the sight of him.

"Hi."

He strides down the hall to erase the distance between us. His hockey bag and stick thuds on the floor as he wraps me in a tight hug that I really need. I melt into it.

"Hi," he says against my hair. "Missed you. Are you okay?"

"I am now."

We stay like that until I pull back. He cups my cheek, thumb brushing back and forth softly.

He follows me inside, leaving his duffel bag next to mine by the door. "Do you want to tell me what happened?"

My teeth rake across my lip. "I thought someone broke in."

"What?" He takes me by the hips and pins me to the counter in the kitchenette, eyes searching my face. "What the hell happened?"

Before I answer, he combs through the entire apartment to check if it's safe. I stay in the kitchen area, trying not to be distracted by the hard set of his jaw or the way he moves through each room with a powerful sense of strength that I'm drawn to. Is it weird I sort of want him to bend me over the nearest surface and unleash that wildness on me?

"It wasn't what you're thinking. He's not here anymore. You know that Jeep Gladiator that almost ran you down? That was him."

"How do you know?"

Easton braces his hands on the opposite side of the small island when he finds the apartment empty. I sigh.

"It's my ex's truck. Johnny Werner, my brother's teammate."

His jaw clenches, a muscle twitching in his cheek. "Fucking *Wiener*? I knew I should've broken his other arm."

I blink. "What?"

"Nothing. You dated that asswipe?"

"In high school. For two years, until—" I cut off, not wanting to get into the whole mess. "I'd bet anything he's probably just messing with me because I finally blocked his number like I should've done years ago."

While I'm unblocking it with agitated movements to tell him off, Easton rumbles in frustration.

"Are you calling campus security? Report him for breaking in."

"No. And technically he didn't." Grimacing, I motion towards the door. "I keep a spare key in the flower pot that hangs from our message board."

"Maya." He blows out a breath, sinking his fingers into his hair. "Then you should tell them you lost your keys so they'll change your locks. Keep the spare key with you."

"I'll do it in the morning," I promise. "But I don't think he'll come back."

Easton scrubs his jaw, pacing the short length of the island. "There's no way to know that. Only psychos think it's funny to scare people with shit like this."

He's not wrong. Johnny was good at making me think I wanted what he did. I refuse to let him get to me now because he's already done enough damage. I hate giving him any power over me. There's no way I'll let his bullshit scare me.

I text Johnny, fingers stabbing the screen in irritation. It doesn't take him long to respond, as if he's been waiting for me to put the pieces together.

Maya
You're not funny. I know it was you. If you ever do that again, I'm reporting you to the cops.

Johnny
You should chill. I was just having a little fun since you blocked me. It was a joke, babe.

Maya
I'm not laughing.

Johnny
Relax. I was just checking in on my teammate's little sister. My orthopedic specialist is nearby and I wanted to see you again since you ran off from the bar with another man. Remember when I used to surprise you like this and be waiting in your bedroom? You loved it.

A sickening lurch unsettles my gut at the memories he's talking about. My skin crawls at the way he still talks to me like he believes I'll always belong to him.

Easton is at my back, reading over my shoulder. My cheeks prickle with uncomfortable heat. My phone rings and I feel the rough sound of anger in his chest when he sees the name on the screen. He takes the phone and answers it for me.

"You're lucky you got away. If you come back here, you're a dead man."

I shiver. His arm wraps around my shoulders and he presses a kiss to the top of my head. I turn in his embrace, watching his fierce expression.

"Who is this?" Johnny asks sharply. "Where's Maya?"

Easton stares at me. "She's busy. Lose this fucking number."

He hangs up. My phone clatters on the counter behind me when he sets it down. He swoops down to kiss me, palm splaying at the small of my back. He chases away every bad memory of Johnny, erasing every ounce of fear and frustration that coursed through me tonight. All that remains is him, and I can't get enough.

"What do you need?" His breath is hot ghosting across my lips.

"Just this." I suppress a shudder. "Just you."

With a ragged noise, he captures my lips again. I open for him, allowing his kiss to consume me. His hand drags down my side and I gasp when he grabs my thighs to lift me on the counter. I spread my legs and he moves between them.

My breath hitches when he grabs my ass in a firm grip, tugging me against his body. We're wild, touches growing desperate.

"Maya," he pushes out roughly.

I cry out as he kisses my neck, clinging to his shoulders. His fingers push down the waistband of the HU sweatpants I wore to be comfortable on the drive. The moment his fingertips brush over my clit through my panties, I arch my back.

"Please."

"Fuck, you're wet. How are you so wet, baby?" His lips drag over my feverish skin as he traces teasing circles over my panties, making me more and more needy to have nothing between us. "You want to come?"

I gasp. "Yes."

He captures my lips again, matching his movements to his tongue sweeping into my mouth. I tremble, stomach concaving in pleasure when he slides my panties aside and finds my clit. My hips move instinctively with his touch. He doesn't tease me anymore, giving me what I want.

My nipples tighten and tingles spread across my body as he brings me closer to the brink.

I choke back a cry as my orgasm hits, thighs clamping against him. I break away from the kiss, a moan tearing from me as my pussy throbs, the pleasure spiraling through my core.

"That's it, baby. Ride that wave." He brushes light kisses along my jaw. "You're such a good girl, coming for me."

Still floating, I reach for the rigid bulge in his pants as I kiss him deeply.

Easton's the one to slow us down from going any further. A band tightens around my heart. A noise of protest escapes me when he pulls back. He hushes me, stealing another quick kiss that we nearly get lost in again.

"God, I want you so fucking bad, Maya," he rasps.

"Yeah? So have me." I squeeze my legs tighter around his waist to keep him in place. "Right here. Come on. Reagan's gone for the night."

"I—" He rests his forehead against mine with a rueful laugh. "I can't believe I'm doing this. But I think I'm afraid you'd regret it if we did anything else right now."

I wilt against him, unable to help circling my hips against his firm torso, wanting to feel his hardness against my center. He groans, massaging my waist.

"Fuck. You make me crazy. Promise me this?" He takes my chin between his thumb and finger, eyes darkened with desire when they bounce between mine. "If you still want this in the morning, you're mine. I don't want to rush you. You're not some dare to win, Maya. You're the whole damn package for me."

The exhale I let out is shaky, but it helps clear my head. I nod, swallowing past the lump forming in my throat.

"Okay."

His mouth quirks up at the corners. "Deal?"

"Deal."

Tingles race through my body, converging with a hot pulse in my core when he helps me down from the counter.

"Are you sure you're alright?" His brow wrinkles as he studies me.

It should probably tell me something that his reaction to my ex breaking into my apartment is far more worried than my own warped perception.

A bitter, humorless laugh leaves me before I clench my teeth fiercely. "Johnny Werner doesn't get to dictate any of my emotions. He's a pathetic narcissist and that's the only reason he joined a hockey team. Fuck that guy."

He nods, watching me closely as he echoes, "Fuck that guy."

Easton hangs around until I insist I'm okay. We end up watching a movie with far less making out than I fantasized when I was thinking about it earlier. He pulls my legs across his lap, resting a hand on my knee. More than my annoyance at my ex, I feel safe because he promised to always be there when I need him.

When I'm struggling to keep my eyes open near the end, he chuckles. "Come on."

I allow him to pull me to my feet, stretching languidly with a huge yawn. "Are you staying?"

"I won't leave. You rest easy, baby. I've got you."

I might be tired, but the resolute promise he rasps makes me sway. He catches me in his embrace, then walks me to my room.

"Goodnight, Maya."

"Night." I linger by the door, tracing a thick lump of paint.

He smiles. "I'm not going anywhere."

An answering smile breaks free.

For so long, I believed all hockey players were heartless playboys who weren't capable of giving a damn about anyone but themselves.

Easton Blake proves me wrong at every turn. When I'm with him, it's not just that he makes me feel safe. He makes me want to trust him. To give him the pieces of myself I've kept locked away tight.

SEVENTEEN
EASTON

By morning, I haven't moved from guarding Maya's door. My stick lays across my lap, ready for Wiener to come back. I wish he wasn't still on the injured list this season. If he was on the ice, I'd put his ass right back on it.

My fists close around my stick, wishing it was his fucking neck. In my mind, I'm checking his ass so hard all his teeth get knocked out.

Cameron texts me to remind me about practice this afternoon since I didn't come back last night. I let him know I'll be there. The door opens behind me when I'm sliding my phone back in my pocket, making me catch my balance so I don't fall when Maya leans into the hall.

She's wearing dark gray leggings and my faded green Heston University t-shirt.

"You're still here." Her words are teasing, back to her usual self. There's a hint of warmth beneath them. "When I didn't find you on the couch, I thought you left last night after I went to bed."

I tip my head back to grin at her. "You're sharp. I told you I wouldn't leave. I sat out here all night ready to handle any trouble."

"You don't have to babysit me." She leans against the door frame with a sigh, offering the steaming mug of coffee she has. "I doubt he's coming back to do anything again. He's not a follow through kind of guy. He gets bored and moves onto the next thing pretty quickly.

Anyway, I'm sure that you answering the phone like that was enough to make him back off."

I frown, not liking her implication that she was something Wiener got bored of. That guy's a fucking idiot.

"I still think you should report this to campus security at least. There are cameras all over, so there should be a feed from the parking lot they can check for proof he was here when he almost ran me over."

"Okay, I will. Right now I'd rather forget about him."

"Does your brother know? I'd never stand for any of my teammates pulling shit like this if I had a sister."

She gives a sharp laugh, waving me off. "I'm not dealing with Ryan this early. It's fine, okay?"

Setting aside the coffee, my fingers grip my stick tightly. "For real, though. If he bothers you again, tell me." I blow out a breath, shooting her a lopsided smirk. "At least now everyone on your floor knows not to mess with you. I think I scared the shit out of your neighbor two doors down when he came back last night and saw me out here with this."

She lifts her brows. "You could've been asleep in my bed. All warm and comfortable."

"If I did that, I don't know if I could've kept our promise. You're too tempting."

I rake my gaze over her, heat rushing south as my need for her reignites. Her blush is gorgeous.

"Thank you," she murmurs.

"For what?"

"Everything. Coming here without question. Watching out for me."

"Watching out for everyone is a captain's job."

She smirks. "I'm not one of your teammates, but I appreciate it."

I pull her down, guiding her to sit on my lap, careful not to spill the coffee. She rests her head on my shoulder. Something warm tugs in my chest as I rub her back, enjoying the small, content sound that escapes her.

"No, you're my girl. I'll protect you from anything."

"It's morning now," she murmurs after a beat.

"Yeah?" My fingers sneak beneath the hem of the shirt she slept in, seeking skin.

Before I capture her lips for a kiss, we're interrupted by Reagan's arrival. She peers between us with an amused hum, eyeing my hockey stick with a raised brow.

"What's going on here?"

Maya catches my eye to give me a pleading look. I think Reagan should know about what happened last night, but for now I'll keep it quiet if that's what she wants.

"Just having coffee." I pick up the mug, smirking as I take a sip.

"Uh huh," she says doubtfully. "Well, watch out. I've got class soon and I haven't had breakfast yet."

"Here." I help Maya up, then take Reagan's bag and follow the girls inside. "I'm making breakfast. What do you have?"

"Sorry, you're going to cook for us?" Reagan leans against the island with a broad grin. "That changes everything. You can stay forever."

I smirk while Maya rummages through the cabinets, pushing up the sleeves of my warm up jacket. She falters, attention lingering on my forearms. I flex my hands while I wash them, chuckling when her lids grow heavy as the corded muscles in my arms tense.

"We haven't gone grocery shopping yet since we were both gone for break," Reagan says.

"Our options are cereal, instant oatmeal, and I think we have some eggs," Maya lists off.

"I make damn good omelets. Do you want cheese?"

"When don't I want cheese?" She sets out the egg carton. "You're lucky I get free eggs from Marnie."

"No cheese on mine." Reagan starts an electric kettle and gets out a comically large mug.

Maya sets me up with a bowl and a pan. We move around each other in the tiny kitchen.

While Reagan isn't looking, I sneak over to Maya to kiss her neck. She smothers a gasp, catching my hands when I hold her waist. My tongue swipes across her skin.

We break apart before her roommate catches us, and I enjoy the shy way she ducks her head while peeling oranges to go with breakfast.

"This kitchen isn't big enough for two people," she says.

I take her hips from behind to shift her to the side, murmuring in her ear. "You could have breakfast at my place instead. The kitchen is way bigger."

My old no sleepovers rule flies out the window when it comes to the idea of Maya in my bed.

It hits me how much I'd want that. Waking up with her soft warm body tangled with mine. Taking care of her.

"Go sit over there, I said I'm cooking for you." I give her hips a squeeze, reluctant to let go.

She retreats to the other side of the small island, ears pink. Reagan nudges her, wriggling her brows while sipping her tea. The pan crackles on the stove when I pour the first omelet on it.

Keeping the smug grin off my face is impossible when my girl keeps sneaking those cute little glances at me while I cook for her and her friend.

"This is nice, you serving me for a change," Reagan jokes.

I laugh. "You work hard to keep all of Heston Lake happily watered when you bartend."

She turns to Maya. "How was your break?"

"Good." Maya smiles softly, propping her cheek against her fist. "Grandpa's up on his feet again after the hospital scare."

Reagan hugs her. "I'm so glad to hear that."

"What about yours?" Maya asks.

"Can't complain. I wrote a new song. It's rough, but I'll show you later."

I finish the first two omelets and give them to the girls. Maya's expression when she takes a bite sends a wave of satisfaction through me.

While I'm cooking my eggs, Reagan points her fork at me. "Maya, you need to keep him. He understands that girls need to eat. Stop bringing home emo bassists who don't get that cigarettes aren't a food group."

Maya covers her face. "Oh my god. Can you not tell him the story about Luke?"

"Who's this?" I move the pan to the back of the stove to cool, switch off the burner, and take my plate to stand next to Maya on her other side.

"The last guy she was seeing at the beginning of spring semester. Total emo boy with the tortured soul thing going on. He was hot," Reagan says.

"He was hot," Maya echoes.

"But the dude didn't believe that girls needed to eat." Reagan rolls her eyes. "Took her out to a small show he was playing, but while his band ate pizza backstage, he didn't bring any out for her or offer her anything."

Maya groans in annoyance. "God, I was fucking starving. I left before his set to eat since the venue didn't serve food. Thankfully there was an all-you-can eat wings buffet on the corner." She laughs. "When he found me eating my weight in teriyaki wings, he looked so shocked and said *that's not a salad*."

She breaks down in giggles, leaning heavily on me.

"He sounds like a complete idiot," I say. "Do all your ex-boyfriends suck?"

"To be fair, they never made it to the boyfriend-girlfriend stage," Reagan says.

"To be fair, I only wanted to sleep with him, not marry him," Maya counters in exasperation. "It wasn't serious or deep."

"You can forget about other guys. I'll take good care of you." I drop my voice, my words only for her. "In every way you need, baby."

She bites her lip, her shoulder brushing mine.

"Oh, shoot. I need to leave, like, five minutes ago." Reagan puts her dishes in the sink and hurries to her room.

Once she's gone, I trap Maya between my arms for a kiss. She melts against me, mouth opening with a needy sound that goes right to my cock.

"She won't be long," she mumbles against my mouth. "When she's late, she gets ready in about five seconds."

"Let me make them count, then. One, two..."

A soft sigh escapes her. She tips her head to grant me better access. I pull her hair out of my way, trailing my lips over her skin.

"Three, four..." I count with each grazing kiss.

She shudders, slipping her arms around my waist. "Easton."

My counting makes it to a little over two minutes before I hear a door open.

"Okay," Reagan announces pointedly before she emerges from her room.

Maya gasps, pushing me away. I grab a towel to wipe the counter with, gaze burning into her back.

"Thanks for breakfast. I've got class and a reserved production studio calling my name. Have fun, bye," Reagan finishes in a rush, grabbing her bag on her way out.

I stop pretending to wipe down the counter. "Later."

After the front door closes, Maya gives me a look I have no trouble interpreting. Her gorgeous features broadcast her desire.

"Are you tired? You were up all night."

I shake my head, staring at her mouth.

As much as I want to devour her, I'm enjoying savoring this. I want to know if it's making her as crazy as I've been with my obsession for her.

She leans against the counter. I close the distance between us and brace my hands against it on either side of her. My chin dips to bring our faces closer together. She closes her eyes, looking so damn inviting.

"Looks like we're all alone."

EIGHTEEN
MAYA

WITHOUT REAGAN HERE FOR BUFFER, it's impossible to resist the tension that's been building between me and Easton throughout breakfast with his sneaky touches. He keeps brushing against me while we wash up.

I thought he was going to tear my clothes off the minute Reagan left for class, but after being all seductive saying we're alone, he turned on the sink. My neck still tingles from those torturous stolen kisses, and I want more.

He glances at me. "Are you going to tell Reagan?"

"I will. We tell each other everything. Sorry, I didn't mean to put you in a weird spot."

"It's okay. I'm glad you're going to talk to her. Want me to go with you to campus security?"

"I'll stop by after class. And yes, before you insist again, I'm going to get the locks changed."

"And?" he prompts.

"*And* stop hiding my spare outside."

"Good girl."

"It's morning," I point out again.

Easton accepts the plate I hand him to dry. His eyes hood, moving over me in a slow perusal that makes me rub my thighs together.

I tilt my head to the side, peering up through my lashes. "Reagan won't be back for a while. I don't have to go to my morning class because I already submitted my paper early before break. So..."

His tongue swipes across his lower lip, then he sets aside the last plate on the drying rack. I angle my body to face his, more than ready for him to take care of the unbearable ache between my legs.

He doesn't swoop in to capture my mouth in a searing kiss. Or crush my body to his. Or toss me over his shoulder to take me to bed, like all of the spicy romance books I borrow from Reagan promise.

Rather than any of that, he rests his hips against the island, widening his stance so there's not as much of a height difference between us.

Holding my gaze, his hand pushes beneath his shirt to do that irresistibly sexy thing guys do when they scratch their torso with long, slow strokes. It gives me a tantalizing flash of his abs. Desire burns through my veins and my throat goes dry.

God, he's so hot.

And I *want* him.

I resisted that truth for far too long, but I'm not denying it any longer.

"Are you going to make me spell it out?" I step into him, sliding my palms up his firm chest.

He gives me a slow grin. "Spell what out?"

My mouth pops open. I know what he's doing. He's holding out on me so I'll be the one to make the first move after he got me all hot and bothered.

Part of me wants to turn it back around on him to see who breaks first, but I don't want to play around anymore. I want this too much.

Rising on tiptoe, I wrap my arms around his neck and draw him down for the kiss I'm craving. My breath hitches as my nipples graze the hard planes of his body through the shirt I stole from him.

His chuckle ghosts across my lips when he breaks the kiss, sliding his palms up my back to hold me closer. "Hi."

"Hi." I lift higher on my toes to press my lips to the corner of his mouth, encouraging him to take it further.

Again, he stalls. I release a frustrated noise that makes him rumble in amusement. He tips my chin up, watching me.

"You sure you want me, Maya?"

His gritty tone goes right to my core, sparking a pulse of desire. My fingers curl around the sides of his warm up jacket, tugging insistently.

"*Yes.*"

His mouth curves into a devastating smile. "Can I take you to your room?"

Finally. "Yes."

I yelp as he bends, throwing me over his shoulder. Laughter bubbles out of me while arousal coils tighter in my stomach. He smacks my ass.

When he drops me on the bed, he pauses for a minute, admiring the sight of me sprawled out for him. After shrugging off his jacket, he crawls over me, one leg fitting between my thighs.

I moan against his mouth when he kisses me, shamelessly grinding against his leg. His mouth moves relentlessly against mine, intent on taking me apart.

Arousal spirals through me. I've never felt like this with anyone else, already so turned on.

Not only is Easton a good kisser, but everything with him feels more intense. His touch when his big hand massages my waist before sliding beneath my shirt to tease my breast. The weight of his sculpted body over mine. His scent surrounding me, driving me wild with desire. All of it.

It's like my body was asleep with everyone else, and it's finally awake with someone who knows what I need before I have to voice what feels good for me.

The thought makes my throat sting for a moment before Easton distracts me by circling my sensitive nipple with his thumb as his tongue glides against mine. I arch, clamping my thighs around his.

My pussy throbs with need. It's crazy, but I'm so close to coming just from making out with him while he presses his thigh against me.

A ringtone filters through the haze of pleasure. It takes a minute to register that my phone's going off at the worst possible time.

My gut clenches. The last time I ignored a phone call, it was bad news about Grandpa that I had to hear about by text.

I put my hand on Easton's chest. "Wait, wait."

He stills, pressing his forehead to mine. "Are you okay?"

"Yeah."

I sit up, brushing hair from my face as I grab my phone. When I read the screen, I scrub a hand over my face.

"It's Ryan. If I don't answer, he'll keep blowing my phone up."

Easton rises on his knees, catching my wrist before I answer my phone. "Make him wait and wonder who his sister's with."

My eyes close as he kisses me. His fingers sink into my hair and tug just hard enough to stir an answering throb in my clit.

I break away, trying to catch my breath. "He only calls me on FaceTime when it's important. It might be about my grandpa."

He sobers, nodding. "Okay."

Covering his face when he tries to slide in next to me, I push him down out of frame and answer. He folds his arms behind his head while I wait for it to connect. My attention snags on his erection tenting his pants, and that's the moment my brother answers.

"Why is your face all red? Were you working out?"

"What? No." I clear my throat. "What is it? Is Grandpa okay?"

"Yeah, last I heard from Dad. That's not why I called."

I blow out an irritated sigh, wishing I hadn't answered his call. "What's up?"

"I have an away game at UConn this Saturday. Want to come?"

I rub the space between my brows. "You called about that? Seriously?"

Easton snorts, I throw a pillow at him. He catches it and blows me a kiss.

"Is someone with you?" Ryan asks.

"No," I answer sharply. "I can't go to your game, sorry. I'm busy."

Ryan narrows his eyes. "You're not seeing Blake again, are you?"

Easton's face splits in a cocky grin. I press my lips together, shifting around so I don't break and give us away.

"We're—" I falter over the truth, aware of him hiding out of sight. "—friends, Ryan. Get over it."

Easton hums low enough that I hope the phone doesn't pick it up. He edges into my field of view, staying out of frame stretched along the edge of my bed while sliding his hands over my lower half. My breath catches when his fingers delve between my legs to cup me through my leggings.

Cheeks flaming, I fling my leg out. He overbalances and tips off the side of the bed, thumping to the floor with a grunt.

"Shit!" I squeak.

"What's wrong?" Ryan asks suspiciously.

"Nothing. I thought I saw a spider on my bed," I blurt. "I have to go—bye."

I hang up on him, covering my face.

"Did you just push me off the bed?"

"My brother was on the phone, what did you expect me to do when you touched me like that?"

Easton rolls onto his back on the floor, tucking an arm behind his head. "Take your shirt off and come kiss me better."

"Oh, come on. You get hit harder in a game."

"Fine, no playing doctor. How about we play with this, then?" He reaches beneath my bed and takes out the box covered in cat stickers.

My eyes widen. I'm not ashamed to own vibrators and other toys, but I brace for what inevitably happens when guys discover them. I hate having to deal with bruised egos because I'm better at getting myself off with a toy than with any guy.

He didn't have any problems last night, my mind supplies.

"Easton—"

He opens it, eyes gleaming. "Oh, hell yeah." He waves the lid at me. "This is adorable. I like that you put cat stickers on your pussy box."

I blink. "I—my what?"

Blowing out a breath, I pop off the bed to take it from him, but he holds it out of reach. I prop my hands on my hips.

"What, you think girls don't like some me time between classes? We get horny, too. And these get the job done better than anything you could do to me."

"I love that you have them. It's sexy." He shoots me a crooked smirk that freezes me in place. "No one's ever used them on you?"

I shake my head, face growing hot at the thought.

"You know, hockey is all about your dynamic with the team. There's no one guy on the ice—we're all the team when we score, when we attack, and defend. I'm a team player, baby. I know how to work with my teammates." He selects my favorite vibrator, meeting my wide eyes. "These right here are my partners in crime, not the enemy. I want to use them while I play with you."

My stomach dips pleasantly. He's the first guy I've ever met who doesn't hate the sight of my vibrator or think of it as competition. Rather than be afraid of a girl with sex toys, he accepts it enthusiastically.

"Okay."

He gets to his feet, stepping into me. I'm lost when he kisses me, vaguely aware of the vibrator landing on the bed behind us. As his tongue makes me dizzy with each stroke, he works the Heston University t-shirt up.

The cool air makes my nipples harden. We pause for him to whip the shirt over my head, then he strips out of his. I bite my lip and skim my fingertips over the sculpted planes of his chest while he's captivated for a moment by my bare tits. He cups them, making me bite back a soft noise of pleasure as he teases them.

"God, you're fucking gorgeous," he says. "And still wearing too many clothes. I want to see all of you."

His hands drag down my sides to push my leggings down. I hold onto his shoulders as he helps me step out of them. When they're off, he kneels, lifting his gaze to mine. My stomach quivers when he places a kiss above my panties, then strips them off, leaving me completely bare.

Kneading the soft flare of my hips, he trails more teasing kisses along my pelvis. I cry out when he buries his face against me to taste my pussy. He encourages me to open my legs, nudging my thigh until I blindly find the bed frame to prop my foot on while his mouth seals over my clit. I sink my fingers in his thick brown hair, holding on.

"Oh god," I whimper.

"Does it feel good?" His hot breath ghosting across my sensitive skin makes me shudder.

"Yes."

He lavishes my pussy with more attention until my chest heaves with each breath and my hips rock with every sensual swipe of his tongue. But he pulls back before I come. I smother a disappointed noise as he gets to his feet and pulls me against him.

Easton's mouth hovers over mine. "Maya."

"Yes?"

"I'm going to make you forget the word friend when I'm around."

My breath hitches. "What do you mean?"

"If I haven't made it crystal clear, I don't want to be your friend whenever I do this."

He claims my mouth, the kiss burning me up as much as his roaming touch.

"There's no one else. Do you understand?" he rasps against my lips.

I nod. "You want to be my boyfriend, not my friend."

"Boyfriend," he repeats with a cocky tilt to his lips. "Yeah, I like the sound of that. Say it again, baby."

I thought I'd never be someone who dated hockey players again, but there's nothing making me uneasy. This isn't the wrong decision.

A laugh puffs out of me. "Easton Blake is my boyfriend."

He rumbles in approval, arms cinching tighter around me. "Damn right I am. You're all mine. And I don't share."

I bite my lip. "I'm not telling my brother until after your second game against Elmwood. I don't want him trying to kill you on the ice for being my boyfriend."

"Let's forget about your brother right now."

I gasp as he picks me up and takes us to the bed, covering my body with his. He chuckles against my throat, the rough noise causing a delicious tug in my stomach.

"What?"

"Your neck is all red." His fingertips trace a shape, then he seals his lips over it. "I like you wearing my marks."

I wrap my legs around him, scraping my nails across his shoulder. "Then I need to give you a matching hickey."

"You can mark me all you want, baby." His teeth graze my throat. "But right now, I want to play with that pretty pussy while I eat it."

His lips map a path across every curve of my body before he settles between my thighs with my vibrator in one hand and a wicked smile. He starts off with just his mouth, sucking lightly on my clit. I melt against the sheets with a sigh.

The buzz of the toy turning on makes my stomach tighten in

anticipation. My breathing thickens when he spends a moment working it over my pussy. Each time he finds a spot that makes my hips buck, he keeps the toy there.

By the time he uses it on my clit, I'm unable to keep still. My legs tremble, opening wider, then squeezing around him.

"Oh god," I breathe. "Yes. Please."

He pushes the vibrator into my hand. I'm so dizzy with pleasure, I automatically grip it, allowing him to guide me to use it on myself. I rub it right where I like it, shuddering at the filthy noises he makes while he eats me out.

The sensations of his mouth and the vibrations stimulating my clit overwhelm me. His fingers clamp around my wrist when I try to move the vibrator away. He guides my hand back in place to keep the toy against my clit.

"Keep holding this here. You're going to be a good girl and come on my tongue."

A strangled noise catches in my throat when he pins my hips to the bed and takes me apart by paying attention to every sign my body gives him that I'm close.

It's too much.

With a strangled gasp, I fall over the edge. The orgasm hits me hard, the pleasure far more heightened than anything I've experienced alone. My core erupts with wave after wave of ecstasy that seems to go on forever.

"That's it. I've got you," he rasps. "Let me taste you."

He groans against me, the noise electrifying me. He takes control of the vibrator again. My mouth drops open and I arch, arousal cresting once more before the first orgasm fades.

"Fuck," I whimper. "I—I'm coming again."

He still doesn't stop. Not until I finally push him away three more mind-melting orgasms later.

While I'm catching my breath, Easton sets the toy aside, stretching out next to me. He props on his elbow, blue eyes roaming my face with awe.

"Damn, baby. You're such a beautiful sight." His knuckles brush my cheek. "You okay?"

I manage a nod. "That was..."

"So fucking hot," he finishes for me.

I nod again, a laugh escaping me. Rolling into him, I press my lips to his. He kisses me back with a languid hum, stroking my spine with his fingertips.

"Why am I the only one who's naked? Lose these." I give his sweats an insistent tug.

His grin is smug. "You want to see my cock?"

"See it. Taste it." I wriggle closer. "Feel it inside me."

He pins me to the mattress with a gravelly rumble. "Yeah?" He grinds his erection against my sensitive pussy. "You want me to fuck you?"

I bite my lip, meeting his eyes while I roll my hips to meet his. They flare with lust, pupils darkening.

"You are..." He pushes out a ragged breath. "So damn sexy. But I won't fuck you today. Not yet."

I blink. "What? Why?"

My body still craves more.

He cups my face, kissing me deeply. "I'm just getting you warmed up so when I do fuck you, I have you begging for it."

I narrow my eyes without any heat. "I told you I don't beg."

"I heard you begging to come when my tongue was inside you."

He smirks, moving to sit on the edge of the bed. His palm splays on my stomach and teases the underside of my tits.

"As much as I want to stay and make you come again and again, I have to go back to my place before practice." He leans down to brush his mouth over mine, then takes the vibrator and drags the tip over my nipple. "But I want you to stay in this bed and use this on your pussy while you think about how good it'll be when I fill you up with my cock."

My thighs clamp together and I fight back a shiver. "Don't listen to any voice chats I send you until you're alone, then. Unless you want everyone to hear what I sound like when I come."

"Fuck, Maya."

Threading his fingers through my hair, he steals another kiss. I take the vibrator and click it on before slipping it between my legs. He swallows my moans, grip tightening in my hair until I tremble with another orgasm.

When he pulls back, I give him a hazy smile.

"You're killing me." Chuckling ruefully, he kisses my forehead. "If I don't leave right now, I'm going to say fuck it."

"I wouldn't complain."

"I really have to go." He gets dressed, lingering by the door on his way out. "Make yourself come a lot for me, baby."

I haven't stopped teasing myself with the toy, smirking at him while my lashes flutter. "Have a good practice. Make sure you focus instead of thinking about me coming over and over."

"Jesus." He scrubs a hand over his face and adjusts his dick in his sweats so his erection isn't as obvious. "You're going to be the death of me, woman."

My laugh breaks off into a moan. "And you'll love every second of it."

He rakes a hand through his hair, giving me one of the heart-stopping smiles that floods me with a warm glow.

"Yeah. I have no doubt I will."

Easton watches me come again, then leaves me in my bed, naked and indulgently enjoying wringing every ounce of pleasure with the help of my toys.

NINETEEN
MAYA

One of Reagan's playlists streams on my phone's connection to the smart speaker we share while I shower on Friday. It's mostly her songs she's put online, along with some other indie artists she's connected with.

I have extra time before my work shift because my class ended early, so I'm taking full advantage.

It's been a long week. I've earned a nice shower with some *me* time.

After telling Reagan about what happened and giving a report about Johnny's prank to campus security, I'm working on getting myself back to a positive mindset.

Easton's been busy, and I've spent the week getting started on my last assignments due before finals. We haven't seen each other for more than grabbing a bite to eat together on campus. This morning the donut truck was here and we got our favorite donuts to share.

Tomorrow night's our first date, technically. He convinced me that girlfriends go watch their boyfriends play hockey. I haven't been a girlfriend cheering her hockey boyfriend on in a long time, but I'm actually looking forward to going to his game. I'm eager to see him play and excited to enjoy the exhilarating experience of being at a game again.

When I'm done washing, I grab the pink toy waiting for me on the shelf. This one vibrates and has an air pulse head that feels incredible.

I let the pulsing head tease my folds while my mind wanders, biting my lip as the scene unfolds in my head. At first it's a faceless guy while I concentrate on the sensations, but he quickly becomes Easton. I shudder as I move the toy to seal over my clit, imagining him commanding me to sit on his face.

The toy's resonation makes my clit feel like his tongue strokes over it.

An exhale rushes past my lips as the fantasy becomes more vivid. His hands grip my hips as he devours me, encouraging me to lose control and ride his face until I come.

"Oh! Yes," I cry as my orgasm hits.

The smart speaker's AI voice barely registers when it announces, "*Incoming call, Hat Trick King sweat droplets. Answer?*"

"Yes. Fuck, *yes*." A moan slips out as I rock my hips against the toy, chasing ecstasy for as long as possible.

"*That's it, baby. Come for me,*" I imagine Easton crooning to me.

The music doesn't return, but I'm not paying attention, too wrapped up in pleasure.

"—got you two tickets for the home game tomorrow night if you want to bring one of your fr—"

Easton's voice overlaps with the fantasy in my head. It takes another few seconds for me to recognize what's going on, and I jolt, smacking into the wall.

"Fuck, baby," he grits out, voice going deeper. "Are you playing with yourself without me? That's so goddamn hot."

My chest heaves, body still thrumming with arousal. I turn the vibrator off.

Though I'm surprised, there's no shame. It makes me feel sexy to know he heard me.

"Yes," I answer thickly. "I'm in the shower."

He mutters another curse, groaning under his breath. "Naked, wet, soapy. Shit, I bet you look so good right now."

I brace my back against the wall, skimming my hand over my stomach with soft caresses, traveling lower. "I didn't mean to answer the call, but I guess there's no differentiation between *yes*, as in answer the phone, and *yes*, as in *oh shit, yes, I'm coming, I'm coming*."

He releases a raspy chuckle at my fake orgasm voice. I close my eyes, picturing him here in the shower with me, chest and jaw beaded with water while he rakes his wet hair back.

"Were you thinking about me?"

"Yes," I murmur.

He groans and mumbles something to someone talking in the background. There's a rustle, a muted thumping, then he stops whispering.

"Now I'm trying to hide a raging boner from the guys. I haven't had to run to my room like this since I was a teenager."

"You're welcome?" I quip.

"You've got me all out of whack," he admits in a gravelly tone tinged with amusement. "I'm serious. I've never felt like this with anyone before."

My stomach dips. Knowing he's that affected by me is such a turn on.

"Smooth line, hotshot."

"It's not a line, it's the truth," he rasps.

Warmth spreads through me. It turns into a rush of tingles that leave me shivering at the wrecked sound he makes. My teeth scrape my lip and my thighs slide together.

"Tell me what you were thinking about," he urges.

"Are you the one touching yourself now?"

"Yeah." His breathing becomes thick and ragged. "If I didn't have to get on the team bus for our away game in twenty minutes, I'd be hauling ass to come join you in that shower. Help me get there, baby. Tell me."

Air rushes past my lips and my clit throbs. He's jerking off, wanting to know what fantasy was in my head so he can get off to it.

"You made me sit on your face."

"Oh, fuck. Yeah," he grits out.

"You gripped my hips and made me ride your face." As I set the scene, I turn my toy back on, closing my eyes as I move it over my throbbing clit. "Mm, I want your tongue inside me again."

"You gonna come with me?"

"Yes," I answer hoarsely. "It feels so good."

"Gonna eat your pussy until you're dripping down my chin." The sound he makes is sinful. "I'm close."

I bite my lip, straining my ears to listen to the muted noises of his hand stroking his cock. Tipping my head back against the wall, I moan. He chokes out a garbled curse that sets off my orgasm.

"Shit. I'm coming. You coming with me, baby?"

"Yes."

It's just as hot to come together over the phone as it was when he went down on me with my vibrator the other day.

A laugh leaves me when I recover first. "That was my first time having phone sex."

"Did you like it?" He sounds sleepy and relaxed after coming.

"Yeah."

"We can do it again while I'm on the road if you want."

I grin, rinsing off before getting out of the shower. "Are you saying you want a booty call?"

"It's a definite perk of having a girlfriend." He chuckles. "Now I see why there are some guys on the team that spend hours shut up in their rooms on the phone with their girls."

"Uh huh," I tease. "You're going to be late. Aren't you supposed to leave?"

"I'm cleaning up now." The tap runs in the background while he washes his hands. "Shit."

"What's wrong?"

"My cock is still hard. You got me too worked up with that hot little fantasy of yours."

The corners of my eyes crinkle. "Not sorry."

"I can hear you grinning."

"Oh yeah?"

"Yes, and it's fucking hot."

Warmth spirals through me. "Easton?"

"Yeah?"

"Good luck. I have work during the game, but I'll check the score."

"Thanks, baby. You know I'll be lighting up the lamp for you."

I huff in amusement. "See you tomorrow."

"Can't wait. I'll text you. Have a good shift at the farm."

* * *

Later at work, I'm in an awesome mood that's kept me smiling all day. Though it's chilly out now that winter has truly set in with the start of December, an ember glowing from within me keeps the dreary cold at bay. For the first time in a long while, it feels like everything in my life is going great.

Grandpa called on my walk to the farm sounding better than he has in months. His voice was clear and strong while we made plans for when I go back home for winter break. Hearing him sounding so healthy soothes my constant worries about his health.

My advisor emailed me earlier to let me know the situation with the senior seminar that was up in the air is sorted. Another professor agreed to oversee the course. I'll be able to take it next semester after all, so I'm right on track for my plans to graduate in May.

And...the guy who just might steal my heart keeps texting me.

Hat Trick King 💦
Still thinking about earlier.

Maya
Isn't your game about to start?

Hat Trick King 💦
This is now part of my pregame ritual to get in the right headspace.

Maya
How's that working out?

Hat Trick King 💦
Might need to hide another boner. If I tell Coach I need to tape my stick again, it could buy me ten minutes to jerk off.

Maya
Omg 😂 I really need to change your contact name.

Hat Trick King 💦
Why? I proved it was true when I had your sexy thighs wrapped around my head, didn't I?

Maya
Keep it up and you'll be named after this year's least favorite mascot.

Hat Trick King 💦
Nah, my girl wouldn't do me dirty like that.

Maya
Try me 😇

Hat Trick King 💦
Fine. But add a heart to my name.

Maya
Why? You're so cheesy.

Hat Trick King 💦
Because it's all yours, baby. You've gotta keep it safe for me.

My cheeks hurt from smiling. Once I edit his name in my phone, I send him a screenshot. He sends back a selfie of his pleased grin. My heart swells.

Hana helps me with the AA group that visits the farm for a horse bonding session. We teach people about grooming with a pair of lazy mares that are more than happy to enjoy the pampering and attention.

Pride makes my heart swell each time I watch someone tear up or release heavy sighs of relief when they meet the horse's eyes. One woman starts to cry as she's taking her turn brushing the horse.

I hand her a tissue from the pack I bring to these sessions. "It's okay. Whatever you're feeling, that's what you need to. This is a safe space to let out what we've been holding back."

She nods in thanks, stroking the mare's neck. I back away to let her work through her overflowing emotions.

I join Hana by the paddock fence, leaning against a wooden post. "Are you doing anything tomorrow night?"

"No."

"I have an extra ticket to the hockey game. Want to come with me? They're great seats."

"Really? Yeah, okay. That sounds fun." Her cheeks tinge with a pretty shade of pink. "Do you know if Elijah Adler will be playing?"

A slow grin spreads across my face. "I can ask Easton."

Hana waves her hands. "No, no. Don't do that."

"So you're in?"

"Yeah."

"Cool. It'll be fun!" Excitement bubbles up inside me. "Come over to my place before the game. We can pregame with pizza and wings while we get ready."

"Perfect." She beams. "I'll be over after my meeting for our final performances. Thanks for inviting me."

TWENTY
EASTON

When I arrive at the arena for Saturday night's home game, I feel unstoppable. We fought hard with UMass at yesterday's away game and came out on top when Elijah scored the winning goal with a beautiful wrister. Tonight we're playing against them again and I already taste victory.

Noah's waiting at the bottom of the steps outside the back entrance to the locker and equipment area, phone at the ready. I smirk, smoothing a hand down my tie.

"Captain arriving an hour and forty-five minutes early before game time, that's what we like to see," he says. "Strut it, East. That suit looks sharp on you. People go nuts when I post the team's arrival looks."

Giving a salute with my sticks, I start down the steps. As I reach the bottom, I hear girls cheering. I spot Maya hanging out with Reeves and her friend from work nearby. He nods with his chin.

My attention locks on Maya. I've been waiting all day to see her. She looks cute as hell wearing a navy crewneck with Heston U Hockey emblazoned across the chest, and has her hair pulled half up in two sections of braided pigtails. Her cheeks are painted with #24 inside green hearts, making me break out in a slow smile.

A smug chuckle leaves me when she stares at me in a suit like a slab of meat. She steps into my embrace when I open my arms.

"You're here." My gaze dips to her sweatshirt again. "Still not wearing my jersey. At least it's the right team colors this time. You're also early."

"There was a free cookie on the line," she says. "Clocktower Brew House has a tent set up in front of the arena. We had to show our school spirit to get them."

I open my mouth and she gives me the last small bite. Then I have to kiss her pretty grin.

"Mm, tastes sweet. You like the suit?"

Her lashes flutter and she tries to fight a smile. "Um, that would be a yes. Definitely."

"More reasons for you to come to my games." I waggle my brows. "Are you going to be warm enough? I still have time to get you one of my alternate jerseys to wear over that."

"God, I almost forgot how needy hockey players are as boyfriends," she sasses, dropping her voice in imitation. "My girlfriend has to go to my games, wear my jersey, chant my name—"

Grinning, I swallow her words when I capture her mouth for another kiss. She keeps mumbling against my lips until she melts into it, wrapping her arms around my waist. I could kiss her like this all day.

"I wouldn't complain about any of that, but I only want it if you want it."

Her gaze flickers between mine. "I know."

"Good." I touch her cheek, carefully grazing the face paint with my number, then bring my lips to her ear. "Scream my name nice and loud for me, baby."

She shivers, peering up through her lashes with a look I love seeing in her gorgeous hazel eyes.

"Good luck, captain."

My chest expands, filled with a sensation that's soft and warm. A happy laugh slips out of me.

"Thanks. Have fun tonight. When we're done, I'll meet you back here and we can all head to The Landmark together."

"Okay."

She presses on her toes to claim one more kiss, and I'm not about to deny her. I don't think there's anything I'll ever be able to deny her.

Hiking my gear bag higher on my shoulder, I back away in the direction of the player entrance, keeping her in view for as long as I can.

"Where's my good luck, captain? You gonna give me a kiss, too?" Cam falls into step with me, elbowing my side.

I return it with a smirk. We both snicker. He can give me shit for being all sappy now that I have a girlfriend. It does nothing to conquer the way being with her makes me feel.

We pass the open door to the coachs' office on our way to the locker rooms. Neil Cannon is talking with Coach Lombard. They pause their conversation and he lifts his coffee in greeting.

"Give 'em hell tonight, boys," he says.

"Yes, sir," I say.

My mood only gets better gearing up in the locker room. The guys joke around until it's time to get in the zone as game time approaches. The coaches go over our best plays and the weak moments we need to tighten up from playing against UMass last night.

I stand in the middle of the locker room, surveying my team. "We're entering that rink ahead tonight."

"Hell yeah," Manning whoops.

"We're going to leave the ice as winners," I continue. "UMass passed on me and half of you in this locker room. They didn't see what Lombard and all of Heston know. We're a team of the best damn talent in Hockey East."

When I finish, the room erupts in a ruckus of cheers and whistles. We leave the locker room unified and fired up to take the win tonight.

During warm-ups, I find Maya in the crowd. Do I show off for her?

Of fucking course I do.

I'm glad I scored her rinkside seats. This time she's here for me, not her brother.

After they're over, I gather at the bench with the guys until the ice is cleared of loose pucks. My gaze doesn't leave her during the opening before puck drop. One by one, our names are called by the game announcer to introduce us to the arena.

"Introducing tonight's lineup. For the Heston University Knights, in goal, number thirty-three, Cameron Reeves."

Cameron skates to the blue line, waving as the crowd showers him with support for their goaltender.

"At left wing, number sixteen, Daniel Hutchinson."

Hutch zooms to the line like his ass is on fire.

"At right wing, number fourteen, Theo Boucher."

Theo joins them while the crowd chants his nickname.

"On defense, number forty-five, Noah Porter."

Noah flirts with the crowd, skating in a meandering zigzag to reach the boys. Reeves pretends to swoon, leaning against Boucher to catch him. The crowd eats it up.

"Also on defense, number forty-seven, Jake Brody."

Brody takes off, inspiring a burst of high-pitched screams from girls at the swagger in his stop.

"And at center, your team captain. Number twenty-four, Easton Blake," the announcer finishes, energetically hyping up my name.

The crowd cheers, but it's Maya who has me grinning as I skate towards my teammates at the blue line. She cups her hands around her mouth.

It might be my imagination, but I swear I hear her scream my name as I send snow flying when I stop on the edge of my blades to join my linemates.

I exchange looks with the guys. "Let's fucking go."

They echo my sentiment, tapping gloves before it's time to take our starting positions.

Once the game begins, the pace moves lightning quick. We can feel UMass' desperation to put up points and come out of this on top, but we're not letting that happen.

By the end of first period, the air is tinged with their rashness. Coach directs us to stay focused on keeping our pace steady.

In the middle of the second, they're getting sloppy trying to rush this. We take advantage, pressing their players hard when they make mistakes. We're the first to score on them and it's only making them play more wildly.

Early in the third period while I'm on the bench, McKinley moves with the puck. One of the defenders slams into him to steal it.

He takes the hit, then shakes out his wrist when UMass goes for the breakaway once they have the puck. He's having trouble, lagging while our guys chase down our opponents to stop the play.

"Coach," I say.

"Go."

I surge over the boards. "McKinley!"

Jack hears me, heading for the bench as I switch in for him. Our D-men shut down any play UMass tries to get through their wall. Nick Briggs pries the puck away from one of the forwards and barrels his way through.

Noah gets to an open spot, taking it when three UMass players converge on Briggs. He moves the puck across the red line and passes to Madden.

"Go! Let's make it happen!" I yell.

Madden has a zippy UMass guy on his ass. It screws up the shot he sets up, sending him on a goose chase to outskate him.

"Here, here!" I move into position to receive the puck.

He sends it so fast, I catch it off my blade to control it. Then I'm off, racing to attack.

When the game moves fast, you have to be faster. Not only to see what's going on, but to be two steps ahead of the other guys.

Being able to read the ice in a matter of seconds while the pressure is on is where I excel. I find my opening. The sound when I slap the puck is pure fucking magic.

Once it's in the net, I search the crowd for Maya's face in the section where she's sitting.

"Hell yeah, man! That was a damn beauty," Noah says.

"Buy me two minutes," I say in a rush when he collides into me for a celebratory hug.

"On it."

He heads for our equipment manager, holding up his stick to change it out before the next play starts. A couple of our teammates switch out.

It gives me just enough time to reach Maya's section. She goes from clapping and smiling with excitement to gaping at me when I wave at her.

Everyone around her in Heston's student section gets hyped,

chanting my name. She swings her gaze around, wide-eyed. I point at UMass' net, then at her, mouth stretching in a broad grin as it dawns on her what I'm doing.

"Oh my god." Her words are barely audible, muffled by the noises surrounding us, but I make them out by reading her plush lips.

She hides her face, shoulders trembling with laughter. Her friend nudges her while I wait.

The clock won't start again until the puck drops. I don't have much time, and I'm risking a penalty if I delay the game. The ref gives me a warning to get my ass in gear with a pointed blow of his whistle, but I'm not moving until she knows.

I tap on the glass with my glove. "Maya! Come on, baby. Look up for me. It's important."

At last she drops her hands and meets my eyes. Her embarrassed exasperation is cute as hell.

I lean closer, my helmet resting against the plexiglass as I mouth *that was for you*. She gives me a slow smile, shaking her head wryly. I nod, blowing her a kiss that makes her cheeks turn the prettiest shade of pink.

The fans in the section shout at her in encouragement. When she stands to press her palm to the glass where my glove is, they go wild, erupting in frenzied cheers.

With a cocksure grin and a wink, I push away from the boards. The ref gives me a flat look when I scrape to a stop at center ice.

"Finished with your girlfriend?" UMass' center sneers.

The corner of my mouth lifts as I sink into position to face off with him. "You wish. I'll never be done with her. Now, are we ready to play some hockey, princess? Or do you guys plan to skate around with your dicks in your hands some more?"

His outraged growl is hilarious. I smirk, adjusting my grip on my stick, ready for the puck to hit the ice.

It feels damn good when I win the face-off against him.

Even better when we take the W for this game.

And knowing Maya will be waiting for me after she watched me play?

Sweet fucking victory.

TWENTY-ONE
MAYA

After the game, we migrated to The Landmark. My stomach hurts from laughing. Easton keeps his arm locked around my waist to hold me up.

"Work it, rookie." Noah cups his hands around his mouth and whoops.

Elijah's face is beet red while he plants his hands on his thighs and attempts to gyrate his hips to the seductive beat of Pony by Ginuwine while all of us cheer him on.

"Why is he doing this?" I ask through uncontrollable giggles.

"It's tradition," Easton explains. "I don't know who started it, but the rookies every year have to dance when we come out, win or lose. You missed out on me and Cam. We really took our duty to heart."

"You guys are ridiculous."

He brings his lips to my ear and I feel the shape of his amused smile. "Yeah, and you love it, baby."

Yeah, I think I just might.

It's official. I'm a hockey girlfriend once again.

And this time I don't hate it. Not in the slightest.

The game was a blast, even when Easton made sure the entire arena knew the goal he scored was for me. Warmth floods me all over again at the thought. I couldn't believe he stopped in the middle of the game to skate over to our seats.

Reagan points the bar's drink nozzle at Elijah to spritz him with water. He rolls with it, smearing the wetness across his face, pushing his fingers into his hair while he slides his other hand up his shirt. He starts getting into it, letting go of his embarrassment. She keeps spraying him while we all holler in approval until he's nearly soaked.

He shakes out the damp tendrils of his hair as the song comes to an end, shooting Hana an affectionate grin. "What do you think? Do I have a shot at joining one of your dance classes?"

Hana tucks her hair behind her ear. "Don't audition for Magic Mike Live just yet. But..." She lifts her shoulder and grins. "Your moves have definitely improved since high school."

With a rueful laugh, he covers his face with his hands. "When will you let me live that down?"

"Never." She ducks her face to hide her smile.

Easton's arm squeezes my waist and his lips find my ear again. "Feel like getting up on the bar to dance? I'll pay Reagan for an encore."

I flash him a flirtatious smile. "Why, are you still dreaming about it?"

"Every damn day, baby."

A huff of laughter leaves me. "The night I turned you down?"

His arm tightens and his lips brush my skin. "The night we met."

My stomach dips pleasantly as his face presses into my neck. He hugs me against him.

I hum. "We should stay just like this."

"Forever? I love the way you think."

I swat him in amusement. "I mean so I don't have to cram for finals the rest of the weekend."

They start on Thursday and last for the next two weeks. I lucked out because my professors scheduled all of my exams early. I get to leave by the following Wednesday after my last one to go home for winter break.

He grumbles. "I wish we had more time together this semester before you leave for break."

"Me too. But I am looking forward to seeing my grandfather. My dad said he had really great blood work results at today's appointment with one of his doctors."

"That's good." His fingertips sneak beneath my Heston U

Hockey sweatshirt to graze my skin. "We can still talk. I'll be here until the end of semester, then home with my mom and Asher for Christmas, and then I have to be back here for a game right before the new year, so I'll probably just stay to train until next semester starts up."

"Talk or *talk*?"

I press my ass against him, grinning when he grabs my hips to hold me still.

"Woman," he rumbles. "Both."

"Uh huh. We're back in booty call territory." I break off in a giggle when he tickles me. "Hey!"

He apologizes with a trail of kisses, moving up my neck to end at my cheek. "For real, don't go silent on me over break. I'll miss your voice too much."

"I won't."

A flutter moves through my chest. I twist around to kiss him. It only lasts a moment before his teammates make loud kissing noises.

"Alright, alright," Easton says.

"Five orders of wings and jumbo fries?" A waitress balances a tray packed with food.

"You can bring those right over here," one of the senior players says.

The waitress gives him a shy smile. "Great win tonight, guys."

He lowers his chin, the corners of his mouth curling. "Thanks. Care to help me celebrate later?"

Her eyes widen and dart around the group. "Oh, really? Um, I—"

"Don't hit on the wait staff while they're working," Madden mutters when he comes over to get a basket of wings. "She's just trying to do her job."

She turns even redder, her focus shifting to him and his rugged look. Easton grabs my fries while she distributes the food, eyeing them longingly.

"Oh, just eat a fry, Easton." I pick one out and stuff it in his mouth before he can wrestle with himself about what he's supposed to eat during the season.

"Hammy's falling in love with you, Brody," Noah says with a laugh.

The Landing's sweet bar dog, Hambone, sits between Jake's knees with a wide, blissed out pittie smile as he gets his ears rubbed. His tongue lolls out and he paws at the air whenever Jake stops.

"You're done for. That's your job now," Theo says. "Time to hang up your skates. You're my dog's ear rub bitch now."

Jake snorts, showering Hambone with attention. "I just can't say no to his sad boy face."

"Coach Kincaid!" Cameron raises an arm in the air.

A good-looking guy in his twenties nods to our group. I think he's one of the assistant coaches. I recognize his name from the opening announcement before puck drop. He has a beautiful woman around his age tucked against his side. They make their way over to the corner we've taken over.

"Great game, guys! I was cheering for you," she says.

"Thanks, Eve," Jake says. "You're our good luck charm. We always play better when you're there to root for us."

Kincaid's brows flatten. "She'd better not be."

"She's our head coach's daughter," Easton murmurs in my ear. "This is my girlfriend, Maya. And her friend Hana."

"Hi. It's nice to meet you." I offer a friendly wave. "I love your earrings."

Eve touches them, her cute features lighting up in delight. "Thank you! I make them. I mostly sell them online, but I'm opening a boutique and have some wholesale partnerships for bigger stores to carry my creations."

"Really? That's awesome."

"Hey, Eve!" Reagan slips out from behind the bar to hug her. "Good to see you. It's been a while."

"Hi! I know, I keep missing you on the days you're working. I miss hearing you sing. It always got me through my shifts here."

Reagan waves her off. "Okay, but now you're doing what you've always wanted instead of bartending." She gives her one of the smiles that never fails to uplift even the crappiest mood. "Proud of you, girl."

Eve hugs her again. "Thank you."

"We're all proud of you," Kincaid murmurs to her.

They share a secretive smile before saying goodbye and finding a secluded spot.

"Guys, look at this photo of Hammy," Jake says.

"Aww," I say.

Reagan pouts at the cuteness. "Oh god, I can't handle it when his lip gets stuck on his teeth like that. Sweetest boy. Who's my best work buddy?"

She gets some dog biscuits from the jar behind the bar and comes out to give them to him for doing tricks. Madden pauses eating to join her, holding out his hand for a biscuit. She leaves the last two with him before going to take a customer's drink order when they flag her down.

"I'm saving this. Chicks dig dogs." Jake bounces his brows and taps on his phone.

"He's not even your dog," Theo points out.

"Won't matter. It's just an opener," Jake says.

Easton shakes his head. "Nice. Some of us don't need any help picking up girls. Right, baby?"

I hold up my hands. "Don't bring me into this."

"Wait, you've got to see what this guy has on his camera roll," Theo taunts.

He steals Easton's phone, evading him when he tries to get it back.

"Boys. Play nice in my bar, or I'll get the water bottle to squirt you." Reagan brandishes the drink nozzle from behind the bar, one eyebrow lifted in warning.

Theo cackles as two of the guys take his side, holding Easton back. He swipes through photos, showing them off. There are photos of a cat, of me, and of him hanging out with his teammates.

"This is your nationally ranked captain, gentlemen. This is the cheesy shit on his camera roll."

"Laugh it up now," Easton says. "I'm a patient man, and when I get you assholes back for this, you won't see it coming."

"When did you take that?" I lean in to get a better look at the photo of me sleeping.

"Okay, that's it. " Easton breaks free of his teammates' hold and swipes his phone back. "Let's see what's on your phones. Who wants to go first?"

Cameron snickers from his spot leaning against the bar, elbowing

Madden seated on the stool beside him, back to tearing through a basket of grilled wings.

"We've all seen your dick, man. There's nothing to hide," Cameron says.

Easton pokes his cheek with his tongue, then lunges for his best friend's phone sitting next to Madden's wings. Cameron grunts, bracing his arms over it like a fortress.

"What's wrong, Reeves? Got shit you don't want us to see?" Easton goads.

Madden picks up his basket and moves to lean against the wall where Hana and Elijah are talking. He looks stunned when Elijah steals two wings from him, offering one to Hana.

I hop onto a stool, exchanging a smirk with Reagan. She refills my drink. Hana makes her way over to me a few minutes later.

"Maya, I'm going to head out," she says.

"Oh, already? Okay. Thanks for coming with me tonight."

She beams. "Of course. Thanks for inviting me, I had a great time."

"You're leaving?" Elijah asks.

She stares at him for a beat. "Yeah. I need to study for finals."

"I'll walk you back."

"No, you don't have to do that. I'll be okay."

He dips his chin to level her with a look that says he isn't budging on this. "My sister will kill me if she catches wind I let you go home on your own. She made me swear to keep an eye on you after she graduated."

Hana lifts her brows. "Oh, so now that extends to college?"

He grins and shrugs. "Let me walk you?"

"Fine."

"Later, rookie," Easton says.

Elijah offers a brief wave, trailing after Hana. Easton abandons his attack on Cameron to stand behind me, hands absently settling on my waist.

"Having a good time?"

I lean back against him, the corners of my eyes crinkling. "Yeah."

He kisses my cheek. "Good. That's what I like to hear."

This is a night that will be ingrained in my memories for years to come, one I'll look back on to remember the good times from college. I want it to last forever.

TWENTY-TWO
EASTON

Our group makes our way back to the house when Reagan's shift ends. I keep Maya tucked beneath my arm, keeping her warm against the frigid chill in the winter air.

Kit-cat waits for me on the porch, pacing back and forth when we start up the path to the house.

"Oh, is this where you hang out?" Maya moves ahead to crouch in front of my cat. "Do these boys give you all the food?"

"That's all Easton," Theo says on his way to the door. "He started feeding her freshman year. Then brushing her. Now she's claimed this as her place."

"She likes it when her coat is shiny." I squeeze the back of my neck as heat creeps up it.

Maya shoots me a pleased look. "Of course she does. I met her a while back on one of my night walks. What's her name?"

"She sort of doesn't have an official one," I admit. "We call her a bunch of things, but usually I land on Kit-cat."

She hums, petting the cat beneath her chin. "I think she looks more like a Turnip."

"Turnip?"

"What? It's a great name for a cat."

Kit-cat follows us and Maya picks her up, expression softening with affection at the loud purring. My steps falter, heart thudding. Kit-cat can be shy, but she's warmed right up to my girl.

"She likes you. She doesn't usually let other people pick her up."

"I'm good with animals. Always have been." She lets Kit-cat sniff her nose, puckering her lips to kiss the air. "Actually, I like animals better than people most days."

"Most people," Reagan interjects.

"Most people," Maya agrees. "The tolerable ones get a pass."

"Do I count as most people?"

She laughs at the charming grin I offer and bumps her shoulder against my chest.

"You count."

I turn around and raise my voice to tell the empty street the good news. "I count!"

"Shh." She tugs on my sleeve, careful not to upset the cat. "You're going to wake up the whole town."

"Come on."

We go into the house. I pause in the entryway, taking the cat into my arms. Her purring sounds like the motor of the world's smallest pickup truck when I nuzzle my nose against her head and smooth a hand down her back.

"Did you eat all the field mice you could find today, pretty girl? What about the coffee shop, they gave you some milk again, didn't they?"

Maya stares at me, the corners of her parted lips tugging up.

I might be six-five, built, and the captain of the hockey team. Doesn't mean I'm not man enough to baby talk my cat.

I smirk at her awestruck expression. "What?"

"Nothing, you doing that is just really hot for some reason."

My mouth stretches into a cocky grin. "Is it the baby talk or the way my biceps bulge when I cradle her like this, like she's my baby girl?"

She shakes her head with a wry smile. "Shut up."

Her cheeks flush, eyes dancing with mirth. She takes the cat from me and goes to find everyone else.

"Which one is it?" I call after her.

"I'll never tell."

We end up piled onto the plush couches and chairs in the living room. Kit-cat hasn't left Maya's lap. Whenever she's not looking, I take about twenty photos of my two favorite girls cuddling together. My chest expands so much it feels like it might burst open, no longer able to contain my happiness.

Someone starts the PlayStation and Reagan connects her phone to our speaker system to play music while we hang out. The chill vibe is nice. Tonight is the most fun I've had at the house in years.

I never minded the parties, but they pale in comparison. I'd take a hundred nights like this over the way things used to be before I met Maya.

I'm given the controller when Manning taps out against Cameron. He gets us set up for the next match.

"I'll be back," Maya says.

She kisses my cheek before getting up. My gaze tracks her through the room, the edges of my mouth quirking up.

"Oh!" Cameron pumps his fist in the air when he obliterates me because I'm not paying attention to the game. "That's how it's done boys."

I hand off the controller to Elijah when he gets in from walking Hana home. "Here, rookie. Smoke Reeves for us. You're the only one who can beat him. Avenge me."

Elijah snorts, dropping into the open seat on the couch. "What, you old guys can't make your fingers move fast enough? I bet that's disappointing for the girls you hook up with."

A round of protests and boos sound from the upperclassmen.

"I've never had any complaints." Brody smirks, wiggling his fingers. "It's more along the lines of *oh god, oh god, yes, yes, yes, ahhhh*!"

"I know, I hear it every time you have someone over," Theo says.

Noah leans over the back of the couch to mess with Elijah. "Come to the club with me. I'll show you how the big boys keep all the girls happy."

Elijah pushes him off, but it's too late. Cameron wins again.

My brow furrows when I realize Maya's been gone for a while. I search the living room, back den, and kitchen. In the front hall, Reagan is shrugging on her coat.

"Have you seen where Maya went?"

Reagan pauses, shooting me a sly smirk. "Upstairs to use your bathroom, I think. I'm out."

I'm torn between making sure she has someone to walk her home in the dark and finding my girlfriend. I open my mouth and she cuts me off with a laugh.

"Relax, Hutch is waiting outside already. He's driving me to campus. See ya."

"Later."

I take the steps at a quick clip, then stop in my goddamn tracks when I open the door and find what's waiting for me, because *holy shit*.

"I thought you'd never find me," Maya sasses.

She's on my bed looking more exquisite than I've ever seen her. The green hearts have been washed off her cheeks, and her hair spills down loosely around her shoulders. She ditched the jeans she had on, legs bare and inviting when she skims a hand up her thigh.

And she's wearing nothing but my jersey.

I repeat, *holy shit*.

The fantasies I've had of this have nothing on the real deal. My hungry gaze rakes over her, a thousand and one thoughts racing through my head of what I want to do to her first.

I want to fuck her. My hands flex, already imagining spreading those gorgeous thighs and sinking my cock into the tight heat of her perfect body.

No, I have to fuck her *mouth* while she's on her knees.

No, shit, I need to taste her pussy with my hands fisted in my jersey and my name on her lips, knowing she's *all fucking mine*.

"You're wearing my number."

The obvious statement is the first dumb thing to tumble from my lips. She tilts her head coyly, offering a sexy little smirk that sends blood rushing to my dick.

"I know how much you've wanted to see me in your jersey. I wanted to wear it just for you first."

"Fuck. Maya, you look..."

She hums in amused agreement. "So, you like it?"

"*Fuck yes*."

Finally, I find the ability to move. I slam the door and reach her in two urgent strides. She rises on her knees to meet me. When I collide with her I take both of us to the bed, mouth already slotting over hers in a scorching kiss full of unchecked need.

My hands drag up her legs, dipping beneath the jersey to find she's not wearing anything underneath. A groan scrapes my throat as my fingers dig into the soft flesh of her hips.

I kiss my way to her neck, pausing there to pay attention to the spot that makes her shudder. She grips my hair, squirming beneath me as my mouth moves against her skin. I work a knee between her thighs and waste no time sliding my fingers over her pussy to tease her clit.

Maya's back arches. "Oh!"

My teeth scrape her throat and I enjoy the way her thighs clamp around my hand. She's so responsive. It drives me insane.

I map a path down her body, kneading her breast as I close my lips around her nipple to suck it through my jersey. She writhes against my hand.

"Easton," she whimpers.

I keep moving lower, lifting the hockey sweater to trace her stomach with my tongue until I reach her mound. Pausing, I draw back just long enough to strip my clothes impatiently, almost ripping them in my rush to get naked.

She sits up to peel off my jersey. My fist closes around the hem and I shake my head.

"No. Leave this on. I want to see how you look wearing it when I make you come."

Her eyes darken with arousal, pupils blown wide to eat up the flecks of green and gold in her hazel irises.

I hold her gaze while I position myself between her legs, teasing her with grazes of my lips until she lifts her hips and pushes my head down to eat her. I chuckle against her pussy and get to work.

She pants, faint moans slipping out of her as I enjoy myself, licking and sucking with unrelenting focus until my face drips with her wetness. I grip the material of my jersey with both fists, holding it up while I devour her.

"Oh god, there. Please, I—I'm—"

Maya breaks off with a hazy cry, her body trembling with her orgasm. I don't stop, determined to extend her pleasure. Her fingers scrabble across my shoulders trying to direct me up.

I continue lapping at her pussy because I'm addicted to the sounds she makes when she comes. It's not until I have her shuddering for me again that I finally move, covering her body with mine.

"Taste it," I mutter against her lips before I kiss her.

She sucks on my tongue when I sweep it into her mouth, making my grasp on her tighten. I grind my cock against her. She gasps when it rubs her clit.

The sensation is addictive. The slickness of her folds coats my shaft the more I glide the tip between them until the head pushes inside her.

Both of us groan. Fuck, she feels amazing. I want to keep going, desperate with the need to slam inside her and fill her pussy with my entire length without any barriers.

Tearing away from her is damn near impossible. I fumble through the drawer of my nightstand, but she pulls me back to her with an insistent tug and the most irresistible pleading noise.

I settle over her again, bracing my arms on either side of her body. She meets my eyes and bites her lip.

"Don't," she whispers.

My heart drums. "Don't what?"

Maya wraps her legs around me and tilts her hips to rub against my cock. Air punches out of me in a rush as the tip enters her again. It penetrates deeper as she closes her eyes and encourages me to move with her heels pressing against my ass.

"Oh, shit, Maya," I mutter hoarsely.

"Don't put a condom on. I don't want anything between us. I want to feel you." Her breath hitches with a strangled sound of pleasure as she keeps moving to take more of me. "Just like this."

My stomach clenches with desire and I have to lock every muscle to withstand the growing urge to fuck her senseless. Her wishes mirror my own and the fragile thread of my control is about to snap.

I drop my forehead against hers, swallowing hard. "Are you sure? I'm tested for everything regularly for the team, but I've never slept with anyone without one."

"Yes. I'm on birth control. And even if I wasn't... I'd still want this. I need to feel you, Easton."

My mouth crashes against hers in a fiery kiss. With a growl, I draw my hips back and drive into her with a sharp thrust, swallowing her cries as I fuck her raw.

Her pussy squeezes me like it doesn't want my dick to leave. It's hot, tight perfection. Too perfect.

With a grunt, I freeze with my cock buried inside her, trying to catch my breath while I concentrate on *not coming*.

"Don't stop," she begs.

"Fuck," I grit through my teeth when she clenches around me.

I capture her lips, then flip us to put her on top. God, she looks sexy straddling me like this. I gather the jersey in my grip, holding it up to see her pussy stretched around my cock. Jesus, that's a nice fucking sight.

"You look damn good sitting on my cock, baby."

She goes still for a moment, staring at me like she's seeing me for the first time. I caress her thigh soothingly.

"What is it?"

"Nothing. It's just... I've never done it this way before. With me on top."

The corner of my mouth lifts. "No? Then I get to show you how fucking amazing it is while I lay back with this excellent view."

She looks down at herself, splaying a hand over the softness of her stomach on display. Typically she's confident, but the moment of vulnerability makes something fierce and protective tug in my chest. I capture her wrist and bring her hand to my lips to kiss.

"You're beautiful, Maya. Every damn inch of you." The tightness in my chest loosens when she relaxes. "Now chase what feels good."

It takes her a minute of trying different angles, first circling her hips, then grinding back and forth. When she does find the sweet spot for what she needs, I know it immediately from the sigh that slips out of her.

She's stunning riding my cock.

I love that she loses herself in her pleasure now that she's found the motion she likes. Her eyes close and her head tips back with a little moan as she dictates the pace.

Shit, she still feels way too damn good. The fire in my veins builds again, taking me closer and closer to exploding. I'm fighting for my life trying to make this last, holding off as long as I can so she comes first. I've never struggled like this before.

With a groan, I knead her hips. "If you keep that up, I'm not going to last."

Maya smirks, planting her hands on my chest for balance as she rides me faster.

"You're the one that put me on top. This is for *me*, so you'll just have to take it."

Another wrecked noise tears from me. I love it when she's confident like this, it's so fucking sexy. I urge her on, grip flexing on her hips.

Her lids grow heavy and her mouth parts as she stares at the strained expression melting from my face because I can't hold it off any longer. My cock throbs and the orgasm that rips through me leaves me lightheaded.

"Oh!" She gasps, hips still moving as my come fills her.

"Fuck, I'm sorry, baby," I breathe raggedly.

"I'm not," she manages. "I—ah!"

Her thighs clench and her pussy flutters around me. She sighs in satisfaction, riding out her orgasm with languid movements as she grinds on my cock.

I can make her come harder than that.

Grabbing her waist, I curl up for leverage, thrusting to keep hitting the spot that makes her gasp. It's muffled against my mouth when I press it to hers.

My hands roam her body as we kiss. I fight my softening cock, fucking her as long as I can before I flip her onto her back. Moving between her legs and tugging them over my shoulders, my mouth covers her pussy with a groan.

I taste both of us.

Despite coming moments ago, heat sears through my veins from it, and from the sexy fucking noises she makes while I devour her.

Her hands sink into my hair, gripping to hold me in place swirling my tongue over her clit. "You're going to make me come again."

"That's the idea."

My fingers dig into her hips and my mouth hovers over her glistening pussy. I look up the length of her body, pinning her with my gaze. A shiver racks her body from my breath ghosting across her sensitive folds.

"We're not stopping until I make you scream my name louder than you did at the game. Ready to lose your voice, baby?"

She pushes out a breath, nodding. I put my mouth back where it belongs and worship her body.

Sucking two fingers to wet them, I sink them inside her, fucking her slowly. It lights up a primal side of me knowing I'm pushing my come back inside her pussy.

Maya tangles her fists in the sheets, rocking her hips against my face with abandon. Then she tenses with a shattered cry.

"That's it," I croon. "I've got you."

The sounds she makes when she comes are better than anything I've ever heard in my life.

I'm rock hard again, cock throbbing. She makes me so wild.

"Fuck," I rasp. "I need you again."

I'm a man possessed when I reposition myself and push inside her with one long stroke. Her back bows and her mouth drops open, nails scratching rough lines down my back. My vision goes hazy for a second as lust courses through me.

"Yes," she cries.

"Goddamn, your pussy squeezes my cock so good."

"More. I need more."

"More? You want fast?" I pick up the pace, grinning at her strangled gasp, then slow back down with steady, sharp thrusts. "Or hard?"

"Hard," she whimpers. "Fuck me harder."

Gritting my teeth, I give her what she needs. Each time I slam into her, her tits bounce as it jolts her body up the mattress.

My name flies from her lips with a desperate cry. She's close again, her body trembling. I catch her hands, pinning them beside her head and claim her mouth.

When she comes, my hips stutter. Her pussy grips me like a vice.

My vision blacks out for a moment as I bury my cock inside her, shuddering with the force of my orgasm.

I do my best not to collapse on her like an asshole, managing to keep myself braced on one arm. I caress her with gentle touches, cupping her face. She loops her fingers around my wrist, rubbing her cheek against my palm.

We remain like that until we both catch our breath, exchanging lazy kisses with no purpose other than keeping the sense of connection going.

"You're incredible," I say against her lips.

"Back at you, lady killer. That was—" She pushes out an amused breath, running her fingers through her tangled hair. "Yeah, I think it's safe to say you're good at that."

I chuckle. "It's okay, sweetheart. You can admit I'm the best you've ever had."

"There's that cocky ego."

With a sly smirk, she covers my face with both hands. I kiss her palms.

She traces my jaw and a flush creeps up her neck. "Should we go back downstairs? If they somehow didn't hear us, there's no way they haven't guessed what we're doing."

"No doubt."

She socks me in the arm. I drop against her, burying my laughter in the crook of her neck.

"Sorry, sorry." I get myself under control, trailing kisses up her throat. "We're a house full of hockey players."

"Water is wet, you mean," she sasses.

"Yeah, basically." Sitting up, I scoop her into my arms and carry her to the bathroom. "Anyway, I don't want to go back downstairs."

"Oh? What are we doing instead? Because I think I'm tapped out."

I pause at the small grimace that flickers across her face, stomach dropping. "Did I hurt you?"

"No, I think I'm just a little sore."

I kiss her temple. "Then let me take care of you."

Setting her on the counter, I turn on the shower and get a washcloth. When the water feels warm enough, I soak the cloth and nudge her legs apart to gently clean her.

"I wish I had a tub for you to soak in, but it's too small in here."

She drags her teeth over her lips. "It's okay. This is nice. No one's ever done this for me before."

I brush my mouth over her cheek, then rinse the rag and wet it again to hold it between her legs while I get us towels. Once I return, I lift the hem of the hockey sweater to pull it over her head.

When I have it off, I pause. A rough noise vibrates in my chest at the sight of the fresh hickeys dotting her neck and collar bone. Stepping close, I brush her cheek with my thumb.

"Come on."

Taking her hand, I help her down from the counter and follow her into the shower. It's a tight fit, but I kind of like that. Water cascades over our bodies as they press together and steam envelops us.

She closes her eyes, expression blissful while I take my time gliding soapy hands over her body, kneading her muscles until she's fully relaxed.

This is my first time truly washing someone I'm showering with. It's far more intimate than sharing the space because of sex or two people washing themselves.

My arms lock around her waist and I press a reverent kiss to the top of her head. She leans against me with a soft sigh while I care for her.

A profound sense of contentment settles over me and I know without a doubt she's it for me. There's no one else who could ever fit as perfectly with me as she does.

TWENTY-THREE
MAYA

On the first day back at campus in January after winter break, I'm curled up on the couch with half a bag of potato chips and some left-over chocolate chips I found in the freezer, watching a Korean romcom series Hana recommended.

When another wave of cramps hits, I wrap my comforter tighter around me.

Reagan commiserated with me for a while before she had to leave for class. We huddled together beneath a cocoon of blankets while watching the first episode. Now I'm starting the third one, but things are about to get dire because my snacks are running low.

I grab my phone, ready to say fuck it and order delivery so I don't have to go out. A knock at the door interrupts me. Sighing, I leave the comfort of my blanket to answer it.

Easton leans against the frame with his forearm when I open the door. He holds up a packed grocery bag.

"Hi," I stammer in surprise.

He slips past me, dropping a quick kiss on my lips before taking his stuff to the kitchen island. I close the door and watch from the other side as he unloads everything.

"I wasn't sure what you were in the mood for, so I figured it was best to cover the bases. Salty, sweet, savory." He shakes the box of nuggets before setting them on the counter. "And I brought this heating pad from the house."

Tears prick my eyes. Stupid hormones.

"You got me all this?"

He gives me a soft smile. "You said you had your period and were dying from cramps. Of course I'm going to take care of my girl."

A lump forms in my throat. "I expected not to see you for a few days when I texted you that. Guys typically run in fear of a girl on her period."

He stops unloading the snacks in the kitchen and gives me an insulted look. "I'm not afraid of blood." Stalking around the island, he backs me against it, trapping me between his arms. "And it doesn't make me want to be around you or have you any less. I don't care if you're on your period, because I find you hot as fuck when you're all done up shaking your sexy ass on the bar and when you're wearing those cute little fuzzy socks. You make me want to earn my red wings with you over and over again. Okay?"

"O-okay."

He takes me by the waist, eyeing me up and down with a smirk that makes my insides twist pleasantly. "Want me to go down on you? Lay down on the couch. I'll suck on your clit and finger you while you watch your show."

I rub my forehead, torn between the arousal pulsing through me and the urge to sit around in a burrito blanket all day. "No, you don't have to."

Guiding me back to the couch, he sits me down and plugs in the heating pad. I set the lukewarm hot water bottle I was using on the coffee table, then spread the pad across my abdomen with a relieved sigh as the heat starts to kick in.

"Thank you," I mumble.

"I told you, Maya. You need me? I'm there." He sits down with me, wrapping the blanket around both of us. "I have something else, too."

"A magic way to scoop out my uterus?"

He chuckles. "No."

I wave a hand. "Sorry. I'm just being dramatic. I hate suffering through cramps every month."

"Let it all out. Rage as much as you want, baby. I'm here for anything you need." He kisses my temple and rubs my back.

I shift to curl against his side. "This. I just need this."

"Me too. Missed you over break."

My face presses into his neck. "I missed you, too." A small laugh slips out of me. "I thought Ryan was going to catch us every time you called me."

"Worth it."

Any moment I wasn't with Grandpa and Easton wasn't playing hockey or with his family, we talked. He called almost every night of winter break. Sometimes it was over Facetime with a wicked gleam in his eye, lighting me up with desire from his dirty mouth. Other times it was just because he wanted to hear my voice while we fell asleep.

I draw in a deep breath, closing my eyes at his calming scent. It feels good to be back in his arms.

"Here, this is what I got you." He takes my hand and slips something into it. "I've noticed you like to move around when you get anxious or stressed. I went to this holiday market with my mom on Christmas Eve and saw these at a stall. I thought of you—thought that you might like them."

The gold ring loops in a coil to create three rings with a set of matching beads that can be spun or moved freely around the loops. I slide it on my thumb, tracing the beads. It's soothing to roll them.

My heart climbs into my throat at his thoughtfulness. "Easton. This is..."

"Is it okay?"

I give him a soft smile. "Yes. I love it."

His arms loop around me, kneading the aches out of my lower back. I groan pitifully in appreciation.

"Did you spoil all the girls with this treatment? You're being the perfect boyfriend. If anyone finds out, I'm going to have to fight to keep you."

He scoffs, his embrace tightening. "No. This is all for you and only you. Forget the guy you might've heard about or think I was before we met, because I'm not him anymore. The only thing I am now is yours."

I roll my lips between my teeth and a tender glow fills my chest. "Thank you."

"What are we watching?"

"Don't you have class today?"

"It's a short one just to go over the syllabus. I'll get the notes from Cam and email the professor later. I'd rather stay here with you."

"What about practice?"

"We had practice early this morning. I skipped weight training when I saw your text, but I can make it up later." He tugs me back against him. "Now stop worrying that pretty little head about me."

I huff, battling a smile. "You really want to hang out all day and watch a romcom with me?"

He sighs in exasperation, tipping my chin up to meet my eyes. "Baby, I don't know how to be any clearer. Every second spent with you is my favorite. Stop trying to put yourself last when you're number one for me."

It's difficult to breathe for a moment, my cycle making me sensitive to getting emotional over something as simple as my boyfriend wanting to be here with me while I feel gross.

He drops a kiss on my forehead. "Catch me up on the show's plot."

I give him a rundown of the characters, gaining enthusiasm as I go on. His smile is full of affection at my animated explanation while I talk with my hands.

We put on the next episode and contentment washes over me. He gets as sucked into the show as I am, both of us gasping when drama unfolds to keep the two love interests apart. When the episode ends on an epic cliffhanger, we both scramble for the remote to tell Netflix we're still watching.

He beats me to it, starting the next episode.

"If they don't end up together by the end of this, I'm gonna be so pissed," he mutters.

"Right? They're so perfect for each other."

The show puts me through the wringer, taking my emotions on a rollercoaster ride. When the couple has the slightest brush of their hands, I clutch at Easton, feet kicking with excitement.

"Oh my god, look! It's happening!"

He shakes his head. "Nah, they're gonna blue ball us some more. Watch. I bet they get interrupted."

I slump against him when he turns out to be right. He chuckles, clasping my chin with his fingers to angle my head for a kiss.

"They might have to suffer through a slow burn, but we can do this whenever we want."

My face splits into a brilliant smile. I get the remote to rewind the part we missed so we can read the subtitles.

"Oh, damn. We watched three episodes already?"

"It's addictive," he admits.

I smirk, reaching for the snacks he brought me. "Hana warned I would put it on and not stop until I finished watching it. Which is exactly how I wanted my day to go with a nice veg out."

"I honestly can't remember the last time I've had a day of doing nothing."

"We're practicing self-care and resting. It's good for you."

"You're good for me," he counters.

It amazes me how happy I am with him. And if I hadn't let my walls down for him, I would've ruined this because of my fear of going through another awful heartbreak. I'm glad he never stopped chasing me until I could learn to let him in.

Easton would never treat me the way Johnny did.

I want him to know I trust him. To do that, I need to tell him everything.

Instead of starting the episode again, I pause the show and sit up. He gives me his attention immediately.

Reagan's the only one I've ever talked to about this, but something loosens inside my chest once I have the urge to share it with him.

"You remember the night we thought there was a break in at the end of last semester?"

He grunts. "You report that asshole to campus security, right?"

"Yes. They have his plates and won't allow him back on campus."

"Good." The tension ebbs from him and he caresses my spine. "I feel better knowing you're safe from him."

I sigh. "He's a total egotistical dickhead who's obsessed with himself, but I wasn't in danger. He hasn't tried to contact me again."

"Doesn't make me want to make sure you're protected any less."

I toy with the ring he gave me, nudging the balls along the loop.

"Johnny's the one who made me hate hockey players. I wanted nothing to do with any of them ever again after we broke up."

Easton lifts my chin with a crooked finger. His jaw is set, eyes blazing fiercely.

"He hurt you, didn't he? What did he do to you?"

I swallow, gathering my courage. "At first, nothing. Johnny had a big personality, and since I was close with Ryan in high school we were around each other a lot. At the end of their season in mine and Ryan's sophomore year, he came onto me at a party. I thought it was cool an upperclassmen was flirting with me."

The memory makes me frown. Looking back, I now have the clarity to see how much he flirted with other girls at the same party. I was simply the first one to say yes when he wanted me to go with him.

Frustration at my naivety burns in my chest. I rub at it, flashing Easton a thin smile when he soothes me with his own touches while he listens.

"I guess he knew my brother wouldn't stand for one of his teammates sleeping me then ditching me, so he asked me out. It seemed fine enough through the summer. I mean, other than the fact he would pressure me into sex and never cared if I came or not." A dry laugh leaves me and he narrows his eyes in disapproval. "I don't know if it was happening during the off season, but probably when it started back up, especially when the team traveled for away games."

Easton's brows wrinkle. "If what was happening?"

I give him a resigned look, aware that he's already guessed by his brittle tone.

"Cheating on me. We dated all through his senior year and long distance his first year at Elmwood, but it wasn't until I was touring colleges that I caught him."

Easton goes still, breathing heavily. He clears his throat and twines our fingers together.

"Sorry. Go on," he says gruffly.

I squeeze his hand, grateful for his fixation with tracing patterns on the inside of my wrist as I go on.

"I was such an idiot. I thought it would be cute to surprise him, so

I showed up for the tour early. When I found him, he was screwing a sorority girl."

"You weren't," he grumbles. "He was the fucking idiot."

"Well, yeah, I know that now. In the moment, I was a wreck. The betrayal cut me deep, but that wasn't the worst of it. He was consumed by the glory of being a hockey player and the attention that brought him. He made me believe the entire team knew he was cheating on me regularly the entire time we dated." I close my eyes. "Even Ryan. So I didn't have the guts to tell him. I was too afraid to know if he knew the truth or not."

A growl tears from Easton, but he holds my hand gently. He works his jaw, scrubbing a hand over his mouth.

"I think if you told your brother, he would've killed this guy. There's no way anyone would be able to play alongside a teammate that did that."

My shoulder lifts. "Johnny was a champion gaslighter to the end, even as I broke up with him."

I sigh. It feels great to get this out, but it does make the pain of his betrayal resurface.

"I hated what he did to me. That he lied and twisted my emotions around to suit his narrative like he was *owed* the chance to get with other girls whenever he wanted."

My voice wavers. I pause for a moment to collect myself, throat sore with tightness to keep myself from falling apart.

"And because I was so torn up over the thought of being around him, I stayed away from hockey, which I loved before he did a number on me. After that, I drifted from Ryan and I couldn't stomach going to a game." I chew the corner of my lip. "I didn't want to give myself over to any kind of serious relationship again."

He remains quiet through the rest of my story other than the dangerous rumbles of outrage and a hard glint in his eyes. His jaw clenches, a muscle jumping in his cheek, and he flexes his fist.

"If I ever catch him alone, I'm making him pay for that," he grits through his teeth.

My breath hitches. His fierce protectiveness is tinged with the promise of violence. It shouldn't turn me on so much, but I can't help the way it makes my heart race with excitement.

This is what always attracted me to hockey players in the first place. Their intensity. Their wild nature. Their need to fight for what's theirs.

It wasn't like this with Johnny. He only had an endless amount of arrogance. The only person he'll ever love is himself.

"I'm the one who dumped him, so at least I have that to be proud of. I wish I'd recognized what was happening sooner, or never dated him at all. After him, I didn't want anything to do with guys like him, so I took the safest routes."

His angry expression softens. "You didn't want to get burned again. It makes sense. I'm sorry you went through that and felt like you couldn't let your guard down around people."

I nod and swipe beneath my eyes. "I shouldn't have told you while I'm on my period. I always get all weepy over the littlest things."

He gently bats my hand away to catch my tears with his thumb. "I'm glad you told me. I want to know everything about you. The good things and the bad. You can always lean on me."

Heart in my throat, I press my lips to his in a soft kiss.

"Now let me erase all the ways he wronged my girl." His forehead presses to mine and he holds the back of my neck, squeezing to drive his point home. "Because I will never let him or anyone else hurt you again."

The kiss he gives me starts out sweet and gentle. It only lasts for a few moments before I want more. Warmth spreads through me as I swing a leg over his lap and wrap my arms around his neck.

His cock hardens the more I grind against it. He eats up the tiny sounds I make, holding my ass in a firm grip to encourage me to rub against him until I stiffen, pleasure erupting in my core.

"That's it, sweetheart," he says against my lips. "Did that feel good?"

Releasing a shaking breath, I nod. My hips continue rocking, savoring the delicious sensation of the thick ridge pressed against my pussy. His jeans and my thin leggings are the only barrier between us.

He slides a hand up my back. "When does your roommate get back?"

"Not until later. We have time."

"Go get yourself ready for me. Then come right back here."

The rough, commanding tone sparks an intense pulse of arousal that takes a long moment to ebb away. I start to get up, but he slips his fingers in my hair and kisses me hard before he lets me go.

I take care of what I need to in the bathroom, then strip down to just his big Heston University t-shirt I've claimed as my own to sleep in.

When I return to the living room, he's put a towel on the couch where he sits. His shirt is off and he strokes the huge bulge in his boxers without hurry. He admires me with hooded eyes, patting his thigh.

My nipples harden and his mouth tugs into a slow, smug grin. I lick my lips, padding closer.

"Are you sure?" I really want him to say yes, body thrumming with desire now that I'm all worked up. "We're probably going to make a mess if we do this."

He grasps my wrist and jerks me onto his lap sideways. "I'm not afraid to get dirty or make a mess with you. I just want to make you feel good. Let me take care of you, Maya."

I shiver at the drag of his fingertips moving up my leg to tuck between my thighs. He nudges them apart and strokes my folds with a light touch until I push against him, legs falling open.

He hums, giving me more pressure. "You want to come, baby?"

"Yes."

"Turn all the way around for me."

Easton helps me twist around so I'm straddling him in reverse, my back resting against his chest. I bite my lip, feeling oddly on display in a way that makes my insides coil sensuously.

He pulls the shirt up and his other hand delves between my legs, fingers spreading me. A dizzying exhale rushes out of me when he slips a finger inside while grinding the heel of his palm against my clit.

I tip my head back on his shoulder with a bitten off cry as he adds another and plunges them deep inside to tease the spot that makes me gasp. He toys with my nipple, plucking it with the same pace as his fingers fucking me.

My entire body aches with arousal that builds and builds, finally snapping with an orgasm that makes my thighs tremble.

He takes his time fingering me while kissing my neck. I don't know how long it goes on for, all I know is boundless pleasure from him playing with me.

"Have you had enough?" he asks after what seems like ages.

"More," I plead. "Feels so good."

"Yeah? You need my cock to fill you up."

I don't have to answer. He knows how much I want him by the way my pussy squeezes his fingers.

"Kneel up."

He keeps one hand on my hip to hold me steady while he works his boxers off. My mouth drops open when I finally sink down and feel his cock stretching me until I'm completely full of him.

Somehow it's even better like this than it is when I'm not on my period, my nerve endings lit up, more sensitive to everything.

"How does that feel?" His lips map my throat and he squeezes my breasts while he lets me adjust to the size of him. "Is that what you need, Maya?"

"Yes." I gasp at the deep angle when he scoots down slightly to fuck me in a slow, steady pace. "Oh, god, that's so—"

"I know, baby. Just relax for me. I've got you."

One of his hands drops down, touching where our bodies are joined before he presses against my clit, rubbing in the same gentle pace as before to build me up to an epic release. The long time he spent leisurely playing with my pussy has me balancing on the edge of another orgasm within moments, keeping me floating in ecstasy that's even more incredible with his cock inside me.

It's less about his desires. He's one hundred percent focused on me, groaning in enjoyment from every ounce of pleasure he wrings from me with the same unwavering drive he has when he's playing hockey.

"Fuck, look at you, Maya. You're so perfect. A gorgeous mess for me."

I let go, unable to think of anything but the sensual tingles that build in my core each time his cock glides into me in long strokes to make me feel every inch. I no longer care about bleeding on him or anything outside of being fucked into oblivion.

Any sense of time becomes lost to me. All I know is the bliss of slipping from one orgasm into the next while Easton kisses my skin, murmuring praise and encouragement when he feels me clamping on him each time I come.

When I've lost track of how many times he's pushed me over the edge, he tenses with a rough groan.

His arms lock around me and he buries a curse against my neck. The pulse of his cock deep inside as his come floods my pussy makes me moan. I fall back against his chest, both of us panting and worn out.

I'm too out of it, drifting in the aftershocks of overstimulation. He takes care of cleaning both of us up in the shower and rinses the towel. I stop him when he tries to figure out how to insert a tampon, laughing sleepily at his attempts.

When we're done, he makes me drink a bottle of water while he cooks us dinner now that it's dark out, then holds me in his arms on the couch while we watch the final two episodes of the show.

I feel weightless in the best way, like I don't have to worry about anything because no matter what I have him there to support me. For the first time since I caught my ex cheating on me, I truly feel like I can move on from it.

I thought I never wanted to fall for another hockey player as a way to keep my heart safe, but now I know it's okay. Even if I didn't want this, it's too late. He has my heart and I know he'll do everything to cherish it.

Snuggling closer to Easton, a soft smile breaks free when his embrace cinches tighter to envelop me in his warm, loving comfort.

TWENTY-FOUR
MAYA

When the first month of the semester comes to an end, Reagan declares we need a girls' night. We're getting ready to go out with Hana at the apartment on Thursday, music blasting while we get sidetracked with an impromptu fashion show that leaves us all cracking up.

"Oh my god, yes," Reagan says from her seat on my bed. "Hana, you have to wear that."

"Really?" Hana splays her hands over her flat, toned stomach. "I've worn crop tops for dance costumes, but I've never had the confidence to rock it for a regular outfit. I don't have any boobs to fill it out with like you both do."

"Make tonight the night, because you look so hot in that," I say. "Look."

I take her by the shoulders and put her in front of the mirror hanging on the back of my door. The black crop is form fitting with three cut outs across the chest. Subtle sparkles in the material catch the light.

"We'll do your hair like this and do a cat eye. I have a shadow palette of pinks and reds that'll look great on you." I mess with her hair and her eyes light up. "Yeah?"

"Yes. Reagan, hand me those high-waisted pants."

While we're putting the finishing touches on our outfits, I text Easton photos of how I look.

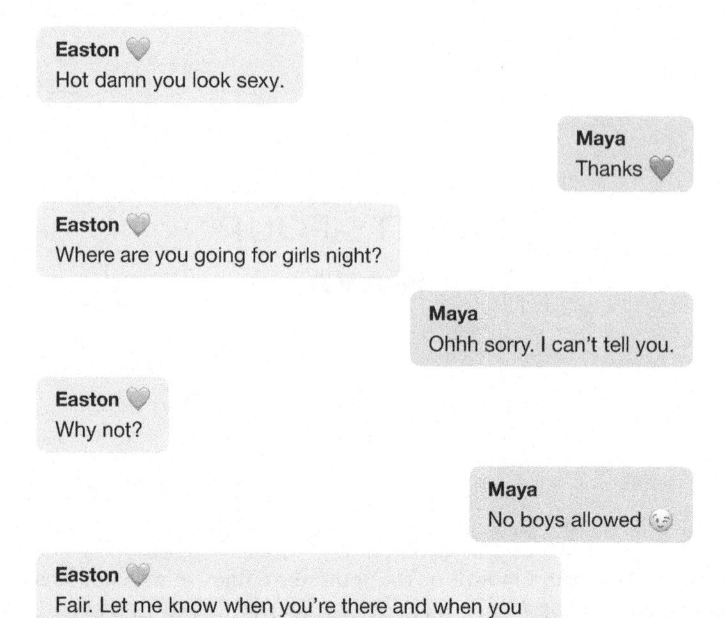

My teeth scrape my lip, but I can't hold a smile back.

"Aww, look at her. She's so in love," Reagan teases. "Don't even pretend you're not texting your boyfriend. That's the way your face looks every time you talk to him."

My mouth pops open and I hold my phone against my chest. "I—Okay, fine. Easton said to have fun."

"He's so sweet," Hana says.

Reagan smirks. "Did he also tell you that you look sexy in that dress?"

I catch her eye in the mirror while I apply a bold red lipstick. "Yes. Are we ready?"

"Yup. I'll order our Uber," Reagan says. "Let's go shake our asses off until our feet go numb."

"Hell yeah," I say with a laugh.

* * *

The nightclub is in a neighboring town. It's the only one nearby with a decent dancing space and a good DJ. It's crowded and lively for a Thursday when we arrive.

"Okay, girls," Reagan announces as we survey the room. "Let's go break some hearts and make some damn good memories."

She takes mine and Hana's hands and leads us to the dance floor. We find an open spot to fill, moving to the music. I get into it, gliding my hands down my sides and winding my body.

Reagan holds up her phone and we all squeeze together to take selfies.

When the next song starts, Hana busts out some techniques that blow us away. Reagan and I become her hype girls and she draws a small crowd until the song is over. She grins and bows to the applause from people around us.

We move back into a tight circle for the three of us. A short girl with red hair almost trips when she passes our spot. Hana grabs her arm before she falls, pulling her into our dance circle.

"Thanks. Someone spilled a drink and I slipped," she says.

"No problem. Oh, wait," Hana says. "I know you, right? Do you go to Heston?"

"I do! I'm Corinne."

"I've seen you around the arts buildings," Hana says. "I'm studying dance."

"Awesome. You girls go to Heston, too?" Corinne asks me and Reagan.

"Psych major with a minor in physical therapy," I say.

"Music and production," Reagan answers.

"Well, I'm glad I tripped near you," Corinne says.

"Did you come out alone?" Hana asks.

Corinne shakes her head. "No, but I think the people I came with ditched me. They're out on a mission to hunt some good dick."

Reagan smirks. "A fair and noble endeavor. But shitty of them to bail on you."

Corinne shrugs. "It's cool. I don't mind. I'll call an Uber when I'm ready to go back to campus."

"Stay with us. We'll give you a ride when we leave. We're here for a girls' night," I say. "We have a no girl left behind policy."

She grins. "Perfect."

Within minutes of meeting, we're enjoying ourselves as we dance. Corinne fits right in like she's always been our friend.

We're absorbed in the next song when two guys make moves to get closer. They start off at the edge of our circle until they catch our eye. Reagan exchanges a look with me and shrugs.

"Ladies," one guy says. "You look like you're having a good time. Can we get in on that?"

For the first song, they just dance with us. It's okay, until the second guy takes Corinne by the hips and doesn't let up until she stomps on his foot.

"Don't wear out your welcome," she warns. "I might be short, but I've got heels on that I'm not afraid to use on your balls if you try that shit again."

He backs up, arms raised in surrender. "It's cool, I didn't mean to come on too strong. You were giving me those eyes that said you wanted to feel this."

I pull a face when he reaches down to squeeze his junk. His smug expression falters when he looks beyond my shoulder. Tapping his friend on the shoulder, both of them back away.

"Are you okay?" I ask Corinne.

"Yeah. Nothing we couldn't handle. They moved on easily enough."

"Maybe that's why." Reagan points and I turn around.

A familiar face appears through the dancing crowd.

Easton glares at the guys who tried to hit on us before making his way to me. His protective expression melts into adoration when his eyes roam over me.

"Wow. The photo was one thing, but the real deal is something else."

"What are you doing here?" I'm surprised, but not mad to see my boyfriend.

His touch skims down my bare arms to capture my wrists in a gentle hold. He cocks his head, brows lifting.

"It wasn't difficult to figure out. This is the only place people go out when they want a more lively scene than The Landmark has to offer."

"Are you crashing girls' night?" Reagan pokes Easton's arm. "No hockey players allowed."

He holds up his hands. "I'm not here to crash. I just came as DD so you don't have to wait for a ride back. You can let loose and enjoy girls' night. I've got your back." The corner of his mouth quirks up and he winks at me. "I'm an excellent bodyguard."

I bite the corner of my lip, touched he came just to watch over us. "I'm good with that."

Reagan nods. "Okay, same. You can stay. Damn it, why do you have to be such a great guy, Easton?"

He chuckles and points to the bar. "I'll keep an eye out from over there. Don't accept drinks from anyone you don't know or haven't seen poured yourself."

I sway into him, my chest expanding with affection. "Thank you."

He kisses the top of my head. "Anything for my girl."

"You guys know the hockey team?" Corinne asks when he navigates to the bar.

"He's Maya's boyfriend," Hana answers.

"Oh, shit. Nice." She holds out her fist and I bump mine against it. "Is it true the players fuck like animals? Seems like they would with all that raw energy during the games."

Reagan and I snort, leaning heavily on each other for support. I've told her about what it's like with Easton because we tell each other just about everything.

"I can't speak for all hockey players, but, uh, yes?" I stammer. "Can't complain, ten out of ten."

"More like twenty out of ten at least after what you told me," Reagan says.

The four of us break into giggles, then the song changes. Corinne and I hold our arms in the air.

She bounces on the balls of her feet. "Oh, oh! Here we go."

"Let's do it," I say with a wide grin.

Hana backs her ass up against Reagan and Corinne pairs off with me. We belt the lyrics of the song while we dance our hearts out. I sink low, waving my hands along Corinne's petite frame while she rolls her body, then pop back up with my arms twisting above my head.

When the song ends, we're out of breath and laughing. I catch

Easton's eyes on me. He's watching with a mix of amusement and desire that makes me feel amazing. It reminds me of the way we met.

Another song starts up that gets us just as hyped, and we lose ourselves to having the best night.

TWENTY-FIVE
EASTON

THE GIRLS ARE HAVING the time of their lives. Seeing Maya smiling and laughing while she dances with her friends makes me want to be by her side. It's a challenge to remain at the bar watching over them to guard them from douchebags and creeps, but I lean on my elbows and stay rooted to my spot.

They draw attention from guys. How could they not? They're beautiful and radiate confidence with their dancing.

There are a few times I have to get up, giving anyone that looks at Maya and her friends too long a glare that says if they touch her, they'll answer to me.

When I'm satisfied they're safe for the moment, I turn back to the bar for a refill on my water. The bartender is chatting with me when I spot someone coming up to order a drink in my peripheral vision.

The blood in my veins rages to life in a violent boil at the sight of *Wiener*. What the hell is he doing here? It's almost two hours from Elmwood.

That's far to go for a night out, and too close to Heston Lake for my comfort after the shit he pulled a couple of months ago.

He's with a girl and he's spotted Maya.

If he looks at her again, we're going to have a huge fucking problem.

The conversation with Maya about how things ended between

them before she started college runs through my head. My hand balls into a fist and I temper the urge to go over there and knock him the fuck out.

Swallowing hard, I concentrate on the memory of Dad's voice to calm down. I don't need an assault charge on my record or I can kiss my NHL dreams goodbye.

I eye his arm. It's no longer in a thick cast, now resting against his chest in a sling. Seems like he's playing it up for the girl he's here with.

There's an open tab on my phone's browser that I refresh every day to check if he's still benched with his injury.

If this asshole wasn't still on the IR list, I'd wipe the ice with him. The severe penalty for fighting in an NCAA game and any game suspensions after would be worth it to make him pay for everything he's done to Maya.

Anger burns through my veins when he says something to his date after their drinks are delivered, then weaves through the dance floor in Maya's direction.

Oh, hell no.

I push off the bar and stalk after him with purposeful strides. Just before he reaches her and her friends, I shoulder him aside.

Maya stops dancing, staring warily at her ex. Reagan shifts closer to her with a pissed off expression and holds her hand.

"Boyfriend," the redhead I haven't met greets.

"Uh, friend?" I return.

She grins and gives me a thumbs up.

Maya tears her attention from Wiener. "Sorry, I should've said earlier. Corinne, Easton. Easton, this is Corinne."

Wiener clears his throat. Maya rolls her eyes, flapping a hand at him.

"That's Johnny. He's just leaving, right?" There's a hard edge to her voice that makes me proud.

He smirks. "Relax, I only came over to say hi when I saw you were here." He points to the bar where the girl he left sits. "I'm on a date."

"Congratulations."

When he doesn't immediately move on, I pull Maya into my

arms and give her a quick kiss. "Have a good time. You know where I am if you need me." Turning on my heel, I level Wiener with a glare. "Follow me, or I'll drag you there."

He narrows his eyes. "You're the guy who answered her phone. Shit, you were at that bar in Heston Lake, too. The guy she left with."

"Yeah, I'm her boyfriend," I grit out.

Wiener tucks his good hand in his pockets and steps past me. He looks back at Maya and I clench my jaw as a wave of possessiveness crashes over me. He will *never* touch her again.

I fist the collar of his shirt and force him to walk away. Once we're back at the bar a few spots down from his date, I don't release him right away, leaning closer.

"It's my name she screams. At games and all night long."

He lurches out of my grasp. "That's because she's nothing more than a nasty little puck slut. Does she still suck cock like shit?"

My vision swims and I need to breathe harshly for a moment to control myself so I don't kill him on the spot. My hands flex and I jerk my head.

"You're something else, Wiener."

He frowns. "It's Werner."

"No, I had it right, dickhead." I get in his face. "I'm only going to say this once, so listen closely because I'm dead fucking serious."

He leans against the bar with a punchable arrogant expression, gesturing for me to go on. I grab his sling and twist just enough to make my warning clear. His face pales and he tries to move back, but I won't let him.

"Never break into Maya's apartment again."

"I didn't break in, I had the key from that ugly plastic flower pot where she keeps the spare." He tries to play it smug again, but it doesn't quite land when I tighten my grip.

I'm about to deck him because I can't keep my anger in check anymore. He fucking deserves it.

Maya stops me by slipping right between us to flag down the bartender. She spares Wiener the briefest glance, flipping him off, then ignoring his existence while his gaze bores into her.

"Four waters, please!"

The anger swallowing me whole calms down. I huff out a ragged laugh, sliding an arm around her waist. She amazes me.

She downs her water first, then beams at me before giving me a sweet kiss. I try to extend it, wanting to rub it in Wiener's face. She breaks away with a sly little smirk.

Turning to him, she props her hands on her hips. "Easton's dick is bigger than yours. Oh, and I told your date everything you did to me."

He gapes, looking in the direction Maya indicates with her thumb. The girl has joined Maya's friends. All of them look our way and give Wiener the finger.

A deep laugh tears from me. I'm proud of her and so fucking in love.

"Bye forever, you pathetic asshole. Hope I never see your face again." With a bright smile, Maya leaves us.

I'm thoroughly enjoying the way his smugness has been obliterated by my girl.

I stop him before he storms off, lowering my voice seriously. "Key or not, campus security keeps logs of every car and has extensive surveillance cameras in place around the grounds. She reported the incident, and they have your plates and description." I drop my attention to his sling, a threat creeping into my tone. "Stay the fuck away from Maya."

Lip curling, he mutters under his breath and leaves the club. I don't relax, not until I know he's gone.

Blowing out a breath, I take up my post as the girls' bodyguard again.

When the girls are ready to leave two hours later, we squeeze into my car and I make sure they all get home safe.

After dropping off Wiener's date at a townhouse off-campus in Heston Lake, I take Reagan home. She makes her way into the apartment building singing the last song that was on the radio. When Hana gets out, Corinne joins her. They both take off their heels and the pair of them hook arms, leaning on each other for support while they walk gingerly up the path to their dorms.

Then it's just me and Maya in the peacefulness of my car, the music station she picked playing low in the background.

I reach across the console to tuck a hand between her thighs. "Ready to go home, baby?"

She gives me a soft smile, fighting to keep her eyes open. "Yeah. Take me home."

Easy. That's wherever she is.

TWENTY-SIX
EASTON

When Maya wakes up, she always makes a grumpy sound before opening her eyes, like it's an offense to be pulled from sleep. It's so fucking cute it makes my chest feel funny. Once she's up, she's what I'd consider a morning person, but those first moments she fights consciousness are my favorite to watch.

She's cuddled close to my side and has one leg hooked around mine. She nuzzles my arm, nose scrunching. Then she makes the little sound I love before exhaling sleepily.

"Morning," I rasp.

"Mhm," she responds, still keeping her eyes closed.

I draw her closer, arms tightening around her when she shifts to lay on top of me. My dick is already awake because it's morning and that's what it does, but with her naked body pressed against mine it throbs with another pulse of heat, growing harder.

Still not fully awake, she moves against me with torturously sensual movements, her body naturally seeking out what it needs. I groan, fingertips moving down her spine to grab a handful of her delectably thick ass.

"Keep that up and I'm going to slip it in." My mutter is rough, tinged with sleep.

"Mm, please," she murmurs.

"Fuck, Maya," I say hoarsely when she scoots down so she's straddling me to grind her pussy against my cock.

She lifts her head, eyes hooded and brimming with desire. "You woke me up from all those touches. I was dreaming your mouth was everywhere."

"It will be in a minute."

With a rumbling noise, I roll her over and slot my mouth over hers with a hungry kiss. Before things heat up further, the cat interrupts us with an affronted meow. She snickers, holding out a hand.

"Sorry, kitty. Are we bothering you?"

Kit-cat stays at the end of the bed by our feet, where she spent the night curled up until we woke her up. The cat surveys us both, meowing again before she hops to the floor.

"Ah, shit. That's her *feed me* meow," I say.

Maya grins. "You know her different sounds. I love that about animals—the ways we learn to communicate with each other."

I go for another kiss, but she pulls away with a frown.

"I still taste last night's drinks. Do you have an extra toothbrush?"

"Yes."

I rub my cock against her tempting body for another moment before I let her up. Collapsing against the pillow, I muffle a jagged sigh at the loss.

"Aren't you coming?"

My head pops up. She stands at the edge of my bed, capturing my hand. Her chin dips in a mimic of my mannerisms.

"Want to shower?"

I scramble out of bed so fast. She laughs at me when I almost trip from getting tangled in the sheets.

"I'm going to finish what you started."

"What *you* started," she sasses. "I don't think you realize how much you touch me all the time."

Kit-cat stops me in my tracks, winding around my legs.

"You want to be fed," I say. "Okay. C'mere."

Before I follow Maya to the bathroom, I let the cat into the hall. She races down the steps, acting like we don't feed her as much as she wants. Cameron nods to me with his chin, scratching at his stomach on his way out of the room we used to share.

"Morning. Can you feed the cat?"

"Yeah." Before going downstairs, he yells at the top of the steps,

"Breakfast will be ready in twenty minutes. Be downstairs fast if you want any."

Damn, that doesn't give me as much time as I want to worship my girl.

Maya's already in the shower when I come in. The thought of her smelling like me from using my stuff sends a rush of possessive satisfaction racing through me. I brush my teeth quickly and join her beneath the warm spray, running my hands over her wet, sudsy skin as my body presses against hers.

She tilts her head back. "Oh, hi."

"Hi, beautiful. Give me that."

I take the shampoo bottle from her and squirt it into my hand. Steam envelops us while I massage it into her hair, enjoying the way she sways against me with cute little blissed out moans.

"This is the life," she says.

"Keep your eyes closed." I guide her beneath the water to rinse, carefully checking there's no soap left before I tug her against me. My arms wrap around her and I drop a kiss on her head. "This is how it will always be, baby. Even when I make the pros, you're my priority. I'll take care of you no matter what."

She doesn't quite smother a surprised gasp at my serious promise, angling her head to stare at me wide-eyed. I turn her around and lean down, needing to feel my forehead resting against hers.

I can already tell what's going through her head. I've learned to read her. Her features are torn, wavering between that radiant smile I'm obsessed with and her practical side that's probably saying some shit about how it's too soon to be talking about the future when we've only been together for a short while.

But I don't need an arbitrary length of time to confirm what I already know: I love her.

"Easton..."

"You don't have to say anything. I just want you to know that I'm all in with you. This isn't just for fun while I'm in college. You're my forever."

Her throat convulses with a swallow. She nods, eyes shining.

I stiffen as she lowers to her knees without breaking eye contact. My cock appreciates the view of her plush lips parting.

"What are you doing?"

"It's my turn to take care of you."

My arm braces against the wall and a garbled curse flies out of me when she takes me into her mouth. Fuck, it's wet, hot paradise.

"Maya." With a wrecked groan, my hand cups the back of her head, fingers sliding into her wet hair. "God, you're so—"

The words die because she bobs her head, stretched lips sucking me deeper. She manages to fit most of my cock into her mouth and it's the hottest thing I've ever experienced.

My thighs tense from her gripping the base and swirling her tongue. She's bringing me right to the edge, but I don't want this to be over yet. I want to make her come.

Tightening my grip on her hair to stop her, I pull her to her feet and kiss her hard. She holds my jaw between her hands and opens for me with a wickedly sexy noise in her throat. Tearing away, I press two fingers against her lips, my eyelids growing heavy when she sucks on them.

Both of us are panting with need when I reach down, rubbing through her slippery folds before sinking inside her. She looks gorgeous, cheeks flushed, eyes closed, mouth open with a silent cry while I spend a minute fingering her.

Her hand flies down to tug insistently at my forearm. "Okay. Come on, I want to feel you."

"I've got you."

Gripping her by the thighs, I lift her. She chokes back a surprised sound, locking her legs around me when I press her back to the tiles. Capturing her gaze, I line up and drive my cock into her pussy in a long, continuous thrust.

She clamps around me, her moan echoing off the shower walls. All she can do is hold on while I fuck her with sharp strokes that hit her nice and deep.

When she throws her head back, I nuzzle into her bared throat, kissing and biting to leave my mark. My fingers dig into her and the force of my thrusts makes her body shake.

Her lashes flutter, then her eyes find mine. We're locked in a stare that kicks my heartbeat into the next gear.

It blows me away how intense every single touch and kiss is with her. Each sensation is overwhelming, blinding me to anything except her existence.

"I'm going to come," she murmurs.

Our hold on each other tightens. My mouth slams against hers when I feel her pussy fluttering with her orgasm just before I sink into her one last time, my cock throbbing in divine fucking ecstasy.

We kiss through our shared pleasure until she melts against me.

"Can I take you somewhere today?" I whisper against her lips.

"Okay. Where are we going?"

My hum is full of contentment. "It's a surprise. Not telling."

"Yet," she teases.

I grin at the word I used whenever I wanted to convince her to give me a chance. "*Yet*. Come on, let's go eat. Otherwise the animals in this house will leave us with nothing."

We finish showering and make it downstairs just in time. Maya wears my clothes so she doesn't have to go downstairs in that hot little dress I peeled off her last night.

Reeves has a dish towel draped over his shoulder and mans two pans at once on the stovetop while everyone else who's up early enough to eat is spread around the kitchen.

Madden balances plates, trying to get the utensil drawer open at the same time. Maya goes over to help him while I clap Cam on the shoulder.

"Smells great, man."

"You always say that when you're hungry," he replies with a smirk.

"Who's having coffee?" Noah counts the hands that go up with a round of jumbled responses.

"Rookie, books off the table. It's time to eat," I say.

"Okay, I just have to finish this part. My professor has been on my ass about citing my sources."

His tongue sticks out from the corner of his mouth and his face scrunches in concentration while he jots down a quote in his outline for a paper. Maya ruffles his hair on her way around the table with Madden to set it.

Theo and Hutch trail in one after the other, hair standing on end from sleep. They both mutter good morning, heading straight for the coffee pot Noah brandishes.

When we all sit down, it feels like a family meal. One that Maya fits right into.

She has no trouble fighting hungry hockey players to fill her plate with her share. I rub her back with a stupid smile on my face, pride unfurling in my chest.

"There's no room for me?" Brody stumbles in, leaning around occupied chairs to steal food.

"Grab a plate and sit with me." Hutch pats the back of the couch where he's perched.

"Here." Maya scoots her plate closer to mine and slides onto my lap.

Humming contentedly, my arm winds around her waist. I finish a sip of orange juice and kiss her shoulder.

Noah pretends to pout. "Why don't any of you sit on my lap?"

Several of the guys ball up napkins and toss them at him. He bats them away with a laugh.

After we finish breakfast, I wash the dishes with Madden's help. The others scatter through the house with the assignments they need to finish up before our next roadie to take on Elmwood for our second matchup of the season. Elijah and Cameron share the kitchen island while studying.

They all know they have to finish early to turn them in to their professors while we're away. I've got it on lock, but it's Cam who worries me. Out of all of us, he has to put the most effort into his classes.

He sinks his fingers into his hair, making it messier before he crams his worn baseball cap onto his head with a sigh.

I lean against the island next to him. "You good?"

"I'm struggling," he admits gruffly.

"You know I'm here if you need help. All of us will make sure you get through it."

"Me too," Maya says when she joins us. "What's the class?"

He pinches the bridge of his nose, rubbing his eyes. It's rough to see him so torn up when he's the team's rock. He always has our backs.

"Calculus. I tried to see if I can drop it, but apparently it's a required course for the major I picked. The other classes are full, so I'm stuck." He shakes his head and blows out a breath. "I already scrape by to maintain the GPA required to stay on the team as an active player."

"Shit," I mutter. "We need you. Holland is a decent backup, but we're not making it to Frozen Four without you."

"I know," Cam laments. "I'll make it work. I swear."

Maya frowns. "I wish I could do more for you. Math and I don't get along. Any other subject and I'm there."

He shoots her a grateful smile. "Thanks. It's okay." He checks his phone. "Actually, I need all of you to clear out. Go do your shit elsewhere."

My brows wrinkle. "Why?"

He squeezes his nape. "I've got someone coming over that agreed to help me study."

"Why are you all shifty about a tutor?"

"It's a girl," Maya guesses.

Reeves turns to her with a harassed expression. I chuckle, slipping an arm around her waist.

"Oh, that changes everything," I say. "You think she's cute, huh?"

"I—well," he stammers. "Shit. Look, she's really quiet and shy. Hockey players freak her out. She thinks we're too intense and it took a lot to convince her to help me. So I need everyone to fuck off for an hour if you want me saving goals for us."

As he talks, he strides between the kitchen and living room until the guys clear out. They put up mild complaints, but pack up their stuff and move elsewhere. Maya exchanges a glance with me, both of us bouncing our brows in amusement. He comes back to herd us away.

"Relax, we're going. We've got plans anyway," I say.

We go up to my room to get Maya's purse and my keys. I change into jeans and layer a hoodie over my t-shirt. On our way back downstairs, Reeves blocks the open door, talking to someone.

"No, it'll be just us," he says. "Not like a da—no. I need to pass this class. If I don't, I won't be able to play."

The response from his mystery tutor is too muted to hear, but his shoulders slump in relief. He moves aside. A girl with curly brown hair and tan skin bundled in a fuzzy cream coat with bear paws on the sleeves steps through the door. She pauses when she sees us on the stairs.

Cameron clears his throat. "That's Easton and his girlfriend Maya."

"Hi," Maya says in a welcoming tone.

The girl shifts closer to Cameron, as if she trusts him more in the face of the unfamiliar. "I'm Elodie. From his calc class."

"Nice to meet you. Don't mind us, we're just heading out," Maya says.

I follow her down the steps and give Cameron a supportive pat on the arm. "Good luck with studying."

When the door closes behind us, Maya hugs my arm. "She's so pretty."

I hum in agreement. "Ready to go?"

She threads her fingers with mine. "Are you going to tell me where we're going?"

"Nope. Not until we get there."

We stop at her apartment for a change of clothes. Reagan is still asleep when she pokes her head in to check on her. She sets out a fresh bottle of water for her and writes a note to say she's out with me before we go to her room.

I sit on her bed while she rummages for an outfit. "If you don't let me know what we're doing, I don't know what to wear."

"Dress warm," I advise cryptically.

She levels me with a look that's a mix of exasperation and affection, swatting me with a stray pair of leggings. Once I deem her bundled enough, we get back in the car. During the ride, I rest one hand over the steering wheel and tuck the other between her thighs, thumb brushing her jeans.

When I pull up at the Heston Lake public rink, she grins.

"We're going ice skating," she says with certainty.

I squeeze her leg. "You know how to skate, right?"

"Of course I do," she answers with an amused huff. "You think I let Ryan learn to skate by himself? As soon as he got his first pair of Bauers, I wanted them, too. I remember being so mad my dad got me figure skates instead of what Ryan had because I thought his were cooler."

"That's my girl."

Once we rent skates for her, I sit her on a bench and tie them for her before I put mine on. I squeeze her ankle.

"How's that feel?"

She wiggles her feet. "Good."

Stepping onto the ice is ingrained in my muscle memory. Maya takes a minute to find her balance, cheeks coloring as she clutches me.

"Don't laugh. I can skate, it's just been a while. I've been too busy for stuff like this."

I rub her elbows encouragingly, supporting her until she gains confidence. "I'm not in a hurry. We could spend the whole date like this if we need to. I just wanted to get you on the ice with me."

The last of the stiffness leaves her. With a slight push, she coasts right into me. My arms circle her waist as I lower my head to meet her kiss.

"I'm pretty sure for an ice skating date, you're supposed to skate," she says when we part.

"I'm good with this."

"If you want another kiss, you'll have to come and get me."

She pushes away, keeping just out of reach when I follow her.

My brows lift at the challenge. "Is that so? You know you're asking an NHL draft prospect to chase you, right?"

The prospect rankings won't be released until next month, but I've seen sports blogs talking about my plays this season. After each game we have more sports journalists wanting to talk to us. This time I know my name will be on that list.

She grins. "I dare you."

"Oh, baby. When are you gonna learn?"

I keep my speed slow and easy while she skates off. When she has a far enough lead, I fly across the ice to close the distance between us. I scrape to a stop with inches to spare, using the slowed momentum to wrap her in my arms smoothly.

"I'll never stop chasing you." I tip her chin up for a kiss. "And I'll always catch you."

"That's one," she whispers.

I let her escape my grasp, eager to chase her down and capture her again and again. She hides behind giggling kids using the penguin aids for balance, weaving through the bustling rink.

By the fourth time I catch her, she knows she doesn't stand a chance against me on the ice. I pin her against the boards separating the rink from the frozen lake to kiss her until we're both dizzy. We rest our foreheads together, our thick warm breaths fanning our mouths.

When our game stops, we join the general flow of other people circling the outdoor rink.

After several loops of easy skating, the wind picks up. She typically doesn't mind the cold, but the biting February chill cuts through our layers, making both of us shiver.

"Want some hot chocolate?"

"Yeah, I could use something to warm up."

I glide closer and take her by the hips, muttering low words meant only for her. "I know how to warm you up."

"Shh." She covers her laughter with a hand. "Save it for later."

"Come on."

Holding her hand, I lead us to the cabin-style hut. It has a rough-hewn wooden bar open to the rink for skaters to take a break. I order drinks for us, adding on a cone of waffle fries because I know she'll want them.

Once we have our food, we move to an open spot at the end of the wooden counter where it's quieter. She digs into her fries, trying to eat them even though they're freshly made.

"Don't hurt yourself."

"I'm okay. They're too good to wait for them to cool down."

"You have ketchup. Here." Warmth spreads through me when I thumb it away from the corner of her mouth.

She murmurs a thank you, then moves closer to lean against me. I rub her back, sipping my hot chocolate while we take in the beautiful view of the lake.

"Thanks for today. I haven't done this in forever," she says.

"It's nice to get on the ice for fun. Brings me back to the reasons I fell in love with it when I was a kid." Nostalgia washes over me. "The first time my dad put a pair of skates on me, it changed my world."

"You skate like you belong on the ice. I can't imagine you doing anything else."

I huff, raising my eyes to the sky. "He used to say that, too. You would've liked him."

And he would've adored her.

She presses closer, resting her chin on my chest. "I wish I could've met him."

"Me too." A ghost of a smile twists my lips.

"So even though you're earning a degree, it's hockey all the way?"

"That's the goal." I rub my jaw. "If I don't make the draft cut this summer..."

She hugs me when I trail off. "You can still get there after college if not, right? Ryan never shut up about it before we found out he was drafted after last season."

"Yeah, as a free agent. The contracts aren't as good, though. First round picks have it made, then for each one after it's less money and a lower chance of ever seeing game play. Out of seven rounds of picks from the pool of players within the eligible age range, it's only about sixty players that go all the way every year. Even less that actually go on to have an NHL career."

"Wow. That's more intense than I realized."

"Yeah. I still won't give up on it, though. My dad built this dream with me." I rub my chest. "I always feel like I have him with me when I play. I want to make it there for me and for him. So I can take care of my mom and my little brother."

My gaze shifts to her. I want to take care of everyone important to me.

"I still have a chance this year. For some guys it still works out, like Elijah's older brother was a third round pick. He was traded after his team didn't make the playoffs. Now he plays for the Seattle Kraken and he's gone from two minutes of game time with his previous contract to a regular on Seattle's roster. And you know Alex Keller."

"So Heston has produced choice players."

I lift a shoulder. "We're definitely up there with the top schools draft picks tend to come out of. I just have to keep working hard to get there."

She hugs me again, resting her cheek on my arm. "I've seen how you play. I believe in you with my whole heart."

Something loosens in me knowing I have her support.

It doesn't matter what we face. I'll work to keep this because she's too important to let go. It's not her or my dreams. There's no choice to make between the two—she's become part of my dreams.

If anything, I have more to fight for to earn my spot on NHL ice. One more important person in my life to take care of.

I turn to her. "There's something else I learned because of my dad." My heartrate kicks up in anticipation. "I love you."

It comes out simple and easy.

Her lips part. "You—?"

"Yeah." Smiling, I cup her face and brush my lips against hers. "I love you, Maya Donnelly."

She blinks rapidly, beautiful hazel eyes glimmering. "I—why now?"

"Why not? It's how I feel. When I lost my dad, all I wanted was to tell him I loved him one more time. After that, I decided to always make sure the people I care about know it. I don't need to wait to tell you when I already know."

Her expression melts. She throws her arms around me with a strangled noise.

"You are the most infuriating, stubborn, ridiculous guy I've ever met. You drive me crazy."

My embrace tightens at the affection filling her tone. "That's a funny way of saying you love me."

"Yeah, I guess it is." She laughs thickly. "Because somehow you barreled into my life whether I wanted you to or not and made me fall for you. I need you."

I hover my mouth over hers, unable to stop grinning. "You have me, baby. Now and always."

TWENTY-SEVEN
EASTON

When I step off the team bus at Elmwood University's campus, Maya is talking to her brother near the players' entrance. She texted me when she got here early with her friends so she could see him before the game.

Donnelly glares at me as I saunter over. It probably has to do with the fact his sister is wearing my jersey. The corner of my mouth lifts in a smirk.

"Hey," Maya says.

We've snuck around so her brother didn't know, but we're past that now. If we weren't, she wouldn't be wearing my number to his game. The urge to claim her right in front of him crashes over me.

No more hiding this. Not when I want everyone to know she's mine.

I fist the jersey and pull her in for a kiss. She freezes for a beat, then welcomes it with a little laugh.

"Hi, baby," I murmur against her lips.

Donnelly crosses his arms and mutters in annoyance under his breath. "I fucking knew it. Can't believe you're with him."

"Ryan," Maya chides without looking away from me, her gorgeous eyes gleaming brightly. "You'll just have to get over it."

My smug expression softens. I give her one more tame kiss.

"Make sure you cheer for me," I say. "Loud enough that I hear you over everyone else."

She gives a small shake of her head, the corners of her mouth curled up. "Good luck—both of you," she adds, cutting off my victorious chuckle. "Don't give me that look, Easton. I can cheer for my boyfriend and my brother."

"But more for me, right? You're wearing my number this time." I dodge with another laugh when she swats at me. "I guess I'll just have to score to get your attention."

Her eyes widen. "Don't you dare risk a penalty to dedic—"

"Maya, every goal I score will always be for you." I cradle her face with one hand, brushing my thumb over her cheek as it turns pink. "Every single one from now until my career ends."

"I'm not sitting though this sick, sappy shit," Donnelly grumbles. "I hope you enjoy eating those words when we beat Heston again."

I don't take my eyes off my girl. "Nah. I've got all the luck on my side tonight."

"Blake!" Coach Kincaid calls from the doorway. "Let's go."

After one last peck to her forehead, I hike my bag higher on my shoulder and head inside. My focus through gearing up and getting ready for the game is honed in on the W.

Not only because that's the outcome I want for every game, but to get revenge for the loss when we played our first game against them at home.

My team is ready to take Elmwood on and beat them and everyone else in Hockey East out for everything—from our conference title all the way to Frozen Four.

We hit the ice as warriors ready for battle, tapping our gloves together.

"Tonight we come out on top," I say.

My team responds with competitive enthusiasm that makes me damn proud to be their captain.

Near the end of warm-ups, I glide by Maya's section, winking at her and her friends. They tease her, pretending to swoon. She laughs and takes photos of the four of them decked out with support for Heston.

I circle around after shooting a few pucks on the net, none of which Reeves lets in. He's in the zone tonight.

Slowing to a stop at the boards, I touch the glass with a broad smile. Maya mirrors it, looking so damn gorgeous.

She's always beautiful, but something about seeing her wearing my jersey does me in.

Donnelly breaks the unwritten rule not to cross the red line to interrupt the moment. He checks into my side just light enough the referee nearby won't call him on it before the game starts.

"Finish warming up," he mutters as he herds me away.

Once he's satisfied I'm separated from his sister, he changes directions to head for his team's end.

I twist to shoot Maya a wink, then glide across the ice after him.

"What's wrong, Donnelly? Jealous it's me your sister cheers for now?" My cocky tone lowers as I slip my glove off to grab the back of his collar. "That it's *my* jersey she wears to games?"

He shrugs me off with an irritated grunt. "Don't even try me right now."

I watch him with narrowed eyes.

"You ready?" Noah comes to a stop at my side.

"Yeah."

"Let's go."

I bump fists with him and head off the ice as warm-ups finish.

When I face Donnelly for puck drop, I'm more determined than ever to clinch this win. The puck hits the ice and I move in a blink, slamming into him while our sticks work to win the face-off.

I edge him out and pass to Theo. The first five minutes after the game starts are standard for two rival teams fighting to be the first with points on the board.

Before my starting shift is due to switch out with the second line, Donnelly comes flying at me from behind, almost taking me down. I catch my balance, banking left to get away from him.

Ignoring him, I follow the puck.

Fifteen seconds later he jabs me with his elbow when I block him from stealing the puck away from Hutch. When I swing around, his lip curls and he squints in dissatisfaction.

I crack my neck side to side, smirking. He's being creative to get some cheap shots in—ones we both know the referees won't call out.

If that's how we're playing, I won't take it lying down.

I don't get the chance to retaliate until I'm put back in for the next shift, high-fiving Elijah when his line trades places with mine. I shoot from the bench, launching over the boards to join game play, angling toward the puck's location before my skates fully touch the ice.

"Let's make it happen!" I yell.

"Hell yeah," Theo whoops when he zooms past me, paired up with Hutchinson.

Adrenaline floods my veins, heart pounding while the three of us get the puck and link up to take it down the ice towards Elmwood's crease. It looks like a solid play, the hair on my body standing on end with the anticipation of scoring.

It goes great until it doesn't. Hutch gets tripped by a stick from a guy on defense. He swerves into the path of another player and the collision is brutal. A referee blows his whistle to stop the clock. Hutch gets to his feet, wincing when he puts his weight on his knee.

"Shake it off, Hutch." I skate to his side, Theo and Noah coming up on the other to help get him to the bench. "You good, man?"

"For sure. Give me five to stretch it out. It just feels like I jarred it."

I give him a supportive pat on the shoulder. "Good. We'll take care of things on the ice until you're back."

Coach puts Madden in for the power play.

Elmwood's down one defensive player, but they won't make it easy on us. Their team drops one of their wingers back to cover when game play resumes.

At first, Elmwood has possession after winning the puck drop. They get deep into our zone, but Noah stops them. Madden picks up the pass from him and skates so fast I swear the ice should be melted in his wake.

He's fucking fast, maybe quicker than me. It takes serious effort to catch up to him to provide the assist when Elmwood comes for us.

I keep an eye on our opponents and call for a pass, but when I turn around Madden is tangled with Donnelly. Both of them fling their sticks down. Jesus christ.

"Theo," I shout.

"On it." He's already moving in for the puck.

I wedge between Madden and Donnelly to break it up, but the nearest ref isn't having it. He pushes me away and takes Madden by the arm. Graves has a wild look in his eyes. His control seems seconds from snapping.

Shit. We can't have him lose it on a game official.

"Come on, that guy started it."

"Settle down," the ref barks at me. "Unless you want to be booted from the game?"

I give him a stiff, forceful shake of my head. He lets us off with a strong warning and sends Madden back to the penalty box.

First period comes to an end without either side scoring. I slap Madden on the back when we head through the tunnel for the break, tuning out Coach yelling about waking up and putting up points in the second.

"I screwed up," Madden mutters.

"Nothing you can do about it now, man. No point in dwelling on it."

"Take your own advice, East," Cameron says. "You need to leave it off the ice if you want to finish this game."

"I'll be fine. Donnelly's just having a fucking pissy fit." I swipe a hand over my mouth. "Do you guys have my back? He's been getting in too many dirty shots the refs are missing."

"Yeah," Cameron answers without hesitation. "But watch it. We're too close to playoffs to screw around."

"I know. We're kicking Elmwood's ass tonight. Right?"

A chorus of cheers sounds around me from our teammates.

For the first half of second period, I remain focused on the game. Both teams get the puck in the net, tying the score.

I'm moving the puck down the center, looking for a winger to evade Elmwood's defense when Donnelly trips me with his stick.

He covers it by checking into me, sending both of us crashing to the ice.

"You're asking for it, you dick," I snap.

Once again, the refs are ignorant to the shit he's getting by their radar.

I shoot him a glare as I get to my feet and retrieve my stick, then chase down the puck. He's right on my ass.

It was fun to clash with him at the beginning, two rivals duking out our frustrations.

Now he's really pissing me off.

I ram my shoulder into him, sending him sideways before he comes at me with another cheap shot.

"What's your problem, Donnelly?"

"You!" He bares his teeth, charging me when he should be chasing the puck in his team's possession.

That's it.

"You wanna go? Let's fucking go."

Donnelly shoves me, growing more heated. His gloves hit the ice and he comes at me.

I'm ready for him, tossing off my gloves to catch his jersey. He throws punches I block and dodge, then I get a good hit in. It sends a rush of gratification coursing through me.

We jerk and swing each other around in circles, ignoring the shouts from our teammates and the game officials.

"Why my sister, huh, asshole? You think you can toy with her? She deserves better than a player like you using her."

Fury rips through me. We struggle, both of us unable to land another blow. I drag him closer by my grip on his jersey.

"*Using* her? You think I'm bad for her? That's bullshit when your own teammate couldn't treat her right."

"What the hell are you talking about?"

My head jerks in disbelief. I open my mouth, more than ready to fucking unleash on him for being so blind to what Maya went through, but before I can get another word out the refs are in our faces to break up the fight.

The benches are empty, both our full rosters on the ice fighting. It's an all-out brawl.

"You're a liar, Blake," Donnelly bellows while he's dragged away from me.

I struggle against the guy holding me back, gritting my teeth. Once they're sure we're not going to go for each other's throats, they corral us.

"You're done," the other ref says.

I stiffen, thumbing the huddle of players being pulled apart from their scuffles. "What, are you going to kick all of us to the sin bin? Who's left to play the game?"

The refs exchange a look.

Donnelly lurches forward. "I didn't do shit."

"Shut up, idiot." I yank him back, growing annoyed all over again. "Look, we started this. Just give us the max penalty."

The older ref narrows his eyes. "You both deserve a two-game suspension for that display of misconduct."

I grit my teeth. We can't afford that.

"Get your asses to the penalty box," he says.

Relief loosens the knot in my chest. I nod, eyeing Donnelly. He looks me up and down, lip curled.

We're not done. But it will have to wait.

After a beat, I head for the penalty box, tearing off my helmet to shake out my damp hair. As much as I want to smash his face into the ice for what he said, I can't risk another fight because there's no way the referees will be so lenient after this. They'll look for any excuse to throw us out of the game.

I spend ten straight minutes glaring at Donnelly, arms crossed, knee bouncing.

The clock for second period runs out while Donnelly and I sit out. Coach Kincaid comes over with a grim look once I'm released. He pats my shoulder.

"Good luck, kid."

"Don't call me that. I hate it when you do that," I mutter.

Before I head into the underbelly of the arena, I scan the crowd for Maya. She's on her feet at the opposite end of the ice, hands pressed to the glass. It's too difficult to make out her expression from here, but just seeing her is enough to anchor me and calm me down.

Coach Lombard waits for me in the tunnel. He folds his arms across his chest, leveling me with a look that makes me feel two inches tall. I dip my chin before he has to say anything.

"Get it together, Blake."

"Yes, sir."

There's no point explaining why it happened. He gets what it's like out there from a lifetime playing the game, then coaching it from the sidelines.

Hockey is a fast-paced, high-intensity sport fueled by adrenaline and physicality. Emotions boil over faster than the puck hitting the ice when you have guys on both sides flying around with sharp blades strapped to our feet hunting down a hunk of rubber.

When I get back out there for my shift in the third period, I'm not fucking around anymore. The moment I have the opportunity, I get revenge against Donnelly with a merciless check that pins him to the boards.

"Fuck off, asshole!" He struggles, aiming to keep the puck from me, but I've got him where I want him.

The refs watch us like hawks. I need to make this quick and keep it clean.

"Listen to me carefully, because I'm only saying it once." I jab my glove against his chest. "I would never lie about Maya. Family is supposed to protect each other and you failed at that when it counted. If you're still friends with that dick, we're gonna have a problem."

"You need to start making sense, Blake."

His brows furrow. I don't have an ounce of patience left in me.

"Don't give me that look. Johnny Werner. The asshole who cheated on Maya and made her feel like shit about it. If that wasn't enough to make you want to kill him, a few months ago the psycho thought it was funny to break into her apartment as a joke."

He freezes, forgetting about the puck. "What the fuck? He did *what*?"

"Come on, there's no way you didn't know something was off."

"No," he spits.

I grit my teeth to keep my temper in check. "It doesn't matter. She has me now. I'm not going anywhere, so if you ever disrespect her the way you have by staying friends with shitheads like Werner, know that I will make you pay for it just as much as anyone else that's hurt her."

"Oh, shit." He goes slack, gaping at me. "You're in love with her."

"Damn right I am." While he's distracted, I flick the puck away from him to the blur of blue and green on my left.

His expression darkens, searching the crowd. "I'm gonna fucking kill him."

Finally, we're on the same page.

"First, I'm beating your ass."

Smirking, I rush off to assist Theo as he flies down the ice with the puck.

TWENTY-EIGHT
MAYA

"FIGHT! YEAH, LET'S GO," someone yells in the crowd near us.

"Maya, wait!" Reagan grabs hold of me to stop me from racing out of my seat the minute the gloves come off.

We're all on our feet with the rest of the arena—me, her, Hana, and Corinne. Phones are out and people eat up my brother and my boyfriend colliding. I clutch the front of the jersey I'm wearing.

Maybe it would've been better to tell Ryan about us.

Within moments, both teams spill onto the ice. The brawl between Heston and Elmwood turns the ice into complete chaos. It takes the referees several long minutes to get the fighting under control, then they take an eternity debating with the players. Ryan gets in the ref's face and Easton yanks him back.

At last, the referee announces, "Numbers twenty-nine from Elmwood and twenty-four from Heston, penalties for misconduct. Ten minutes in the penalty box."

"There, see? It's all good." Reagan encourages me to sit down, patting my leg. "I thought you grew up around this watching Ryan play all the time?"

I sigh. "It's still my brother and my boyfriend attacking each other. I didn't want them fighting. They're seriously lucky they only got penalties instead of getting kicked out of the game. Usually the college league is really strict about the no fighting policy."

"I can't lie. It's hot." Reagan shivers with a smirk. "All that pent up emotion exploding. Really gets a girl going, y'know?"

The breath that huffs out of me is tinged with wry amusement. "Yeah, I do know."

She's not wrong at all. Beneath the uncertainty, there's a current of warmth pulsing between my legs from seeing Easton go wild like that. I bite my lip, seeking him out as he takes off his helmet and shakes out his thick messy brown hair on his way off the ice.

The rest of the period plays out with Easton and Ryan glaring at each other from their respective penalty boxes, separated only by a wall of plexiglass. When the teams break before the last period, I rise to my feet again and text Easton, unsure if he'll check his phone. I stare at the screen until the three dots pop up.

Maya
Are you okay?

Easton 🩶
Yeah all good. We just have some shit to work out.

It sets me at ease through the break. Then my heart leaps back into my throat in the final when Easton crashes against Ryan with another fierce check. Whatever he says leaves Ryan stunned when he speeds off with his teammate to make a play that earns Heston the winning goal of the game.

Once the game lets out, I tell the girls I'll meet them by Reagan's car and hurry through the building. Reporters for sports blogs and podcasts crowd the way to the locker rooms and equipment area. The arena's security isn't letting anyone through.

"Damn."

I head outside to see if I can go in through the door the guys entered when the team bus arrived, whipping my phone out to try to reach Easton.

Maya
I'm trying to get to the locker area to see you but it's totally locked down.

Easton 🩶
I'd come out to get you but Coach is on a rampage. I'm risking life and limb to text you. I'll meet you back at campus.

Maya
Okay. Going to ride back with the girls, see you soon.

The green heart he responds with makes my lips twitch. Changing directions, I head off to meet back up with Reagan and the girls. They're raving about the excitement of the game through the traffic jam of fans leaving that makes it take forever to leave Elmwood U's campus.

When we reach the highway, I pull up Ryan's contact and Face-Time him during the drive back to Heston Lake to check on him.

"Hey," he answers.

It's dark, but it looks like he's in an alleyway between the old brick buildings of his campus. I frown.

"Where are you?"

"Outside." A commotion behind him interrupts us. "Yo, shut up for a minute. It's my sister."

When he turns to them, I spot some of his teammates in the background. Including Johnny.

My eyes widen. His face is red and mottled, one eye swelling shut with the beginnings of a black eye. Two big guys that have to play on defense have him pinned to the wall.

"Um..."

"Don't worry about that piece of shit," Ryan says through his teeth.

I blink, startled at the complete one-eighty from his friendship. His hard expression cracks and he stares at me sadly through the small screen.

Oh. My stomach clenches.

Ryan knows. There's no question about the angry hatred that blazed in his eyes a moment ago.

I don't know how he learned what Johnny did to me, but my intuition has a strong guess.

Ryan scrubs a hand over his face. "You know you can talk to me, right?"

"I—yeah." I swallow. "You didn't have to—"

"Yes I did, Maya. I'm your brother." He blows out a breath, lifting his brows. "I hope next time I don't have to hear about important shit from your boyfriend."

A wet laugh leaves me as a knot that's been tangled for far too many years finally loosens in my chest. I wish I was still at his school so I could hug him. Damn Johnny for twisting my belief in my brother. I should've been able to trust that he'd be on my side if I'd had the courage to tell him sooner.

"Okay," I promise.

His throat bobs. "I'm sorry. I should've seen through that asshole right away."

I shake my head. "I didn't have the guts to tell you, so it's not like you could've known."

"It doesn't matter. I should've had your back."

"Thanks."

He sighs, mouth lifting at the corner. "What a way to end my college hockey career."

"What? Come on, you could still make the playoffs."

"Doubt it. We've had a really shitty season." He snorts. "It's fine. Buffalo sent a contract with their official offer. Once I sign it, I can't play in the NCAA league anyway."

"Oh my god, Ry! You didn't tell me, dick," I say in excitement. "Congratulations. Are you going to sign with them?"

"It just happened before yesterday's game. I've been busy." He gives me the same smile that he's always had when he lured me into something mischievous when we were growing up. "Come see your brother in the NHL."

"You bet. I'm proud of you."

"Thanks. Oh, shit. Coach is calling. I'd better go before he kills us."

"Bye."

"Later."

I rest my head against the window, a weight lifted from my shoulders that I've carried with me since the moment I ended my joke of a relationship with Johnny. He created a rift between me and my brother that I know I'll be able to repair. With Easton's help, Ryan started the bridge that will bring us back together.

Reagan reaches from the driver's seat to squeeze my hand. "You good?"

"Yes. Thanks."

She gives another supportive squeeze.

The rest of the ride is spent with all four of us belting out songs with the windows down despite the brisk late February weather. It doesn't matter to us. Nothing can touch us when we're having fun.

By the time we make it back to Heston Lake, Easton lets me know the team bus isn't far behind us. He invites me to let myself into the hockey house with the spare key he gave me after our ice skating date.

"Thanks for dropping me off here," I tell Reagan when she parks out front.

"Of course. Tonight was wicked fun." She winks and shimmies her shoulders. "All that excitement."

"Hell yes," Corinne cheers from the back seat. "I'm so glad I came out for this. Now I want to go see a professional game."

"I think we've converted a new fan," Hana says through laughter.

"What are you guys going to do now?" I ask.

"Dance around at our place and drink the box of wine in the fridge," Reagan says. "You'll be missed while you get dicked down. Enjoy that."

I smirk at her saucy tone. "Thanks, I will."

"Bring me all the dirty details when you come back," she calls after me as I get out of her car. "Don't leave anything out, we want to know everything!"

I grin and wave to my friends while they drive off. On my way inside, Easton's cat gets up from her napping spot on the porch to rub against my leg. I fill her bowl with food and get her fresh water before heading upstairs. She follows me, hopping on the bed when I sit down with the overnight bag I dropped off earlier before we left for the away game.

She explores my stuff when I put the bag on the floor, trying to climb in when I get the latest romance book I borrowed from Reagan.

I take a photo of her head poking out of my bag to send to Easton. "You fit. Is that your new spot?"

She hops right back out when I stretch out on the bed to read, purring as she curls up at my side. It's peaceful getting lost in reading with her company.

"I like coming home to this. You in my bed."

Easton's leaning in the door with a handsome crooked smile. A warm glow echoes within my chest, spreading through me. He pops off the door frame and I save my page, setting the book on the nightstand.

The cat gives a faint trilling sound in greeting without moving from her spot. He chuckles, strolling to the bed to let her sniff his hand.

I clasp it, examining his busted knuckles with a frown. "You shouldn't have fought during the game. What if you'd been suspended? There aren't many games left before the season ends. You're working so hard to stand out when you play so you can achieve your dreams."

"This isn't from the game." He laces his fingers with mine, gazing at our joined hands. "I was blocking your brother's hits more than hitting him back."

"What do you mean?"

The cat grows bored with us when we stop paying attention to her. She jumps off the bed and pads from the room.

Easton sits beside me, bringing my hand to his lips for a soft kiss. "Ryan came to find me before the bus was due to leave, wanting me to go with him. We worked things out between us." His blue eyes pierce mine. "I got my moment alone. Your ex knows not to even look at you ever again."

The gritty, protective tone he uses sends heat racing through me. With my worries about the game gone, all that's left is the sensual need this wild side of him stirs in me.

I want to feel what his fiery savageness is like when it's unleashed on my body. My desires are reflected in his darkening gaze as it drops to my mouth, then rakes over me.

"Maya," he rasps.

I move first. He catches me in his arms and we collide in a passionate kiss. We're more desperate than we've ever been for each other, yanking and tugging at our clothes while teeth nip at lips and nails scrape across skin.

A moan flies out of me when he roughly flips me over, body covering mine as he reaches around to squeeze my breast and work my jeans and thong down. He gets them off, then his palm pushes on the middle of my back.

"Head down, ass up, baby," he grits out.

Arousal throbs in my clit as the tip of his cock glides against my folds. I grip the sheets, pushing back to get what I want.

He squeezes my ass. "Oh, you want it, huh? Did you get all hot and wet from watching me tonight?"

"Yes."

A rumble sounds from him. "You want to get fucked hard, Maya?"

I cry out in response as his cock begins to stretch me. He stops at just the tip, driving me crazy. I wriggle, attempting to take more of his length. He holds me steady, outmatching me for strength.

"Come on. Fuck me now."

"How do you want it? Tell me."

"Rough."

The pleading admission makes me hot all over, my core pulsing with excitement.

A scream catches in my throat when he slams into me, fingers gripping my hips firm enough to leave marks. I shiver at the thought of finding proof of this moment later. The angle is divine, each thrust lighting me up from his cock hitting me deep.

He takes a fistful of my hair. It's just tight enough to add pressure, keeping my head where he wants it. My mouth drops open with another moan.

"Fuck, you take my cock so good. You're my good fucking girl, aren't you?"

"Yes," I chant breathlessly over and over.

Every inch of my body is taut with pleasure from my nipples to my clit to my pussy until I explode. The orgasm blindsides me, making my thighs quiver from the intense force of red hot waves of ecstasy crashing over me.

"Jesus—fuck, Maya," he grits out. "That's it. Come all over my cock."

He releases my hair and leans down so he's braced over me, holding one of my wrists in a possessive grip. It makes his cock reach even deeper as he drives inside me.

"Oh god," I choke out.

"Give me another one," he growls in my ear. "I want your pussy soaking my cock."

My insides clamp around his dick as another overwhelming bolt of arousal spears through me. His fingers find my clit, circling it with a firm touch. Combined with the consuming sensations of everything else, he sends me right to the edge.

The scream trying to escape me catches in my throat. My back arches as I unravel, giving myself over to oblivion.

I'm faintly aware of his hips stuttering and the throb of his cock filling me with his come.

He collapses next to me for a moment, leg pressed against mine. Panting, he rolls to his side and finds my hand.

I'm too worn out to move, still shivering and tingly all over as the orgasm ebbs away.

"That was—amazing," I get out between heaving breaths.

"Yeah." He slings an arm over his eyes. "Holy shit, baby."

A tired laugh leaves me. We catch our breaths in comfortable silence. He traces random patterns on the inside of my arm. I close my eyes, relaxing from the soothing feel of his fingertips gently grazing my skin.

He recovers first, lifting me into his arms with ease. My thighs slide together in response to his incredible strength and stamina.

"Where are you taking me?" I manage.

"I gave it to you rough. Now it's time to worship you," he explains as he takes us into the bathroom.

"You don't have to. I asked for it because I wanted it like that." My lips twitch. "And I enjoyed every second of it."

He gives me a soft smile, kissing my temple before setting me on the counter. "I know. So did I. It was hot as hell. But I want to do this now. This is my way of taking care of you every way you need it."

Once he turns on the shower, he kneels between my legs. I bite my lip as he scoots my hips to the edge of the counter and pulls my legs over his shoulders. Then his mouth descends on my pussy and I'm lost to his skilled tongue.

Steam fills the room while he takes me apart all over again.

I tip over the edge from the slow build up, pleasure rolling through me in delicious ripples. He peers up to watch me come, caressing my thighs.

Nudging him up to his feet, I loop my arms around his neck for a kiss, tasting both of us. His palms trace my spine before he hugs me tightly. Both of us say how we feel without words.

The hot water feels amazing while we shower. He washes me, big hands mapping every inch of my skin with reverence.

When we're done and dried off, he takes me to bed, pulling me close to rest my head on his chest. His hands thread through my damp hair.

"I've got you, baby," he whispers before I drift off.

TWENTY-NINE
MAYA

Donnelly Dairy might not be an operating farm anymore, but it's still one of my favorite places in the world. Grandpa and I take a slow stroll through the grounds as part of the daily exercise his physical therapist wants him to get in.

I was supposed to work this weekend, but Marnie wasn't having it. She wanted me to take a break.

Since I'm ahead on my assignments and my schedule for the spring semester is even lighter than the credits I took in the fall, I borrowed Reagan's car after my last class on Thursday and drove home to visit my grandfather. We have one more day together before I need to head back tomorrow afternoon for my Monday morning class.

Grandpa pauses with a tired sigh, leaning heavily on the cane he graduated to when his mobility improved. I'm by his side in an instant.

"Do you want to stop for a rest? We can sit down in the old milking barn."

He waves me off, stoically smoothing his features to hide his grimace of discomfort. "I'm okay, chicken. Just need to catch my breath. No need to fuss over me."

"I'm right here if you need me."

"Tell me more about your work."

"Right." I trace the worn stitching on the Donnelly Dairy hat on my head and continue where I left off explaining what animal therapies I get to learn about through Merrywood Farms. "Honestly, it never fails to amaze me how well the animals read us. They're so smart."

The soft smile he gives me is full of love. "I'm very proud of you, Maya. You know that, right?"

I nod. "It's all because you set me on this path."

"No." He shakes his head. "You've done far more than I could dream to in my lifetime. This is all you, my brilliant girl."

A wobbly smile tugs at my lips. "I can't believe I'm almost done, though. In a few more months, I'll finish this degree. Mom and Dad are starting to plan how we'll celebrate after the graduation ceremony."

He hums in acknowledgement.

"They were saying you guys might take a trip down to spend the week in Heston Lake until the ceremony. Then Mom was thinking we could go out for a big dinner together."

Grandpa goes quiet for a long time. Sometimes he gets like this when he's going through a bout of pain, but doesn't want to burden anyone.

Worried, I touch his arm. "Are you okay?"

His somber expression crumples. The gutting turmoil written across his face steals my breath away. He chokes out a broken sob that cleaves my heart in half and sinks my stomach with dread.

"I'm going to make it, Maya. I promise."

An icy spike drives into my chest with an aching blow at the defeated confession, pain radiating through me. My emotions unravel as quickly as his, my breath catching with a whimpering gasp. Tears overflow and stream down my cheeks.

I throw my arms around him, clutching him as if my desperation could keep him here as long as I need him. God, please. I don't want to lose him.

His body feels so frail, trembling with his wheezing sobs.

A world without him is unfathomable. As he's aged and weathered his illness attacking his body, he's remained happy. It unnerves me to see his fortitude rattled to reveal the truth he hides from all of us.

Since I was a little girl, he's the one that held me up with a strength I always believed was infinite and unstoppable. Seeing him break down completely, swearing he'll live long enough to see what I've been working towards so hard, absolutely decimates me.

"I'm sorry," he pleads. "I promise I'll still be here."

I have no words. Everything I try to say can't escape, trapped by the lump lodged in my throat. All I'm able to do is bury my tear-streaked face into his shoulder with a devastated nod.

"I promise," he repeats again and again.

I hug him tighter, willing my heart not to shatter into a thousand pieces.

* * *

A week later, I have the apartment to myself while Reagan goes down to the city for a small show. Easton's away for the weekend, too. The team left after last night's game and won't return until late tomorrow night.

Other than going to class, I've spent the week holed up in my room or at the library. I can't stop working. Guilt plagues me if I take a break because I could be productive instead. It's the only thing I could think to do after I got back from seeing my grandfather.

The one thing that keeps me sane is fiddling with the gold spiral ring Easton got for me when I get overwhelmed by everything I want to get done to the point of paralysis.

My phone screen lights up with Easton's name and a goofy photo he took of us while I'm taking notes at my desk. He texted me an hour ago to say his game was done and he'd call when he got to the hotel. I set my notes aside and answer the video call.

The world stops spinning out of my control and every worry on my mind slips away when he appears on screen.

"Hi."

"Hey. What are you doing?"

"Research for the topic I need to present on. Did you win?"

He sighs, scraping a hand through his hair. "Nah. It wasn't a bad loss, we just didn't have it together to put up more points. Cam might have a groin injury. He's still getting it checked out now."

"I'm sorry. I hope he's okay."

He huffs out a dry laugh. "Fucker tried to play through it before the coaches pulled him to put in our backup goalie, Holland. Eric is feeling the pressure to perform."

I lean closer to the small screen to study him, wishing we were together. "You don't seem that worried about losing."

"I'm staying positive, like that paper you were writing last week."

My lips twitch. "The law of attraction and its application in mind-brain sciences for alternative therapies?"

"That's the one." He snaps his fingers. "We should be okay. Losing this one shouldn't affect our overall standing since we've been on fire. As long as Reeves didn't hurt himself too badly, we'll be fine."

I fold my arms on my desk and rest my head, closing my eyes to listen to his soothing voice. It washes over me, allowing me to pretend he's here.

"You, on the other hand," he says slowly.

I crack an eye open, finding him leveling me with a pointed look. "What about me?"

"You told me you finished all your assignments for the next couple of weeks. What are you working on?"

"Um..." I sit up, scanning the array of books surrounding my laptop on my desk. "I figured I should get ahead. I mean, I might as well. Right?"

"What happened to that break Marnie made you take last week-end? This is why she gave you time off." His brows furrow. "Maya, you're gonna work yourself into the ground."

An uncomfortable heat burns in my chest because he's paying close attention. And he's right, I'm working myself too hard.

His eyes pierce into me, but I don't have to explain what's driving me on again. When I came back from visiting my grandfather, he was the first person I went to. He stroked my hair and listened as I recounted what happened.

I'm still shaken by it. Seeing Grandpa crying has always killed me, but seeing the fear and desperation in his eyes absolutely shat-tered my soul and stole away the hope I've been grasping to that he was getting better.

My grandfather is the strongest person I know, but even he isn't strong enough to fight death. It comes for us all eventually. It's a truth we can't outrun.

Releasing a tight exhale, I swallow past the lump in my throat in an effort to keep my emotions in check.

"I just want to finish," I push out.

"You will. You don't have to rush it all."

"But I'm running out of time." My voice breaks, throat aching with an agonizing sting as Grandpa's breakdown hits me again. "I have to finish."

Easton gives me a heartbreaking look, bringing the phone closer as if it could bring us together from the miles separating us. A band constricts around my heart. I need him and he knows it.

"I wish I was there with you right now," he says gruffly. "I want to hold you in my arms."

"Me too. I could really use one of your hugs."

"The minute the bus gets back to campus, I'll be there. If you're already asleep, know you'll be waking up in my arms on Monday."

"Thank you for putting up with me." I sigh, giving myself a squeeze.

"Baby, it's not a hardship. I'm not putting up with anything. You need my support? You've got it. Just like you do for me. We're a team, right?"

"Yeah."

"A team has to be open with each other. If we don't communicate, we're in the shit, you know?"

"You're right. I know it's better to do that instead of holding it in on my own. I'm still getting used to having someone I trust enough to see me fall apart when I'm frustrated or afraid."

"It's okay. I'm here for all of it." His expression softens when I nod. "You just have to let me be there for you instead of bottling it up."

It's amazing how much better I feel after talking to him. I'm able to breathe easier just knowing I have him to lean on.

"How about when I'm back we load up on snacks and find a show to binge watch? Just us."

"I like the sound of that."

"Good. Now close your computer and put away the books."

Laughing, I do as he says, lifting my hands to show it's done. He nods with a smile.

"Don't even think about touching those for the rest of the weekend."

My lips twitch. I flutter my lashes playfully, dropping my voice to a husky lilt.

"Yes, sir."

Easton gives a rough hum, eyes hooding. "That's my good girl." His gaze passes over me in a slow drag and the tip of his tongue traces his bottom lip. "I can still help you relax. Will you let me make you feel better?"

I bite my lip, heart fluttering. Even when he's not beside me, he's here for me in every way I need him. No distance will matter between us wherever life takes us.

"What do you have in mind?"

He brings his face close to the camera, grinning wickedly. Warmth blooms in the pit of my stomach in anticipation.

"Go get your favorite toy."

THIRTY
MAYA

By the time I turn my attention back to the phone, he's stripped out of his shirt and sits against the headboard of his hotel bed. Arousal coils within me as his shoulder flexes, arm moving suggestively out of frame.

"Are you starting without me?"

"Just taking off the edge. You know it only takes the thought of you to get me hard enough to drill through a wall. Did you get a toy?"

"Yeah. I couldn't decide."

I hold up the vibrator we picked out together earlier in the month for Valentine's Day. It has an app that he can control on his phone. In my other hand, I have a soft purple and pink silicone dildo I bought from an online boutique I discovered on social media.

His gaze brims with lust. "Your pretty little pussy wants to be filled up with my cock, doesn't it?"

My core clenches with desire. Releasing a thick breath, I nod. He groans, arm flexing at the edge of the frame again while his grip on his shaft tightens.

"You're so fucking sexy, you know that?"

"Not as sexy as I'll be riding you."

He forces out a ragged breath. "Yeah? Show me, baby. I want to see all of you."

It takes a moment to get set up. Rather than lay down on the bed,

I prop the phone on the pillows to get the right angle to look like I'm straddling Easton's waist when I fuck myself with the dildo.

I want to be hands free to use the vibrator, so I grab a heavy glass jar with a flat lid that I use for storage on my desk. It's short enough that when I stick the dildo's suction cup to the top, it brings it to the right height to make it easier for me to ride it while he watches. I tested the toy this way once before and it works out nicely to keep it in place, allowing me to move how I want.

When I'm ready, I climb onto the mattress.

He's speechless for a moment, staring at every inch of me. His stare stops on my chest.

"If I was there, I'd be all over those tits."

I trace a nipple, teasing it until it hardens. Closing my eyes, I picture how it feels when his mouth is on me.

"Now move your hand down. Slowly," he corrects when I go too fast. "That's it. I want to get you shivering before I touch your pussy."

My stomach dips and a rush of hot and cold tingles race across my skin when I caress myself. "It's working."

He chuckles when I try to dip my fingers between my thighs before he directs me to. "Not yet. I'm the one making you feel good, remember?"

A small frustrated noise escapes me, but I let him set the pace. Each caress to erogenous spots of my body ignites sparks of desire until I'm warm all over.

"Tell me what you want."

My stomach clenches while I trace patterns on my inner thigh. I move higher, stopping short of where I'm throbbing.

"I need you here."

He makes me wait a torturous beat. "Now let me take care of you, baby. I'm going to play with your clit just how you like it."

A needy sound escapes me the moment I graze my fingers over my folds and find my clit. The fantasy we're creating becomes my reality when I close my eyes, picturing Easton kneeling behind me, callused fingers rubbing between my legs while the heat of his hard body presses to my back.

"Tell me how it feels when I touch you."

Air rushes past my lips. "Good. So good."

"Get the vibrator," he rasps.

My insides tangle in a knot of arousal as I press it against my clit with a gasp. The pulsing sensation feels incredible, and I have no idea when he's going to change it up on me. He watches my reactions intently, teasing me with light spikes in the vibrating speed.

"Does that feel good, baby?"

"Yes," I breathe. "Really nice."

"But we're not done yet. You need to be filled up."

I gulp. When his voice gets all gritty and commanding like that, it gets me so hot.

A tremor moves through me as I position myself over the dildo. At first, I glide the head against my folds, testing the stretch of my body as I begin to drop to let it penetrate me. I'm so wet already, it slips right in. My head drops back with a breathless moan.

"Sink that pussy down my cock. Take every inch." His chin dips and I faintly hear the slap of skin on skin while he jerks off. "Ride me, Maya."

"Fuck." I gasp at the stretch, circling my hips until I feel so full. Normally I use lube with this toy, but I'm so turned on I'm dripping, thighs slick. "Oh god."

"Look at you," he praises. "So fucking gorgeous riding my cock. So damn perfect for me."

My lips part as the vibrations of the toy steadily increase, as if he's circling his thumb across the app's controls. His gaze sears into me while I fuck the toy I'm pretending is him.

"Harder. I love watching your tits bounce." A note of desperation creeps into his tone as he gets closer to finishing.

I rise up on my knees and sink back down at a faster pace, releasing soft noises of pleasure. The closer I get to the brink of coming, the more he increases the strength of the pulsing toy pressed to my clit.

The vibration pattern changes again just as I'm about to reach my orgasm. My pussy squeezes the dildo and I move my hips faster, chasing what I need.

"Easton," I whimper. "Please. I'm so close."

"You ready to come for me?"

"*Yes.*"

The vibrator pulses, hitting my clit with powerful stimulation that leaves me breathless. My mouth drops open as I reach the cliff and begin to tip over into oblivion.

"Scream my name, baby."

"Easton! *Easton*!"

I don't care if my cries wake the entire building because the orgasm that crashes over me takes over every one of my senses, overwhelming me with pleasure. My lashes flutter, body still grinding on the toy as I watch his movements stutter.

"Fuck." He chokes out the word as his features twist in ecstasy while he comes. "Oh—*fuck*, baby."

It takes both of us a minute to recover. I'm still moving my hips in tiny motions, getting hit with jolts of pleasure from the vibrator when he triggers it from the app. He watches me, the corner of his mouth lifting in satisfaction when I shake apart again with a strangled moan.

"So damn pretty when you come," he murmurs. "How do you feel?"

"Better. Very relaxed." I shift around, stretching out on the bed and holding the phone up. "Still wish you were here for the real deal."

He chuckles and cleans up with a tissue. "Me too. Are you tired?"

I hum, struggling to keep my eyes open. My limbs feel heavy as I finally allow myself to slow down.

"Get some rest. I—" He cuts off, looking up sharply with a caught out expression. "You're back."

"Your dick is out," Cameron states the obvious off screen.

I bury a snicker into the pillow, reaching for his t-shirt I claimed for myself before I wipe everything down and put it away.

Easton clears his throat, keeping the phone angled to himself as he tucks himself away. "I'm going to shower real quick." He pauses in the door to the bathroom to face his friend. "What did the doctor say?"

"It's not as bad as they were worried about. I have to rest it, but it should be all good."

Relief crosses Easton's face. "Good."

He ducks into the bathroom, starting the water in the shower stall without ending the call. When he turns his attention back to me, I'm tucked beneath the covers with a soft smile from watching him.

"I'm glad Cam's okay," I say.

He nods with a reassured sigh. "Yeah, me too. We're too close to the end of our season to suffer any bad injuries."

"Go shower. I'm sleepy."

The corners of his eyes crinkle. "Sorry, am I keeping you up?"

"Mm, you could if I get the vibrator back out. You could keep me up all night while you shower."

He braces an arm against the wall, covering his face. "God, Maya, you drive me so crazy. You're going to make me hard again." A rough, sexy laugh escapes him. "You need to rest. I can see you're about to pass out any second because you've worked yourself to the point of exhaustion."

I nod, fighting a yawn.

"See? That's not good. But tomorrow, I want you to stay in bed and play with yourself all day. No working. Deal?"

"You drive a hard bargain."

He smirks. "That's my girl." He's quiet for a beat, eyes bouncing between mine. "I'll see you soon. I—"

"I know," I say in a rush, unable to contain my affectionate smile.

His mouth tugs into the crooked grin that's captured my whole heart. "I'm gonna say it anyway because I want to. I never want you to doubt it or go without hearing that I love you."

The warmest glow swells to fill my chest as his words envelop me.

"I love you," I murmur.

His blue eyes soften with tender adoration. "Everything will be okay. Goodnight."

THIRTY-ONE
EASTON

Ending the season victorious after a win on home ice, then another against Boston College tonight is one of the best feelings in the world. My teammates crash against me on the ice the moment we finish, all of us hugging because we clinched it.

We're bound for playoffs and I can already taste the crisp air of the arena for the championship tournament at the end of the road.

Best of all? My girl waits for me outside the locker room, looking cute as hell in my alternate jersey.

Her cheeks have green hearts with number twenty-four painted on them. She beams at me proudly for our stellar win.

I match her expression, my grin unstoppable. In one smooth move I pick her up with one arm.

"Easton!"

She wraps her arms around me with a laugh. A pleased rumble vibrates in my chest as I hold her up.

Yeah, this beats everything else on my list as my favorite feeling ever.

I carry her, starting toward the gauntlet of reporters lining the hall that leads to our exit. I'm not hiding that she's my girl.

Their cameras flash and they call my name, firing off questions about the game, my team, and about the draft prospect ranks that were released with my name coming in at the top of the standings. It feels damn good.

Someone sticks a recorder in my face. "Heston's entering the playoffs as the defending champions. You won Frozen Four last year. Do you hope to do the same again?"

"Of course. The Knights always fight to win when we're on the ice," I say.

"How are you feeling finishing the season in the top ten of the prospects for this year's draft? This is your first time on the list—what's changed in your strategy from last year to stand out?"

No lie, when the list released on all the biggest online sports media outlets centered on hockey news, the entire house lost our shit in celebration. Of all the guys who played for Heston that went on to be drafted out of college, none of them ranked as high as my name on that prospect list.

It was surreal to see my name mentioned on ESPN and Sportsnet's websites.

"It's an incredible honor to be recognized among this year's amazing players, for sure. I've got a lot of motivation that keeps me focused. Most of all, this year I've had an amazing support system through my teammates and family." I flash a smile at Maya. "Oh, and this is my girl, Maya. Make sure you put that in your article, too. I'm a taken man."

The guy shifts his camera to her with interest. She buries her face in my neck. I chuckle, rubbing her leg.

More cameras flash blind us. I give a brief wave in thanks and hustle through the gauntlet to reach the door for the parking lot.

I brace against the bitter early March wind, buffing Maya's side to keep her warm. She wraps her legs around me and tightens her arms with a hum.

She peeks out now that we're in the clear from the media. "You really just did that."

"Did what? Win?" I tease. "Because I'm awesome."

She clicks her tongue, eyes dancing with humor. "You know what I'm talking about, hotshot."

A prideful grin twists my lips. "No doubt. Thousands of people read those sports blogs and articles online. I want everyone to know I'm yours."

Stopping in my tracks, I cup her face to draw her in for a kiss.

"Ow, ow," Noah heckles.

Cameron's voice booms when he puts his hands around his mouth. "Get a room."

Maya keeps the kiss going for another minute, lifting her arm away from me. I grin against her lips, suspecting that she's flipping them off. I hold up my own finger.

"That's cute, they match," Noah says with a snort.

We break apart and I hoist her to keep her in my arms. "Let's give it up for our true MVP."

I steal Cam's hat off his head and wave it in the air while we all whoop.

He laughs as the guys circle around him. Thankfully his injury wasn't as bad as everyone worried it was. He was back in business for our final two games, on fire while defending the crease.

"You were on fire tonight," Maya says.

"Thanks." Cameron gives her a fist bump.

"What about me?" Noah prompts. "You saw that sick save I had in the second, right?"

She laughs. "No doubt."

"And what about me?" I clasp her chin, drawing her attention back. "Your eyes were on me, weren't they?"

Someone pretends to gag. She shakes her head, cradling my face as she bumps her nose with mine.

Her back pocket vibrates against my forearm. "Oh. Hang on, someone's calling."

She fishes out her phone while I keep her balanced in my arms. I spot her brother's name on the screen and swipe it to answer with a cocky grin.

"Look at that, my rival's called to congratulate me for making it to the playoffs." I chuckle, wanting to bust his balls. "You'd better watch us when we win Frozen Four again, Donnelly."

"What—Blake?" He's far from amused, snapping at me seriously. "Put Maya on the phone, *now*."

I blink at his demand, offering the phone back to her. "He's not in a good mood."

She huffs at my antics. "When is he ever? Hello? What's up, Ry?" She listens for a moment, her joyful smile falling. "What?"

When she taps frantically to be let down, I set her feet on the ground, brows furrowing. She covers her mouth, features stricken.

"No."

Worried, I rub her arm. "What is it?"

She shakes her head, hunching her shoulders as she turns away. The first spark of panic flickers to life as I follow her through the parking lot.

"When? I thought everything was b—" Her voice cracks with anguish.

It does me in. She hangs up, chest heaving with deep gulps of air as she digs through her purse. A jagged band of steel locks around my heart when she rips Reagan's borrowed keys from the bag.

There's no way I'm letting her drive in this state. A snowstorm just blew through the entire northeast, leaving the roads a wreck with black ice.

"Maya." She's not listening. I snatch the keys away, catching her when she tries to fight me for them. "Maya, stop. Just wait a second. Tell me what's wrong."

With a strangled gasp, her distraught gaze collides with mine. Her chin wobbles, breaking my fucking heart.

"I can't help if you don't talk to me," I encourage gently.

Her throat bobs. "It's—it's my grandpa. He's dying."

"Fuck, I'm sorry." I haul her into a hug, cradling the back of her head and neck, squeezing as I hush her. "I'm so sorry."

"I—I can't. Easton," she whimpers. "I don't want to lose him."

"Blake," Coach Lombard calls.

Damn it. I look across the parking lot, clenching my jaw.

I kiss her forehead, eyes boring into hers. "Wait one minute, okay? I'll be right back. The last thing I'll do right now is leave you alone."

She nods, clutching at me like she doesn't want me to go. It kills me to leave her like this for even a second to talk to the coaches.

"I'm coming right back. Just wait here for me."

My teammates cheer as I jog over to the bus, pausing from loading all our gear to chant *captain, captain*. For the first time ever, I ignore them, not stopping until I nearly crash into Coach Lombard's back.

"Sir."

He's not paying attention, going over a checklist with our equipment manager. "Let's go. Get on the bus. We're starting practice early tomorrow. We've got work to put in before the first playoff game."

"I can't." Finally, he turns his attention to me. I gesture to Maya. "I know it's against the rules and the team is supposed to ride the bus, but I'm asking for one exception. It's a family emergency."

"Family?" He lifts a brow.

"Yes. She's about to lose someone extremely important because he's dying, and I need her to be able to say goodbye."

The insistent words scrape my throat, overlapped by my own grief rising to the surface. I blow out a breath, trying to hold myself together while I relive how much it hurt to know I couldn't tell Dad I loved him one more time. To know I couldn't talk to him about my problems or ask his advice about hockey or life. To know I'd never hear his voice outside of old home videos and saved voicemails where he's giving me shit for blocking his car because I parked my bike in the driveway again.

I don't want her to find out what that's like if she has the chance to see her grandfather before he passes and find some of the closure I wasn't able to experience.

"I don't want her driving alone while she's upset. The roads are a mess from the storm."

Coach hums gruffly in acknowledgement. He hands the checklist to the equipment manager and grasps my shoulder to lead me away from the bus.

"Playoffs don't wait for anyone, son," he reminds me. "Topping the draft prospect ranks for the season doesn't mean you've made it yet. Your current team can't go without their captain. We're on the road to the championships now."

"I know," I answer tightly.

"You'll need to be back for practice."

My conflicted gaze finds my girl. I'm torn between my love for her and how that fits into the goal I've worked towards. I'll never choose anything over her. She's part of my future now.

I rub at the burn in my chest. I know this is what Dad would expect of me. To take care of the people important to me, the way he always did before we lost him.

Ah, shit. I blink away the sting in my eyes, swallowing thickly.

Death and loss fucking suck. There's no denying that truth. But as long as we hold on to the people we love, everything will be okay.

And I'll never let go of Maya Donnelly, especially not when my girl needs me.

Even if it costs me my dream of being drafted. I'll still fight my way to the NHL one way or another.

"Coach, with all due respect, I'm not really asking permission here. She comes first. No question." I raise my chin. "I'll do everything in my power to make this work. You can count on me. I won't abandon my team, but I have to go right now."

Coach surveys me in silence, then nods. "You make me proud, Blake." He squeezes my shoulder, leaning closer. "I've never been more honored to coach a player like you. Cannon and I look forward to seeing the long career I know you're going to have in this game."

My throat closes. I clear it and scrub my eyes before sprinting back to Maya's side.

She's trembling, struggling to hold back her emotions. I pull her into my embrace, wanting to carry all her pain for her.

"Come on. I've got you. I've always got you."

She loses the battle once she's in my arms, hiccuping as she presses her face against my chest. Jarring shudders rack her frame and she clutches at me with a desperate white-knuckled grip. She tries to speak, but can't get anything out past her heaving breaths.

Seeing her like this destroys me. I gather my strength in order to keep it together because she needs me to lean on more than ever. We'll get through this together.

"It'll be okay, sweetheart. Let's hit the road. We're going to see him right now."

THIRTY-TWO
MAYA

The ride from Boston College's hockey arena to my hometown is a little over two hours. An accident slows us down because a car spun out on the ice and has blocked two lanes on the highway. It makes it take forever to get out of the backed up traffic, pushing our arrival time on the GPS.

Every minute added is torture.

We checked flights first, but everything's still grounded because of the fresh snowfall.

Our only option is to drive and the slow progress only makes my anxiety worse. My stomach is a messy tangle that won't settle while I methodically move the balls on the spiral ring Easton got me back and forth on the prongs.

My parents send me a photo of Grandpa in his hospice bed and it hits me harder than I expect to see him like that. His body looks so frail and his wrinkled hands have a mottled grayish tinge. I'm only able to look at the photo for so long before a stabbing pain lances through my gut. I put the phone back on the grip mounted to the dashboard.

Not long after we left, Easton told Reagan I wouldn't be home, but he'd bring her car back in the morning. She sent me a long, supportive message. I can't read through all of it before my vision blurs again because I don't want to believe this is even happening.

I call Mom on speakerphone shortly after to give her an update on our progress once we finally leave Boston city limits, biting my lip raw. As soon as it connects, I don't give her a second to talk.

"Mom?"

"Yes, sweetheart."

"We're just getting out of the city now. How is he?"

She pauses, saying something to Dad. "He, um. He's out of it, but the nurses have assured us that he's not in any pain. Dad's sitting with him now and holding his hand. They told us it's comforting if we keep talking to him so he knows we're with him."

My throat grows hot, muscles strained. "I'm on my way. Tell him I'm coming."

"Okay. Drive safe."

"We are."

Easton's jaw is set when I glance at him in the shadows of the car. He goes as fast as he can, though I can tell from the way his knuckles turn white when his grip tightens on the wheel that if it was safe, he would floor it for me to get me there as quickly as possible.

My aching heart squeezes in gratitude. I'd never get through this if I didn't have him by my side.

Without looking, he reaches for my hand, always able to sense when I need him. I grab it as a lifeline, closing my eyes.

Grandpa's smiling face is there when I do. Pressure builds in my head and tears seep beneath my lids, clumping my lashes when they spill down my cheeks.

At some point, exhaustion gets the best of me. I drift off in a fitful sleep.

I startle awake when I hear Easton talking in a low, serious tone. I don't know how long I was out for, but I dreamed of Grandpa hugging me the day I told him I got accepted into Heston. The sense of hope and peace from the dream shreds to pieces as reality slams back into me.

We're still on the highway. It's after midnight and we're about thirty minutes away.

"Yeah." Easton glances at me. My phone is pressed to his ear. "Okay. We'll head to your parents' place. Send me the address. Thanks. I'll have her there soon."

His sympathetic expression puts me on high alert. I fiddle with the strap on my purse, sitting forward when he puts the phone back on the dash mount.

"What's going on? Why are we going to my parents' house when Grandpa's at the hospice center? I need to be with him right now."

He sighs, reaching for my hand. I tense, heart pounding. His thumb rubs my knuckles.

"I'm sorry," he starts quietly. "That was Ryan. Your grandfather just passed away ten minutes ago. Ryan said he was holding on, but then it happened quickly."

"No," I whisper brokenly.

He can't be g—

My throat closes with a sharp pain, eyes searing as they brim with a fresh wave of devastated tears. I shake my head, refusing to believe this is happening.

No. Please, no.

But we were so close. I was almost there so I could be with him.

My entire family got the chance to say goodbye except me.

It hurts to breathe. To swallow. To talk.

Everything fucking *hurts*.

"I didn't make it," I choke out hoarsely.

Easton holds my hand tighter. He pulls off to the side of the road and turns on the hazards, letting go only long enough to come around the side of the car. Opening my door, he tugs me against him while my world falls apart.

"Shh, I know. I'm so sorry." He sounds as anguished as I do, consoling me with gruff words while stroking my hair and clutching me in his embrace. "It's okay. I've got you."

He unbuckles me and lifts me to hold me closer, sliding into my seat with me on his lap. I bury my face against his chest and hug him with every ounce of strength I have left. I'm no longer in control of my body, tremors racking me as blood rushes in my ears.

Everything I've held back breaks through in an overwhelming rush. I cry so hard it's a struggle to drag air into my lungs. Through my breakdown, Easton never lets me go.

"No," I sob in utter defeat.

"I'm here, Maya," Easton whispers thickly as his own emotions splinter through his composure. "I'm sorry, baby. He knows how much you love him. He knows."

He locks me in his strong arms, murmuring against my temple while I soak his hoodie with my tears. Every part of me aches with unbearable pain.

I wish I'd hugged Grandpa tighter the last time I saw him. Wish I'd spent longer with him.

How was I supposed to know that day we walked through the grounds would be the last time I saw him?

Another tormented sob racks through me.

Grandpa promised me. He promised to see me graduate. Two months. He was supposed to make it two more months for me.

He didn't make it, and neither did I.

My grandpa is gone, and I didn't get to talk to him one last time. I don't know how life will ever be the same again without him.

THIRTY-THREE
MAYA

Ryan and my parents are at the house when we get in. Mom reaches me first, catching me in her arms when my knees go weak. Dad comes up behind her and fits his arms around both of us while Ryan comes up at my side to rub my back. I'm numb, yet also feel like I'm balancing on the edge of breaking down again at the smallest trigger.

"I wanted to be faster," I say hoarsely.

"It's okay," Dad says. "It was tough to go through. Maybe it's better this way."

I look back at Easton, vision going blurry. Would he agree? Both of us lost our chances to say goodbye. He knows what I'm feeling better than they do, although his loss was so sudden he wasn't able to prepare at all.

Maybe there is no good way to face losing your loved ones, whether it's in an accident or by illness, or when it's simply their time to go.

Easton rests his palm at the small of my back when my family gives me room to breathe and holds out a hand.

"I'm sorry for your loss. I'm also sorry we're meeting this way."

"Easton, right?" Dad asks.

"Yes, sir. Easton Blake."

"I've seen some of your games. You've got one hell of a slapshot."

A surprised exhale escapes him. "Thank you."

"Quit fluffing up his ego, Dad. Trust me, he doesn't need it to grow any bigger," Ryan mutters.

It's odd to talk about normal stuff with fresh grief hanging over our heads.

"Why don't we go inside," Mom suggests.

As we sit around the kitchen table with decaf coffee, my family recounts Grandpa's final moments. Mom rubs Dad's shoulders when his voice thickens. Ryan frowns into his mug.

I stare at my parents and brother, jealousy trickling into the hollow well inside me. They got to have something with Grandpa that I was robbed of. I chew on the inside of my cheek, feeling guilty for even getting angry about something that isn't anyone's fault. It was out of our control.

Easton clasps my wrist, thumb tracing a pattern. I concentrate on that, needing a tether to calm down.

I feel out of it when we finally go up to my room. He tucks me in, knuckles grazing my cheek. I wrap my fingers around his forearm.

"Thank you. I would've been such a mess without you to get me home."

He sits on the edge of the bed. "I wish I could stay with you tonight. If I don't leave now—"

"Go." My heart rushes into my throat. "I understand."

His hand unfurls and cups my face. I nuzzle against it, kissing the center of his palm.

"I'm proud of you for making playoffs. You're going to be amazing."

"Get some sleep. I'll see you soon."

He lingers until I close my eyes. I peek them open to find him still by my side. The second time my eyelids shut, they're too heavy to open again.

The next afternoon, Easton's back. I'm on the couch, failing to occupy myself with the book I'm trying to read to get my mind off things. It's always been a favorite, but every few sentences, my thoughts drift. When I get up to answer the door, he's there holding a huge pot with a duffel bag slung over his shoulder.

I didn't expect to see him. He texted me throughout the day, and called this morning when he made it back to campus. I thought he'd throw himself into training for the first round of playoffs that begins later this week.

"What are you doing?" I blurt.

The corners of his mouth tilt up. "Taking care of you."

He sidesteps me, navigating my house like he belongs here. I follow him to the kitchen.

"Hi, Mrs. Donnelly. One of my teammates made this for you to help out."

Mom looks up from the paperwork she has spread on the table to make arrangements for the funeral. She slips off her reading glasses and smiles.

"That was very thoughtful of him. Tell him thank you."

"I will. Cameron's meatballs are a big hit when we need some comfort food." He turns to me. "All the guys send their condolences. Noah said he's offering free hugs whenever you need one. He got the guys to record a video for you before practice this morning."

My lip quivers. I manage to swallow back the wave of emotion.

"Can I see your phone?"

He unlocks it and hands it over without question. First, he plays the video. Noah starts, then he pans down the entire lineup in the empty ice rink. Even Madden has something brief yet sympathetic to say. After it's over I pull up the group chat with the team I've seen him use. Their responses flood the message thread within moments.

Easton 🩶
Hi guys, it's Maya. Thank you for the food and sweet messages. You didn't have to do any of that. Good luck this week!

Noah
Anything for our fans. But seriously, I'm sorry to hear about your Grandpa.

Elijah
You're in our thoughts.

Cameron
Happy to help however we can. Let me know if there's anything else we're able to do for your family.

Theo
Really sorry for you and your family. I let Lainey know and she's going to see if she can come visit you.

Madden
Sorry for your loss.

"Set it on the stove, Easton. I'll heat it up now," Mom directs. "When it's ready, I'll call you in."

He does as she asks, then we go upstairs. He sets his bag down and rummages through it.

"This time I can stay longer. I also got this from Reagan when I went by your place to return her car keys. She said she'd pack more if you need it."

He pulls out some of my clothes, my laptop and phone charger, then some envelopes. One of them has Hana and Reagan's handwriting, and the other has beautiful flowers illustrated all over it.

I'm touched when I open it to find it's a handmade card from Corinne. It says *thinking of you, remember even after the heaviest rainfall flowers will bloom.*

"I ran into her when I went to your apartment. When she found out what happened, she drew this in like ten minutes."

"Wow." I trace the drawings.

The card from Hana and Reagan is just as kind, wishing me well and letting me know to take my time. Hana says she'll cover my shifts at work for as long as I need her to, and Reagan promises to get me anything I need.

Easton loops his arms around me. I sigh in relief, basking in the masculine scent I now associate with everything good in my life.

"Is this you and him?"

I turn to the wall of photos. He's pointing at one where I'm around twelve. Grandpa's mounted on the horse next to mine, mid-laugh and waving at the camera.

"Yeah. He taught me to ride. I loved when we took the horses out on the trails."

It aches to look at, though my lips still twitch into a soft smile. I touch the edge of the frame, wishing more than anything I could relive this moment of pure joy.

A weak laugh leaves me. "He kicked up the biggest fuss because I wanted to do the harder trail that cut through the woods. I got my way, but he wouldn't let me hear the end of it because my horse spooked when we got to jumping a small stream and I ended up falling in. I was soaked and I lost one of my boots." I swipe at my eyes. "He fished me out and held me the whole ride back on his horse while I cried about how sorry I was for getting him wet."

His arms cinch tighter. "It's nice you got to grow up so close with him. You'll always be able to look back on the special relationship you two had."

Memories are all I'll have left. It's such a strange thing to get used to.

I can't go see my grandfather or hug him or tell him about what's going on with me anymore.

"Come eat," Mom calls from downstairs.

"Come on. Food will help." Easton laces our fingers together.

When we climb into bed at the end of the night, it's the first thing to feel right. I didn't realize how much I've grown used to sleeping with him until last night. I woke up twice after he left, unable to drift off as easily as I did when he waited for me to fall asleep. This time I'm able to get a better night's rest.

* * *

On Tuesday, I block Easton from getting in his car when he's getting ready to leave for tonight's practice again after arriving at lunchtime. I'm thankful he's driven the entire way back and forth from Heston Lake every spare second he can to be with me while I'm home, calling me before and after practices when he can't.

He's done more than enough to be there for me while I grieve.

"I wish I could stay longer, too." He steps into me. "I told the coaches I'd make this work."

"You're being crazy going back and forth like this every day." My fingers tangle in his hoodie as his fresh, comforting scent encompasses me.

"I'm in love. People in love do crazy stuff all the time. Besides—" He presses his lips to my hair. "—you're worth every moment of insanity."

"Easton," I mumble.

"Maya."

He twists my reluctant tone to a stubborn one, lifting his brows. My heart pangs, affection breaking through the constant fog of sadness clouding my mind.

"You shouldn't be worried about me. You need to focus on hockey. This isn't helping to split yourself like this. You need to rest and prepare for playoffs, not spend hours on the road just to see me for a little bit."

"It's fine. I can handle it."

I lick my lips, tugging on his sweater. "Please, Easton. I don't want you to sacrifice your dreams for me."

He clasps my chin between his fingers, lifting it to make me look him in the eye. I swallow at his serious expression.

"I'm focused on the most important part of my future. That's not a sacrifice at all." His chin dips and his eyes bounce between mine. "You, Maya."

Damn him. My throat constricts and I sniffle, eyes watering for the millionth time this week.

"I don't want to cry again. I've cried so much."

His expression softens and he cradles my face between his hands. "I know. I didn't mean to make you cry." His thumbs caress my cheeks. "I'm not going anywhere, so lean on me, baby, because you'll always have me to hold you up when you need help."

I slide my arms around him, burying my face against his chest.

"I love you," he murmurs.

My arms tighten. I get it now, why he says it so often. We never know when it will be the last time we get to say it, so we have to make every moment count.

This headstrong, cocky man swept into my life and turned it upside down. He taught me what it's like to love harder than I ever thought possible. I wouldn't give him up for anything.

"I love you more," I confess.

"Impossible."

"Well, we have the rest of our lives together to see who wins this time."

His chest shakes with his chuckle. "Challenge accepted."

I press on tiptoe and he meets me in a kiss.

* * *

The funeral is on Wednesday. Because of the short notice, we end up having the events out of order due to the church and the funeral home being overbooked. The viewing is after today's memorial service, then the burial is tomorrow.

I sit through the service tucked into Ryan's side. Dad gives the eulogy, but Mom has to finish it for him when he becomes too emotional to speak about his father's life.

Easton doesn't make it until just before the viewing in the afternoon. He's partway through changing into a suit when I go outside to meet him. Ryan hands him a jacket he brought with him while Easton buttons up his shirt.

"Thanks. I didn't want to be wrinkled when I got here."

"Thanks for coming." Ryan rubs his nape. "It's got to be tough to drive back and forth right before playoffs. I know everything you've been doing the last few days means a lot to her."

"Of course I came. She needs me, I'm there." Easton's gaze finds me and he strides over. "Hey. I'm sorry I missed the service. We had a team meeting that ran long."

I shake my head, stepping into his embrace when he opens his arms. "This is good."

His cheek rests against the top of my head. "How are you holding up?"

I shrug. "Sucky."

He squeezes me. "That's okay. I'm here now."

"The funeral home won't open to the public for another half hour. It's just the family inside now."

"Do you want to go in?"

Taking a shaky breath, I nod. "I haven't seen him yet. I want to, before it's too late and I lose the chance."

He keeps his arm around me on our way in. We wait for one of my aunts to finish first.

Dread knots my stomach as we approach for my turn. I wasn't

able to see him once I got home. This is the first time I'll face him since he passed away.

The cushion to kneel on beside the casket feels strange against my tights. All the fresh flower arrangements tickle my nose with their strong perfume.

I stare at the pastel blue cushion, willing myself to look up. My chest heaves in trepidation.

"It's okay." Easton rubs my back, kneeling beside me. "You have all the time you need, Maya. Breathe for me."

I'm not prepared when I lift my gaze.

It's—wrong to see him lying so still. So stiff.

Whenever I caught him napping on the couch when I visited his house in high school, he'd sleep hard with his mouth open, snoring loud enough to wake the neighbors on either side of the dairy farm.

He's like a waxy doll. His hands are arranged over his stomach. They're far more frail and bony than when I last saw him.

Sliding my lips together, I gather the courage to hold his hand. A startled noise catches in my throat.

"It's cold," I whisper.

Cold. Rigid. Unable to hold my hand like he did when I was a little girl.

Easton covers my hand with his. I close my eyes as more memories with Grandpa hit me.

All the times we spent together in the stable. The day he gave me the Donnelly Dairy hat I love so much. When I was younger and so excited when me and Ryan got to have a sleepover with him at the farm. The first time the car broke down while I was driving and calling him to walk me through what to do.

He's always been there and now he won't be.

In my head, I hear his voice calling me chicken.

I cover my face, breath quickening into sharp gasps. Easton helps me to my feet and tugs me into his arms. He guides me away from the casket to find us a private corner for my breakdown.

"I know, baby," he says gruffly. "I know."

When I calm down, he's massaging my nape. I lift my head from his chest, frowning at the wet spot and mascara smearing his shirt. At this rate, I think I've cried off all the makeup I reapplied after the service.

"You're a mess now. I'm sorry."

"What are you apologizing for? Come on." He captures my hand and finds the bathroom. "I don't care about my suit."

"Why can't I stop?" I mumble. "No one else is losing it as much as I am."

"Because loss fucking hurts. Everyone handles it differently. So no shame—cry your eyes out. Feel whatever you're feeling as long as you don't bottle it up. Trust me, it doesn't work." His lips twist ruefully. "It'll still come out."

He picks through the basket stocked with toiletries, finding a packet of makeup wipes. Grasping my chin, he carefully wipes my face clean with a cool, soothing wipe.

"What about you?"

"Don't worry about me. I'm good." Once he's done, he wets a thick napkin and holds it over my puffy eyes. "How's that feel?"

"Nice," I murmur.

A few minutes later, he tosses the damp napkin and swipes hair from my face. My lips wobble, not quite forming a smile.

Determined to be useful in some way, I pin him against the counter when he tries to leave the bathroom. He dutifully lets me do what I can to clean the makeup stains off his shirt. I'm not sure if I've made it better or worse.

"Should've worn a black one instead of white," he says with a snort. "It's fine. This jacket's a little tight, but I think I can get it buttoned if you want."

I shake my head. We linger in the bathroom for another moment, but I can't hide out forever. Eventually, we make our way back out.

After the viewing, most of my extended family and close friends move to a pub Grandpa liked to celebrate his life. More memories of times we spent here flood me while they laugh and toast to Grandpa, telling stories about the good times and the bad.

My aunts help put Dad in better spirits until he's the one telling most of the stories. They laugh and cry, their tears tinged with fond happiness and love for the man who was the pillar of our entire family.

Easton chuckles at the funny ones, keeping an arm wrapped around me. My heart might be crushed right now, but I'm so glad to have him here with me. I rest my head against him, shaking it when he tries to get me to eat something.

"I just need you," I whisper.

"You've got me. Here, at least nibble on the bread. It'll help your stomach settle."

It takes me all night, but I get down small bites.

He's right. The food does help.

It's hours after dark by the time we get back to my family's house from the pub. Easton follows me upstairs and sits me on the bed, removing my heels to rub my tired feet. I drop my head back with a grateful sigh.

"You're the best."

The corner of his mouth kicks up. "That's always what I strive for. Tell me what else you need right now."

I bite my lip as I think it over. "A walk."

His handsome warm blue eyes crinkle while he starts humming the tune for the chorus of I'm Gonna Be (500 Miles) by The Proclaimers. My tall, muscled hockey player boyfriend kneels at my feet, humming a song to tell me he'd go anywhere for me—*with* me.

The cracks of my grieving broken heart fuse together as it swells in my chest with a tender glow. Even though this is all so hard, I know I'll be okay because I have him there to catch me whenever I fall. And I want to be that same comfort for him, too.

For the first time in the last few long, draining days, a genuine smile breaks free.

"There's my girl," Easton murmurs.

I bite my lip. "Are you sure? I could go by myself. You're probably exhausted. You need to sleep since you have to get up early."

His fingers loop around my ankles, gliding up my calves. "What did I say about you going out alone?"

I hunch forward to hug him, not needing to repeat his promise when he first found out I like to walk at night to calm my anxiety. "Okay. I don't think I need a long one."

"Change while I run to the car to get my bag. I picked up more of your stuff from Reagan before today's practice. I'm pretty sure she packed your running shoes."

Once I throw on comfortable clothes to walk in, I stand at the wall of photos. Even though Easton won't be with me when we bury Grandpa I think I'll be okay. His advice from earlier when he wiped off my makeup has stuck with me all night.

I don't know that I'll ever fully be ready to say goodbye to Grandpa, but I can allow myself to feel whatever I need to.

THIRTY-FOUR
MAYA

Easton and the guys make it through playoffs. I watch every game from home, sticking around to help my parents with whatever they need after the funeral. Dad joins me whenever I turn the games on because he needs a distraction.

On Sunday Heston is up against Penn State in the quarterfinal. Whoever wins will advance to the championships.

I dart a look at Dad in disbelief when he cheers for Penn State scoring the first goal.

Dad chuckles. "I still root for my alma mater."

"I hope you like losing." I smirk, getting into the game as Heston fires back with a lighting-quick play. "Heston is taking this. They're going to the championships again."

It's a tense game. No one's able to stay ahead for long. It comes down to a play during overtime.

Easton—no, Lainey's brother has the puck now. He passes it back to Easton.

I jump to my feet clutching a pillow to my chest, eyes wide. The players move so fast, the camera has trouble keeping up with them. It's so different from watching in person.

I miss the moment they score, but the lamp lights up and they're going wild with their arms in the air.

They did it. Heston won.

Dad gets up from his armchair with a resigned sigh. He opens his arms and I fall against him with a giddy noise.

"Your boyfriend dusted my school."

Laughter bubbles out of me. "Yeah, he did."

He doesn't let go, hugging me tighter. I sense he needs a minute and return it. The last week since I got home has been like this. For the most part he holds it together, but at random moments his emotions unravel whenever he remembers something he'll miss about Grandpa. I understand, going through the same bouts when I see something that reminds me of him.

"Love you, sweetie," he utters hoarsely.

"Love you too, Dad."

When I pull back, I catch a glimpse of Easton on TV, helmet off, grinning that silly big grin that makes my heart beat faster, laughing at the center of his teammates jostling him in celebration.

More than anything, I want to be with him right now. I can picture his ecstatic laughter and it makes me want to be there for him, to support him and his team the way he's supported me.

I can't stay at home frozen in time forever, missing Grandpa. The world won't stand still. At some point, we have to go on even though he's not with us anymore.

It's time for me to face that sometimes we plan our life out, but one small thing can make it all fall apart. But it doesn't change the fact Grandpa is proud of me no matter what.

He might not be with me, he might not be here to call up whenever I want to talk. I close my eyes, feeling how much he loved me in all the memories of growing up with an amazing grandfather like him.

Grandpa knows how important it was to me to graduate this semester. I'm not giving up on that goal. I've put three years of hard work into this degree and I want to see it through to the end.

I was so afraid of losing him. It's the most difficult thing I've ever experienced.

But Easton's shown me that even though loss is inevitable, it doesn't mean there isn't love to help heal the broken pieces of my heart.

"Where's Ryan?" I ask.

"Upstairs, I think. I'm surprised he didn't watch the game with us."

I cover my smile with my fingers. "When I asked earlier he told me he didn't want to watch Easton's team since they beat Elmwood."

I find Ryan in his room, chin propped in his hand while a show plays on his laptop. I lean in the doorway.

"Hey. Can you do me a favor tomorrow?"

"What?"

"Give me a ride back to Heston Lake?"

He sighs, then nods. "You're ready to go back?"

"I am. It's been over a week. It feels weird, like we're stuck in a bubble here." I shrug. "But I've got to get back into the swing of my life and prepare for finals and graduation."

"I don't think I'm going back to finish classes," he mumbles. "Just to see the guys and get my stuff. I need to find a place close to the Sabres' practice facility and move in before I'm due to report for training."

I blink in surprise. "You could at least finish the semester. You don't have to be there until August, right?"

He shakes his head. "No point. Maybe I'll transfer my credits and finish it online, but my job now is being a professional hockey player."

The concept to just let it go unfinished is mind boggling to me after working my ass off to earn my degree. If Easton gets a draft pick, I wonder if he'll feel the same. I've read over his papers and other assignments when we worked together. He was right about not slacking off in his classes.

"I'll go pack up everything after I shower. Let's head out early," I say.

"Sure."

"Thanks."

"Hey," he says before I walk away. "Are you okay?"

I run my fingers through my limp three-day old ponytail, nodding. "I think I will be."

"Good. I don't like to worry about you."

I huff in amusement, then go to him and wind my arms around him in a crushing hug. He twists to return it.

"And what about you?"

He grunts and nods. "Yeah. Me too."

"Good," I parrot. "I don't like worrying about you, either. Love you."

"Love you too," he says gruffly.

* * *

It feels good to return to Heston Lake. I've only been away for just over a week, yet it feels like it's been ages.

I spend the morning emailing my professors and my advisor to apologize for my absence and explain the situation. Easton said he stopped by my classes, but I still want to tell them myself. My advisor replies to invite me for a meeting during office hours this week to get everything in order for my early graduation.

A relieved sigh escapes me. I flop back on my bed, balancing my laptop on my stomach.

The homepage for the student portal has a banner congratulating the hockey team for advancing to Frozen Four. The championship tournament begins next weekend.

Sitting back up, I check the ticketing sites for any available seats. They can be the crappiest seats, I'll take them just to surprise Easton so he knows I'm there to cheer him on when he steps on the ice.

"Damn. Sold out for both games, really?"

I shouldn't be shocked. Exhaling, I scour Facebook and auction sites for any opportunities. My stomach clenches when I find a listing.

Reagan comes in while I'm bidding and losing, close to emptying my savings account for these tickets.

"Come on," I mutter. "No—No, no! Ugh!"

She sits on my bed. "What's up?"

"I lost the tickets I was bidding on."

"Concert tickets?"

I give her a flat look. "You know every concert playing before I do. No, hockey tickets. I wanted to figure out something last minute for Easton's big game."

"Oh, well lucky for you, I got you something."

She messes with her phone, then shows me a ticket package that covers access for the semifinal and championship games. There's also a hotel reservation in my name.

"Oh my god." I grab her phone, holding it close. "What? How?"

"Me, Hana, and some of the guys on the team all chipped in to get you this and make sure you're staying at the same hotel they'll be at. I've saved up all those extra tips they were giving me for making sure their song played. We wanted you to have something fun to do after everything you've been through."

"Rea." I move my laptop out of the way and tackle her with a thankful hug. "You're the best bestie ever."

"Love you. You'd better write this into your wedding vows," she teases. "And don't leave out the part how I helped him get your number, either."

Both of us are consumed with a fit of giggles.

It feels really good to find the ability to laugh again.

"I have to pack." I spring out of bed and flit around my room.

"You've got days to pack."

"I've got to go. The guys are off this week before the tournament starts, so I want to go there."

She laughs. "You just got back and you're already leaving me."

I pause, clutching all of the clean underwear in my arms to divide between the bag I'll take to the hockey house and the one I'm packing for my surprise trip.

"I'm just joking," she assures me with a wave of her hand. "Go, shoo. Have fun. There's a very sexy tattooed drummer coming over later that's great at pounding things with his stick, anyway."

I snort. "Nice."

She winks. "I mean when he makes music. He's doing the percussion track for the song I'm working on. Then he'll pound me."

"Enjoy."

"Oh, I will, babe." She spreads out on my bed with a dramatic moan. "So much."

"You're ridiculous. I love you."

She grins. "Back at you."

Once I finish cramming two bags full of clothes, I take one, hurrying across campus and through the square to get to Easton. He's sitting on the porch brushing the cat.

Everything feels right again once he looks up, face splitting into a broad, heart-stopping smile.

"Maya."

The warmth spreading through me at his affectionate tone fills me to the brim until I can't contain a smile.

I start towards him slowly. My pace quickens when he stands, opening his arms. I fly right into them, jumping on the last step. He catches me in his strong embrace, a content rumble sounding in his chest.

"I'm glad you're back."

"I was ready."

I smoosh my face into his hoodie, savoring the comforting fresh masculine scent that is so distinctly *him*. The scent that tells me I'm where I belong—the home I've found in my person.

He strokes my back. The bag on my shoulder slips and he takes it for me.

"You didn't say you were coming back."

I rest my chin against his chest, peering up at him. Another happy flutter moves through me.

"Ryan drove me back early this morning. I had to talk to my professors to make sure I was on track first, but I wanted to tell you in person that I was ready to find my normal again."

He hums, hugging me tighter. "That's an important step. Proud of you."

"It's thanks to you for keeping me afloat through this. Thank you."

"You don't have to thank me for being there for you. You needed me."

God, I love him. I love him so much it overwhelms me. How is it possible to feel everything this deeply for one person?

"I did. But now it's my turn. I promise I'll be watching and cheering you on."

He brings his face close to mine, staring into my eyes before he kisses me. I smile into it, thinking about my surprise trip.

"Are you staying a while?"

He hoists my bag, resting a hand at the small of my back to guide me inside.

"Until you leave." I shoot him a sassy smirk. "So you'd better run upstairs and kick out whoever's been warming your bed because your girlfriend's here."

He chuckles, smacking my ass with a shake of his head. "The only other girl in my bed is Kit-cat. You two are the only ladies for me."

"Smooth, captain."

He tilts his head back slightly, eyes hooding in pleasure, the tip of his tongue tracing his lip. My heart beats faster. I step towards him, drawn to him like a magnet.

"The others are in the living room. I'm going to put your stuff upstairs."

I linger for a moment, taking in the way his gray sweatpants accentuate his ass and sculpted legs. Part of me wants to chase him up those stairs, but I want to see the guys, too.

Cameron and his tutor from class, Elodie, are on the couch with game controllers. Hers is customized with a pretty pastel green skin and cat paw covers on the joysticks. Elijah and Madden are sprawled in the armchairs watching the game they're playing together.

Noah spots me first when he's coming in from the back den in gym shorts and a Heston Hockey hoodie.

"Hey, there she is." He holds up a hand for a high five. "Good to see you."

I slap my hand against his and hug him. "You guys, too. Thanks again for all the messages and food you sent."

"No problem," Cameron says without taking his eyes off his character.

He's dressed like a medieval knight and Elodie's character uses magic. I fold my arms over the back of the couch. They've been playing this a lot lately during their study breaks.

"What are you guys playing again?"

"It's an open world RPG with a fantasy setting. You play single player or multiplayer if you form a party, like we have," Elodie answers quietly. "The main storyline is loose enough that we can create our own around the major quests. We're working on a new base to store our supplies before we take on the next boss."

It's taken her a while to get comfortable with the boisterous atmosphere of the hockey house and open up to us. She's introverted until it comes to gaming, then she's more talkative with a rush of information to dump. It's really cute to see her get animated about things she's interested in. I like her, she's a calming presence to hang out with.

After a few minutes of watching them explore the scenic area, I'm bouncing behind the couch. "Ohh, on your left, Cam! No, left! Dude, how are you so good in the net but you can't stop your enemy from hitting you?"

"I—don't—know," he mutters. "Shit. El? A little help here?"

Elodie laughs quietly at my enthusiastic commentary. He games with his whole body, jerking side to side. In contrast, she keeps her eyes glued to the screen while her hands move in quick patterns on the controller.

Muscled arms lock around my waist and Easton's scent surrounds me as he presses his body against mine. I tangle my fingers with his, leaning into him with an appreciative hum.

"There's my girl," he murmurs.

THIRTY-FIVE
EASTON

Frozen Four is hosted in Boston this year. It feels like fate to be playing the championships in the city I want to play for professionally.

This morning I left Maya in my bed. We spent so long saying goodbye—my lips fused to hers, tempted to sink into her—before three of my teammates banged on the door with warnings to get going. She curled up with a book and the cat, wishing me luck. Well, I had to kiss her one last time after that, didn't I?

It took four more guys knocking and barging in to get me to leave.

They're just lucky Maya pulled one of my t-shirts on while I got my stuff together, or we'd be down in players if they'd seen her naked.

The coaching staff gets us checked in at the hotel once our bus arrives, then we're told to meet back downstairs for a team dinner. We're up against Denver in our bracket of the semifinal tomorrow night. Whichever two teams make it through to the top two will face off Sunday night for the national title.

After dinner, Coach stops us in the hotel lobby.

"We're meeting at ten tomorrow." He dips his chin, surveying each of us. "Don't go wild tonight or stay up too late. I expect you ready for tomorrow's game."

"Yes, sir," I answer for all of us.

He nods, waving us off. We split up at the bank of elevators, me, Theo, Cameron, Madden, Noah, and the rookie piling into one.

"We're gonna kill it tomorrow." Noah stretches, folding his hands behind his head, his suit jacket straining to contain his bulky muscles.

"If I'm honest, I thought Penn State had us," Elijah admits sheepishly. "It's crazy we made it to the top four."

"You gotta have faith, rookie." I slap him on the back. "Let's keep this going, right?"

"Right," Madden answers with a burning look of determination. "All the way."

"That's what I like to hear," I say.

They exit the elevator in pairs, Theo and Elijah leaving first, then Madden and Noah when we reach their floor.

"We've made it here again," Cameron says when it's just us left.

We shoot each other matching grins, clasping hands to bump our shoulders together. He said something similar back in freshman year, sounding bewildered compared to the pride he has now.

"Hell yeah, man. Three years running. I wouldn't want it any other way."

"Let's do this."

"Let's fucking do it," I echo confidently.

I'm not nervous. If anything, I'm strangely at peace, my mind clear and eager to get on the ice to prove myself.

The elevator reaches our floor. We exchange a look as the doors open. Smirking, I dart forward. He moves at the same time. We snort and choke back laughter, wrestling each other down the hall until we reach the room we're sharing.

He gets me in a headlock and I nudge my elbow into his side before we manage to unlock the door and practically trip through it.

"I win," he crows.

"Like hell you did."

He waggles his brows, backing further into the room. I flick on the light, loosening the tie I wore to dinner and undo my top button.

"It's not too late yet. Should we watch something?" I grab the remote, surfing the channels.

He's absorbed in his phone. Muttering to himself, he freezes. His eyes widen, then he rushes for the door like he's diving to save a loose puck.

"Dude, where are you going?" I call after him.

"Uh, getting snacks," he blurts.

I lift my brows. Maybe I'm the only one who's calm. Every player has a different ritual before a game, and the pressure of the championship only makes those habits more intense.

Sitting on the edge of the bed, I check my phone. Mom texted to wish me good luck when I told her we made it to the city and were getting dinner. She liked all the photos I sent her of the hotel and the skyline as the bus drove into Boston.

Maya asked if I ran into anyone famous while the team was at dinner.

Easton
No. Noah lost his shit when he thought he saw Brad Marchand at the place where we got dinner. No dice though.

Maya
Oh damn that would've been cool.

Easton
I know. We just got back to the hotel.

Maya
Yeah? Going to bed yet?

Easton
Not yet. It's only 9, that feels too early.

Maya
Are you nervous?

Easton
Nah. Not when I know I've got to show off for my girl 😏

Maya
Good luck. I'll be watching you 🩶

Easton
Those are the magic words. Now I know we'll win this.

A knock at the door makes me tear my attention from smiling at my phone like an idiot in love. Maybe Cameron needs help carrying in the snacks he muttered about when he left.

It's not Reeves outside the door when I open it.

Maya steals my breath, her tan peacoat open to show off the nice dress beneath. The green velvet bodice hugs her body with a plunging neckline that gives me a tempting view, then the dress follows the shape of her curves, flaring from the hips down to her calves with a sexy slit that shoots right up to her thigh.

I stare at her, heart beating hard. "You're here."

"Surprise," she says with a little wiggle of her hands. "Reagan and the others scored me tickets for this weekend so I could be here in person to support you."

"You look..."

Sexy as fuck.

Several things jump to mind as blood rushes south to my hardening dick. Her tits make me want to bury my face in her cleavage and peel those dainty straps off her shoulders to lick, bite, and suck on them. The craving to touch her barrels into me, but she probably put effort into getting dressed up, so I shouldn't maul her.

"Amazing," I finish, pulling her in for a kiss, then murmuring against her lips. "Wow."

She laughs. "Thank you." She smooths her palms up the lapels of my jacket. "You too. I like when you wear a suit."

"How did you know where to find me?"

A playful smile tugs at the corners of her mouth. "Cameron let me know your room number."

Is that why he left in a rush? I'll definitely have to thank him later for being an excellent best friend. I grin, arms circling her waist beneath the coat, stroking the plush material of her outfit.

"I'm really glad you're here, baby."

"You've done so much for me, and showed up for me when I needed you. I wanted to do the same for you, because this isn't one sided." She admires my suit again, her eyes hooding. "And you're already dressed to go."

"Where are we going?"

It doesn't matter. I'll go anywhere she wants. I'm already

following her out into the hall once I grab my coat, lacing our fingers together.

"That's a surprise, too."

Fuck, I love this girl. I can't believe I thought I didn't want a girlfriend in order to focus, because being with her proved me wrong again and again. She grounds me, makes my focus sharper than ever.

Boston at night is beautiful. The city overflows with a sense of history in every brick and cobblestone. We walk aimlessly, taking in the sights hand in hand.

"This is a nice part of the city," she says when we're passing through a spot with cool apartments.

"Yeah. Look at that one."

"I like it, too. I always thought I'd end up in Boston when I was growing up. Maybe we'll get a place like that if you end up playing here."

We.

The side of my mouth kicks up and I squeeze her hand. "I love the way you think."

She grants me a brilliant smile. The wind moves through her hair. I stop in my tracks, then step into her, tucking her hair back in place. With a smile that forms slowly, I kiss her.

"Where are we heading? I thought maybe you made reservations or something since you're dressed up."

I trace the dip in her waist. She peers up through her lashes, moving closer.

"I thought about it. Then I decided I didn't want to have a table or anything else separating us so we could be free to do this as much as we want."

She grasps my lapels and draws me into another kiss. I take my time, pouring everything I want to say without words into it.

When we part, her hazel eyes gleam. "I have a better idea than fancy dinner."

"Yeah?"

She takes my hand with a delighted sound. Two blocks later, we find a place to get chicken nuggets.

We stroll and eat, sharing them between us. I let her have most of them, knowing the gravity of keeping my girl fed.

"Let's sit down here."

My arm drapes behind her on the bench while we people watch. She looks beautiful—not because her hair and makeup are done and she's wearing a nice outfit, but because she's here for me. Because she's mine.

It gives me the strong urge to get down on one knee right here and now to ask her something important. I don't have a ring or a plan, but I do have my heart to give her over and over again.

"What are you thinking about?"

I stroke the soft material of her coat with a muted hum. "I'm thinking about doing something a little crazy."

"Hold that thought." She shows me a list of nearby places on the map on her phone. "There's a gourmet donut shop around the corner. Can we go?"

"Don't you know by now?"

Her eyes bounce between mine, shining radiantly. "What?"

I take her hand. "I'll always go anywhere you ask."

We run down the block, our laughter echoing into the night. The donut shop is minutes from closing when we reach it, and I buy up four of the remaining ones in the display case.

She samples them first, then feeds me a bite.

"This one, oh my god. Try this."

I open my mouth, lips dragging against her fingertips when she pops the piece in my mouth. It's good, but I'm not paying much attention to the flavors.

"Mm."

She steps in front of me, planting her hands on my chest and tilting her head. "Let's head back. I have one more part to my big surprise."

My dick is very interested in the sinful lilt in her words. The walk back should only take a half hour, but I keep stopping to kiss her until she's breathless.

By the time we're in the elevator, I'm all over her, face buried in the crook of her neck, seeking out more skin to map with my tongue and teeth.

"Easton," she breathes throatily. "Aren't there cameras on these?"

"Don't care," I mutter against her throat. "Too busy doing this."

She clings to me when I kiss a sensitive spot that makes her sway. The elevator stops. I keep her pinned in the corner for another beat.

"What room number?" I rasp.

"Uh, shit. I forget." She releases a faint giggle, digging for the keycard in her small purse. "504."

She yelps when I haul her over my shoulder and start down the hall. One of my hands slips beneath her dress to grasp the back of her thigh.

"Easton!" She folds over my back, smoothing her hands down my spine to rest just above my ass.

"Just like the first night we met. Key."

I reach around, blindly feeling for her to drop it in my hand. Once her door unlocks, I take her inside and allow my hands to roam where I want, squeezing her plump ass before tossing her on one of the beds.

She bounces, then rises on her elbows with a sexy fucking look that makes me want to take her apart.

"Wait." She slides off the bed. "The surprise."

"Baby." I brace my forearm against the door frame leading to the bathroom while she takes her bag inside. "You don't have to put on lingerie or anything for me. I want you just as you are. I'm three seconds from tearing that dress off you."

"Don't you dare," she says through the door in an amused tone. "This is one of my favorites."

I rest my face in the crook of my arm, pressing a palm to my straining erection to take off the edge. "You have two minutes to get your cute ass out here before I bust this door down."

She giggles. "You're going to ruin the surprise."

"Screw the surprise. I want you too badly," I rumble.

The door opens, revealing her wearing nothing but my alternate jersey. My mouth drops open. She tips her chin up.

"Screw the surprise?"

"Fuck."

She grins, teasing the hem of the oversized sweater higher up her leg to reveal she's not wearing panties, either. "Oh, so now it's fuck the surprise? Well, that is the idea."

"You—" With a playful growl, I capture her in my arms. "Mine."

I swallow her fond laugh, kissing her hard. My touch explores her body beneath my jersey, one hand on her ass and the other snaking up to play with her nipple until she arches against me.

She starts towards the bed when I release her, but I want something else. I grab her hips and redirect her towards the window, plastering myself against her back to walk her over to the excellent view of the Boston skyline.

I splay my hands over her stomach while fitting the ridge of my cock against her ass. "Put your hands on the window."

Air rushes past her lips. She does as I say, my cock pulsing at the sight. I drop to a knee behind her, ripping out of my suit jacket. Pushing the bottom of the hockey sweater up to expose her mouthwatering ass, I spread her, a rough sound catching in my throat at the sight.

Not wasting a minute, I bury my face against her pussy, covering it with my mouth to work her with my tongue.

"Oh!" Her hips tilt to give me better access. "Oh my god, that's—ah!"

I groan against her folds, feasting on her like a starving man. My tongue swirls around her clit, then presses against it, stroking it until her legs begin to tremble.

"I'm so close," she pushes out between moans.

My fingers dig into her thighs and ass, holding her open further while I worship her body.

"Oh, shit, shit." She cries out and scrabbles at the glass, rising on her toes.

I yank her back against my face, not done enjoying my meal. Her pussy soaks me, coating my jaw, dripping down my throat.

"You're going to make me come again," she whimpers.

"Good," I say against her folds. "Give it to me. Come on my face."

Her body goes rigid and her breath hitches before she grinds against my face with a moan. I'm panting when I shoot to my feet, fumbling to unbuckle my belt. I slap her ass when she drops one of her hands between her legs to play with her pussy while I nearly rip the buttons on my shirt in my haste to get undressed.

"Keep those hands on the window, baby."

She twists to look at me. "Hurry up, then."

Holding my gaze, she braces both hands against the glass, looking gorgeous as fuck with my jersey hanging around her waist, pussy glistening and begging to be fucked.

"Good girl."

I finish stripping and slot behind her. My nose dips to graze her hair, inhaling her sweet scent. She nudges her hips back, her folds gliding over my length.

I line up, covering one of her hands with mine as I sink in slowly, making her take my cock inch by inch.

"Easton." Her head thumps against my shoulder, face angling towards me.

"I know." My eyes hood when I fill her completely. "Hold on."

Keeping her steady by gripping her hip, I drag my cock out slowly, then slam back in. Her mouth drops open in the reflection. My thrusts are slow and sharp, making her tits bounce with each one.

We fuck against the window with the city as our view.

Her sounds of pleasure grow louder and her back arches when she's close to coming. I find her clit, circling it with my fingers while I trail kisses down her throat to her shoulder. Her pussy clamps and she chokes out a plea.

I pull out, silencing her protest with a kiss as I pick her up, wrapping her legs around me. Taking her to the bed, I lay her down and enter her again. She throws her head back, arms locking around my neck.

She's all mine. My girl, wearing my jersey.

A groan tears from me and my hips stutter, cock pulsing with my release. She welcomes it with a sound of pleasure, body squeezing me tight while she hums and rocks her hips languidly.

"Maya," I rasp.

I bury my face against her neck. We're both panting and wrecked. Her fingers run through my hair. Pushing up to brace over her, I brush my lips over hers.

"So, good surprise?" she murmurs.

"Best fucking surprise."

I roll to my back, tugging her on top of me. My palm splays over her spine, tracing it in long sweeps as our gazes meet. Those stunning hazel eyes that stopped me in my damn tracks crease with love. Threading my fingers into her hair, I draw her down for another kiss, needing to tell her with my lips once more that she's my world.

Whatever the future holds for both of us, we'll have each other. Nothing will separate us.

Maya Donnelly is it for me and I want to spend my life with her.

EPILOGUE

EASTON

July, Three Months Later

THE SUMMER HEAT bakes me alive while I allow Lainey and Reagan to lead me around town for "errands". They're doing a decent job with the secret they're supposed to keep from me.

They haven't realized I already found out about the surprise party Maya organized to celebrate my number one draft pick and the contract I signed with the Bruins.

Don't get me wrong, I'm happy as fuck about achieving my dreams. I still can't believe I'll step on the ice at TD Garden wearing the jersey of mine and my dad's favorite team. Fucking surreal.

And I think it's sweet that she wants to surprise me just like she did a few months ago when she turned up in Boston to watch us win Frozen Four in person. That weekend is cemented in my mind as one of my favorite memories from the moment I found her waiting outside my hotel room to winning to celebrating with her all night long.

She's gone through all the trouble to put this together, so I'm playing along for now.

What she doesn't know is that I got the guys to help me double down for the real celebration: her early graduation.

We had dinner with her parents and brother after watching her walk with honors in the cap and gown ceremony in May. As much as she smiled that day at her accomplishment, there was a bittersweetness for her to go through it without her grandfather there to see it.

After the NHL draft, she was there for me when I went through the same thing, wishing Dad was with us to see another important moment of my life.

All we can do is carry them with us to get through the times we'd do anything to rewrite the universe to have one more minute with them.

I saw today's party as the perfect opportunity to congratulate her with our friends. I'm so damn proud of my girl and I want her to get all the recognition she deserves for her hard work.

"Is that the last of it?" I ask when I accept another bag to carry for the girls.

Reagan checks her phone. "Looks like it. Thanks again for helping us out." She pats my arm. "We appreciate you doing the heavy lifting when Alex had to bail on us."

Yeah, I bet. Last I saw when I looked at the group text with the guys, Alex was helping Cameron season and marinate the meat for the grill."

"No problem."

"Let's drop this off at the house," Lainey suggests.

I lift my eyes to the sky, begging Dad for the patience to finish playing along without giving myself away. I should've told the girls when they wrangled me into these errands to get me out of the house that I knew what was going on.

The walk back isn't more than a few minutes, but I'm loaded down with everything we bought. Half of it I know is for the party, but I swear Lainey and Reagan picked out a bunch of books at Derby Book Shop just to fuck with me because I've got to be carrying about thirty pounds worth of romance novels.

By the time we walk up the path to the house, I've definitely gotten arm day done.

They pause outside the door, making a show of petting Kit-cat stretched out in a puddle of sun. Reagan pretends to take a photo of the cat, except I'm tall enough to see her texting rather than using her camera app.

"Such a sweet girl," Lainey coos louder than usual.

I cough to cover my snort. Is that the code phrase? They're terrible at this whole distracting the guest of honor thing.

It's not me, anyway, the real guest of honor is inside, probably finding a hiding spot to jump out at me as soon as I walk through the door. My lips twitch. I'm more than ready to see her.

At last, they reach for the door, peeking over their shoulders at me. I smirk.

As soon as it swings open, everyone shouts, "Surprise!"

Maya is nothing more than a blur flying at me from her spot at the bottom of the steps. I quickly set down the bags before she crashes against me. Locking my arms around her, I lift her up.

"What's all this?" I ask despite knowing the answer.

The guys barely contain their amusement. Cameron brandishes grill tongs, gesturing to the hand-painted banner in Heston colors declaring *#24 is #1 Congratulations Easton* with the NHL and Bruins logos.

"We couldn't send you off when you report for training without a party, captain," Maya says.

God, I fucking love her and that sassy tone she uses to tease me.

"Is that so? I don't know." Signaling to the guys with my chin, I bring my face close to hers. "I think you should look again."

Noah records us to get her reaction while the rest of my teammates shuffle around the entryway, unrolling the poster they helped me finish yesterday after I was sure Maya was asleep. It reads *Maya Donnelly is smarter than me, congrats on graduating love Easton.*

Her eyes go wide, then she cracks up, tucking her face into my neck. I kiss her head.

"Surprise, baby."

"You knew, didn't you? How did you find out?" she manages to get out between joyous laughter.

"You're not as sneaky as you think. Me, on the other hand. Very sneaky."

Noah moves in for a closeup on us. "Annnnd kiss."

We look at him, then I take her chin to turn it back to me, capturing her gaze for a beat before I close the gap between us and press my mouth to hers.

"What are we waiting for? Everyone out back. Let's get it going." Cameron ties an apron over his head that says grill king. "Burgers will be ready soon."

"No one come in the upstairs bathroom, we're going to put our bathing suits on," Reagan announces, grabbing Lainey's hand.

"Babe, that's like dangling a steak in front of a starving dog. Now all I'm going to think about is two hot chicks naked together right next to my room."

"Hey," Alex says sharply, pausing from moving Lainey's bags of books into a separate pile. "Don't you dare think about my girl, Porter."

Reagan laughs and smacks his chest lightly. "Shut up, you big flirt."

"Are you sure you don't need help?" He saunters closer. "I tie great knots."

Madden jerks him aside with a forceful grip on the back of his open Hawaiian shirt, thick brows flattening.

"That's not funny," he mutters.

Noah holds up his hand. "Relax, Graves. Didn't mean any harm."

Reagan grins, shaking her head. She puts a hand on Madden's shoulder when he steps between them, standing guard at the steps.

"Thanks, Madden. You're the MVP Knight."

"I thought that was me?" I joke.

"You're the rookie now." Maya waggles her brows.

Alex snorts. "That's right."

"Go change," she says when I set her on her feet.

I admire her outfit, the green bikini top giving me plenty of ideas. Her skirt is long and flowing, the sheer floral material split up to her hips in two spots to show off her luscious tan legs. I'm a genius for suggesting to the guys to make Maya think it was her idea to put kiddie pools in the yard.

"I'll meet you out back."

I jog upstairs to put swim trunks on, rifle through my shorts to get a folded slip of paper from the pocket, then head outside.

The yard has blue, green, and white streamers hanging from every tree and fence post. Logs burn and crackle in the fire pit. They set up a kid's version of a rink on the grass to play 1v1 with mini sticks, improvising a slip n' slide to serve as ice.

Cameron and Alex talk while manning the grill. It smells fantastic. The girls have cans of hard seltzer and sit with their feet in the pools.

McKinley puts a beer in my hand and clinks his bottle with mine. "Fuckin' wild, bro. It won't be the same without you."

I huff in agreement, running a hand through my hair. "Yeah. It still doesn't feel real."

The next step of my future is about to start, but I'm going to miss this when I leave for Boston next month. Hanging out with people who have become as close as family.

College hockey is officially over for me. Part of me is still adjusting to that reality.

Madden and Elijah hustle by us, shoving each other with challenging smirks. They face off against each other with mini sticks on the play rink in the corner of the yard, some of our teammates heckling them.

Next year these guys won't have me. It's wild to think of them winning the next Frozen Four with me watching from the sidelines. They'll be skating with new recruits to the team. Someone else will take over for me as captain. My money's on Cameron, but he thinks it should be Noah.

Even though I'm moving up to the pros, I know these guys are my brothers for life.

Just like I know I want forever with Maya.

I head in her direction, led by the invisible tether she has tied around my heart.

"Hey, you." I capture her wrist, reaching into my pocket for the folded piece of paper I've been carrying. "Want to sneak away with me for a minute? I got you something."

"Ohh, mysterious," she jokes.

I tip my head in the direction of the magnolia tree full of pink blooms. We only make it a few steps before someone asks if a phone is buzzing.

"Oh, hang on." Maya grabs her bag off the picnic table, pressing it to her ear. "Yup, that's me."

She pulls her phone out and moves to the side of the yard. I follow, throwing a glance over my shoulder. I wanted this to be a surprise, but maybe I should've told some of our friends to help this go smoothly.

"What's up, Ry?"

My gaze snaps back to her. Is this for real?

I snag the phone from her to talk to him. "Is this life and death?"

"What—Blake? Why are you always grabbing the phone when I'm trying to talk to my sister, man?"

Weird. Years of playing against this guy, and somehow he'll go from being my rival to my brother in law.

If I can ever finish proposing to Maya.

"I can't wait to get you back for this," I mutter.

"Big talk, Blake."

A competitive grin twists my mouth. "That's rich coming from a second round pick. You'd better bring it, Donnelly. Now fuck off."

While I'm getting off the phone with her brother, Maya takes the paper in my hand. I open and close my mouth, holding back a laugh at how this idea has fallen apart.

"What's this?"

She unfolds it, finding the heart I drew on it. I picked out the ring I want to get her, but my signing bonus hasn't hit my account yet to pay it off before today's party. Even without the ring in hand, I've wanted to ask her for months, and being surrounded by our friends seemed like the perfect chance to do it.

I sigh, smiling softly as my fingertips trail down her arms before grasping her waist. "My heart, baby. Keep taking care of it because it's all yours."

Her eyes meet mine, crinkling at the corners. "You and your lines, hotshot."

"I only speak the truth."

"In that case..."

She turns away to rummage through it for a pen. When she faces me again, she holds up the paper. She's drawn a heart that overlaps mine, both hearts labeled with our names.

"You've got mine, too."

"Come here."

I knead her waist, tugging her against me. Neither of us stop smiling as we kiss.

"Where did—? Never mind. Found them!" Noah shouts when he rounds the side of the house. "They snuck away to make out again."

"Typical," Reagan calls from the other side of the yard.

Maya laughs and rejoins the party. I hang back a moment, watching her hugging Reagan and accepting a drink while they splash their feet in the kiddie pool.

There will be time. I don't have to rush anything.

All that matters is that we have each other.

EPILOGUE

MAYA

October, 3 Months Later

It's thrilling to be at TD Garden for Easton's first NHL game. He's worked hard since the start of training to get to this point and tonight he's making his debut as a professional hockey player. My heart swells, overflowing with how proud I am of his work ethic and determination.

The tickets he got us are great seats a few rows back from the glass with a fantastic view of the action. We file in next to an older man who seems familiar when it's close to the pregame show. I think I've seen him around Heston Lake. He has a Bruins cap tugged low over his face and fiddles with a radio.

A nostalgic smile tugs at my lips. He reminds me of Grandpa. He'd always listen to the radio to get commentary from his favorite sports station while watching games live, too.

I miss him. It catches me off guard some days. Sometimes I'm able to laugh, then other times I need a minute to gather myself, shedding a few tears. Whenever it happens, Easton is always there to remind me it's okay.

When Easton found an apartment in Boston, I moved in with him. I haven't determined my next step yet. For now, I'm taking time off before deciding on grad schools and enjoying life in a new city. In the meantime, I've been volunteering at a local animal shelter and I scored a part-time job at a physical therapy clinic.

Asher freezes at my side instead of sitting down in our row.

"Holy crap, you're Neil Cannon," he gushes.

"Asher," Mrs. Blake chides. "Sorry, sir."

The older man adjusts his hat, giving us a better view of his face. "It's fine."

"It really is you." Asher's eyes are wide. "You're my brother's favorite. He has your picture on a poster."

Mr. Cannon chuckles, surveying the rink with a knowing gaze. "Who's your brother?"

The answer isn't hard to guess. I'm wearing Easton's Heston U jersey and Asher has his new Bruins number on his.

"Easton Blake. He's playing tonight," Asher says.

"Thought so. He's who I'm here to see."

Asher gasps, whispering to his mom. "He knows Easton."

"Nice to meet you," she says.

"He's a good kid," Mr. Cannon says.

His gaze moves to me, turning curious. I hold out a hand.

"Hi. I'm Maya, Easton's girlfriend."

He hums and nods as if this is intriguing information. "Ah, so it's you."

"What do you mean?"

He shakes his head. "Nothing. He said things turned out right when he paid me a visit to invite me for tonight's game."

I'm still not sure what he's talking about, but my phone vibrates with a notification. Pulling it out, I grin at Easton's name on the screen.

Easton 🩶
We'll be out on that ice soon.

Maya
I can't wait.

Easton 🩶
Eyes on me. I'm going to score a hat trick for you.

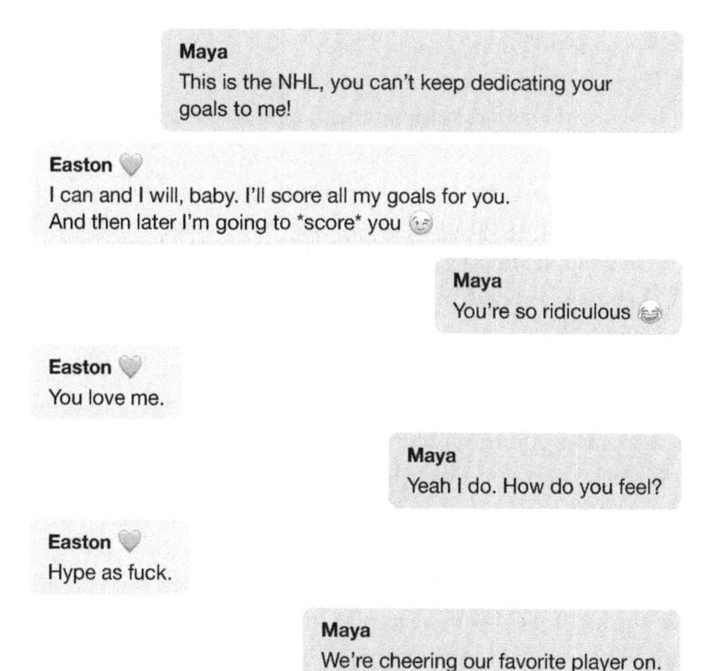

I send him a selfie of us in our seats, managing to squeeze in Mr. Cannon.

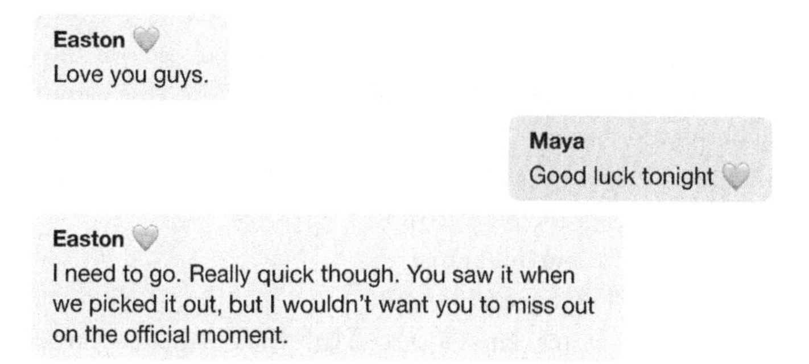

He sends a photo of him in his suit from when he arrived earlier at the arena. I bite my lip because he looks incredibly attractive when he's dressed up.

The lights flash and an announcer booms over the speaker system to kick things off. The players spill onto the ice one by one as their names are introduced.

"Welcome to Boston, Easton Blake."

"There he is," I say warmly.

He scans the crowd with an awed expression as he skates to the blue line.

When the players start their warm-ups, he looks up at our section. He spots us, grinning big enough to light up the entire arena. We wave when he lifts a gloved hand.

"Mom, you've taken a million photos of him already," Asher says. "Are you watching?"

"I know. Don't worry, I'm watching. I'm a proud, Mom, okay?" She winks at me and ruffles his hair, turning the camera to capture a shot of them together. "Of both my boys."

At puck drop, I'm taken back to all the times I went to Bruins games growing up. It's even more exciting now.

Me and Easton's family get excited when he swings his legs over the boards to join the game near the end of second period. We weren't sure if he would get play time as a rookie, but I'm not surprised to see him meshing with his teammates and seamlessly finding his place amongst them.

He's more focused and driven than I've ever seen him in a game, not hesitating for a second to play right alongside seasoned pros. He knows he belongs on that ice just as much as they do.

There's only a few minutes left on the clock before the next break before third period. Both teams put their all into the game.

The players bunch up near center ice along the boards, fighting for the puck. Easton provides support, then races down the ice when his teammate passes the puck to him.

My heart leaps into my throat.

"Go, Easton!" Asher and I shout.

I reach across his lap to take Mrs. Blake's hand. Two guys converge on Easton, but he's faster.

The opponent's goalie dives into a split to block the shot he takes, looking around in bewilderment when the lamp lights up.

"Oh my god!" I leap to my feet, squeezing his mom's hand. "He scored!"

The jumbotron plays a repeat of the goal, slowing it down as the arena erupts in excitement.

Mrs. Blake pulls her hand free to press her fingers to her mouth, eyes shining with elated tears. Asher throws his fists in the air, chanting his brother's name.

Easton laps the ice. The jumbotron follows him, capturing his grin when he slows in front of our section, pointing up at us. His eyes lock on me and he blows me a kiss.

"Maya, look! We're on the big screen." Asher points at the jumbotron.

My cheeks heat at the sight of us shown next to the camera angle of Easton on the huge monitor hanging above the ice.

The sports commentary on Mr. Cannon's radio filters through the clamor of the fans.

"An excellent play from promising rookie and number one NHL draft pick, Easton Blake. We got the chance to have a few words with him before the game. He told us he's got his dad with him tonight, a longtime inspiration for him, as well as his family and fiancé cheering him on in the audience."

My head whips to the side. Did the commentators call me his fiancé?

We've talked about marriage before—murmuring to each other late at night before we fall asleep, on our walks through the city to explore the area where we live together, and over chicken nuggets.

But technically we're not engaged yet.

Neil Cannon laughs. "Not holding back anymore, kid."

I turn my attention back to the ice, laying a hand over my rapidly beating heart. I can't stop smiling.

To the world, he's making a name for himself as the rookie to watch this season.

To me, Easton Blake is always going to be the cocky hockey captain that tossed me over his shoulder the night I danced on the bar and stole my heart.

* * *

Thank you so much for reading ICED OUT! If you can't get enough swoony Heston U hockey players, keep reading to enjoy two free bonus deleted scenes of Maya and Easton.

Download the free bonus scenes: bit.ly/vebonuscontent

Need more new adult romance with another irresistible book boyfriend? Meet Cooper Vale in THE DEVIL YOU KNOW. Enjoy the brother's best friend standalone with spicy lessons.

Start THE DEVIL YOU KNOW now!

BONUS DELETED SCENES

If you can't get enough of Easton and Maya, enjoy two bonus scenes! Additional bonus content is available on my website. Visit the address below or scan the QR code to collect all available bonus content.

BONUS CONTENT:
www.veronicaedenauthor.com/bonus-content

MAYA

DELETED SCENE BETWEEN CHAPTERS 11 AND 12

THE BUZZING WILL. Not. Stop.

Easton keeps texting me while I'm in class. At first I try to pretend it's not my purse vibrating every few minutes, but the unimpressed look my professor shoots me when it goes off for the fifth time makes me dig it out to silence it.

Maya
Dude, I'm in class.

Hat Trick King 💦
Oh, my bad. What class?

Maya
Does it matter?

Hat Trick King 💦
Yes? I want to know what you're studying. All part of getting to know you ;)

I don't have time for this. The professor is going over what she expects for the topics we select in our next essay. I shove my phone into the folds of the sweater piled next to my notebook. I always come into class cold, but the heat in here is usually cranked all the way up and I get too hot.

It doesn't work. Now I'm self conscious about the vibrations muffled by my sweater. A girl sharing the wide desk with me peeks over when it goes off again.

That's it.

If telling him I'm currently in class isn't enough to shut him down, then I'll need to resort to other measures.

I ignore him for a few more minutes before I drop the bomb on him.

Maya
heyy daddy

Maya
oh shit sorry haha, that was for someone else, wrong number

It only takes him seconds to go feral.

Hat Trick King 🥶
What????

Hat Trick King 🥶
Who?

Hat Trick King 🥶
Don't leave me on read, come back here

Hat Trick King 🥶
Maya

Hat Trick King 🥶
Seriously who tf are you talking to

I cover my mouth to contain my amusement. He's losing it now that I've disappeared and left read receipts on.

He goes from texting to bombarding me with calls. After the first one startles me, I decline it with a jab of my finger. He calls back right away, blowing my phone up each time I decline it or silence it and let it go to voicemail.

With ten minutes left of the lecture, he finally goes radio silent.

When class ends, I'm busy thinking about topics I'd like to explore for our paper as I pack up. I'm lost in brainstorming when I nearly crash into a firm wall standing in my way.

An apology dies on the tip of my tongue when I look up and meet Easton's gleaming blue eyes.

Oh no. *Fuck*, he's doing the thing. The super hot door lean.

His big hands casually reach up to grasp the frame while his broad, muscled body blocks my path as he smirks at me.

"Hey," he says, cool and cocky.

My face—no, my body—is too warm for this. I duck around him and squeeze through the doorway.

I thought I knew how to handle him. The plan to keep him in check with that daddy prank while he texted me through today's lecture has totally been shut down. I didn't expect him to show up and wait for me at the end of class.

Easton's a man on a mission.

I only make it two steps before he catches me in his arms. God, why does he have to smell so good?

"Where are you going, baby?"

A noise crossed between a smothered scream and a laugh escapes me when he lifts me off my feet from behind like my curves weigh nothing at all to him.

I hate to admit it stirs warmth in my core. I'm not what I'd consider plus sized, but I've got an ass and big boobs. The last guy I dated was smaller than me since he survived mainly on cigarettes and melancholy. He couldn't pick me up at all.

"Put me down," I say through laughter.

We draw some stares from other students as he carries me down the hall towards the doors that exit to a courtyard.

"Hmm, pass." His arms tighten around my waist and he murmurs low enough that only I hear him. "Daddy likes this better."

Why am I smiling so much? I can't stop.

"Oh my god. It was a joke. You wouldn't leave me alone during class."

His chest vibrates against my back with a rumble of amusement. "You think I wasn't going to haul ass all over campus to make sure my girl wasn't calling some other dude her daddy?"

"I'm not your girl," I remind him. "And you're definitely not *that*, either."

"Yet," he says cheerfully.

I don't know which part he's referring to.

"Easton."

He still won't let me down. His lips brush my ear.

"That's not my name. Say it right if you want me to let you go."

I bite my lip, squirming. He holds me steady, carrying me outside to a secluded spot. I expect him to drop me, but he only adjusts his grip and waits.

Oh my god, he's seriously going to make me say it, isn't he?

"Fine. Let me down, daddy," I sass.

He hums in consideration. "No. Only good girls get what they want." His voice dips. "Are you going to be my good girl, baby?"

I shiver at his gravelly tone, lit up by him calling me good girl.

Before I figure out something to say, he chokes back a snort and sets me down. I blink, facing him warily. He offers a crooked, charming smile.

"Sorry if I distracted you in class. Next time I'll know you need me to shut up for real."

I—what?

"What?" I blurt.

He winks. "I've got to get to the weight room. See you later."

"Just like that?" I call.

He twists to walk backwards. "Just like that." Glancing around to the emptying courtyard, he flashes me a devious look "Be daddy's good girl."

My mouth drops open when he turns around and jogs off.

I'm so going to get him back for this.

EASTON

DELETED SCENE BETWEEN CHAPTERS 34 AND 35

Soft kisses pull me to consciousness with a pleased groan the morning we're due to leave for Boston.

Maya plants her lips across my chest, then my jaw. I pretend to be asleep, then pounce on her with a joking roar, rolling on top of her.

"Good morning," she says.

"Any morning you wake me up with your mouth is a good one, baby." I graze my nose alongside hers. "I've got somewhere else you can kiss."

She huffs in amusement when I rock my morning wood against her thigh. She opens her legs and I settle between them. Threading a hand in her hair, I cover her mouth with a burning kiss. We become tangled in each other, the movements of our bodies naturally seeking out what we both want. It'll take nothing to sink into her.

"I don't think we have time for a quickie," she murmurs against my lips.

"That's where you're wrong. There's always time for a quickie."

Someone bangs on the door.

"Time to go," Cameron calls.

I don't move. Yeah, we're headed to Frozen Four.

Rather than getting out of bed, I dip my chin to kiss Maya again. A minute later, someone knocks again.

Not my best moment as captain, but when I'm fitted between my girlfriend's luscious thighs, can they blame me?

Maya smirks, stretching her arms overhead. It presses her tits right up to the perfect position to nuzzle my face into them.

Another teammate rattles the door with his fist. "E, get a move on!"

"Don't make us get Lombard," Hutch warns.

Oh, shit. I freeze, debating how long I can push it before they send in the coach.

"You'd better go," she says.

"Five more minutes."

Leaving the paradise of her body is pure torture.

"Go!" She giggles when I shower her with more kisses. "I don't want to show your coach my boobs today."

A growl works its way out of me. "Hell no. I'm the only one that gets to see these."

Diving back beneath the covers, I suck her nipple into my mouth, loving the way it makes her sigh and arch for me.

"Easton," she breathes.

I hum, skimming my hands down her sides to map her hourglass figure. When the cat jumps on the bed, I sigh, finally admitting defeat.

Dragging myself from bed, I get dressed and gather my stuff. It's all packed. The gear is already loaded onto the bus. I chuck my phone charger in my backpack and wheel my suitcase to the door. My gaze lands on Maya when I make sure I'm not forgetting anything.

She watches with a sweet, pretty smile.

I brace an arm against the wall, leaning over her. "What's that look for?"

"Not much. Just that I love you."

A grin splits my face. "Oh, is that all?"

She lifts a shoulder with an amused expression. Sitting up, she snags one of my discarded shirts and shrugs it on, lifting her hair out from the neckline. Then she stretches towards the nightstand to get the book she started last night.

"You going to finish that today?"

She holds it open, peering at the top to check the amount left. "Oh, definitely. Probably before lunch."

The corner of my mouth kicks up. "Send me pictures of the parts we can use as inspiration."

Her cheeks turn a gorgeous shade of pink and a spark of interest lights up her hazel eyes. I brush my knuckles along her cheek.

"There's my girl."

She bites her lip. "Good luck this weekend. I know you're going to play some amazing hockey."

Hell, I've got to kiss her again. There's no way I'm leaving without one more.

I climb over her, pinning her beneath the sheets to keep myself from giving into temptation again. Her arms loop around my neck while we kiss.

The door bursts open and four of my teammates barge in. I use my body to cover Maya's even though she's not exposed, twisting to shoot them a look of disbelief.

"What the hell?"

Noah taps his bare wrist. "Dude, you're late."

"We don't have to leave at ten on the dot," I say.

"Coach said ten," Madden mutters. "So it's ten."

I swing around to Maya. "You believe this?"

She shrugs. "You do need to go at some point."

"Listen to your girl," Cameron advises.

He grabs hold of my calves and tugs. I claw at the sheets, holding on to Maya. She snickers, pecking me before they drag me out.

"Wait—"

"Time to go, man." Noah helps him, hoisting me into the air.

"Guys—"

"Rookie, get the suitcase," Cameron instructs.

"Got it," Elijah says.

They carry me across the room. Maya's openly laughing now. I grab the doorframe, flashing her a grin.

"Watch me. I'll score for you, baby."

ACKNOWLEDGMENTS

For my Poppop. I miss you forever.

* * *

Readers, I'm endlessly grateful for you! Thanks for reading this book. It means the world to me that you supported my work. I wouldn't be here at all without you! I love all of the comments and messages you send and live for your excitement for my characters!

Thanks to my husband for being you! He doesn't read these, but he's my biggest supporter. He keeps me fed and watered while I'm in the writer cave, and doesn't complain when I fling myself out of bed at odd hours with an idea to frantically scribble down.

Thank you always to my girls! Ramzi, Kat, Sara, Becca, Jade, Sarah, Mia, Bre, Heather, Katie, Erica, and Jennifer for the supportive chats and keeping me on track until the end! And to my beta queens for reading my raw words and offering your time, attention to detail, and consideration of the characters and storyline in my books! With every book I write my little tribe grows and I'm so thankful to have each of you as friends to lean on and share my book creation process with!

To my lovely PA Heather, thank you for taking things off my plate and allowing me to disappear into the writing cave without having to worry. And for letting me infodump at you, because that's my love language hahaha! You rock and I'm so glad to have you on my team!

To Silver, thank you for your amazing artwork for this series!

To my street team and reader group, y'all are the best babes around! Huge thanks to my street team for being the best hype girls! To see you guys get as excited as I do seriously makes my day. I'm endlessly grateful you love my characters and words! Thank you for your help in sharing my books and for your support of my work!

To Shauna and Becca and The Author Agency, thank you so much for all your hard work and being so awesome! I appreciate everything that you do!

To the bloggers and bookstagrammers, thank you for being the most wonderful community! Your creativity and beautiful edits, reviews, and videos are something I come back to visit again and again to brighten my day. Thank you for trying out my books. You guys are incredible and blow me away with your passion for romance!

ABOUT THE AUTHOR

STAY UP ALL NIGHT FALLING IN LOVE

Veronica Eden is a USA Today & international bestselling author of addictive romances that keep you up all night falling in love with spitfire heroines and irresistible heroes.

She loves exploring complicated feelings, magical worlds, epic adventures, and the bond of characters that embrace *us against the world*. She has always been drawn to gruff bad boys, swoony *sin*namon rolls with devastating smirks, clever villains, and the twisty-turns of a morally gray character. When not writing, she can be found soaking up sunshine at the beach, snuggling in a pile with her untamed pack of animals (her husband, dog and cats), and surrounding herself with as many plants as she can get her hands on.

* * *

CONTACT + FOLLOW

Email: veronicaedenauthor@gmail.com

Website: http://veronicaedenauthor.com

FB Reader Group: bit.ly/veronicafbgroup

Amazon: amazon.com/author/veronicaeden

facebook.com/veronicaedenauthor

instagram.com/veronicaedenauthor

pinterest.com/veronicaedenauthor

bookbub.com/profile/veronica-eden

goodreads.com/veronicaedenauthor

ALSO BY VERONICA EDEN

Sign up for the mailing list to get first access and ARC opportunities!
Follow Veronica on BookBub for new release alerts!

New Adult Romance

Sinners and Saints Series

Wicked Saint

Tempting Devil

Ruthless Bishop

Savage Wilder

Sinners and Saints: The Complete Series

Crowned Crows Series

Crowned Crows of Thorne Point

Loyalty in the Shadows

A Fractured Reign

Heston U Hotshots Series

Iced Out

Standalone

The Devil You Know

The Player You Need

Unmasked Heart

Devil on the Lake

Jingle Wars

Haze

Reverse Harem Romance

Standalone

Hell Gate